FORTUNES FOR EDEN

A CLEAN ENEMIES TO LOVE ROMANCE

TINA NEWCOMB

Dedication

To William, Aiden, Ava, Wesley, Matthew, and Archer
This Grandma gig is pretty awesome!

CONTENTS

CHAPTER 1

*I*sadora Adams waved goodbye to her youngest sister from her parents' front porch. Her mom and dad would be gone all morning on the five-hour round trip to the Seattle airport.

Back inside, she wandered from room to room of her childhood home, lost in memories. Five girls and a wife under one roof—her poor dad was the most patient man on earth. In the kitchen, Izzy ran a hand over the table, which had stood up under countless meals and late-night study sessions. The whole house echoed of laughter and tears, territorial squabbles, hormones, whispered secrets, and screaming matches.

On a small desk in the corner, she spotted a copy of the *Eden Falls Chronicle*. A picture on the front page showed Stella and her new husband, Rowdy, working side by side on a Fourth of July float. Below the article another picture captured the finished product, three tiers of cupcakes advertising Patsy's Pastries. "You always were the crafty one, Stella," she said to the empty house.

After a quick shower, Izzy grabbed a jacket and headed

out the door for Town Square, which was only a few blocks away. She and her friend Joanna were meeting at The Roasted Bean after Joanna dropped her twin boys at school. Izzy and Joanna, along with Ariel, were so inseparable in high school, Joanna's mom had called them Peanut, Butter, and Jelly.

Ariel's devilishly handsome older brother had attended Stella and Rowdy's wedding reception on Saturday night. As hard as she tried not to look in his direction, her traitorous gaze had different ideas. Every time their eyes met, Gunner Stone glared as he'd done since she was sixteen.

Ever since The Kiss.

She turned onto Main Street, enjoying the morning air and familiar sights. As long as she'd lived in San Francisco, she still considered Eden Falls her home.

Outside The Roasted Bean, police chief JT Garrett pulled to the curb in a shiny patrol car. "Hey, Izzy, I didn't get a chance to talk to you at the wedding reception. How's San Francisco?"

"It's still there. I miss running into Carolyn, though. I ate at her restaurant at least twice a month until she moved back here and you made her a better offer. By the way, congrats on your marriage."

"Thanks. Move back to Eden Falls and you can run into Carolyn all the time."

I'm thinking about it.

JT held up a hand. "I've got to go. Mr. Polanski spotted Sasquatch near his chicken coop again."

Izzy laughed. Mr. Polanski had been chasing Bigfoot for as long as she could remember. She waved back, turned to go inside, and collided with a solid mass. The plastic top on a coffee cup flipped off and scorching liquid sloshed down her blouse and soaked the muscular chest in front of her.

Sucking in a gasp and plucking her shirt away from her skin, she glanced up, apology on the tip of her tongue and froze. *No!* Her mind screamed. Anyone—*anyone!*—but Gunner Stone.

Based on the you-are-the-bane-of-my-existence look on his face, he felt the same way about this fun little encounter.

"I'm sorry, Gunner." She waved a hand at the road. "I was talking to JT and turned...I should have looked...I just...my attention was on him and..." She covered her mouth as a giggle burst out in one of the most awkward moments of her life—a horrible habit she wished she could break.

He cocked his jaw to one side and narrowed his gaze. She found his one brown eye and one green eye mesmerizing. So much so, she'd looked up the term for it—heterochromia iridis—when she was in middle school. They could appear so stormy one minute, so sad, so burdened the next.

"I really am sorry." Another giggle bubbled up, so she pressed her lips together and bit down while she swiped a hand down his T-shirted chest like she could magically dry him off.

He caught her wrist and an energy—so intense, so tangible she felt it in her toes—crackled between them. His nostrils flared, and the look in his eyes hardened like he'd just locked gazes with Medusa.

Ahh, nice job, brain. If only the Medusa analogy were true. Turned to stone, I wouldn't have to put up with Gunner's loathing anymore.

He lowered her hand but didn't release his hold, his palm hot. Was it just him, or was his skin heated from the coffee he was now wearing? When his gaze dropped to her lips, her stomach dipped like she was on a roller coaster. Something flashed across his face...desire? But that couldn't be right. He hated her. She looked at his lips and fire flashed over her cheeks so suddenly it startled her.

"I really am sorry." She tipped her head toward The Roasted Bean. "Come inside and I'll buy you another cup."

He dropped her wrist and, with a look of complete disgust, tossed his empty cup into a nearby trash can and stalked away.

Oka-a-ay. "Good to see you again, Gunner. Have a nice day. Buh-bye."

Anyone—anyone but Gunner.

"I see you ran into Mr. Hot and Handsome," Joanna said, joining her on the sidewalk.

"Oh, now you show up! You couldn't have arrived five minutes earlier? Or two? Thirty seconds?"

Joanna ruffled her still-wet hair with her fingertips. "Sorry. Cody couldn't decide between his black Batman shirt, his yellow Pokémon shirt, or his green Incredible Hulk shirt."

Izzy hadn't seen Joanna's adorable twin boys—the spitting image of their dad—in a year. "Which one did he choose?"

"The blue Spiderman one."

Izzy laughed. The release soothed the lingering Gunner-encounter tension.

"Clothes are an everyday battle with Cody. Everything is too tight, too loose, too scratchy. Food is Caleb's battle. The kid won't eat anything without a fight. If I fix hot dogs, he wants spaghetti. If I fix spaghetti, he wants tacos." She ran a hand over her pregnant belly. "I'm not sure what Troy and I were thinking when we decided to have another baby."

"You were thinking a little girl would calm the snakes and snails and puppy dog tails of a house full of boys." Izzy hated the longing that tinged her tone. The desire for a baby was so deeply embedded, she'd considered adoption—a decision her parents would frown upon if there wasn't a husband. Not her first choice, but not unheard of. "Is your mom still driving you crazy about a name?"

Joanna groaned. "Driving us crazy is putting it lightly."

"Clearly, you should choose Isadora. What little girl

doesn't want to go through life being called Isadorable?" she asked, waving a hand down the front of herself like a game show hostess, which got the laugh she'd hoped for.

She glanced down the street. Gunner's scowl was visible from where they stood as he backed out of a parking spot.

"He doesn't look very happy," Joanna said.

"Isn't that the normal I-hate-everyone expression he always wears?"

Joanna looked from Gunner to her with crinkled brows. "Gunner is really friendly around town. He smiled a lot while he and Dahlia were dating."

Izzy closed her gaping mouth. "Gunner and nice Dahlia Dallas dated?"

"For a few months after his divorce."

If possible, her jaw dropped even farther. "I can't believe someone actually married that cranky crosspatch. Why didn't anyone tell me?"

"Cranky crosspatch?" Joanna said with a laugh. "That sounds like something your mom or a four-year-old girl would say."

Izzy opened the coffee shop door and followed Joanna inside. "I learned from the best. So, what happened to the wife?"

"She left after three—or six—months. Not really sure of the details. They were in the Army together."

"Was she pretty?"

"Halle Berry gorgeous."

"Geez, you move to California for a few years—"

"Thirteen."

"—and everything changes."

Joanna looked over her shoulder. "Did you expect things to stay the same as they were in high school?"

"No." But she wasn't sure how she felt about Gunner

having been married. Then again, why did it matter to her? He was free to marry anyone he liked.

Joanna pointed at Izzy. "Could that be the reason Gunner looks so angry?"

Izzy pulled her coffee-covered blouse away from her chest. "Could be a small part of the reason."

"Izzy! Wow, I didn't know you were in town."

The second person she'd rather not run into. Ever. She mustered a smile for her high school sweetheart. "Tim. Hi."

Joanna pointed toward the counter. "I'm going to order."

Izzy didn't want to get into a back-and-forth *"You look great." "So do you." "How've you been?"* conversation with Tim.

They hadn't exactly parted on good terms when she left for college. He wanted to keep up a long-distance relationship, but she wasn't interested. She suspected he was seeing someone else, which he vehemently denied, but not quite convincingly enough. College in a new city had been just what she needed for a fresh start.

The man standing in front of her was as tanned and handsome as the boy had been, his smile just as charming.

"Are you in Eden Falls for a visit?"

"Wedding." She winced inwardly. Stella, probably wanting to avoid awkwardness, hadn't invited Tim.

"Right. I heard Stella and Rowdy got married." He reached out like he might take her hand, but stopped. "How long are you in town for?"

"I leave on Friday."

"Do you still live in San Francisco?"

She nodded.

He'd visited once in her freshman year, making her even more certain their relationship had run its course.

"We should get together while you're here."

"Oh…uh…"

"How about dinner tomorrow at East Winds? You used to love that place."

"Ah…" She couldn't think of an excuse fast enough. "Okay."

"I'll pick you up at—"

"Actually, I'll meet you there." She didn't want him coming to the house, where her mom and dad would see him and start asking questions. "Does seven work for you?"

"Sure. I'll see you tomorrow night at seven. Bye Iz."

She waited until he walked out before sidling up to the counter next to Joanna. "Thanks for abandoning me."

Joanna laughed. "You're a big girl. I figured you could handle Tim yourself."

"Being able to and wanting to handle Tim myself are two different things."

"He didn't bite you, did he?"

Izzy fluttered her eyelashes. "Not since senior year."

"He's single, you're single…"

Izzy held up a hand. "Don't go there."

"Why? Tim is a nice guy."

"That flame was doused before I even left for college. There's no going back."

"Thank you," Joanna said when the barista handed her two mugs. She held out one. "Hope chamomile tea is still a favorite. My treat after your two unpleasant encounters."

"Love it. Thank you. And the unpleasant encounters continue tomorrow night. I told Tim I'd meet him for dinner at East Winds."

Joanna slid into a chair at a vacant table. "Why didn't you say no?"

Izzy pulled out a chair across from her. "I couldn't think of an excuse fast enough."

"Why do you need an excuse? Just say no."

Izzy thought of her San Francisco job and all she did for

Baron Van Buren and the Van Buren Gallery. "I've never been very good at saying no."

"You could have used me."

"Nice to know if I need an excuse in the future." Izzy held the mug to her nose and breathed in the lemony fragrance.

Joanna smiled. "The way you say that makes it sound like there's going to be a future in Eden Falls...I say hopefully."

It would feel good to tell someone the secret she'd been carrying around for over a week. "The gallery had a big event last weekend. I planned every detail myself. When I reminded my boss I wouldn't be attending because of Stella's wedding"—Izzy lowered her voice so word didn't get back to her parents before she had a chance to tell them—"he threatened to fire me, so I quit."

"Izzy!" Joanna sat forward and touched her arm. "I'm sorry. You loved that job."

"A long time ago I did." She'd loved every aspect of her job at first. "But after I accepted the manager's position, things changed. I wanted that promotion more than anything, but Baron expects me to be on call twenty-four seven. A day off is rare." Dating the man had only made things worse. He was a major manipulator. Details Joanna didn't need to know.

"Even after gallery hours?"

"I attend fundraisers and cocktail parties and committee meetings representing the gallery. I meet with new artists and organize events and socials. I even plan weddings held at the gallery."

"People hold wedding in art galleries?"

"All the time."

Joanna settled her mug on her extended belly. "What are you going to do?"

Izzy shrugged because she didn't have an answer. "It's only been a week, so I haven't had time to look for another job."

"Do you think you'll stay in Washington?"

She didn't say that the thought had occurred to her more than once. Her mom and dad had tag-teamed her about coming home, even without knowing the situation. The cost of living would certainly be lower here than in Northern California. There were art galleries in Seattle and the surrounding areas, though nothing like the Van Buren Gallery. She had a sizable savings account, but only because she'd been stashing her money and sharing a rickety old house with four other women.

"They're building a big country club and golf course between here and Harrisville. Maybe you could organize their events. Sounds like you have plenty of experience."

The idea of opening her own event planning business had also occurred to her, but she didn't think Eden Falls was big enough to support such a job.

"You should talk to Alex. She does the flowers for weddings all over the area. I bet she'd know if you could make a living around here," Joanna said, as if reading her mind.

"I guess it wouldn't hurt. I have three more days before I go back to California."

Joanna sipped from her mug, then grimaced. "I miss coffee. Herbal tea isn't strong enough to get me through a day with two boys."

"You are an adorable pregnant lady."

Her friend laughed. "I look like a beached whale."

"That's so cliché. Your husband works in advertising. Have him come up with something more original."

"I'll tell him you said so."

"How is Troy?"

Joanna's expression softened. "He's doing well. Business is good and, despite my complaining, life is good."

"I'm happy for you, my friend. Did you think you'd end

up married to your high school boyfriend with two point five kids thirteen years after graduation?"

Joanna laughed again. "Absolutely not." She nodded toward Izzy. "What about you? Where did you picture yourself by now?"

"I thought I'd be married and have the two point five kids. Instead, my career took over my life." She shook her head trying to clear away the melancholy. "Tell me about the boys."

"You mean the heathens? Caleb clogged the toilet yesterday morning before church, trying to flush his plastic Army guys to China, and Cody decided to melt his crayons in the microwave because he couldn't find the watercolors."

Izzy laughed.

"You laugh now. Just wait."

Izzy didn't want to wait. She was anxious for those clogged-toilet and microwave disasters if it meant she got to kiss a sweet forehead goodnight after tucking him or her into bed.

Joanna set her cup on the table. "I thought you'd stick around for social hour after church yesterday."

"Mom and Dad had to take Georgiana to the airport, so I went home to spend time with Oops. She left this morning."

"I can't believe you still call your little sister Oops," Joanna said with a laugh.

"We say it with love."

Joanna pushed back from the table. "I need a donut. Let's walk across the square to Patsy's Pastries."

unner backed into the street and drove around the square, flexing and releasing his hands on the steering wheel. Too little sleep had him on edge.

Running into Isadora Adams hadn't helped. She'd kept him awake for the last two nights.

Or at least thoughts of her had.

Ever since seeing her at her sister's wedding reception, she'd been front and center in his mind.

His cell phone rang and he grabbed it from the console of his truck, grateful for the interruption. "This is Gunner."

"Hi, Gunner, it's Karen over at The Dew Drop Inn."

"Hey, Karen."

"A maid discovered a hole in a bathroom wall over the weekend. Do you have any time in the next couple of days to take a look?"

He glanced at the clock on his dashboard. "I have a few minutes right now. Is the room empty?"

"Yes."

"I'm on my way."

"Thanks, Gun."

He disconnected the call and waved to Rance Johnson who'd just stepped out of The Fly Shop and placed a side-walk sale sign on a table filled with tackle boxes. Second Monday in September. Changing leaves and cooler days were ahead. Shop owners would be clearing out summer merchandise and bringing out the fall and winter stock. Porches would soon be decorated with pumpkins and cornstalks.

Once the cold hit, his outside jobs would dwindle, followed by everyone tightening their belts to save for the holidays. Then he'd have to tighten his own belt until spring.

The cons of owning a handyman business in a small town were worth the freedom of setting his own hours and not answering to anyone but himself. He would never be rich, but he'd come a long way from his white-trash upbringing. People who used to look down on him as a thug when he was a kid now trusted him to repair their roofs or fix the leaky faucets—in their homes. Sometimes when they weren't even there.

More thoughts of Isadora muscled their way forward. She was at the wedding reception alone, wearing an orange dress and no wedding ring. She danced with a couple of local guys and her dad, then made the rounds, saying hello to Eden Falls' residents, careful to stay as far away from him as possible.

At one point she and her four sisters converged on the dance floor and gyrated to the pulsing beat of a crazy country love song. Nothing could have torn his gaze away from her. The eyes of every guy in the place were riveted on the sisters as they swiveled and wiggled and giggled to the tune. That's when he decided it was time to leave.

Isadora. Everyone called her Izzy. He knew she'd be at the wedding reception, knew if he attended he'd see her, knew if he saw her it would take weeks to forget her.

She didn't visit Eden Falls often. He'd only spotted her a handful of times over the years since she left for college, and then only from a distance. A quick glimpse across Town Square, going into one of the shops, picking up takeout from Renaldo's Italian Kitchen or East Winds Chinese, coming out of the movies with a sister or a friend.

Rumor had it she ran some swanky art gallery in California. A job that suited her. He could imagine her in fancy clothes commanding a small army of employees. Though he was six years older than she, he knew from his younger sister that Izzy was a leader. Well liked. Surrounded by friends. Heading committees and getting kids involved in causes was her MO even in high school.

She'd befriended his quiet younger sister, Ariel, during her crucial junior high school years, taken her under wing, turned a trailer kid into a fashionable, popular girl. Izzy was there for Ariel when he enlisted in the Army and left her with their unstable mother, something he had to do and wished he could undo at the same time.

Since the wedding reception was held at The Dew Drop, walking through the door made him think of Izzy again. Being so near her this morning, so close, yet so untouchable... She'd be back in California soon, and he'd try to forget her until the next time he spotted her in town.

Karen scanned his T-shirt when he stopped at the check-in desk. "Looks like you're wearing your coffee."

"Ran into someone."

She nodded toward the kitchen. "Let's get you a fresh cup before we go upstairs."

A few minutes later, he followed Karen to a second-floor room where she pointed out a hole behind the bathroom door.

"A group of fishermen got a little unruly over the weekend."

"It will take a few days for the patch to dry."

"Not a problem. I don't need this room until Friday afternoon. I have a big party coming in."

"I can get to it before then. Do you have matching paint?"

"In a storage room in the basement. If I'm not here, whoever's at the front desk can get it for you."

"I have to get to another job, but I'll swing by later this afternoon and start patching it up."

"Thanks, Gunner. Here, take this." She pressed a key card into his palm. "This will get you in when you need to."

He refilled his coffee and walked around the back of the inn to a path that led to the river. Standing on the bank, he watched the water burbling over rocks. The level was low due to the dry summer, but that would soon change with winter snowfall.

A butterfly floated past and landed on a wildflower close by. He took a step closer, but it lifted into the air and fluttered away. The breeze rustling the leaves on the trees brought the smell of rain.

Today would be long and dirty. The team he'd hired would have to wear masks while clearing the damage left by a wildfire that destroyed several mountain homes last month. He hoped the storm would hold off until tonight. Driving a bulldozer through soot would be messy enough without rain making the ground a gloppy mess.

He squatted down and scooped a handful of water. At one point Izzy left the reception and came down to the river. Her father joined her a few minutes later. Gunner had watched them from the windows above, wondering what it would be like to have a good talk with his dad, who deserted his mom and him when he was four.

Gunner had discovered the man had a new family in a town close by. A wife and kids who depended on him. He'd waited outside his father's house early one morning, right before his high school graduation. When his father backed out of the driveway on his way to work, Gunner followed and intercepted before his dad could go into his Harrisville office.

The man recognized him immediately. Their conversation entailed a brief greeting, with no exchange of hugs or even a handshake, Gunner's mumbled request for help with college, his father's denial of responsibility—because Gunner was eighteen by that time—and an exit. The man never gave his mom a dime to help with expenses after he abandoned them.

So Gunner was on his own. The only way for him to generate a steady, reliable income for himself and his dependent mom and sister was to join the Army. He'd serve his time, then use the GI bill to go to college and at least get some business courses under his belt.

He straightened. Enough with the bad memories. Time to get up the mountain to work.

~

*I*zzy had planned to go back to her parents' house after she and Joanna parted. Instead she walked through Town Square and down a side street to three Victorian houses lined up like pretty sisters dressed in their Easter Sunday finery. She'd loved these houses since she was a little girl. The gingerbread trim, the attention to detail, the original wavy glass in the windows…their history fascinated her.

The first was painted a lovely blue with navy and white trim. Attorney Owen Danielson had refurbished the house for his offices. He'd made slight changes to the interior, but kept the integrity of the house intact.

When the second Victorian, which sat back on the lot a little, came into view, Izzy plopped down on the curb and stared. The house, once painted a soft yellow, was now a garish green, which, along with the black trim, was flaking off in brittle chunks. The beautiful front garden was overgrown with weeds, the lush lawn brown from neglect. A tree had fallen across the driveway. The only pretty feature left on the property was the maple in the front, its leaves just beginning to turn with the cooling weather.

"It's a crying shame, isn't it?"

Izzy turned to find Lily and Rance Johnson standing behind her on the sidewalk. "What happened?"

"We had a fortune-teller move into town," replied the town librarian.

"After painting the house the color of puke and destroying the yard, Madam Venus, *Goddess of Love*, pulled up stakes," her husband added. "I guess not many people in our small town wanted to know what their futures held."

"She doesn't live here anymore?" The sight of the house made Izzy heartsick.

Rance shook his head. "She moved in and out within a year."

"How long has the house been empty?"

"Gosh, going on two years...right, honey?" Lily asked.

Removing his fishing hat, Rance scratched his bald dome. "At least two years."

Izzy stood and got up on tiptoe to see over the weeds that grew as tall as the fence. Had it really been that long since she'd come to admire the Victorians? Two windows above the porch overhang, which sagged on each end, made the house look like it was frowning. "I don't see a *For Sale* sign in the yard. Is she going to keep it?"

Rance lifted bushy eyebrows. "Your dad should have the answer to that question."

True. If not her dad, at least someone in his real estate office should know what was going on with the dismal Victorian.

"Are you staying in town long, Izzy?" Lily asked.

"I leave Friday. How are you both? We didn't get a chance to visit Saturday night."

"We've got a new grandbaby on the way." Rance took his wife's hand and settled it in the crook of his arm.

"Congratulations. I heard Mac got married."

"We're so lucky Mac found Noelle," Lily said. "She's a wonderful addition to our family, such a sweet stepmother to Beck."

"I haven't met her yet. I'll have to stop by her café for breakfast while I'm in town."

After they walked away, Izzy crossed the street. She wrapped her hands around the ornamental iron fencing that circled the yard. The sun-warmed metal felt oddly comforting. She studied the worn, forlorn house and wondered if the interior was as abused as the exterior.

Unhooking the gate, she picked her way over the tangle of

vines covering the walk. She wasn't sure what drew her forward, but knew she had to take a closer look. The steps needed repair work. Pots with plants that had seen much better days, along with leaves and debris, littered the peeling painted porch. The front door screen hung by only one of three hinges. She tried the knob. Locked up tight. Cupping her hands, she tried to see through the oval window, but film over the inside of the glass blocked her view.

After polishing a tiny spot on one of two front picture windows, she peered inside. Trash littered the floor, which looked to be hardwood. The walls were painted black or navy or brown...she couldn't tell for sure. She also couldn't see beyond the one room which looked huge.

The windows on the side of the house were too high, so she picked her way around to the back. The glass in the door was cracked, but she could see into a mudroom. Again, the floor was littered with rags and leaves and trash. Only a small section of the kitchen was visible. The cupboards were painted flamingo pink with lime green walls. She imagined the house sobbing while the painters applied the shocking colors.

She didn't dare climb the rickety stairs that led to some kind of screened-in sunporch.

Disappointed, she stumbled through the overgrowth and around the downed tree. On the other side of the house, she noticed a bird's nest under the eaves and several wasps disappearing behind a shutter.

Izzy crossed the street and stared at the gloomy Victorian, remembering how the house used to look. With a little tender loving care, she could possibly be restored to her majestic glory.

CHAPTER 2

*I*zzy woke to a muffled giggle from down the hall and decided her parents were worse than a couple of newlyweds. In fact, she was surprised she only had four sisters rather than twenty-four.

When she walked into the kitchen after her shower, her dad had his nose buried in the once-a-week *Eden Falls Chronicle* and her mom was busy at the stove. The smell of coffee—probably the reason she'd never acquired a taste for the stuff—was strong.

She set a kettle of water on the stove and flipped on the flame.

"Want some eggs, honey?" her mom asked.

"No thanks. I think I'll drag Phoebe out of bed. I haven't seen much of her since I've been home."

There it was again, the feeling that Eden Falls would always be home.

Her dad chuckled. "Good luck. Phoebe has Tuesdays off and usually doesn't get out of bed before noon."

"I'll guilt her into it. I told Rance and Lily I'd try to stop by Noelle's Café to meet their new daughter-in-law. I haven't been inside since the renovation. Does the café have a good breakfast?"

"Second only to your mother's."

"Aww... Thanks, sweetheart." Her mother fluttered her eyelashes.

Her dad looked at her from the corner of his eye. "Why are you caressing the table?"

Izzy stopped moving her hand back and forth over the scarred wood. "I did a lot of homework on this table, ate a lot of breakfasts."

"Had a lot of arguments," he added with raised brows.

"My five daughters had many heartfelt moments around this table, too," her mom said, setting a plate of eggs and toast in front of him.

"Notice how you're *her daughters* when having heartfelt moments, but mine when the fighting starts."

Her mom winked at her over her father's head.

The easy way her parents loved each other after years of marriage and a houseful of girls was genuine and warm, moving to watch. Since she was a little girl, she remembered seeing them laugh and joke together and knew what they had was special, something she wanted to have one day.

"I walked past the Victorian houses yesterday."

"Still one of your favorite things to do when visiting." Her dad set the paper aside and took a bite of toast.

"One is a little...different."

He set his toast aside and picked up his fork. "You noticed?"

"Kind of hard not to." She waited a beat. "What did you two think of Madam Venus?"

Her mom pulled out a chair and sat. "How on earth did you hear about her?"

"Lily and Rance Johnson happened to walk past and told me Madam Venus owned the house."

"If you're asking if we visited her for a reading, the answer is no. We don't need a psychic to tell us we have five daughters who drive us crazy, do we, Bev?"

"No, we have firsthand knowledge."

"We don't drive you crazy anymore. I bet you miss the yelling and the smell of nail polish and the heightened emotions during *that* time of month."

Her dad shook his head. "I promise you there is nothing on your list that I miss."

"So, is the Victorian for sale?" Izzy asked her dad.

"If it is, Madam Venus didn't list it with Adams Realty."

"It's shameful what she did to that beautiful house," her mom added as she gathered the paper into a neat pile.

"The house has good bones." Her dad stood, washed off his plate, and put it in the dishwasher. "With a little elbow grease, that house can be restored to what it once was."

"Where did Madam Venus go?"

"Oh, honey, don't waste your money."

"I don't want a reading, Mom. I'm just curious about the house."

"Someone told me she moved to a place just off the highway, closer to Harrisville, where there's more traffic," her dad said.

"Is there any way you could check into the Victorian, Dad? Lily said Madam Venus moved out two years ago. Maybe she's willing to sell."

He picked up a banana and turned to study her for a long minute. "Why the interest?"

"I don't know. I just hate seeing the house in that condition. Maybe the town has money hidden in some historical fund that could be used to fix it up. Turn it into a museum or something."

He bent and kissed the top of her head. "Sure, sweet roll. I can ask around."

Izzy smiled. Neil Adams had tagged each daughter with the name of one of his favorite sweet treats and sometimes remembered those nicknames better than their real ones.

A sudden wave of guilt settled over her. She'd kept her news to herself so far, not wanting to put a damper on Stella's wedding. She could go back to San Francisco on Friday and not mention her joblessness. Her parents would never have to know. She could save them the worry...except she didn't like keeping secrets from them, and she'd waited long enough. "So, I lost my job."

"What?" her parents said in unison.

"I talked to my boss about Stella's wedding as soon as I found out, but he wouldn't give me the time off. When I told him I was going to Washington anyway, he threatened to fire me. I quit before he could."

"Oh, honey." Her mom bent forward and hugged her, her soft scent enfolding Izzy in a mom-blanket of love. "I'm so sorry."

"Don't be. The job was becoming more and more of a drudge. I didn't have any free time at all. Mr. Van Buren"—no reason to tell her parents she'd been dating her boss—"had me working around the clock."

"What will you do?"

Her mom, the worrier. "I've got money saved and the options in San Fran are endless."

"Come home," her dad said with finality, as if the decision was just that easy.

"That's a perfect solution," her mom said, a smile touching her eyes. "I talked to Maude just yesterday. She's hiring at the bookstore."

"Or you could take after your old man and get your real estate license. Speaking of which, I have to get out of here. I have an appointment to look at a new office space."

"You're moving your office?"

"We need more room."

Izzy had noticed her dad's cramped quarters the last time she was in town. He'd moved his business from their home into the vacant office building two doors down from the post office when Izzy was in second grade. Since then, he'd added a receptionist and two agents.

Her mom walked her dad to the back door, their eyes communicating more than Izzy wanted to know. "I'll be home for lunch."

"I'll see you then," her mom answered.

Izzy would stay away from the house until well after lunchtime.

*I*t took several knocks on her apartment door before Phoebe yanked it open.

"What?"

Her gorgeous sister's blond hair was a mass of tangles. "Cute," Izzy said nodding toward Phoebe's giraffe pajama pants.

"Thanks."

"Why are you still in bed?"

"Because it's only eight and my day off." Phoebe opened the door wider so Izzy could step inside. "Why aren't *you* still in bed? You're on vacation."

"Mom and Dad."

"Geez Louise," Phoebe said, pushing the door closed with her hip. "They still going at it like rabbits?"

"Makes it kind of awkward sitting across the breakfast table from them. I plan to stay out of the house until after Dad's lunch hour, too. I'm pretty sure they've got special plans."

Phoebe snorted before she flopped onto the sofa. "You

can stay in Stella's old bedroom if the parents get to be too much."

"Thanks, but I leave Friday. I can bear their lovey-dovey activities for two more nights." She plopped down next to her older sister. "Get dressed and let's go out to breakfast. I've never been to Noelle's Café."

"It's eight o'clock in the morning—"

"I hope they have good French toast."

"—and my only day to sleep in," Phoebe groaned.

Izzy patted Phoebe's leg. "I'll buy. Get dressed."

Thirty minutes later they walked the few short blocks to Town Square. As they passed Patsy's Pastries, Phoebe winked at a handsome man coming out of the door with coffee and donut in hand.

"Who's that?" Izzy asked once they crossed the street.

"A guy I dated for about two months."

Izzy glanced back at the man, who looked older by at least ten years, graying at the temples, and watching Phoebe like she was the main course at an all-you-can-eat buffet. "How did you meet?"

"Maude Stapleton. He's a distant nephew or her tax man... Something like that."

By the look on his face, he wasn't the one who'd broken things off. "Why aren't you still dating?"

Phoebe's brow crinkled in a frown. "He wanted to get married."

"After two months?"

"After two dates."

Her police officer sister amazed Izzy. She wished she'd inherited the easy way Phoebe breezed through life. She met men with a handshake and let them go with a wink. Everyone remained friends with Phoebe. Izzy, on the other hand, was an awkward mess. She knew dating her boss was a mistake the first time he'd asked her to dinner. Their relationship, if you could put a name to what they had, was very one-sided. And now over, since he threatened to fire her after all the time and effort she'd poured into him and the gallery.

She glanced at her sister. "Are you dating now? You didn't bring anyone to Stella's wedding."

"I've been going out with a doctor. He was on call Saturday night."

Izzy opened the door of Noelle's Café, and was oddly comforted by the clank of dishes and buzz of conversation. The smells coming from the kitchen sold Izzy on the food before she tasted a morsel. She loved the retro décor, the welcoming atmosphere, and the shiny jukebox cranking out a 90s love song.

A girl wearing a *Hi, I'm Laura* nametag showed them to a table. Izzy recognized almost everyone in the café, including grumpy Gunner Stone sitting at the end of the counter. He glanced her way and glared. Before she left town, she'd offer to buy him a new T-shirt. *There. One good deed for Mr. Cranky-Pants.*

A lady stopped next to their table. "Morning, Phoebe."

"Hi, Noelle. Izzy, have you met Noelle?"

Noelle smiled. "I've heard your name mentioned. It's nice to meet you, Izzy."

"Same here. Your in-laws said all kinds of nice things about you yesterday. They're both excited about another grandbaby. Congratulations."

Noelle put a hand to her barely-there baby bump. "Thank you. Lily and Rance are sweethearts."

"And I love what you've done with this place. It looks great."

"Thank you again. What can I get you to drink this morning?"

Squawk!

Izzy about jumped out of her skin. She clutched a hand to

her chest as her heart thumped wildly. "Rita, you scared the life out of me."

Rita Reynolds, postal worker and town gossip, flapped her arms like she might take flight any second. "I heard you're moving back to town."

Glancing around, Izzy realized everyone in the café had turned to stare...and wait for her answer. Gunner, hunched over his breakfast, turned to glower over his shoulder. She looked back at Rita. "Where did you hear that?"

Squawk!

Though half expected, Izzy still jumped. She'd forgotten how terrifying the tiny woman could be. The thick lenses in her glasses made Rita's eyes look double their size. She tipped her head at an odd angle, a pigeonlike habit. "Word travels fast in this small town."

"What word? I didn't tell anyone I was moving back to Eden Falls."

Rita pointed a bony finger at Izzy's nose. "This visit is longer than you've ever stayed before. Think you're too good for this town now you have a fancy job in the Big Apple?"

Phoebe snorted. "The Big Apple is New York, Rita. Izzy works in San Francisco."

"Same difference."

"Except they're on opposite sides of the United States."

Rita swatted Phoebe's argument away. "You've got something else up your sleeve, Isadora Adams. You can't fool us. You were in front of Madam Venus's house yesterday. Don't you bring that Goddess of Love back here."

"Relax, Rita. I don't even know Madam Venus."

"And you better not be reading people's fortunes and causing havoc in this town. That last kook had everyone scared to walk past her place for fear she'd cast a spell."

Izzy looked at Phoebe in question.

"Madam Venus didn't have any customers coming to her

door, so she sat in the front yard to conduct business." Phoebe turned her wrist and looked at her watch. "It's almost nine, Rita. Aren't you supposed to be at the post office about now?"

With another ear-shattering squawk, Rita flew out the door.

Phoebe waved a hand as if moving a crowd back from a crime scene. "Okay, everybody, show's over. Catch the next Izzy and Rita episode tomorrow at a shop near you."

"She's still alarmingly loud and…"

"Annoying? Crazy? A busybody?" Phoebe supplied, then flashed a smile. "You'll get used to her again after you've moved back."

*A*fter breakfast they wandered to Riverside Park. How many hours had she spent here with family and friends? More than she could count.

The sun glistened off the water while dragonflies with their iridescent bodies and transparent wings hovered near the bank and then darted quickly away. Pockets of wildflowers bloomed here and there, waving in the gentle breeze. The rain last night had washed everything clean, and today the air was warm and smelled faintly of fall.

Izzy kicked off her shoes and Phoebe followed her lead, each enjoying the still-wet grass tickling the bottoms of her feet. They settled on a nearby bench and took pleasure in the perfect weather, the sun on their faces. Unless she had an outside event, Izzy didn't get to enjoy the out-of-doors much. Managing the gallery kept her busy from early morning until after nightfall.

When Baron told her she wouldn't have a job if she attended Stella's wedding, her initial reaction was anger. After all the time they spent together, after all the hours she devoted to make sure every event ran smoothly, after all the time she invested in planning out details like flowers and food and music, he was willing to replace her without batting an eye. Her second reaction was deep hurt that he wouldn't allow her a week off to be with family.

When he started interviewing for her replacement, she knew he was serious, and she quit on the spot. By the time she took her seat on the flight to Seattle, something had shifted. Though the thought of starting over scared her silly, maybe this change—this shakeup of her very ordered, list-making, ridiculously disciplined life—was exactly what she needed.

"I hear you have a date with Tim tonight."

Izzy glanced at her sister, who had her face tipped up to the sun, her blond braid falling behind the bench. "How on earth did you hear about that?"

"Tim told Patsy who told Maude who told Leo."

"It's not a date. I agreed to meet him for dinner."

"Kind of a date," said a voice behind them. Leo, her sister's ridiculously handsome best friend, plopped down on the bench between them.

"It's not a date if I pay my own way."

Leo rested his arms along the back of the bench, flipping Phoebe's braid out of the way. "I can't believe you're going on a date with your high school boyfriend."

"It's not a date. I'm meeting him for dinner."

"That's a date," Phoebe and Leo said in unison.

"I haven't seen the guy in years. Why would he think meeting for dinner was more than just dinner?"

"He's never married, never dated anyone seriously that I know of." Phoebe leaned forward and looked at Izzy. "He's still grieving over you."

"Poor Tim," Leo said. "You broke his heart. I bet he has pictures of you tacked up on his bedroom walls."

"That's more than a little creepy," Izzy said.

"He lights candles and chants your name every night before bed," Phoebe added.

She pushed to her feet. "You two are cracked."

Leo flashed one of his devastating grins. "Great minds think alike."

"So do crazies." Izzy turned toward Town Square. "I'll see you around."

"Thanks for breakfast," Phoebe hollered over her shoulder.

Izzy ended up in front of the sad Victorian again. Sitting in the same spot on the curb, she stared at the house. *With a little tender loving care…*

The front door on the blue Victorian next door closed and attorney Owen Danielson crossed the street. "This is the second time in two days I've seen you out here, Izzy."

She patted the curb beside her. She'd gone to school with sweet, geeky Owen. He'd always been the kind of man who'd do anything to help a friend or stranger. "Have a seat."

He tugged the legs of his dress pants up and sat. "My wife and I had a nice time at the wedding reception. I was a little surprised when I heard Stella and Rowdy were getting married, but really, they are a perfect match."

"Funny how that happens every once in a while."

Resting his forearms on his thighs, Owen pointed at the middle Victorian. "What do you see when you look over there?"

What did she see? Her dad said the house had good bones. "Something old. Something that holds a lot of memories." She shook her head. "Something full of history and stories." She turned to him. "Did it take you long to renovate that house into your office space?"

"A few weeks, but it was in good condition when I bought

it. I think Madam Venus did a fair amount of painting when she bought that place."

"She did. I peeked through the windows yesterday. 'Yikes' is the kindest word that comes to mind."

"Paint is cheap." He was quiet for a long moment. "What would you do with the house if you owned it?"

As soon as he asked the question, a vivid picture came to mind. The paint colors, a garden full of spring, summer, then fall flowers, Christmas trees in the two big front windows, a fountain in the yard. Possibly a small tearoom overlooking a side garden. A living room that could be converted into a regal setting for special events. Scones and muffins provided by chef *extraordinaire* Carolyn. She imagined Christmas decorations, then Valentine's Day. All the holidays would be special.

The thoughts clamoring for attention made her giddy. People could rent the space for showers and weddings and special birthday celebrations.

She looked at Owen. "Maybe an events venue for anniversary or office parties. Do you think Eden Falls could support such a place?"

He pushed his silver wire-framed glasses higher on his nose with an index finger and nodded. "Yes. With the right advertising, the interest could go well beyond Eden Falls. Besides The Dew Drop Inn, there aren't any places around here to hold parties or events."

Her ideas became clearer, so defined they almost scared her. Her pulse picked up speed, making her short of breath. "My dad is looking for a new office space. I could rent out the second story to him."

"If you put a parking lot in back, you could expand to my lot by simply pulling down that section of fencing on the side."

"Really?"

"Sure. I have more parking than I need."

She looked from him to the tangle in the yard. "There isn't a *For Sale* sign anywhere."

"Your dad should be able to get information about the house. If not, you might talk to Alex McCreed. As mayor, she's usually in the know."

"Good idea. I need to talk to her about something else anyway."

He stood and dusted off his pants. "It'd be nice to have you and your dad as neighbors, Izzy."

She wanted to get inside and see if this picture in her mind was realistic. There was no use investing time in a dream that wouldn't work from the start. "Thanks, Owen. I'll let you know if I find out anything."

Izzy sat where she was long after Owen went back inside his office. While walking the perimeter yesterday she'd noticed windows to a basement, which would give her extra storage space for party supplies. She wondered how many bedrooms the house had, and if the attic was big enough to be converted into a living space. What she told her parents about a healthy savings account was true, but she couldn't afford to buy a house and rent an apartment too. Even sharing the rent with Phoebe would be more than she could afford until money started coming in.

Izzy finally stood and headed toward Pretty Posies. When she stepped inside, she was glad to see nothing had changed. The flower shop had always been a delight for the senses. Even the bell over the door was the same. The smells of flowers, moss, and earth surrounded her in the most pleasant way. Alex had placed pops of fall color—varying hues of orange, yellow, burgundy, purple—all around the shop, which reminded Izzy that Eden Falls' Harvest Festival was next month. She hadn't attended since her senior year of high school.

A girl Izzy saw at the reception came out of the back room. She wore a black dress with green netting over the skirt. Her black hair was pulled into a high ponytail, the ends ratted into a nest of knots, and beaded spiders hung from her ears. "Hello."

"Hi." Izzy stopped at the counter. Stella worked for Alex during her summer months off from teaching second grade, and she'd mentioned the Goth-dressed girl a time or two. "I'm Stella's sister, Izzy."

"Stella has mentioned you." The girl quickly held out her hand. "I'm Tatum Ellis."

Tiny Alex McCreed appeared and flashed her sunshiny smile. Her pregnant belly looked like she was trying to hide a cantaloupe under her shirt. "Hi, Izzy. What a nice surprise."

"Hope I'm not interrupting."

"Absolutely not." Alex waved her into the back room and pulled out a stool. "Have a seat. I have a flower arrangement to finish, but I can work and listen at the same time."

Talking about her idea would make things seem real. Was she ready to do that?

Alex started clipping the stems of roses with quick, efficient movements, yet her attention was on Izzy. Each flower was strategically arranged in a mercury glass vase.

"Do you know where Madam Venus is?"

Alex raised a brow. "You want to see Madam Venus?"

"No. Well, actually, yes. I might want to buy her house."

She could tell by Alex's expression she had her attention. "Really?"

"Do you think there would be enough interest around the area to support an event planner and possibly another venue for small parties and receptions?"

"Yes! I can direct more business your way than you can handle. I always have people in here asking if I know anyone."

That was a fantastic bit of news. "I don't want to step on Karen's toes at The Dew Drop by taking away business."

Alex placed white lilies among the roses. "I don't think that will be a problem. She's had to turn parties away because she only has the one room. You should talk to her."

"Before I worry about anything, I need to find out if the house is even for sale and in my price range. There isn't a sign out front."

"I don't know if she's selling, but I do know where you can find Madam Venus." Alex grabbed a pad of paper and a pencil. "I don't have an address, but I know the general directions." She tore the sheet free and handed the paper to Izzy. "Stella and Phoebe would love it if you moved back to Eden Falls, not to mention your parents."

"Nothing's set in stone. In fact, only you and Owen know about this crazy idea. Can we keep it that way until I know more? I don't want to get my parents' hopes up."

"Of course. We won't tell a soul." Alex glanced toward the door. "Right, Tatum?"

Tatum poked her head around the corner. "My lips are sealed."

Izzy indicated the bouquet Alex was working on. "That's going to be beautiful. Do you still use the language of flowers when creating an arrangement?"

"As much as possible. Sometimes the flowers people choose prevent it, but I can usually throw something in that has special meaning."

The whole idea of using the Victorian language of flowers intrigued Izzy enough that she'd bought a book on the subject from an antiques dealer in San Francisco.

"I hope your plans come to fruition," Alex said when Izzy stood and pushed her stool under the worktable.

"Me too." In fact, she was getting very excited about the

idea. She held up the directions to Madam Venus. "Thanks for this, Alex."

Izzy left Pretty Posies with a sense of triumph, even though the only thing she'd accomplished was to get directions to the fortune-teller's house.

~

*A*ll these years of just catching glimpses of Isadora Adams, then yesterday she literally ran smack into him. Gunner could still see her pretty, amber-colored eyes wide with surprise. He very seldom ate breakfast out but, today at Noelle's Café, there she was again with her sister Phoebe. When Rita accosted her about moving back to Eden Falls, she hadn't denied anything.

He could close his eyes and imagine the smell of her perfume—vanilla with a hint of something exotic. Nothing overpowering like his ex-wife used to wear. For some reason, running into Izzy jarred loose memories of Jessica and his failed marriage.

And Arial, another of his failures. He'd raised her, done what he could to keep her safe, but failed to save her. If there was one day, one hour of his life he wished he could change...

Ridiculous emotions that guys generally ignored were bombarding him because Izzy was in town. Thoughts of Jessica, memories of Ariel—he didn't handle either well.

After a long day of bulldozing rain-soaked debris from the fire-damaged area, the last thing he wanted to do was cook. He showered, took Domino—his black-and-white rescue dog—for a walk, then headed out for dinner.

East Winds was busy for a Tuesday, but the special, Szechuan chicken, was one of Gunner's favorites. He found a small table in the back and ordered dinner. The waitress smiled and tried to initiate small talk.

Juliette was sweet, pretty, and only lived a town away, but he wasn't interested. His ex-wife had flayed his ego. She'd left because she couldn't take small-town living. She hated that he worked all day and went to school at night. While he tried to make their life better, she complained. Her rejection cut deep. He'd never believed he would find real love or be interested in marriage, but everything changed when he met Jessica. She was wild and adventurous, and they melded together so seamlessly he believed their match was fated.

He'd been wrong.

He glanced up when someone took a seat at the table next to his. Tim Cutler nodded in greeting. Gunner nodded back. Tim had gone to school with Ariel, and was out on the ice with the high school hockey team the day his sister died.

Gunner sat back in his chair. After two long days on the bulldozer, he should be able to finish up his part by tomorrow. Mike Stettler from the forest service walked the burn area today, marking trees to be taken down. He'd start that part of the project tomorrow, after he finished patching the hole at The Dew Drop Inn.

Seeing Tim reminded him of the diary he found in Ariel's room after her death. In several places, she agonized over her infatuation with Izzy's boyfriend. Entries later claimed she'd found love, but never divulged a name. Reading her scribble, he'd laughed at her seriousness, because at sixteen, and with him and their mother as role models, Ariel had no idea what love was.

It turned out she wouldn't live long enough after she wrote those entries to find out.

He'd wanted so much more for her than the single-wide their mother rented that should have gone to trailer heaven long before they moved in. She shouldn't have had to worry about wearing hand-me-downs to school or feeling embarrassed that her school lunch was provided by the state.

When not working after school at the local hardware store, he picked up any odd job he could find back then. It was never enough to make a difference in their circumstances.

Sweet, wide-eyed Ariel was only twelve when he enlisted. Brokenhearted, she'd wept at the curb when a cab carried him away, leaving her with their unpredictable, very unqualified mother.

Juliette delivered a bowl of soup just as Izzy came through the restaurant's door. Of course she'd pick here for dinner. He'd gone years barely catching a glimpse of her. Now, he was seeing her twice a day.

Tim jumped up when she reached his table. He moved in with puckered lips, but she turned her head. The look of surprise on Tim's face had appeared on a multitude of rejected men.

Tough luck, buddy.

Izzy didn't look overjoyed to be there, and her look deteriorated even more when she spotted Gunner sitting at the next table. After they sat, Tim asked about her day. Her answer was vague and low. She talked about breakfast with Phoebe, running into Owen Danielson, and visiting Alex at the flower shop.

Gunner signaled to Juliette. "Can I get my dinner to go?"

"The soup too?"

"No, I'll finish that here."

As he ate, he tried not to listen to Izzy and Tim's conversation, which was impossible since they were so close by, adding fuel to his original reason for leaving as soon as possible.

"Tell me about your life, Tim."

"I'm a pharmacist."

"Oh, that's wonderful," Izzy said, her tone genuine.

"Yeah, I work at Harrisville Regional Hospital. Even though it's only fifteen to twenty minutes away, the drive got old so I bought a house there two years ago."

"What made you choose to be a pharmacist?"

Gunner stole a glance their way. Tim was bending forward eagerly, while Izzy leaned back in her chair. During one of their rare overseas phone conversations, Ariel had admitted she was jealous of her best friend having a date to the high school's Homecoming Dance when she didn't. Izzy had everything Ariel didn't—a loving family, money to buy new clothes, a boyfriend. Gunner sent a check home every month, but imagined his mom took most of it to support her drinking habit.

After that call he opened an account in Ariel's name and deposited money for her use only. He wondered if Ariel ever told their mom about the money. He'd expected to find the account drained when he found the statements hidden in a hole in her mattress, but Ariel had been very frugal with the money, which made him sad. He'd wanted her to enjoy what he gave her. He wanted her to buy things and go places that would make her happy.

When Juliette stopped at their table, Izzy ordered the Szechuan chicken.

"I thought you didn't like spicy," Tim said.

Izzy raised both brows. "My tastes have changed since high school. Szechuan is my favorite."

Of course it is. One more thing to remind Gunner of her. Now she'd even invaded his favorite place for dinner.

After ordering, they dove into more small talk. Tim made a fool of himself trying too hard when it was apparent Izzy wasn't interested.

None of my business.

Juliette set the to-go box in front of him. "Can I get you anything else?"

"No thanks." He handed her his credit card.

"Be right back."

Juliette was back in a flash with his card and the receipt... her phone number jotted at the bottom. He left a generous tip, signed the slip, and handed it back to her with a slight shake of his head. "Have a good night."

Time to go home and try to get some sleep. Tomorrow would be another busy day.

~

Izzy watched Gunner's straight back and wide shoulders as he made his way to the door. He'd changed his order to takeout, and she couldn't help but think it was because of her. Well, he'd have to get used to running into her if she decided to move home.

She wished she was leaving, too. Not with Gunner— though hearing his voice after all these years had done funny things to her stomach.

Grateful when the waitress delivered their meals, she dug in, tired of her forced conversation while carefully skirting around the past.

She wasn't about to tell Tim she was thinking of staying in Eden Falls, allowing their conversation to circle back to the job he didn't know she'd lost, and the house she shared with four other women. He seemed fascinated with her life in San Francisco, talking about the possibility of finding a job in the city himself.

It wasn't until her senior year of dating Tim that she finally realized just how possessive he was. He became moody and angry when she spent time with family and friends rather than with him. Manipulation—the name she finally put to his strong suggestions and attempts at reverse psychology.

When she received her acceptance letter to the University of California, Berkeley, she kept the information to herself until graduation night. At first Tim was angry, then insistent that they go to community college together until they could apply to the same university. She left town a few days later.

"You seemed uncomfortable when Gunner was here. Do you two have some old history?"

Her laugh came out more like a dog bark. "Nope. No history."

"I still think about that day Ariel died."

Me too. She thought about her friend often. Tim was on the ice that day with the high school hockey team. The coach had rushed out to help but couldn't get to Ariel in time. She often wondered where her friend would be now if someone had been able to save her.

"Are you dating anyone, Tim?" she asked, ready to change the subject.

"I've been seeing a nurse at the hospital for about a year," he said, watching her closely.

"That's wonderful."

"How about you, Izzy?"

"I just broke up with a man I've been dating for about two years." She left out the boss part.

"Differences of opinion?"

That sounded funny coming from him, especially because they'd been at odds so often during their dating years. "Something like that. My job leaves very little time for dating."

"Is your boss a tyrant?"

"He takes his gallery and the business of art very seriously." After the events of today, she was glad Baron had threatened to fire her. Stella fell in love at the perfect time, and

Rowdy deciding on a very short engagement worked in Izzy's favor even more.

Now all she had to do was find Madam Venus and pray she was willing to sell the Victorian at a price within Izzy's means.

CHAPTER 3

*G*unner finished applying the last layer of mud over the patch at The Dew Drop Inn. He'd sand one last time tonight, and slap on a coat of paint. Another coat tomorrow morning, and he'd be done. Karen walked in as he was packing up his tools.

"You're a lifesaver."

If only. "This was an easy fix."

"How much do I owe you?"

Karen reminded him of his mom. They'd attended high school together, and after his mom passed, Karen told him they were attendants at each other's weddings. Karen had her daughter the same year he was born, and both women suffered through divorces together. The likeness ended there, though. Karen went on to work her way up from maid to owner of The Dew Drop, the only hotel in Eden Falls. His mom worked her way through liquor bottles instead.

"I'll drop by with the bill when I finish up."

"Thanks, Gun." She gestured over her shoulder. "I just made a fresh pot of coffee. Can I get you a cup?"

"I'll take two if you don't mind."

"Got another job?"

"I have to stop at Dahlia's Salon before I head up the mountain."

"Are you on the crew clearing Rowdy's property after that fire?"

"Most of the debris is cleared. Now we're pulling down damaged trees."

"I heard Rowdy's house was a total loss."

Gunner nodded and picked up his bucket of drywall tools. "If you've got that paint, I'll put on the first coat later this afternoon."

"I'll leave the can and a brush in here. Let me get you that coffee."

"One black, the other with a little creamer and two sugars, please."

"You got it."

"Thanks, Karen."

Fifteen minutes later, he entered Dahlia's Salon. She turned from scrubbing out a sink and a smile lit her face. Dahlia had a way of making you feel special without even trying. They'd only dated for a few months after his divorce was final, but he still felt a little uncomfortable when he ran into her. She always put him at ease within minutes. Though they'd tried to fly under the gossip radar, he knew people still talked about them, even though their relationship didn't last and they parted amicably about six months ago. She said he was too quiet, too intense, too closed off. The same things his sister had complained about.

Dahlia wanted more out of a relationship than he was willing to give.

He'd offered his heart once, and Jessica had shredded it raw before breaking it in two. He wouldn't make that mistake again.

"Hey, Gun. How are you?" she asked, her sweet voice echoing through the empty salon.

"Same as always."

She crooked a finger and he followed her into the back room. "Thanks for coming."

"Anytime." He held out one of the cups of coffee.

"Where'd it come from?" she asked, examining the cup.

"I had a job at the inn this morning. Karen doctored it up for you."

She took a sip. "Perfect. Thank you."

"What can I do for you?"

She picked up several sheets of paper and held them out. The top one held a sketch of shelves with compartments. "I need this to hold these"—she plucked a small box of hair color off a table—"in that space on the wall." She pointed to a spot above a counter. The second sketch showed how many boxes each compartment should hold. One thing about Dahlia, she was thorough with details. She liked things as exact as he did.

Dahlia also wanted feelings compartmentalized. All the small things that as a whole made up a relationship had to have meaning, all the feelings had to be lined up and identified. Rather than two people just enjoying each other's company with no strings attached, she needed reassurance that there would be a tomorrow together, and a day after that. He was supposed to know what she meant by a look or a nod of her head. Maybe with time he could have learned to read her signs, but he wasn't willing to step out on that ledge again.

He studied the box of hair color. "Don't companies make cabinets to hold these?"

"Yes, but your custom-built shelves are so much nicer than the plastic junk or particleboard they offer."

Her drawing was very specific, with dimensions jotted on

each side. Neat and precise, like Dahlia herself. He wished she didn't require everything so lined up, organized, and shiny. Though she never said so, he knew he fell short of her expectations.

Still, he missed spending time with her.

"Can I take one of these?" he asked, picking up one of the boxes of color.

She reached behind him and produced a stack of five boxes. "Thought a few would be helpful. Aw," she said pointing at his face. "You almost cracked a smile."

He hooked an arm around her neck and looked down into her pretty blue eyes. "I smile."

"Not often enough." She touched his chest, her hand pressing against his heart.

The sudden desire for physical contact surprised him.

"How are you really doing, Gun? Business good?"

"I'm keeping busy. How about you?"

"Business is great." She looked past him. "Are you seeing anyone?"

"No. You?"

She made eye contact, but her smile was gone. "Phoebe Adams introduced me to one of her exes. He's nice. We've been out a few times."

"Yeah? What does he do?"

"He's a human resources manager for a computer company."

"Does he treat you the way you should be treated?"

She nodded.

"Good." He squeezed her neck gently, then released his hold. "I've got to get to my next job."

"And I have to open the salon."

"I should be able to get this done sometime next week."

"Thank you, Gun."

Once he was in his truck he watched through the window while Dahlia met her first client of the day.

Loneliness had a color. He'd found it recently on a paint swatch at Eden Falls' Hardware and Lumber. *Morning Fog.* There were no blue, yellow, or purple undertones. It was pure, unadulterated gray.

~

*I*zzy borrowed her mom's car, and, following Alex's directions, she took the highway toward Harrisville. Turning off at the right exit, she veered onto a dirt road until she spotted a huge, hand-painted sign directing her to Madam Venus's. At the end of the driveway sat a simple farmhouse. The front was painted solid black except for the bloodred door. Either Madam Venus or the painters hadn't found their way around to the green sides yet.

Seems like a goddess of love would pick a cheerier color.

She climbed out of the car as two black cats skittered across the front yard and scrambled up a spooky dead tree.

At least Madam Venus won't have to decorate for Halloween.

At the front door, she raised her hand to knock.

"Come in," called a female voice.

She stopped short. *How...*

"The door's unlocked."

Izzy turned the knob and stepped inside. The interior was also black, the windows covered by dark curtains. A corner of the room was sectioned off with the same heavy fabric. Hundreds of candles lit the space.

A woman stood near a table wearing a fuchsia top with gold, coin-like fringe around the neck and short sleeves. Her very low-riding turquoise skirt had panels of violet, fuchsia, lime green, and bright yellow, her midriff bare. Several gold necklaces hung long around her neck, and a purple scarf, tied around her head, covered most of her black hair. A walking rainbow.

"Welcome."

"Thank you. I'm Izzy Adams."

The woman—Izzy guessed they were about the same age—held up her hand. "Isadora. I know why you're here. You want to buy my house."

"Uh..."

"I'm ready to sell. This is a much better location for me. People in Eden Falls were a little too...traditional. They weren't willing to give my predictions a chance."

The woman had to make pretty good money if she was able to hang onto the Victorian and still buy this place.

"I do. Make a good living. But I bought the house in Eden Falls with a sizeable settlement from an accident years ago." Madam Venus indicated one of two chairs near the table, a collection of gold bracelets jangling together on her arm. "You seem nervous. Please, have a seat."

Izzy *was* nervous. So nervous her stomach felt twitchy. She took the chair. "Is this where you do your readings?"

"No." The psychic nodded toward the corner. "We go behind the curtain for that." She pulled out a piece of paper from her skirt pocket and set it in front of Izzy before she took the other chair. "That's my asking price."

Izzy glanced at the number. Depending on how much repair work was needed, the price was more reasonable than she'd expected for a house the size of the Victorian. "Why haven't you listed it with a real estate agent?"

"Why pay a middleman? I knew when the right person was interested they'd seek me out."

"Would you consider coming down on the price for paint and other repairs?"

"What's wrong with the paint?" the medium asked, with a completely straight face.

So that's a no, because who doesn't want to live in a garish green house with black trim?

"I'd like to walk through before I make a decision."

Madam Venus tugged a gold chain with a key out from between her breasts. With every movement, the bangles on her arm chimed merrily.

"It's a pity the place isn't haunted. You'll just be getting an ordinary house."

The Victorian was anything but ordinary to Izzy, and she was grateful ghosts didn't haunt the halls. "As a psychic, shouldn't you have known it wasn't haunted before you bought it?"

Madam Venus slowly raised a brow. "Not all secrets are revealed right away."

"Does that mean there might be a ghost wandering around?"

The medium laughed. "No. I can say with certainty that the house is ghost-free."

Izzy appreciated the reassurance. She'd never met a ghost, and didn't want to start now.

"I gave your beautiful sister a reading last summer."

"I have four sisters."

"The youngest. Adelaide. The one you call Oops. She came home to visit your parents, and we talked one night."

Had Adelaide told her about the nickname the family used? Easy enough to check. She and Adelaide had spent a lot of time together, both before and after Stella's wedding, and her sister never mentioned meeting with the psychic. "Why did she come to see you?"

"Same reason most young girls visit me. She asked about love and marriage." The medium looked down. She still held the chain with the key in her hand. "Though she didn't say so,

I sensed a deep resentment toward her high school boyfriend. He broke her heart, and she's still hurting, more than she lets on to her family and friends."

That was news to Izzy. She knew Oops and Cameron Klein had dated for two of their high school years and been friends before that, but she thought their split was amicable. Cameron had gone to school on one coast, Oops on the other.

"When the time is right, her future husband will come into her life. He has rich, dark hair—"

Izzy fought a smile. "Dark hair covers a huge portion of the population."

"—and green eyes."

Okay, that narrows it down some.

"They'll know each other."

"Of course they will, because very few of us marry a complete stranger. We usually date someone before marriage, giving us time to get to know them."

"They'll have to work through some major issues before they enjoy a long, happy life together."

"I hope you're right about that last one."

Madam Venus drew a circle around Izzy's face with an index finger. "Your skepticism is showing."

"Basically, you told her the same thing you tell all young girls who are curious about their future," Izzy said in answer to the psychic's comment. "Common sense will tell them the same things for free."

"When her true love moves to Eden Falls"—she paused, looked down at her hands—"he won't come alone."

Despite her reluctance, Izzy felt herself being reeled in like a fish. "Are you saying Adelaide will move back to Eden Falls to live?"

"Eventually. She, *like you*, will be ready to come home."

"Who does Adelaide's true love come back with?"

"A heavy load."

"So, not a who. A what. What kind of heavy load?"

"Too heavy for him to bear alone. Your sister will help."

The psychic was talking in riddles. This was how she made her money. Drawing people in, piquing their curiosity, then handing them the bill. "You can't just tell me?"

"To reveal the future would be to change things that must happen."

"You're saying Adelaide has to go through misery before she can find happiness?"

This was too much. Izzy wasn't sure if she should pull out her wallet or laugh.

Madam Venus unclasped the chain around her neck and the key slipped into her hand. She held it out. When she dropped it into Izzy's palm, she wrapped both her hands around Izzy's. "That old Victorian has been waiting for you."

A tiny shiver worked its way down Izzy's spine as she searched the woman's unreadable expression.

"You'll find your happiness in that house."

I'll be very happy if my business is a success.

"Your business will be very successful."

Did I say that aloud?

"Your first client will be Ariel."

All the air left Izzy's lungs in a whoosh. She almost whispered, "Ariel's dead," but she could see by the woman's grave expression, she already knew. "Why would you say such a thing?"

"You'll see." Madam Venus slowly shook her head, her nearly-black eyes piercing Izzy's soul. "You'll fall in love in that house. Though you gained a lot of experience in San Francisco, your life there is over. The Victorian, as you call it, has been waiting for you to come home."

"I've never lived there," Izzy said, pulling her hand free of Madam Venus's grasp and pushing up from the chair at the same time.

"No, but you've loved the house since you were a little girl." Madam Venus stood. "Love has a way of finding us at the most unexpected moments, don't you think?"

"Love hasn't exactly found me yet," Izzy said, the words spilling out of her mouth before she could stop them.

"Ah, but it will in your lovely Victorian. You'll fight it and lose. So will the hero of your story. He's been infatuated with you for a long time."

Her thoughts jumped to Tim. She'd felt nothing when she met him for dinner. Their high school romance was over. At least for her. She was glad and a little sad at the same time. Those carefree, youthful days were gone. She couldn't imagine regressing and trying to rekindle anything with him.

She held up the key. "Thank you for trusting me with this. I'll get it back to you tomorrow."

"No need."

Izzy opened her mouth to object, but Madam Venus held up her hand. "You can keep it until the closing. That way you can go inside whenever you want. I'm not going to change my mind. And neither are you."

Izzy was shaking by the time she climbed into her mom's car. The woman's intent stare and predictions unnerved her. She pulled out her phone and scrolled to Adelaide's number.

Her sister didn't answer, but a moment later a text pinged on her phone.

Can't talk now. In class. Call back tonight.

Next she called her dad and he agreed to meet her in front of the Victorian. She was standing on the sidewalk when he pulled to the curb.

"Hey, sweet roll."

"Hi, Daddy. Am I interrupting a busy day?"

"I'm free until three."

She held up the key Madam Venus had dropped into her palm.

His eyebrows shot up. "You met with the medium?"

"I want to see the house."

They picked their way to the front door, where Izzy inserted the key into the rusty lock and fought to turn the old brass knob. As soon as she stepped into the grand foyer, something inside her stirred, an excitement she hadn't experienced in a long time. Her skin tingled and the hair on her arms stood up, as if she was stepping into hallowed halls. She glanced at her dad, expecting to see the same excitement— but nope, he was looking for water spots on the ceiling and damage to the wooden floors.

"Black? Who paints their walls black?"

Izzy laughed. "Just wait till you see the kitchen."

The beauty of the curved staircase shot anticipation through her. To the left was a spacious living room with a commanding fireplace and a bay window that overlooked what she imagined to be the side garden. This would make the perfect events room. The connecting dining room, with another bay window, was big enough for several small tables. The tea and sandwich shop floated through her mind.

A chandelier with gargoyles peering down at them would have to be rehomed. "That's creepy," she said.

"From black to bizarre, that medium sure liked variety," her dad said, pointing to the turquoise walls and red trim.

Beyond the dining room was the very neglected sunporch she'd seen the day before. Plantation shutters opened inward. Her mind was running wild with ideas for the space.

Her dad whistled long and low when he spotted the green walls and Pepto-Bismol-colored cupboards in the butler's pantry and kitchen. They were even brighter than they appeared when she'd looked through the window. "You need sunglasses before walking into this room."

"I warned you," she said with a laugh.

The other side of the house consisted of a mudroom with

laundry hookups, a breakfast nook, and a half bath. A back staircase led up to the second story and down to the basement. A room on the opposite side of the entry was as spacious as the living room.

"What would this room have been used for?" she asked her dad.

"With the low-hanging light, my guess would be billiards."

Back in the foyer, her dad inspected the staircase banister. "Like I said, the house has good bones."

"I counted three fireplaces. Do you think they work?"

"Easy enough to have someone come in and check. So..." He turned to her. "What's your plan here, Iz?"

She took a deep breath, exhaled slowly. "Have you found a new office space yet?"

"No. I'm going to have to build or move my business to Harrisville."

"Or I could buy this place and you could rent the second floor for your offices."

A sudden frown pulled her dad's eyebrows together. "What would you do with the main floor?"

"I'm thinking of becoming an event planner. Alex said there was plenty of business around the area. I've planned hundreds of events for the gallery in San Francisco." She stepped back into the billiards room. "I could make this side of the house my office."

Her dad's face lit with a smile as he pulled her into a hug. "Love the idea. You coming home. And opening a business in what used to be a landmark of Eden Falls. Your mom will be ecstatic."

"It's not set in stone, yet."

"What about the other side of the house?"

"I could use the living and dining room and even the sunporch for small events like birthday and retirement parties.

When not in use, the area could be turned into a tea and sandwich shop. The only problem is I'd need to install public restrooms. But where?"

Her dad took her arm, led her back to the foyer, and pointed to either side of the staircase. "Right there. Two huge areas that are wasted space."

There was plenty of room. "I should have invited Mom to come with us," she said as they climbed the stairs. "She has a good eye for design, too."

"Let's not get her hopes up until you decide for sure. She hates that you, Georgiana, and Adelaide are so far from home. She wants all her little chicks under her wings."

"So," she prompted. "Would you be open to the idea of using the second floor for your offices?"

He stopped on the landing and glanced around at the many doors on the second level. "I'm going to say yes, I'm very open to the idea."

They counted five spacious bedrooms, each with its own bath, and the landing was large enough for a reception area.

Izzy wanted to jump up and down with excitement...and throw up at the same time.

Before they could search the attic or basement, they ran out of time. Her dad left for his three o'clock appointment and Izzy headed to Pretty Posies.

Alex was rearranging some items on an armoire when Izzy entered. "Hi, Izzy. Did you have a chance to find Madam Venus?"

Just hearing her name made Izzy's spine quiver. "I did. That's why I'm here. I need an inspector or...some qualified person to take a look at the house and tell me I'm nuts. Do you have any recommendations?"

"Gunner Stone."

No-o-o! "Really?"

"Gunner is the best in the area. He can fix anything. He's like the town's handyman."

"There's no one else?"

Alex's hands stilled and she studied Izzy. "Do you have a problem with Gunner?"

"More like he has a problem with me."

Now she had Alex's full attention. "Something happened?"

"A long time ago. Ancient history. It's probably just my imagination." Except she knew it wasn't.

~

*A*fter another long day on the mountainside, Gunner climbed into his truck and headed into town.

His first stop was the inn, where he sanded his repair job and applied a coat of paint. One more coat tomorrow and this job would be complete.

Next he drove around the square and found a parking place close to Pretty Posies. Not only had he promised to look at her walk-in cooler, but Alex was a fountain of information about jobs around town.

He opened the door and the jaunty bell jingled overhead. This little shop settled his edgy soul. Sure, it was girly and full of flowers, but his usually impatient interior relaxed at the sights and scents of nature—which was way more pleasant than the sooty earth he'd been disturbing for the last three days.

Alex popped around the corner, her smile in place. "Hi, Gunner. Sorry to call you on the spur of the moment. I'm afraid this can't wait."

"Not a problem." He followed when she beckoned him into the back room. "What's going on?"

"The darn cooler stopped cooling." She climbed onto a

stool and put a hand to her lower back. Alex was five-foot-nothing and pregnant. He wondered how such a tiny woman could carry a baby.

"You okay?"

"Yeah, just a backache."

"Maybe you should take it easy."

She shook her head. "Just tired by the end of the day."

He made sure she wouldn't tumble off the stool before he pulled the cooler door open. "When did it cut out?"

"I don't know. I noticed the temperature wasn't cold enough right before I called you."

He let the door shut behind him. The shelves were lined with buckets of flowers, a riot of colors and textures, which reminded him of his sister. Ariel had loved coming into Pretty Posies. He found the digital thermostat next to the door. The red numbers read forty-eight degrees.

He pushed the door open. "Where do you normally keep the temperature?"

"Thirty-two to thirty-five. Dealing with this right now is completely inconvenient. I have a big wedding next weekend and can't buy the flowers with the cooler on the fritz."

"Where's your circuit breaker panel?"

She waved his question away. "I already checked."

"Is the condenser on the roof or out back?"

"Condenser?"

He thumbed over his shoulder. "I'll check out back first."

The condenser sat near the door on a concrete pad set next to the dumpster. When he let himself inside the shop a few minutes later, Alex was at the worktable clipping the stems of big star-shaped pink flowers with a heady scent.

She wiped her hands on her apron. "Did you find what you were looking for?"

"Yes, the condenser is next to your dumpster in the back."

"Please tell me the problem is fixable."

"It's fixable."

Tears filled her eyes.

"Whoa. Whoa, Alex," he said, holding up his hands. Other than his drunk, sobbing mother, he didn't know how to handle a weepy female. "It's very fixable and should only cost a couple hundred bucks. It looks like the unit was hit when the garbage truck dropped the trash bin a little too close. The fan motor has a bent shaft, which pushed the fan blade into the shroud. I think I can bend the shaft and fan blade back enough to work until I can get a new part in Harrisville."

"I have no clue what you just said, except the fixable part. Thank you." She swiped under her eyes and hugged him. "Sorry about the tears. Hormones are vicious when you're pregnant."

He didn't want to hear about hormones, and calming a weepy pregnant woman was beyond his expertise. He patted her back a couple of times and stepped away. "Tell you what, I'll only charge you for the parts, if you'll keep me in the loop with any jobs that come available."

"I can't let you do that."

He ripped off a paper towel and handed it to her when her eyes filled again. "It's an easy fix, Alex. Just let me know if something around the area comes up."

An hour later he had the fan running and the cooler working. He said goodbye to Alex and crossed the street to Noelle's Café, ready for some dinner. Gertie greeted him with more of a grunt than a hello. She managed the front of Noelle's café with an iron fist while her husband Albert ran the kitchen.

He slid onto a stool at the end of the counter.

"The special is a pork tenderloin sandwich and fries," she said without a smile, which wasn't unusual. He could count on one hand the number of times he'd seen Gertie smile. She probably still thought of him as a degenerate.

"Sounds good."

"Shake?"

"Just water."

While he waited, he sent a text to his fourteen-year-old neighbor. He paid the kid to walk Domino several times a week when he couldn't get home in time. The kid's family didn't have much income, and Gunner understood the bitterness of being left behind when your friends went off to Friday night movies. He'd had to come up with some excuses for why he couldn't join in when friends met for hamburgers after the football games. How many times in his youth had he turned down a loan from a buddy? Even when he got a job at the hardware store, he had to take the money home to pay rent, buy groceries, or fix something.

The kid sent him a riddle in return, something to keep him busy while he waited for his dinner. He heard the door open and Izzy's laugh filled the café. The sound grated up his spine and shot desire through his system at the same time. He glanced over his shoulder as Gertie showed Izzy and Phoebe to a booth by the window. He'd skipped lunch today, so it wouldn't take him long to wolf his dinner down and make a quick getaway.

Even though they chatted in hushed tones, phrases still floated across the room. He heard something about a house, repairs, and paint colors in their quiet conversation. Phoebe's voice was lower and more gravelly than Izzy's. They might be sisters, but the two couldn't look more different. They were about the same height, but that's where the similarities ended. Phoebe was blond, with fair skin and blue eyes. Izzy had dark hair, and her eyes were the color of the sun shining through a glass of whiskey.

Pretty, mesmerizing eyes.

Noelle walked past holding her lower back much the same way Alex had.

For one short month he'd thought he was going to be a father, and an abnormal happiness took hold. He found himself imagining a swing set in the backyard and toys littering the house. Son or a daughter, he didn't care. And he'd be a very different kind of parent than his had been. He would never leave. He would never drink himself into a stupor rather than buy food for his family. He would make sure his son or daughter knew he loved them. He'd be a good father—a good parent.

Noelle set his dinner in front of him. "Here you go, Gunner. Can I get you anything else?"

"No, thanks. This looks great."

"I was wondering if you might have some time this week to look at a fridge that's making a funny noise."

"I'll look at it as soon as I finish here."

"Oh—" She flapped a hand. "I didn't mean tonight."

"Not a problem." If he could diagnose tonight, he could fix it tomorrow. He was finished on the mountain and hoped something substantial would come up soon. And by going into the kitchen, he'd put distance between him and Izzy.

~

*A*fter dinner, as Izzy walked back to her parents' house, her phone rang. Adelaide's cute face popped up on her screen. She connected the call. "Hey, Oopsie. How's school?"

"I got my hardest class out of the way today. The rest of the week should breeze by."

"Good. It was so much fun spending time with you."

"You too. I forget how much I love Eden Falls until I visit."

Perfect opening. "Speaking of Eden Falls, I saw an old friend of yours today."

"Really?" Her sister's voice brightened with happiness or hope. Izzy couldn't be sure without seeing her face. "Who?"

"Madam Venus."

"Madam Venus was never an old friend," Oops scoffed. "I don't even know her."

"But you visited her for a reading. She remembers you and your fortune," she added when Oops didn't respond. "Did you tell her we call you Oops?"

"No. At least I don't remember telling her."

"She called you by that name."

"She must have heard someone call me that."

"Except only your four sisters call you that. Everyone else calls you Addie."

"She must have been around when one of you did."

Izzy sat on her parents' front porch steps. Darkness had fallen and it was getting chilly, but she wanted to finish this conversation out of her mom and dad's hearing. "What did she tell you?"

"Just the usual things. I'll marry one day."

"Was she more specific?"

Adelaide cleared her throat. "She said I'd marry a man with dark hair and green eyes. Cameron has dark hair—"

"And green eyes. You know psychics tell you what you want to hear, right? More than likely she saw you with Cameron before you left for college."

"Probably," Adelaide said without much conviction.

"Don't let what Madam Venus said change your plans."

Her sister's non-answer was answer enough.

"Adelaide?"

"I won't."

"And don't spend any more money on that kind of stuff, Oopsie."

"Several of us went that night. It was just for fun."

"Madam Venus makes her living telling people what they want to hear. She gives vague predictions that could cover so many situations. Don't build your future around what she said. You have to make your own."

CHAPTER 4

*G*unner pushed his cereal bowl aside and stared out the window. Domino paced along the back fence, ears cocked. Something had his dog's interest.

He washed his breakfast dishes, took some clothes out of the dryer, and wheeled the trash to the curb. Then spent thirty minutes in the backyard playing catch with Domino, only stopping long enough to check his phone when it pinged a message from Alex.

Can you meet a couple of people at the house next to Owen's office at ten this morning?

Why? He texted back.

Domino dropped the tennis ball at his feet and yipped.

"We'll go in just a minute, buddy," he said while watching the message bubbles bounce on his screen. Let me line up a job here."

They need a professional opinion about structural damage.

Once a grand old dame, that house was now a dump. If he could get a renovation job out of a professional opinion, he would be set for the next several months, depending on what was needed.

I'll be there.

Thanks, Gunner. Sorry about the late notice. I just found out.

Not a problem.

Ten minutes later, he pulled into a parking space close to Patsy's Pastries. He clipped a leash to Domino's collar and climbed out of his truck. His hound bounced out, ready for one of Patsy's doggie treats. "Patsy spoils you."

He looped Domino's leash around a lamppost and scrubbed him behind the ears. "Be back in a minute, Dom."

"Hi, handsome," Patsy said in her usual greeting when he entered her pastry shop. "Here for some of Carolyn's sweet delights? She's outdone herself this morning with a tantalizing iced raspberry braid. The way the flavors in her cranberry-orange muffins burst in your mouth is sinful. And her cheese Danish...I have no words for the rich flavor that oozes from the puffy, buttery pastry."

Only Patsy could make ordering a pastry sound like the menu at a brothel. Her very fitted V-neck said *My Husband's Wife is Awesome*. Not many women could pull off such a statement T-shirt, but Patsy wore it with her customary flair.

He decided to go for sinful and ordered the cranberry-orange muffin. "And a large black coffee to go."

"Is Domino outside?"

"Sure is. He loves Carolyn's sweet delights as much as I do."

"Hear that, Carolyn?" Patsy hollered loud enough for the dead to hear. "Gunner said he loves your sweet delights!"

"Patsy-y-y," Carolyn groaned from behind the swinging kitchen doors.

"I love to make her blush," Patsy said with a wink as she

snapped a white paper bag open with a flick of her wrist. "I'm adding two treats for your sweet dog."

"Thanks, Patsy."

Gunner took his muffin, coffee, and Dom's treats outside, only to find a female stooped down petting his dog. He stifled a groan when he realized the female was Izzy.

"You are such a good doggy, and so sweet. Yes, you are. Yes, you are," she said like she was talking to a baby. "I love your doggy smile."

Her comment caught him by surprise. He was the only one who ever noticed his dog's silly grin.

She lifted the tags on his collar. "What's your name?"

"Domino."

She popped up like a jack-in-the-box, knocking Gunner's hand, dumping his coffee down the front of his shirt. Again.

He sucked in a quick breath as the hot liquid burned his skin. "Really?"

She giggled, then quickly covered her mouth with both hands. "I'm so sorry."

"You don't sound sorry," he said flatly, plucking at his wet T-shirt in irritation.

Her humor evaporated and she narrowed her eyes. "This time the spilled coffee is your fault."

"It's *my* fault that *you* dumped my coffee down my shirt."

"You startled me. And you're standing too close —"

He held up a hand to stop her. She was right. He shouldn't have been standing close enough to smell her perfume... which was tantalizing.

When Domino realized he wasn't going to get a longer belly rub, he stood and nudged her hand. She petted his head. "You have a sweet dog."

"Hear that, Dom?" he said, untying the leash. "You're sweet."

Domino answered by wagging his tail so hard it whirled like a helicopter rotor.

Izzy bent and ran her hand from Domino's head to his tail. He almost crooned in ecstasy. "I'll be happy to buy you another cup of coffee."

"Why, so you can dump a third down my front? No thanks. Come on, Dom. We'll eat in the truck."

"Okay, bye. Good to see you again," she hollered down the street. "Bye, Domino!"

Domino yipped in reply, smiling all the way to the truck.

Only when he and his traitor dog were safely in the cab did he glance up. Izzy stood in the same place he'd left her, hand on her cocked hip. He threw his truck into reverse and started to back up, then slammed on the brakes and grabbed Dom around the neck to keep him from toppling to the floor when someone honked.

Izzy smirked, which irked him further.

Once the car passed, he circled the square and headed to the library, where Lily Johnson had asked him to look at two cupboard doors in the employee kitchen. He could see what he would need to fix them before he had to meet his possible new client. Luckily he had enough time to stop by his house and change out of his coffee-drenched shirt before that meeting.

Parking in front of the stone library building, he sat for a long minute. He'd visited this library often as a kid, and going inside always inundated him with memories. Books were an escape. They took him to another place or world or dimension. He used to read all the time, and not just for school. He'd read to take his mind off his dad leaving, followed by his mom's drinking. He'd read to Ariel until she decided she was too old. He'd read to free his mind from the worries and frustrations and responsibilities that weighed on him every day of his young life.

In college he took business classes, when really he wanted to study philosophy, which would have taken him down such a different career path. He still read a lot, but not for escape. Now he devoured books to learn about human nature, history, and even religion.

He ruffled his dog's fur. "No reminiscing today, Domino. Cross your paws that our next clients keep us busy and fed and the heat on over the winter." Not that he was hurting for money or jobs, but it would be nice to work on something long-term rather than the odd here and there fix-its.

His dog's tail thumped wildly.

He left Patsy's dog treat on the seat, cracked the windows, and opened the door. "You stay here. I'll be back in five minutes, and then we'll go to the park for a run before my appointment."

Lily Johnson scooted around the checkout desk as soon as she spotted Gunner. Lily and Rance had always been kind to him and Ariel.

"Thanks for coming so quickly, Gunner. I'm afraid one of the kitchen doors will fall off and brain someone." She eyed his coffee-stained shirt. "Looks like you had an accident."

An Isadora Adams accident. "I spilled."

He followed her downstairs to the employee kitchen and immediately spotted the problem. "I have an appointment at ten, but I can come back this afternoon and fix the doors. Until then, I'll take them down to keep the library staff safe."

"You are a lifesaver. What would this town do without you?"

He smiled, though her compliment pained his heart. This was the second time he'd been called a lifesaver this week. If only he'd been able to save his sister.

He wished she were here, wished she lived close so he could drop by her house for a cup of coffee. She would laugh about how this was the second time this week he'd literally bumped into Izzy. He wished he could see her smile once more. Wished he wasn't so…alone in the world.

"I'm sure the town would survive just fine without me. Let me get my drill out of the truck. I'll be right back."

~

*I*zzy waved to Patsy when she entered the pastry shop. She loved the way the enticing smells of cinnamon, powered sugar, and chocolate swirled through the air.

"Is there any truth to the rumors I've heard about you moving home?" Patsy asked.

"There might be a little truth, but let's keep that between us for now. I'm working on something that's still a little iffy."

Patsy pretended to lock her lips. "I won't say another word. What can I get you?"

Izzy perused the wonders behind the pastry window. Everything looked so delicious. "How does anyone decide?"

"It's a dilemma I love to watch."

"I'll try the raspberry braid, and I'll take a slice of lemon-blueberry coffee cake for my dad."

"Perfect choices." Patsy opened the glass door. "Did I notice a little something between you and Gunner out there?"

"Absolutely not. Well, maybe a little rage on his part, but that's nothing new."

"That's hard for me to believe. Gunner is one of the nicest men in a town full of nice men."

"Believe it. He usually views me with disdain, but it gets worse when I dump his coffee down the front of his shirt."

"Oh, no," Patsy said.

"Twice in one week," she added.

Patsy barked out a laugh. "Now, that's funny."

"I know, right? But somehow, he doesn't see the humor in the situation."

"Kill him with kindness."

"He doesn't seem the type who'd appreciate kindness."

Patsy leaned across the counter. "Gunner had a hard life growing up. He was the sole provider for his family after his dad left, and took over for his mom when she started drinking."

"I always heard he was the hoodlum of Eden Falls."

"From who? Rita? Gunner didn't do anything worse than the boy who is now our police chief. People just assumed he was a hoodlum because of where he lived and how he was raised." Patsy straightened. "He's a good man who's faced a lot of heartache."

"Like dealing with a wife who left?"

"She walked out just like his dad did. Gunner was head over heels in love with that girl, and she took off without so much as a goodbye."

Izzy had such a hard time imagining Gunner married...or in love, for that matter. She saw him as a vagabond, traveling from place to place, never growing roots—which didn't make sense either. As far as she knew, other than being away in the Army, he'd never lived anywhere else.

But none of this information changed the fact that he didn't like her.

"Thanks, Patsy," she said, taking the white bag Patsy held out.

An hour later she met her dad at the Victorian for the second day in a row.

"I'm kind of nervous about this," she said with a hand to her stomach. After visiting Patsy, she'd gone to the bank to apply for a loan.

"I'm the opposite. The thought of sharing office space

with my daughter... I was thinking last night, maybe we should buy this place together. I'll have the money from—"

"Too complicated," she interrupted. The thought had also occurred to her, but she quickly squashed it. "What if we decide we can't stand sharing space with each other? What happens if you decide to retire?"

"Honey, I'm a long way from retiring. I like what I do."

"Still..."

He shook his head. "It was just a thought. This place and the renovations could get expensive."

"Hello?" A too-familiar voice called out. What did it say about her that she got a little short of breath?

Her dad leaned into the foyer from the dining room. "Hey, Gunner. How are you?"

Boots thumped on the hardwood floor. "Good. How's it going, Neil?"

"Alex said she was sending someone to meet us, but didn't mention who—did she, Iz?"

She was the one who'd asked Alex to call him. She'd done a quick internet search, but hadn't found anyone who could meet her today. That didn't mean she wouldn't get several quotes.

Gunner stopped at the door. His smile dropped away and his eyes sparked with annoyance. "Alex didn't mention who I was meeting either."

"Well, if anyone can tell us what we're up against in this project, you can," her dad said, patting Gunner's shoulder, completely missing the shroud of tension that settled over the room like a dense fog.

Gunner studied the color of the walls with a thundercloud of a frown. "What is this project?"

"Izzy is thinking of buying this old beauty and turning it into a suite of offices. Maybe adding a sandwich shop."

"Huh." The black look he shot her said he was less than thrilled by the news.

Yep, this would be loads of fun. "You changed your shirt."

"Second time this week, thanks to you."

She looked away from his condescending glare. "My dad says the bones of this house are still good. Can you tell me if that's true?"

Gunner walked closer—close enough that she could pick out the dark flecks of brown in his green eye, which was too close—and glowered down at her. "I'm not a licensed inspector."

"Neither is my dad, but he knows enough about a house to know if it's worth buying."

When his eyes narrowed, she wondered what he was thinking, though she'd never ask. Probably that he wished she was the one who'd died that cold January day. He made it clear he didn't want to be anywhere near her. *Sorry, dude, this is my town too.*

"It's only fair to tell you I charge forty dollars an hour for my services."

"Not a problem," she said with satisfaction. *Take that, you arrogant jackass.*

Her dad was examining the molding around a window. "We'll get a certified inspector in here before she decides to purchase. I can spot water damage and more obvious issues, but we need a professional opinion before she actually makes any major decisions."

Gunner turned his back on her. "I'll take a look around."

"I'll be the one buying the house and paying your forty-dollar-an-hour fee. Not my dad."

He glanced at her, a seven on his Izzy Is A Bore scale. "I'll get a few things from my truck. I usually start outside."

The tension in the room evaporated as soon as Gunner

left. Izzy glanced at her dad to see if he noticed, but he was now inspecting a hole in the wall near a light switch.

When they finished here, she'd pay him—with her own money, thank you very much—and immediately search for someone else to do the work. There had to be another contractor in the area.

~

*I*zzy *is moving to Eden Falls.*

That thought scrolled through his mind like an endless, one-message ticker tape while he walked around the outside of the house.

He kept thinking if he hadn't kissed her that one, fateful, I'm-the-biggest-idiot-alive moment, things wouldn't be so uncomfortable. The kiss was his bright idea, meant to scare her out of her infatuation with him. That part of his plan had worked. She'd been terrified of him ever since. The part of the plan that failed was on his part. He'd never expected to experience any feelings for the teenager. Feelings that still cropped up every time he saw her.

The yard was overgrown and would take some major work. He couldn't imagine Princess Izzy getting dirt under her fingernails or blisters on her palms. She obviously made enough money in San Francisco to buy this historic Victorian, which couldn't be cheap. What would bring her back here after so many years away?

Why was he even thinking like this? What she did wasn't any of his business. She could become mayor of Eden Falls and it wouldn't affect him. Stone was a well-remembered name by most of the town. He could hang the moon and he'd still be known as the delinquent from the trailer park. The kid whose father ran away and whose mother was a drunk. The man who wasn't there to save his sister.

Izzy is moving to Eden Falls.

"Find anything?"

"I'm not a licensed inspector," he repeated, turning to face her.

"Got it the first time, Gunner. Alex obviously thought you were qualified enough to spot rotten siding. Are there any visible holes or cracks I should be worried about? Is the foundation sinking? Signs of termites, mold issues, infestation of rodents? If you can't spot those kinds of things, let me know now and I'll find someone else."

Her irritation was sharp as shards of glass, each word punctuated by her rising voice. He fought a smile, but wasn't sure why. Maybe because he could get a rise out of her with just a few words. Why did that seem like a victory?

"Some of the trim around the windows will need to be replaced. I haven't seen any cracks in the foundation. No sign of rodent infestation. You'll need a professional to check for termites."

"The yard is going to take some major work," he added when she moved past him without a response.

She glanced around, as if seeing the tangle of bushes and vines for the first time. Then she smiled and his heart squeezed uncomfortably.

"What do you think, Gunner?"

He chuckled to himself. She wasn't smiling at him, but at her dad who'd come up behind him.

He picked up a chunk of shingle from the ground and held it out for Neil to see, but made eye contact with Izzy so she didn't get her tender feelings hurt by being left out. "Judging by all the pieces of shingles in the yard, I'll bet the roof needs to be replaced."

"You skipped that detail a minute ago," she stated.

Gunner continued around the house while Izzy and her dad stayed behind. He'd given up hope of a job that would last several months once he found out Izzy might buy the house. Even if she decided to hire him, which she wouldn't, the tension between them wouldn't be worth the paycheck. He didn't need her kind of irritation or temptation.

After circling the house, he went inside and climbed the stairs. He heard Izzy and her dad follow him, so he leaned over the banister. "Do you know where the attic door is?"

Izzy ran up the stairs, her amber eyes shining with excitement. "No. Our first walk-through was so fast we didn't even look in the attic." She ducked into the first room and opened an interior door. "Just a closet. No trapdoor in the ceiling. This room gets great light. Dad, you should consider using this as your office. Come look at the beautiful built-in bookcases."

Her comments caught Gunner's attention. Neil said Izzy was turning the house into a suite of offices. Who would be using them? She could be buying and renovating the house, then renting out the office space while still living in California.

He was surprised by the shot of disappointment that zipped through him, but he shook it off. Her returning to San Francisco would be for the best.

He stood at the top of the stairs as the daddy-daughter duo went into another room. Based on the footprint of the house, the attic would be sizeable. He pointed at a door toward the back of the second story when Izzy reappeared in the hall.

She walked over and pulled the door open, the hinges squeaking. "Bingo. This stairway makes sense, since the back stairway to the kitchen is on the opposite side of the landing."

Gunner trailed Izzy and Neil up a staircase into a huge attic space. Dust and cobwebs covered the windows and sheets masked furniture. Boxes and trunks were stacked haphazardly around, leaving little space between.

In the middle of the room, Izzy spun in a circle. "This is home."

"Don't get your hopes up, yet, sweet roll."

Gunner remembered Mr. Adams calling each daughter by some silly sugary treat nickname. Izzy had always been sweet roll.

A pretty pink touched her cheeks. "I can't help getting my hopes up. This room is so much larger than I expected." She turned to him. "Can a bathroom be added up here?"

"You want a bathroom in the attic?"

"This is going to be my apartment," she said, the excitement vivid in her eyes.

So she was moving back to Eden Falls after all. He wanted to feel another shot of disappointment. Didn't happen. "You're going to live in the attic of a huge house?"

"If things work out, I'll move my real estate office to the second level and Izzy will run her business on the first level," Neil said.

He glanced from Neil to Izzy.

"What?" she asked defensively when he didn't respond. "It's been done before. Can a bathroom be added?"

"Yes."

"Does it have to be over an existing bathroom on the second level?"

"Not necessarily." He circled the attic, looking for damage. The windows, though old, were tight. Only one water leak was visible that he could see. He pointed a flashlight into a corner to show Neil. "Along with a new roof, you may also have to replace some of the fascia and soffits. The roofer can give you an estimate."

"Do you have any recommendations?" Neil asked.

"Apple Valley Roofers will give you a fair price. Their office is in Harrisville."

Gunner hadn't noticed a *For Sale* sign in the yard. He

knew a psychic lived here before, had seen her sign hanging from the fence out front, but didn't know if she actually owned the house. She'd walked around town in colorful skirts, bright scarves, and layers of necklaces. Once she'd touched his hand in passing and said, "You should come see me."

"Excuse me?" He'd never waste money on a medium's opinion.

"I could ease your conscience for fifteen minutes of your time."

"No, thanks. My conscience is just fine."

"We both know it's not. It's time you were released from the guilt you carry."

"Uh-huh."

Suddenly her expression had changed and a bewitching smile appeared. "Love is coming from a very unexpected source, but only if you can move beyond the past which holds you hostage."

He'd walked away, and though he didn't believe, for a couple of weeks he'd half expected Jessica to come home to Eden Falls. She never did, so the psychic was wrong. Imagine that.

For a split second he wondered what ever happened to the woman. He hadn't seen her around town for a while.

Other than the one leak, the attic looked solid, so he moved down to the second floor. Izzy was kicking up a cloud of dust moving boxes and looking under sheets. A kittenish ahh-*choo* escaped her as he hit the bottom step.

The sound stopped him for a moment as a memory rushed forward. Ariel very seldom brought friends to the trailer, but on a weekend, when he was home on leave, she and Izzy were in the bathroom, trying to straighten his sister's extremely curly hair. A hairspray-smelling cloud shot into the hall, and Izzy darted out a moment later and sneezed, sounding like a tiny kitten. The image was so clear in his mind...

That was also the day he kissed her.

He'd bet any amount of money that she remembered. She'd come into the close confines of the kitchen for a glass of water, looked up at him with those big, amber-colored eyes full of teenage lust. He'd been determined to scare it right out of her.

She had no idea the things he'd done growing up to provide for his family. She was experiencing a hero worship or big-brother-of-my-best-friend adoration that he didn't deserve. She was too good for the likes of him. So he'd yanked her close and kissed the living daylights right out of her.

Then he'd chuckled like it was all a big joke. It should have been, but he felt something he'd never felt before. The moment scared him way more than it seemed to scare her. It took everything he had to turn away and act like nothing had happened rather than apologize, because he should have.

What he'd done was unconscionable. She was sixteen to his twenty-two. Yet he'd laughed and walked away with a "Grow up, little girl," and left her standing there with crimson cheeks and tear-filled eyes.

She had no business moving back here. The town didn't have the kind of money needed to support a fancy art gallery.

After inspecting the second floor, where he found more water damage in the room below the leak, he moved to the main level. The wall colors in every room varied from eye-popping teal to purple that was so dense it almost appeared black, bright orange to storm-cloud gray. Every wall would have to be primed before painting. Also, paint had dripped onto the hardwood floor, which would have to be sanded. The moldings would also have to be sanded and cleaned with denatured alcohol. The work wasn't hard, but it would take time and patience.

The kitchen cupboards were flamingo pink against lime green walls. They would have to be replaced or would take days and days of sanding if Izzy wanted to keep what was here.

"Off the top of your head, how much would it cost to replace these cupboards?"

He was surprised to find her only a foot away. He hadn't heard her come down the stairs, let alone enter the kitchen. "Depends on what you want," he said without turning around.

"Not cheap, but not the most expensive, either."

He glanced over his shoulder. She was picking at a piece of flaking paint with a light-purple fingernail. "I assume you want to include the butler's pantry."

"Yes."

When her eyes lit up again, funny things happened in his chest. He had to get out of here before he did something stupid, again. He took a few measurements, then pulled a small calculator out of his back pocket and did some quick calculations while she and her dad continued to look around. When he was done, he found them in the foyer. "Rough estimate, new cupboards will cost somewhere between fifteen to possibly thirty-six thousand. Since I don't know what your idea of midgrade is." Probably much higher than his own.

"How hard would it be to repaint the ones already there?"

"It will take a lot of stripping and sanding before they can be repainted."

Neil frowned. "This is going to be a lot of work, Izzy."

"Do you think it's too much? I can paint the walls, and sand and clean the baseboards myself."

Her dad looked around, hands on hips. "For the price, I think you're getting a gem, but it's going to take a lot of elbow grease and money."

Gunner felt out of place standing in the middle of this daddy-daughter discussion, so he ducked down the basement stairs. He'd expected the same kind of mess as the attic, but there was no clutter. One section held three aisles of sturdy, handmade shelves, and the concrete floor was clear of trash. He didn't see any sign of leaks or cracks in the foundation.

"Any damage down here?" Izzy asked as she joined him.

"Other than one cracked window, I don't see any issues. It will take me another thirty minutes to check the furnace."

"Great." She glanced at the screen of her phone and pulled her wallet from her shoulder bag. "I owe you one hundred dollars."

"I can send a bill with an invoice."

"No. Let's make things nice, neat, and complete." She handed him five twenties.

So much for this job feeding him and Domino through the winter. "I'll send your dad an invoice for tax purposes."

Anger flared in her eyes and she opened her mouth, but he held up a hand. "I know *you're* buying the place, but I have your dad's address. Just keeping things nice, neat—and complete."

Her mouth closed.

He pocketed the money and shook hands with Neil on his way to check the furnace. He had broken hinges to replace at the library.

CHAPTER 5

*G*unner could think of a million places he'd rather be than sitting at a conference table in the basement of the library. Friday night and he was mentally banging his head against the table through what seemed like an endless meeting with Patsy Douglas, as chairwoman, going over each and every detail for the upcoming Harvest Festival.

Most of the members of the town council were present. Patsy always played a big part in organizing the festival, and she set up a pie-throwing booth every year to raise money for the humane society. He'd let her talk him into participating this year. Just what he wanted to do, stand behind a big board painted with a clown's body, stick his head through the hole where the face should be, and get hit with a pie.

Gertie and Albert Rollins had the floor. They were discussing the dance lessons they'd be teaching before the square-dancing exhibition. Though he didn't dance, for some odd reason Gunner had always loved watching petite Gertie and her six-two, three-hundred-pound chef husband square dance. They moved around the floor as if they were one,

mpletely in sync with each other. The idea that two people
uld be so united had always fascinated him. He saw that
id of thing in other couples around town too, but had never
rsonally experienced it in a family. He'd hoped to build that
th Jessica, but she had other plans.

"Have all the sign-ups been turned in?" Patsy asked.

"There's no rush. People can still sign up that morning,"
Gertie replied. She glanced at him. "We just need to make
sure the sound system is working."

Her implication that he wouldn't do his job irritated
Gunner. He'd never failed to have the system up and running
since he took over after his return from the Army. "It will be
working, as always."

"Thanks, Gertie and Albert. We'll get back to you about
the sound system in a minute, Gunner," Patsy said.

Shoot me now.

"Where are we on the craft booths? Are they all rented
out?"

Beam Garrett shuffled through a stack of papers in front
of him. He was filling in for his brother Rowdy, who was still
on his honeymoon. "We have one more spot available."

Madam Venus, with her colorful skirt and bright head-
scarf, swept into the small room. The committee was stunned
into silence when she held out a check to Beam, a line of
bracelets jingling on her arm. "I'd like to take that remaining
booth."

"What you do isn't a craft," Gertie said.

Madam Venus turned with an expression Gunner couldn't
read. "What I do is most certainly a craft."

"Maybe witchcraft," Gertie mumbled.

"I am *not* a witch."

Beam glanced from Madam Venus to Patsy.

"I know this town is full of unbelievers," the psychic
said, her intense dark eyes pausing on each committee

member. "But people from all over are searching for answers to their questions, and the Harvest Festival is well advertised. I won't cause any trouble or force my opinion on anyone. Like other people selling their wares, this is how I make my living."

Patsy nodded. "You're welcome to rent the booth."

When Beam reached for the check, Madam Venus's hand touched his. She smiled at him. "Last night was a success. You'll have a boy in nine months."

Beam, who was six-five and over two hundred thirty pounds, blushed beet red.

Patsy snorted out a laugh. "Well, now we all know what *you* were doing last night."

Beam shook his head. "We aren't trying to have another baby."

"Surprise," Madam Venus said before she swept out much as she'd come in, with bracelets jangling together.

"Congratulations," Noelle said

"The woman is crazy. Sophia isn't even two. She keeps us up half the night. We're both so exhausted we don't have time to think."

Gunner had never seen the big guy look so flustered.

Patsy raised perfectly arched brows. "Obviously you have enough time to...cuddle."

"Welcome to parenthood," Manny Hernandez said with a chuckle. The guy was perpetually happy. Always had been. Even in high school, when he was teased about being short, he grinned and joked right back.

"Sorry, Beam," Patsy said. "At least we have all the booth spaces rented. Now, back to business." She turned to Maude Stapleton. "How about the food vendors? Has everyone turned in their licenses?"

"Yes," Maude said, with a no-nonsense nod of her head. "Everyone is legal."

Patsy made another check mark on one of the papers in front of her with a flourish.

Beam cleared his throat. "Look, can everyone please keep what just happened to themselves? Don't say anything to anyone, including my wife. If Madam Venus is right and Misty is pregnant...She. Will. Freak. And then she'll stab me."

Everyone around the table knew Misty well enough to know she would probably maim Beam in one way or another. She hadn't loved being pregnant with her first baby. At least Rita Reynolds, Eden Falls' gossip train wreck, wasn't on their committee. Rita might be tiny, but she was a mighty force when it came to spreading town secrets.

Gunner had endured the gossipmonger his whole life. His dad leaving set things off, and then his mom's drinking only made it worse. So had his sister's death, but when word of Jessica's leaving got back to him, he'd gone to the post office, aimed his finger at Rita's nose, and told her to stay out of his business. Of course, his warning only made her tongue-wagging harsher. Now he was a bully who preyed on inno-cent women.

"What about games for the children? Have they all been assigned out?"

Tatum Ellis looked over her list. "The fishing booth, apple bobbing, cakewalk, and apple toss will all be manned by volunteers who agreed to serve for two-hour shifts, although one volunteer had to drop out of the ring toss because of a family matter. I still have to fill that ten-to-twelve time slot."

Gunner couldn't believe what he was about to do a second before he raised his hand. "I'll take it."

"Thank you," Tatum said. "Dahlia Dallas volunteered to set up a new activity for the kids. She's providing everything she needs, and asked the girls at the salon to help her run that booth for the day. Everything should be set up by eight and will run from ten to four. Saunders Orchards are donating the apples. I've had fifty people sign up to bring baked goods for the cakewalk, and Colton McCreed has donated money for the children's prizes."

Gunner had never officially met the *New York Times* bestselling author who'd moved to Eden Falls and married Alex, but knew Colton regularly donated both time and money to Alex's hometown.

Patsy sighed. "Gotta love a good-lookin' man who pulls out his checkbook."

"Sounds like everything is set for the little ones, but you didn't mention face-painting. My kids love that booth," Manny said.

"Leo Sawyer worked that booth by himself last year. The line was a mile long, and he couldn't keep up with the demand," Tatum replied. "He said he'd work the booth this year, but he'll need help."

Patsy glanced around. "Do we have any other artistic people in town?"

"We could ask the high school art teacher for recommendations," Noelle suggested. "I bet a few students wouldn't mind helping out."

"Great idea," Patsy said. "Manny, can you take care of that for us?"

Manny made a note on his own stack of papers. "Sure. I heard Izzy Adams is moving back to town. Does she still draw?"

"Oh, Izzy was a wonderful artist! Great idea, Manny," Patsy said. "I talked to Izzy yesterday, but she didn't exactly confirm that she's moving back."

Everyone looked at each other. Gunner played dumb. He didn't know if her moving back depended on buying the Victorian or not, and he wasn't about to get involved.

Patsy tapped the eraser end of her pencil on the table. "I

bet Rita Reynolds would know."

A laugh rippled through the group.

"Gunner, didn't you inspect the house next to Owen's office with Neil and Izzy?" Manny asked.

"Uh…" He hated how fast word traveled through town. It wasn't his job to divulge Izzy's business. "I did do a quick inspection on the house, but I don't know their plans." Which was true. Though he'd walked through the house with them, he didn't have final decision details.

Manny elbowed him. "Is she still in town?"

All eyes were on him, like he should know more than he did. "Last I heard, she flew back to California today."

Patsy pinned him with a look and raised brows. "Well, is she coming back?"

Noelle held up her phone. "I just texted Phoebe. Izzy is moving to Eden Falls and should be back sometime next week."

"The next time you meet with her, can you ask if she'd be willing to help us in the face-painting booth this year, Gunner?"

"I don't plan to meet with her," he was quick to say. "I just walked through the Victorian to see if I could spot any major damage."

Patsy turned to Tatum Ellis, who was acting as secretary of their committee. "Make a note in the minutes to check with Gunner about Izzy painting faces at the next meeting." She glanced at Gunner. "Thank you."

She didn't give him a chance to argue. Instead, she moved on to his responsibilities with sound systems and lighting.

Thirty minutes later he walked out of the meeting he never wanted to be involved with in the first place. Someday he would tell Alex no, referral or not. Most of his jobs came by word of mouth anyway. The quality of his workmanship was advertisement enough. He didn't need all this extra froufrou stuff in his life. Why he'd ever agreed to serve on the committee or be involved in more than his regular duties was beyond him.

He'd let Alex get into his head, she'd sent him on a guilt trip, and then sweet-talked him into volunteering, neat as you please.

Now he had to try to convince Izzy to paint kids' faces in the booth right next to the ring toss.

Thanks, Alex.

When he got home, Domino was waiting by the door, tail thumping. Gunner squatted down and rubbed the belly his dog offered. "Hey, buddy. You ready to go for a walk?"

Domino jumped up and bounced around on all fours until Gunner clipped a leash to his collar.

They walked to the high school, a few blocks away. He stood on the other side of the fence and watched the football game between the Eden Falls Bulldogs and Glenwood Knights, remembering his days on the football field with Beam. Back then he was anything but a carefree high school kid, worrying about things like Ariel needing new shoes and money for her school field trip to the Seattle Space Needle.

After the game, which the Bulldogs won, he and Domino walked to Riverside Park. The sun was down, and the temperature had cooled. He unclipped his dog and watched him nose along the bank of the river while thoughts of Beam and Misty having a second baby and his own failed marriage plagued him.

He and Jessica had met while serving in Iraq, when he'd flown a helicopter in to pick up what was left of her squad. They ran into each other again a few months later. Soon after they were getting together every chance they got.

He'd never been in love before, but Jessica captured his heart and tied it into knots. He returned to the States and started school before her time was up, but she stayed with him everytime she was home on leave. They lived together for a while before he finally talked her into marriage. Soon after, Jessica was pregnant, and lost the baby a month later.

He didn't know she'd tried out and was accepted into LA's SWAT team until he came home from installing a new sink for Maude in Pages Bookstore's employee kitchen and found her things gone. Ninety days later he was served with divorce papers.

Jess had always hated goodbyes. And small towns. And children. She was meant to jump from planes, dodge bullets, and carry a gun—anything for an adrenaline rush.

Their short marriage wasn't very happy. Jess needed action, and after his eight years of service, Gunner was just grateful to be back home, away from the horror of so much death and destruction. He appreciated the quiet of nature. She craved adventure and wanted to be on the go all the time, bored silly with his quiet nights at home.

Gunner believed things happened for a reason. He wasn't sure what purpose was served by falling in love with Jessica, or why she lost their baby. Wasn't sure he wanted to know. If she'd carried the baby to full term, most likely he'd be a single parent now. Which wouldn't be much different from how he'd grown up taking care of his baby sister.

He was just a speck on this earth, along for the ride. So far it hadn't been much fun. Not that he had a bad life. He made it back from the war. The Army put him through college, which he finished while serving in the Reserves. His PTSD wasn't as bad as what most of his buddies suffered. He considered himself one of the lucky ones.

His thoughts turned to his sister and her short life. If Ariel had lived, he would have made sure she went to college. He often wondered what she would have picked as her major. Nothing he suggested, that's for sure. She always went her own direction and fought him every step of the way. Ariel wanted a much different life than the one she was experiencing. She wanted the moon and the stars, and he wanted to give them to her.

After he was shipped out, Ariel, Joanna, and Izzy had been inseparable, for which he was still grateful. Those girls changed his sullen sister, brought joy to her life. Before Izzy befriended her, she'd been quiet and embarrassed by her circumstances. Missing out on extracurricular activities because money was so tight.

He'd done what he could, but Izzy did more. She invited Ariel to go places, included his sister, got her to join school clubs, built her confidence. He'd watched them hug every time they separated. He wasn't much of a hugger, and his mom was usually too drunk to even notice if her daughter had shoes on her feet, but he'd seen Ariel's face and knew she loved the physical contact—the sense of belonging.

Done with his exploration, Domino loped over and nudged Gunner's hand, knocking him out of his reverie.

"Hey, buddy. You ready to go home?"

Domino yipped and wagged his tail.

Gunner gave the dog a good rubdown before they walked back to the house.

~

*T*hings happened quickly in California. When Izzy informed her roommates she was moving, one had a friend looking for a place. And that was that. Since she'd cleaned out her office before she attended Stella's wedding, she wouldn't have to go in and face her ex-boss slash ex-boyfriend, Baron Van Buren. Though she'd love to walk through his beautiful gallery one more time.

Izzy rented a U-Haul and loaded up her belongings, then she made the rounds, telling the friends she'd made over the years goodbye. She and her best friend since college cried on each other's shoulders for thirty minutes. Jasmine was bright and colorful and everything that Izzy felt she herself lacked.

After extracting a promise to visit from her friend, Izzy took off for Eden Falls. She decided to make two days of the fifteen-hour drive since she'd never driven a U-Haul in her life. She didn't own a car. While living in the city, if her destination wasn't within walking distance, she used public transportation. The thought of driving the truck was a little intimidating.

Two hours out of the city, her cell phone rang. Baron's name lit the screen. Which was a surprise since she hadn't heard from him since she left a week earlier. She reached out to press the OK button, then stopped. He didn't have anything to say that she'd want to hear. She declined the call and turned up the radio volume. The phone rang again, and she ignored the call while she car-danced to Justin Timberlake's "Can't Stop the Feeling."

When she pulled over for gas, she called her dad. "Hey, sweet roll," he said after one ring. "You on your way?"

"I left this morning. I should be in Eden Falls by late tomorrow afternoon. Phoebe said I could stay with her until after the closing."

"What about your things?"

"I rented a storage unit."

"You can store everything here."

She didn't really want to get into the reason she didn't have that much stuff. She'd lived lean in San Francisco. "A storage unit will be more convenient. I'm calling because I need the names of two or three contractors."

"Why?" her dad asked after a moment of silence. "Gunner is the best in the area."

"It's smart to get several quotes on a job, isn't it? That's what I've always heard."

"That's good business practice generally, but you can count on Gunner to give you a fair price, Iz. Ask anyone in town—in the area. You'll get the same answer."

"Still…"

He blew out a breath. "Okay, I'll text you the numbers of a couple of guys some of my clients have worked with."

"And a pest control company and a roofer."

"Gunner suggested Apple Valley Roofers," her dad said.

So, we just trust him? "Daddy."

"Okay. I'll ask around about roofing companies, too."

"Thank you. I'll see you Tuesday."

Back on the road, she visualized how she'd arrange furniture and set up desks. She'd need a receptionist slash assistant. The attic would have to serve as her office until the first floor was finished, because she had to have a place to live. More shelves would line the basement's walls for storage. Her dad could use one side to store old files.

Her phone rang. Baron again. She declined the call.

The first time Baron had asked her to dinner, she'd known accepting was a mistake, but the thrill of being noticed by an older man overrode logic. Soon their dinners and outings merged with work and she lost track of her own goals and dreams—lost herself as Baron molded her into the person he wanted her to be when representing the gallery and his name. His constant correction of everything she did had her endlessly doubting herself, which wasn't like her. She started questioning every decision she made, quit believing in herself.

Looking back, she was embarrassed by how she'd allowed him to take over her life so completely, both professionally and personally. She never meant anything to him. She was simply an employee, a puppet he formed to do his will.

The Van Buren Gallery of San Francisco was one of the

most prestigious in the United States, and they had clients from all over the world. Baron lived and breathed for the gallery. Everything he did involved business in the art world. He didn't have room in his life for marriage and children, yet, naïvely, she'd hoped...

Funny thing, even after all the time she devoted to the gallery and Baron, she wasn't that upset about losing the job or ending their relationship.

Her job at the art gallery had been a dream come true. She started as an associate and worked her way up to a manager's position, which kept her busy. When the economy slowed, she worked even harder to keep Baron happy. He only became more demanding, more impossible to please. Her hours were extended until all she did was work and attend social gatherings with him or representing him.

As she drove north, she didn't like how often Gunner Stone and his stormy expression popped into her head. Now she could laugh over her teenage crush on him. He'd been very successful at jolting it right out of her the day they'd kissed. Or rather, he'd kissed her. She was too stunned to move or even breathe, then blushed so hard her cheeks practically burst into flames.

Then she was mortified when her eyes filled with tears.

His sharp words, *Grow up, little girl,* had slashed her young heart to pieces. Crushes were painful anyway, and wanting to be noticed and recognized was agonizing. Gunner's actions had decimated her feelings for him that day.

Before the kiss, he'd been an enigma. She'd always wanted a big brother, and was so jealous that Ariel had one who teased, cared for, and loved her so much.

She'd skittered back to Ariel's bedroom as fast as she could without running.

Ariel died the next day. And Gunner went back overseas immediately after his sister's funeral.

CHAPTER 6

*T*he morning after she got back to Eden Falls, Izzy went to the bank to sign yet another piece of paper to finish the application process for her loan. The bank manager was more interested in discussing her certainty that Madam Venus was a witch rather than a psychic.

"I don't know the woman," Izzy said. "I've only talked to her once."

"You be careful around her. She's put hexes on several people in town."

That was news to her, though Madam Venus scared her a little. Izzy had never wanted to know her future or fortune, but the psychic had made a few predictions for her. She would find love in the Victorian, but to Izzy that could mean anything. She'd fallen in love with the house long ago. Bringing it back to its former glory would be an act of finding love.

Madam Venus predicted her business would be successful. Izzy hoped that insight was right. She was putting a lot of money into this endeavor and wanted things to work out.

"Do you think the loan will go through okay?"

"Sure. I don't see any problems. Did you actually go into Madam Venus's house? I heard there are chicken heads and—"

"How long before I'll know for sure?"

"—feet hanging from the ceiling."

Izzy shook her head. "No. So about the loan…"

The bank manager looked disappointed that Izzy hadn't seen any dangling chicken parts. "We should have an answer by Friday."

Next she checked Town Hall for Alex, but the mayor's office was empty, so she headed over to Pretty Posies. Her dad was only able to provide the name of one other contractor. As mayor of Eden Falls, Alex was a fountain of information. There had to be other reputable handymen or handywomen around the area besides Gunner Stone.

Alex was busy with a customer when Izzy entered, so she wandered around looking at all the fun tchotchkes. When Alex's grandmother had owned Pretty Posies, she'd brought in several gorgeous antique armoires to hold flower displays and local artisans' wares. Alex hadn't changed the interior much since inheriting the shop.

She stopped to look at some blown-glass vases.

"Those are amazing, aren't they?" Alex asked, stopping next to her.

"They are. I love this orange one. So unique. The work actually looks familiar. Who's the artist?"

Alex picked up a business card and handed it to Izzy. "He lives in Bellingham, but he used to work for a company in San Francisco."

Izzy studied the card, positive his work had come through the Van Buren Gallery a couple of years earlier. "Mind if I hang onto this?"

"They're free for the taking," Alex said waving a hand. "So, the Victorian is yours."

"Barring any problems with the loan."

"Everything will go smoothly. Congratulations, and welcome to the Eden Falls business world."

"Thanks. I'm pretty nervous about venturing out on my own."

"I imagine most people are. I was lucky enough to have worked in this shop for years before my grandma left it to me. Still I was nervous I'd do something wrong." Alex straightened a few pots of flowers. "Everyone in town will back you up."

Not everyone, she thought, imagining Gunner's scowl.

"You have to come to the Chamber of Commerce breakfast with me tomorrow morning. We meet at the Senior Center the third Wednesday of every month."

"I'm not a business owner yet."

"You will be." Alex flashed her sunshiny smile.

Izzy wished she felt as confident as she had the two days she walked through the Victorian. Her vision, so clear then, had faded around the edges over the weekend. After the closing she'd have a lot of work to do, but felt pretty confident she could handle most of the interior painting and some of the yardwork herself. "I'm going to need someone to act as contractor for the renovations and hoped you could give me a name or two."

"Hands down, Gunner Stone is the best in the area, and his prices are unbeatable."

Izzy felt like a balloon that had just been pricked with a pin, the air fizzed out of her with a *fffttt...* "He seems to be really busy around town. I'm not sure he'd have time for my job. Is there anyone else?" *Someone who doesn't hate me, or blame me for his sister's death? Someone who doesn't look at me with contempt.*

"There really isn't, not with Gunner's qualifications. He can build or fix anything. He fixed my walk-in cooler last week. He was the contractor on Noelle's café. He fixed the fire damage at the back of Patsy's Pastries. I could go on and on." Alex plucked a withering blossom from a nearby golden chrysanthemum. "Did he do okay with the walk-through for you?"

"Yes," Izzy answered grudgingly. "I'm going to need someone who can really focus on this job until I can open for business. It may take months."

"If Gunner can't do the job, or he's too busy, he can give you the name of someone who can. He might have to subcontract some of the work out, but he always uses companies or men he's worked with for years."

So she'd have to talk to Gunner one way or the other. And how would that look if she asked him for the name of *another* contractor? She forced a smile. "Great."

"You won't be sorry, Izzy. I'm sure he can give you many, many references."

She didn't think there was any air left in her balloon, but nope, a little more leaked out. "Any idea where he might be today?"

"He's at Dahlia's Salon hanging beautiful shelves he built."

"Great," she repeated. Time to put on her big girl panties and face the man with incredible heterochromia eyes, chiseled jaw, and a scowl more intimidating than Baron's.

~

*G*unner sensed when Izzy entered Dahlia's back room before she spoke. Maybe sensed wasn't the right word. He smelled her perfume…warm, sunny, with a touch of flower. She hovered just in his periphery, as if she was unsure about stepping all the way through the door.

He placed a level on the shelf he'd just hung. Perfect.

"Gunner."

He glanced toward her. She had her hair pulled up, a few straggly pieces falling around her face.

"Hey."

She took a quick breath. "I'm looking for a contractor who might be interested in doing some renovations on the Victorian once I close." She waved a hand. "I understand you're really busy. Alex said you might have the name of someone who—"

"I'm not."

"—could...help...me..." she said, her words trailing away.

"I'm not too busy."

"Oh."

He turned to face her. She stiffened and took a step back, like she was afraid he'd attack her. He couldn't blame her after what had happened. Had it really been fifteen years since he kissed her? "When do you close?"

"Well, I'm not sure yet. Possibly four to six weeks. I'm hoping closer to four."

"Can you give me an idea of what you're planning?"

She tugged a piece of paper out of her jeans pocket and spread it out on top of a nearby table. "Alex said you do most of the jobs around town, but this is going to take months."

He put his hand on the mile-long list. Roof was number one. "Can I look over the list, Izzy?"

"Oh. Uh...sure." She glanced down, then back up at him. "There may be more. I just jotted down the most important. Should I...just leave the list with you or..."

She looked cute when she was flustered, and he almost felt sorry for her. Almost. "Can you still get in the house?"

"Yes."

"I'll be done here soon. I can meet you at the house in an hour. You can show me what you want done. I'll work up a quote. You look it over and decide if my price is right. If not, I'll give you the name of two other contractors around the area. Both are reliable and fair."

"Okay," she said, but didn't look happy at his suggestion.

He watched her disappear through the door, all pink-cheeked and frustrated. A minute later, Dahlia walked in.

"The shelf is exactly what I hoped for."

He chuckled. "Your drawing was pretty specific."

"Sorry, I can be a little bossy."

"Not bossy. You're precise. There's nothing wrong with that."

She leaned against the table and picked up Izzy's list. "What's this?"

"Izzy is buying the psychic's Victorian and wants to do some renovations. I told her I'd give her a quote."

Dahlia's smile slipped away. "This is a really long, major list. Add a bathroom in the attic?"

He started packing up his tools. "She plans to live up there."

"She's buying a huge house so she can live in the attic?"

Again, he wasn't going to divulge Izzy's business plan. He put his level in the toolbox with a shrug.

"She likes you."

That stopped him. But only for a split second, then he shook his head.

Dahlia held out the list. "She blushed when she asked if you were here."

"Izzy and I don't exactly...get along." He folded the list and slipped it in his pocket. "I'm giving her a quote, but I'm sure she'll explore her options."

"That's a big job. It'll keep you busy for several months."

"If I get it."

Dahlia crossed her arms and looked down at her shoes.

He walked over and tugged her into a hug. "We didn't work, Dahlia."

"I know." She wrapped her arms around his waist and held him tight. "I know, but I wish we did."

"Yep."

She laughed, her face buried against his shoulder. "You're as talkative as usual."

"Yep." He cupped the back of her head and stuck his nose in her hair, which always smelled like peaches.

~

*I*zzy spotted Gunner wandering around the side of the house when she arrived after discussing business licenses with her dad at his office.

Dried leaves crunched under her tennis shoes as she picked her way over vines and fallen branches. She could start out here even before the closing. She hated yardwork as a kid, probably because it was part of the regular, boring chores her parents assigned. Now, the thought excited her. She could imagine what she wanted the yard to look like. From the shrubs to the flowers to the lush grass, the picture was vivid.

Even if the closing never happened, she'd clean up the worst of the yard before snow fell. Branches and bags of leaves could be stacked along the back fence until she got a dumpster delivered. She glanced up at one of the attic windows. The whole side yard would be visible from there.

Gunner looked over his shoulder and her heart skittered like the dry leaves underfoot. "If you plan to use the garage, you'll have to fix the roof."

"I'll add it to the bottom of my list."

"What are you going to do about parking?"

She stared down at the broken concrete of the driveway. It

would have to be replaced. "I'll add a parking lot in the back. People can pull in on this side of the house, and there's enough room on the other to add an exit driveway." She pointed to the iron fence. "Owen said I could take down that section of fencing and people can use his lot when this one's full. I can add a walkway that leads to the front door, border it with flowers..." Her words petered out when his eyes glazed over.

He would never be a client, so she really didn't care what he thought, but it would be nice if he showed a little interest. *He can't be the only handyman in the area, Alex.* There had to be someone who smiled once in a while.

She peeled a fleck of paint off the house. "Madam Venus couldn't have painted all that long ago, so why is it already flaking off?"

He took the paint fleck from between her fingers. "Probably didn't prep before painting, or used interior paint rather than exterior."

"How long would it take to paint the exterior?"

"A crew can get the job done in a week, maybe less, but it will take them a week of prep before they can start." He glanced from the house to the sky. "If the weather doesn't become an issue."

If she could get a roofer lined up immediately after closing, the painter could follow right after and possibly finish before snow. Izzy tugged out her phone and swiped to the calculator. "How much would that cost?"

A tiny smirk quirked one corner of his mouth. She hadn't realized she'd said anything funny. "I can get you an estimate or two from companies I've used. Do you have colors picked out?"

He was standing too close, his intense stare making her uncomfortable...ly hot. He smelled fresh—soap and sunshine. She took a step away, hoping he'd get the hint. For someone who didn't seem like much of a people person, he sure crowded her space. "Not yet, but I can go to the hardware store after we're finished here."

He turned, hands riding low on his hips. "You leaving the yard until spring?"

"I plan to clear out the worst of it, but yes, the rest will have to wait."

A breeze shook the trees, sending a few leaves fluttering to the ground.

Gunner looked skyward, again, his Adam's apple extended. She was tempted to reach out and touch it.

"Do you still draw?"

The question surprised her. "How do you know I draw?"

His Adam's apple bobbed. "Ariel had a picture you drew of her—of us—on her wall."

She knew the picture, remembered taking time on the details of not only her friend, but the object of her childhood crush. The memory made her sad. It was the first time Ariel had been mentioned to her in years.

He glanced at her with raised brows.

"Occasionally."

"The Harvest Festival committee wondered if you'd consider manning the face-painting booth for a couple of hours, from ten to twelve. They'll supply everything you need. Leo Sawyer usually runs it alone, but he can't keep up with the demand."

Another surprise. "You're on the Harvest Festival Committee?" she asked, fighting a smile.

His frown was instant. "The proceeds go for school supplies."

Gunner Stone was rattled. She weighed the option of drawing out his agitation like he would do to her or let him off the hook. The temptation was strong... "I'd love to help out."

"Tatum has the details. I'll tell her to get in touch with you."

"Who's Tatum?"

"The Goth girl who works for Alex."

"Oh, right. I met her last week. Are there more details than arriving at ten and painting faces?"

Another frown appeared, and she savored a second moment of triumph, which was really mean on her part, but couldn't be helped.

"Should we go inside?" she asked when he didn't answer.

He followed her around to the porch. "You'll need to get the overhang and the porch fixed before you paint."

"Is that something you or another contractor"—she wasn't ready to give in yet—"can do?"

"Yes. It can be repaired while the roofers are working."

"How much will that cost?"

He blew out a breath crammed with frustration. "I can get you a complete, itemized quote as soon as I know what you want done. Are you staying with your parents?"

"I'm at Phoebe's until after I close." She inserted the key into the rusty lock. "Would you have a problem with me doing some of the painting?"

"Once you close, it's your house. You can do whatever you want."

His matter-of-fact comment didn't match his coarse tone, and his expression was unreadable as usual.

"I'm surprised the woman who owns this place gave you access before closing." He took the key from her and inserted it into the rusty lock. "Some WD-40 and a good cleaning will fix this."

She swung the door open, the hinges complaining loudly. "I guess she trusts me."

The second she stepped inside, her vision was back, clear

as a summer sky. A sense of coming home swept over her, so strong she felt dizzy.

"Madam Venus wasn't very impressed with the house. Or the town. I think she was hoping to find ghosts haunting the halls. To her this beauty was just a house."

"And it's more than a house to you?"

She turned at his mocking tone. "Yes." She wondered what he saw when he looked around. Couldn't he imagine the possibilities, or was this just another job? "This old Victorian is a work of art. She has a history, a splendor that most houses don't have. She wants her qualities, though rusty and old, to shine and be remembered."

"You talk about the house like she's a person."

"Ariel told me you called the Army helicopter you flew Persephone—the name of a Greek goddess, queen of the underworld. Did you talk about the hunk of metal as if it was a person? A she?"

His gaze raked over her face, stopping on her lips. She fought the urge to press them together.

"If you love this house so much, why don't you fix it up and live here?" he asked after a long moment. "Why a business?"

"I have to earn a living, and I don't need this much space. I'm—" She stopped short of saying *single, alone, on my own*.

"You could get married and fill it with little Izzys."

You'll fall in love in that house. Madam Venus's prediction came floating back. Even if it came to fruition, she'd have to find another place to live. If her prediction about a successful business came true, the house would already be full.

"Not going to answer?"

"You didn't ask a question."

He nodded, that darned smile barely quirking one side of

his mouth. "Madam Venus hasn't given up on this town yet. She rented a booth at the Harvest Festival."

She turned toward him. "That's the second time you've mentioned the Harvest Festival."

"Since you plan to live in the attic, let's start up there," he said, gesturing toward the stairs.

"Seriously, you don't seem the Harvest Festival type."

"You think you know my *type*?"

"Sure. You're the ornery, festivals-are-too-much-fun type."

He nudged her to get her moving up the stairs. "Just like you're the princess, can't-get-my-hands-dirty type."

She stopped. "Excuse me? You don't know anything about me."

"And you don't know anything about me. I happen to like the festival," he said, nudging her forward again.

She snorted out a laugh. "I doubt it."

Leading the way up the stairs made her feel self-conscious. She'd rather be the one bringing up the rear.

When they reached the attic, she looked around. Heavy work lay ahead up here. "I'll clear all this out before you start. I want to divide the room into three sections. My bedroom will be on that end and the bathroom here," she said pointing one way and then the other, trying to define the space. The room was so clear in her mind. She hoped he could imagine a smidgeon of her vision. "I'll draw everything out."

"You want the space to be left open like a loft, or do you want walls?"

"I want the bathroom and bedroom walled in, but with frosted glass pocket doors if possible. That will allow the light in from all directions. I'll use the kitchen downstairs, so that isn't an issue."

"That's a long way to walk for a cup of coffee."

"I don't drink coffee."

His frown was back. "Everyone drinks coffee."

"Not everyone."

"The first time you ran into me you were going into The Roasted Bean."

"Tea."

"Tea," he muttered under his breath, his look of disgust registering about a seven-point-five. "The attic is wide enough for pocket doors, and there's room for a kitchenette."

A kitchenette. She hadn't thought to add one, but there was plenty of space. And it might be kind of nice for warming up a slice of pizza or a quick cup of hot chocolate.

He glanced around while rubbing his index finger under his lower lip. She wanted to know what he was thinking... and didn't at the same time.

At one of the windows, she stared out at the gray clouds gathering over the mountain peaks.

The sky reminded her of the last time she saw Ariel. That day had started out sunny too. Ariel wore her pink puffy coat and a funny striped hat with bright yellow tassels hanging over her ears.

Izzy swiped away the tear that leaked from one eye before turning back toward Gunner, hoping he hadn't noticed.

His sudden scowl told her he had. "You okay?"

"Dust. I'll lug all this stuff out after the closing."

"I can't get you a quote until I know what you want up here. How big you want your bedroom and the bathroom. How you want everything laid out. Do you want hardwood floors or carpet? How much of the bathroom do you want tiled?"

"Okay. I'll get something drawn up in the next couple of days and drop it off at your place. Do you live in town?"

"Eight-twenty-one Cedar Avenue. Most days I'm not home before six."

She quickly typed the address into her phone. "Do you want to go through the rest of the house, or wait until I've sketched some ideas?"

"Let's finish."

She led him to the second floor. "Each of the five bedrooms will be a different real estate agent's office. I'll have my dad bring them by as soon as I close so they can pick their offices and the colors."

Again, his eyes glazed over.

"The only upgrades will possibly be in the bathrooms," she said getting back to business he might care about. "Dad had an inspection done while I was in California. The report said the plumbing was updated before Madam Venus bought the house, so there's that."

"Once I start, the attic will take three to four weeks, unless I run into problems," he said, thumbs in the back pockets of his jeans. "There might be a little finish work, but you could live there. Do you have the inspection with you?"

"I left it in the car."

Nine shades of irritation flashed over his face. *I've died and gone to hell.*

"I'll be right back." She bounded down the stairs. Grateful to escape. She yanked the front door open and ran smack into Phoebe. They both screamed.

"Why are you screaming?" Phoebe said, hand to heart.

"You're the one screaming. You scared me to death."

They both turned when they heard the thumping of boots. Gunner appeared around the curve of the staircase. "What happened?"

Izzy and her sister pointed at each other. "She scared me," they said in unison.

Phoebe's finger turned from Izzy to Gunner, a lazy smile creeping over her face. "Are you two—"

"No!" she and Gunner said in unison.

Gunner grumbled under his breath and thudded back up the stairs.

"What's up with him?"

Izzy moved past her sister to get the inspection papers from her car. "Same thing as always. His cornflakes were soggy this morning or his underwear is too tight or..." *He hates my guts.* "Who knows? He's Gunner."

"So what's he doing here?"

"He's giving me an estimate for the renovation."

A quick smile zipped across Phoebe's face. "You don't sound very enthusiastic."

"Exactly how he and I both feel."

"I wouldn't mind him being my handyman," Phoebe said with a seductive hum.

"You like Gunner?" Izzy asked.

"Not like that, but you have to admit he's worth looking at."

Yes, he is.

"I can hear you," Gunner called from upstairs. "Sound carries in an empty house."

Izzy ran to her car and grabbed the inspection papers. When she went back inside, Phoebe was staring up at the gargoyle chandelier. "Cool light. I haven't been in here in years."

"When were you in this house?"

"I used to babysit for the Bassett family when they lived here."

"I forgot all about them. Do you know where they moved? The attic is full of stuff. Maybe it's theirs."

"No." Phoebe shook her head. "I can do a little research, though."

"Thanks, Phoebs."

"If you and Gunner don't get along, why not find

someone else?" Phoebe asked in only a slightly lowered voice.

"Both Dad and Alex says he's the best in the area," she whispered. "I plan to get a couple of other quotes, though."

"If anyone would know, it's Alex." Phoebe cupped her mouth. "Hey, Gun! Alex said you're the best handyman in the area. If Izzy hires you, what comes with the package?"

"Phoebe!" Izzy hissed.

"She'll get what she pays for." Gunner's muffled voice came from somewhere above their heads. "Still waiting for that inspection report."

"Oh, right!" Izzy ran up the stairs. She found Gunner squatted in front of one of the bedroom windows, his back to her. His green T-shirt showcased his gorgeously bulging biceps, broad, solid shoulders, and narrow waist. Her eyes moved down to his—

"Whoa, nice view of the assets, Gun. You should be in a jeans commercial with a butt like that."

Izzy jumped, caught gawking at the guy most likely to kill her in her sleep.

Gunner straightened and flashed a rare but extremely knee-quaking smile at Phoebe while she got an *Are you still here?* look.

"No signs of rodents."

Good news. She didn't want rodents. Or spiders. Or snakes. She held out the inspection report.

"Show me around," Phoebe said tugging Izzy out of the room.

"When are you going to finish showing me what you want done?" Gunner called.

"Relax, Gun," Phoebe hollered back as they ran up the attic stairs. "I'll get her back to you in a few minutes."

Izzy decided she'd have to keep Phoebe away if she hired

Gunner, or she'd spend her days fending off Phoebe's crass remarks and blushing. She'd never get anything done.

As soon as Phoebe reached the top of the stairs, she stopped. "Wow, none of this stuff is Madam Venus's?"

"I haven't had a chance to ask her yet."

Phoebe lifted the top off a box. Newspapers and magazines. "So this is where you're going to live? Why don't you take one of the bedrooms? Where's the closest bathroom? And the kitchen is two floors down."

"Gunner said he could install a bathroom and a kitchenette." Izzy pulled a picture up on her phone. "I want the space to look kind of like this." She'd found the picture while surfing through pages and pages of attic space ideas. Airy and open. Her only dilemma was where to fit in a couple of closets.

"You never told me why you're going to live in the attic of a gigantic house."

Izzy shifted a spindle back rocking chair covered in dust. "If I stay up here, Dad can take the second floor for his real estate offices. One side of the first floor will serve as my event planning space. I'll rent out the other side for small birthday or retirement parties. I could even turn the dining room and sunroom into a small tea and sandwich shop."

"Tea shop?" her tough-cop sister laughed. "Who is going to visit a tea shop?"

"If I set it up right, I think it could be really popular."

Phoebe shrugged. "Maybe for women like Rita."

She wasn't going to let Phoebe's pessimism deter her ideas. "I picture a place where women can meet for lunch. I think if I advertise, I can get people from all over the area."

Phoebe opened another box and pulled out a milk glass vase. "This is pretty."

Another box produced a whole set of pink depression glass dishes. Baron would go nuts if he saw this stuff.

"I think you're right, Iz. A tearoom might just make a killing." Phoebe unwrapped a delicate china cup. "You should get Leo to help with advertising. He's great at that kind of thing."

Still inseparable, Phoebe and Leo became fast friends in kindergarten. He'd spent more time at their house than at his sixties-hippie parents' farm. Nerdy Leonard had morphed into smoking hot Leo after he graduated from high school and became a multimillionaire. Amazingly, the money and his spectacular good looks hadn't changed him. He was still just as kind as he'd been as a kid. "Where is Leo?"

"Visiting his parents. We're going to a movie later. Wanna come?"

"I'm not sure I'll have time. I have to draw up attic plans for Gunner. Oh, wow! Look at this, Phoebe. An old Victrola phonograph."

They shifted some boxes out of the way and Phoebe lifted the top. A hinge was loose, but the turntable was in perfect condition. "There's a crank handle in here. Should we try it?"

Izzy glanced around like they might be caught doing something they shouldn't, but what would turning the crank a few times hurt? She opened the cabinet below and hit the jackpot. A pile of records lay in dust-covered sleeves. She slipped one from the cover and wiped it carefully on her jeans. "Stan Kenton and His Orchestra, *His Feet Are Too Big For De Bed*."

"Yeah, that one," Phoebe said, inserting the handle.

She cranked away while Izzy set the record on the turntable, then she gently shifted the needle into place and twisted the arm to rest on the record. *Scratch. Scratch. Scratch.* Then the tinny, slightly garbled, wonderfully nostalgic music came out of the speaker.

Phoebe laughed and bowed, man-style. "May I have this dance?"

"It would be my pleasure." Izzy took her hand and Phoebe led her to an uncluttered spot on the attic floor.

~

*G*unner heard music coming from the attic and wondered what the sisters were up to now. He'd been trying to concentrate on the inspection report, but the voices floating down from above kept distracting him.

Izzy distracted him.

When he heard the laughter above his head, his feet carried him to the attic door. Izzy's voice tugged him up the stairs. At the top, he stopped to watch them dance to an abrasive song playing on an old phonograph.

The way Izzy moved, the way she turned her head, brought a flash of memory. The touch of her lips against his, the astonishment—which had to mirror his own—on her face when he leaned away. A huge, very stupid, moment in his life of regrets and mistakes. The memory sent a solid jolt straight to his chest.

A week after their kiss, he was back in Iraq, but the memory of her mouth lingered.

"Come join us, Gun." Phoebe spun Izzy in a circle.

Izzy's eyes met his for a brief moment before she looked away.

He shook his head and walked down the stairs. He had to concentrate on the quote for Izzy. The work on the second floor would be minimal unless Neil planned to make major changes. According to the inspection, the house was structurally sound. The roof needed to be replaced, which they all knew. Depending on the damage to the soffit, they could probably finish the work in three to five days. The cost of her living space would be contingent on the grade of bathroom fixtures and tile she wanted to go with, but he could give her a quote in the midrange.

The wood floor would have to be refinished. He could hire someone to do that while he worked on the attic.

He walked down the back stairs to the kitchen, the garish colors making him wince. If she didn't want to invest in new cupboards, he'd have to strip and sand the paint off. The linoleum countertops were shot and would need replacing. Luckily Izzy could live here while the work was being done. Same with the upstairs. Only one room would have to be painted for her to move in. All the existing bathrooms were in working order, though she might want to replace the chipped porcelain tubs and sinks.

Phoebe joined him in the kitchen. "Have any idea what you're getting yourself into?"

"A job that will last until after Christmas."

"You wouldn't take advantage of my little sister, would you, Gun?"

For a split second he wondered if Izzy had told Phoebe about the kiss, about how he'd taken advantage of her when she was a teenager. Then she pointed to the pink cupboards and he realized she was talking about the house.

"I don't take advantage."

CHAPTER 7

*H*er dad showed up at the Victorian and walked through the second floor with Gunner, discussing what changes he'd want for his real estate business. The landing, which was like an old library with two walls of beautiful built-in wood bookcases, would become an open office for his receptionist-slash-secretary. No walls would need to be taken down or moved. Rather than let his agents choose a room, he made assignments.

"It'll cause less fuss," he told Izzy. "I'll get a range of neutral colors they can pick from for paint. I don't want wild."

Izzy started a new list. First priority would be the front porch, even before Gunner concentrated on the attic. Her plans for the first floor would have to wait until after the top two floors were completed, since her dad had to be out of his old office by the first of the year. Pending major issues, she didn't see any problem getting him in here before then.

While Izzy talked about her plans, Phoebe became less skeptical and more excited, offering occasional suggestions.

"This is going to be fantastic, Izzy." Phoebe tugged her

into a hug. "At first, I thought you were crazy, but I get it. This place is going to be fabulous."

"Thanks, Phoebs. Hearing you say that means a lot." She pulled back and glanced overhead at the sound of her dad's and Gunner's footsteps. "I'm pretty nervous. This is a huge change in location and job."

"You've made huge changes before. You moved to San Francisco at eighteen, got your degree, and worked your way to the top at a prominent gallery. What happened with *Baron Van Buren*?" Phoebe said with an English accent.

"He's American."

"Well, I don't know how you put up with the guy for so long."

She'd never told Phoebe about Baron. Dating her boss was something she kept to herself. So no need to tell her they'd broken up, either. He'd called several more times since she'd been back, so often she finally turned her phone to vibrate only. He hadn't left a message or texted her what he wanted, and she had no intention of calling him. "It was my job to put up with him. When does Stella get home?"

Phoebe ran a finger over the turquoise paint in the dining room. "Tomorrow. We should take her out for dinner or something."

"Agreed. The first night Rowdy is back at his bar and grill, we'll take her out." She slipped into the butler's pantry and grabbed her purse from the counter. "I'm going to see if Madam Venus plans to clean out the attic before closing. Want to come?"

"Uh…" Phoebe wrinkled her nose like a bunny. "I think I'll pass."

"Why? Come on. I don't want to go alone. She creeps me out."

"That's why I don't want to go."

A male chuckle made them both turn toward the door. Leo

walked into the room. "Phoebe's been creeped out by Madam Venus since she told your sister she was going to have twins."

Izzy turned to her sister. "You got a reading?"

"No," Phoebe said, cutting a hand through the air. "She touched my stomach in passing. I almost arrested her."

"She just touched you and said you'll have twins?"

"She ever touches me again—"

"Still, twins. I mean, if you believe her. That's amazing."

"That's what I said." Leo wrapped his arm around Izzy's neck. "It's like getting two prizes in a box of Cracker Jacks."

Izzy laughed. Leo was comfortable, a friend she'd known her whole life, the brother the Adams girls never had. "That's a positive spin. I loved the little boats."

"Cracker Jacks prizes were replaced a few years ago by a digital code," Phoebe said.

"No-o-o," Leo wailed. "The ring that whistled was the best. What kid wants a digital code? Who do I write to?"

"So, boy and girl? Two boys…"

"None." Phoebe frowned at Izzy. "No twins. The lady is crazy."

Izzy ducked under Leo's arm. "Well, I still need to visit the crazy lady about all that stuff in the attic."

"I'll come with you," Leo said. "I could use a reading."

Phoebe waved as she headed for the front door. "You two have fun. I love the house, Izzy. Congrats. I'll help in any way I can. Bye, Dad. Bye, Gun," she called up the stairs.

"Bye, Phoebe," Gunner said as he and their dad appeared around the banister.

"See you Sunday for family dinner?" their dad asked. "Stella and Rowdy will be there. Gunner, you should join us."

Surprise shot across Gunner's face. "I don't want to intrude."

Despite his disgust with her, Izzy felt sorry for him. He didn't have family to join for Sunday dinner.

"You wouldn't be intruding at all," her dad said. "Leo, Rowdy, you, and me... For the first time in my life the male-female ratio will be even."

"You should come, Gunner," Phoebe said.

He shook hands with her dad. "Thanks for the invite. A home-cooked dinner would be great."

The guy was pleasant to everyone but her. When he glanced her way, she got an expression that said, *And she's still here.*

Yippee. Can't wait for Sunday, she thought.

She locked the door, and everyone trooped down the saggy porch steps and tangled walkway to their cars. Leo opened the passenger door to his truck. "Do you have time for lunch after we see Madam Venus?"

"Yes, if you'll help me buy a car afterward."

"Let's see, spend the afternoon with a beautiful woman or go home and watch TV. Hmmm. That's a tough decision." He tipped his hands up and down as if physically weighing the two. "Deal."

"Don't let those car dealers get the best of my sweet roll, Leo," her dad said.

"We'll get something safe and reliable."

"Not a tank." Izzy really wanted to get busy on the drawings for the attic, but she needed a car.

"You'll get the plans for the attic to me?" Gunner asked, stopping next to her.

"Tonight. Tomorrow at the latest."

She climbed into the passenger seat of Leo's truck. Leo shut the door, spoke to Gunner, then ran around and slid into the driver's seat. "What'd you do to piss off Gunner?"

"Breathed the same air." At Leo's curious glance, she elaborated. "He's treated me like I have a disease since his sister died."

"But that was an accident. There was nothing you could have done to stop it."

"Tell that to Gunner," she said as she watched the subject of their conversation get behind the wheel of his own truck. He glanced up, stared a moment, then drove away.

Leo started his truck. "Want me to talk to him?"

"No, but thanks, big brother. The worst is yet to come. His quote will be too high and I'll go with someone else. That will really give him a reason to hate me." Enough of the topic of Gunner and the house. "How are your parents?"

"Still bead-wearing, tie-dyed hippies." Leo pulled away from the curb.

"They still have their farm?"

"Yep, still farming. They still consider me part of the establishment." He crossed the river and came to a stop sign. "Which way?"

"Right," she said pointing out the side window. "How are you part of the establishment? You dropped out of college and built your own company. You've never worked for anyone but yourself."

"Right, but I moved to Silicon Valley. I was accepted by society."

"You're not estranged, though, are you?" Izzy asked. Leo's parents had never moved past the sixties. They'd never married—free love was still alive and living on an organic farm just outside of Eden Falls.

"Nope, I visit them once a week. Mend a fence or have their driveway graded occasionally."

Izzy pointed to the left. "Turn here."

They bumped along the dirt road until they came to Madam Venus's sign at the end of her driveway.

"Whoa," Leo said when the black house came into view. "Not very welcoming."

"She might have company." Izzy indicated the car parked near the porch.

"I'll wait here."

"I thought you wanted a reading."

"You Adams girls are still so gullible. I already know what my future holds. Fast cars and lots of women."

Izzy laughed. "You're still as humble as always."

She climbed out of the truck and made her way to the porch. A voice called, "Come in," before Izzy could knock on the front door. A young girl, tears running down her face, pushed past her and ran outside.

Madam Venus appeared through the black curtain in the corner of the room.

"Is she okay?"

"Upset. She won't marry the man she has her heart set on. In a few years, she'll be grateful, but for now her heart is broken." Madam Venus scooped up a cat and ran her hand over its black fur. "What can I do for you today? I didn't miss the closing, did I?"

"No. I came because of all the furniture and trunks in the attic."

"It was there when I bought the house, so I guess it's yours. I tried to track down the owner with no luck."

"Were the previous owners the Bennetts?"

"No. The Odenkirks, and before them the Hogans, then the Bennetts. No one claimed the contents."

Okay, that wasn't much help. She'd have to look through the boxes and see if she could find a name. "Well, thank you. Sorry I interrupted."

"You didn't. The reading was over. She just repeated the same question in different ways, hoping for the answer she wanted. By the way, you should answer your phone so it will quit ringing, though that won't stop him."

Izzy pulled out her silent phone.

"I mean the next time your ex-boss calls."

Oh, yeah, this lady gave her the creeps.

"And tell the man you're with congratulations from me."

Izzy glanced out the door where Leo still sat behind the wheel. Madam Venus moved next to her and looked outside. There was no way she could have seen Leo from where she'd been standing.

"I'm not a scary person, Isadora. I just can see things before they happen."

"Why should I tell him congratulations?"

"He's going to have twins."

Izzy's jaw dropped. "Leo?"

"I see your sister has talked to you. Seems I freaked her out, too." She laughed. "And now I'm freaking you out."

"You are."

She touched Izzy's arm. "Tell your old boss no thank you. Your life lies in another direction now."

"Baron?"

"I'll see you at the closing." Madam Venus turned and disappeared behind the black curtain, the cat still in her arms.

"What did she say?" Leo asked when Izzy got back in the truck.

"Uh… The stuff in the attic isn't hers. Let's go."

"What else did she say? You both glanced out here, and now you look like she yanked the rug out from under you."

In more ways than one. Izzy shook her head. There was no reason to freak out Leo, too. "Madam Venus knew my ex-boss has been calling, and she said I should tell him no."

"No to what?"

"I don't know. She didn't say."

"What was wrong with the girl who came out crying?"

"Madam Venus told her she isn't going to marry the man she wants."

Leo leaned forward so she'd look at him. "Are you okay?"

Izzy hid a smile behind her hand. "I'm just excited to be an aunt."

Leo started the truck. "She's still predicting twins?"

"Yes." She laughed. "Let's eat. I'm hungry."

～

Gunner stepped inside and greeted his tail-wagging dog. He was tired, sweaty, and hungry, but Domino came first. He picked up a tennis ball and went into the backyard to play catch for thirty minutes.

He never had a dog as a kid. They couldn't afford food for themselves, let alone a pet.

Domino was like a lifeline for him. Someone who loved him despite his faults or inability to open up and expose things he'd kept hidden for most of his life.

He sat in a lawn chair and Domino lay at his feet until they both cooled off. There weren't many more warm days left where he could relax in the backyard with his dog. Domino usually came with him when he worked outdoors, but that might not be possible if he got the job on the Victorian. Though the yard was fenced, and Domino was calm and didn't bark much, Izzy might not be willing to have a dog hanging around on the porch.

"Come on, Dom. I need a shower and food." His dog jumped to his feet. "You ready for dinner?"

His dog's smile made him think of Izzy.

Inside, he poured dog food into Domino's bowl and hit the shower. When he climbed out ten minutes later, he heard a knock on the door. No one ever came to his door. Domino yipped.

He quickly donned boxers, struggled to pull jeans over

wet legs, and grabbed a T-shirt on his way to the door. "Coming," he hollered, after another knock.

Domino, standing sentinel, yipped again.

He pulled the door open. Izzy, going down the front steps, stopped and turned. "Oh! You are home. I saw your truck, but you didn't answer your door. I was going to look out back."

He hadn't expected her to finish her attic plans so quickly. "I was in the shower."

She looked up at his wet hair like she was verifying his story. Domino's tail thumped his leg and Izzy immediately bent to pet his dog. "Hi, Domino. Hi, pretty boy. How are you?"

"I see you got a car."

"An SUV." Her smile hit him hard in the chest. "My first."

"Your first SUV?"

"Car. I've never owned one. In San Francisco I walked or took—" She waved a hand. "Sorry, I babble when I'm excited."

That statement would revisit him tonight as he tossed and turned while thinking of her.

Straightening, she looked him up and down. "Your shirt has wet spots."

"Because I just got out of the shower."

"You don't seem like the dog type."

Dog, shower, car, dog, her conversation was bouncing all over the place. "What does that mean?"

She shrugged. "You just don't seem like...you'd take the time."

He wasn't the festival type or the dog type. Did she think he wasn't capable of showing affection or emotion? Though if asked, Jessica would probably agree. He pushed the door wider.

She looked past him, as if she was afraid of what he kept in the house.

"All the torture gadgets are locked up where people can't see them."

She narrowed her eyes. "I only had time to draw up the attic plans. I'll just drop them off."

He took the papers she held out. "We should look at these together in case I have any questions. I can't give you a quote if I don't understand what you want. Domino will protect you." His dog was leaning against her like he was deprived of attention. "He loves your 'pretty boy' compliments."

"I'm not scared of you."

"You look pretty scared."

As if to prove him wrong she stepped inside.

He waved her toward the kitchen. "Let's sit at the table." It wouldn't take long to look over her plans, and then he could eat.

He trailed her, catching whiffs of her perfume. They sat kitty-corner from each other and he spread her drawings out. She was good, and her pictures were much more detailed and precise than he'd expected. She'd even drawn little books on a built-in bookshelf and faucets at the bathroom sink.

While he looked over the next design, his dog groaned in ecstasy at the attention Izzy was giving him.

"I like your house."

Something in her voice made him look up. "But, like owning a dog, obviously not what you expected. Did you think I'd still be living in the family trailer with the broken steps?"

"No, I just didn't expect such mature furniture or the beautiful painting over the fireplace."

"You thought you'd find beanbag chairs and sports posters."

Her glance floated around the room. "I'm surprised by the

throw pillows in the living room and"—she struggled to keep a straight face—"the place mats on the table."

"The pillows came with the sofa and the place mats were left by my ex-wife."

Izzy lost the fight and smiled. His heart hit his ribs hard again. She'd always had an amazing smile. She just didn't use it around him.

"Can I ask you a personal question?"

No. He inhaled deeply. "Sure," he said on an exhale.

She averted her gaze and bit her lip. "Why did you get a divorce?"

Not what he'd expected. "I didn't. She divorced me."

"Oh. Because you were...?"

"Because I was what?" he asked, aware of his defensive tone.

Her shoulders lifted around her ears. "Ornery?"

He snorted. "Jessica was—is an adrenaline junkie, and small-town life didn't do it for her. She works for SWAT in LA."

"Was it horrible?"

"The divorce?"

"No. I imagine any divorce is horrible, and I'm sorry. It's just that I never imagined you being married."

She was full of jabs tonight.

"I was asking about Iraq. I..." She glanced around the room again, looking everywhere but at him. "I used to imagine you there, and those images flashing through my head were horrible."

He picked up on what she was saying. She used to think about him. In one brief, very stupid moment, he'd yanked her in for a kiss to terrify her out of her crush on an older guy, but still she pictured him so far away. "Yes. Most of the time it was horrible."

"I'm sorry, but still, thank you for serving our country."

He nodded. He could tell she had more to say by the way she was chewing her lip, so he waited.

"Do you still love your wife?"

Another unexpected question. "Ex-wife, and no." He stood and gathered the papers. He didn't like talking about Iraq, or his personal life with anyone, especially not Izzy. "Did you make copies of these?"

"No."

"Can I?"

"Sure."

He left the room, ready for her to go. Her perfume, though subtle, was taking up too much air in his house. After his copy machine took its sweet time warming up and spitting out her plans, he returned to find her examining the only family photos he owned. One was him holding Ariel just after she was born. He was almost seven in the picture, but he looked much older. Probably because his father had left three years earlier, his mom didn't know who Ariel's father was, and Gunner was worried about how they were going to feed one more person when they didn't even have money for rent.

"I'm sorry about your mom."

His mom. She'd answered the phone five times in the eight years he'd been away from home. The last time she picked up she told him she had lung cancer. He came home to two headstones bearing his last name because he couldn't get back in time to even say goodbye.

He hoped his mom had finally found some peace, because she'd never been happy here, with two kids she really didn't want and no man to help. He and Ariel had lived through plenty of *This guy's the one* or *I can tell this man's a good one. He's in this for the long haul.* None of them ever were.

After a couple of nights with the headboard banging against the wall of their trailer, *The One* always disappeared like all the rest. Then Gunner would hide the booze while

Ariel held their mom's hand as she sobbed over the guy who wasn't quite as perfect as she'd first thought.

"Thanks." He'd heard Preacher Brenner did a really nice job with her funeral, and that it was well-attended despite what people knew about Natalie Stone. Even her funeral was provided by the goodwill of others. She'd made their whole life a charity case. Still, she was his mother, and he loved her.

He handed Izzy her originals. "I think I can put together a quote with what I have here. Remember it will go up or down depending on the bathroom fixtures, tile, flooring, and other things you choose."

She pulled three paint samples out of her back pocket. "I went to the hardware store and picked out paint colors for the exterior. What do you think?"

He held up the three samples against his own wall and her smile disappeared.

"Get five or six samples of each color you like. Tape them up around the outside of the house and look at them during different times of the day, under different light. I promise, you will change your mind about this one."

"I already have." She laughed. "Wow, I actually got a smile out of you."

He blew out a breath.

She grabbed his arm and squeezed. "What is today? Hurry, what's the date? I have to mark this on my calendar. Gunner Stone smiled! With only me in the room!"

"Okay," he said, handing her the paint samples and turning her toward the door by the shoulders.

She was beaming like a kid eating a Popsicle on a hot day. Her eyes sparkled with delight because he smiled at something she said. Imagine if... *Don't go there.*

"I guess I'd better go. That's the second time I've heard your stomach growl."

"I didn't have time to eat dinner."

She bent to give Domino another good scratch behind the ears. "I'll see you around, pretty dog."

"You're destroying his masculinity."

"Oh! Oh!" She pointed at his face. "A smile *and* an attempt at humor. I really have to go. I can't take all this cheerfulness. Next, you'll laugh and... Nope, I just wouldn't know how to handle that."

He opened the front door, determined to keep a straight face.

"Bye, Gunner Stone." She stepped outside. "Go eat."

"Yep." He waited until she backed out of his driveway before he closed the door. He glanced down at his dog. "Hear that, Dom? She thinks you're pretty."

❧

*I*zzy parked her SUV and leaned back in the seat, appreciating the smell of leather. She felt like a sixteen-year-old kid with a brand-new driver's license, she was so excited about her car. In San Francisco she'd taken the trolley or Uber to get around. Now, at thirty-one years old, she had her first car.

Just as she unlocked Phoebe's apartment door, her phone vibrated and Baron's face popped up on her screen.

So much was changing in her life. Might as well cut the strings here as well. She connected the call. "Hello, Baron."

"Isadora. I've been calling for days."

"I know." She closed the door, flipped on a living room lamp, and dropped into a chair. "What do you want?"

"Why haven't you answered?"

Truth. "I didn't want to."

"When are you coming back to work?"

"You tried to fire me. Remember?"

She heard a shuffling followed by a long pause and looked at the screen to see if he'd hung up.

"You're not fired," he stated briskly. "When are you coming back?"

"I'm not. I quit. I moved back to Washington, Baron. You were interviewing my replacement the afternoon I left," she said, starting to lose her patience, which happened often with self-indulgent, demanding Baron. This was just like him to pretend the blowup in his office never occurred.

"That's not acceptable. I need you here at work tomorrow. I'll have a ticket waiting for you at the Seattle airport."

"Not going to happen."

"Izzy, I need you here. Tomorrow."

"Baron, I don't live in California anymore. I bought a car today. I'm buying a house."

"You… What?"

She instilled a little syrup in her tone. "Isn't your new manager working out?"

"I fired her. She doesn't know a Jackson Pollock from a Willem de Kooning. She was worthless. Besides…I miss you."

That part was a lie. Everyone was replaceable in Baron's life. She relaxed into the cushions of her chair, something she wouldn't have dared when talking to Baron before. Being in the same room with him was like watching an action movie where the main actor took an unexpected turn toward danger. "I'm sure she wasn't that bad. Especially if *you* did the interviewing."

"Come back, Izzy. I'll double your salary."

She put a hand to her chest. Double? Baron hadn't been stingy with her salary before she left, but Madam Venus's words came back to her. That chapter of her life was over. "No, thank you."

"Triple. I'll triple your salary."

That stopped her. Triple. That was a whole lot of money. More than she'd ever make as an event planner. But the Victorian... She could fix it up, rent the second floor to her dad and the main level... Her plans for a tearoom would still work. She'd hire someone else to manage the space for her.

Madam Venus's face floated through her mind. Why was she even considering the predictions of a psychic? But the lady had been so serious. Life in San Francisco was fast-paced and hectic, and she'd loved it. Eden Falls was new and slow, and she loved it even more. "I won't be back tomorrow."

"Izzy, you—"

"But I will think about your offer and let you know by the end of the week."

"I can't wait until then. I need your answer now."

"Then my answer is no."

"You have until Friday morning to let me know." *Click*.

She'd never held the cards with Baron. He'd always run the show, always expected and ordered. She'd run herself ragged to please him. For what? Money? Baron's approval? Love? Hers for him, not the other way around. He wasn't going to change, even if their relationship did.

The front door opened and Phoebe and Leo walked in. "Leo showed me your new car, Iz. How do you like it?" Phoebe asked.

"I love it."

"Why are you staring at your phone?" Leo asked.

Izzy smiled. "Funny story."

CHAPTER 8

*I*zzy chose a simple fit-and-flare dress with a side-tie and heels for the Chamber of Commerce breakfast. She met Alex out front of the Senior Center so she wouldn't have to walk in alone. Though she probably knew most of the people in here, she was experiencing impostor syndrome. She wasn't a business owner yet and didn't feel comfortable about being there.

She entered and immediately realized she was overdressed. And of course, out of a room full of people, the first person she spotted was Gunner Stone. He looked her up and down and turned away.

This will be as much fun as the renovations.

She hadn't mentioned to him last night that a second contractor was coming to look over the project today. By getting a second quote, she'd at least have an idea if Gunner's prices, when they came back, were reasonable. If he was the best, his prices would reflect that.

She was welcomed by most of the business owners, hugged by her dad, and had a chance to talk to Karen from The Dew Drop Inn about her plans for the Victorian.

"Please, drop off some of your business cards as soon as you have them. I turn people away because the reception room at the inn is already booked or people only want to rent part of the room for a smaller party."

"You're making me feel better. I didn't want to take business away from the inn."

Karen's smile was friendly. "Not to worry. Believe me, there's plenty of business to go around."

She sat at a table between Alex and Beam Garrett, who co-owned Eden Falls Hardware and Lumber, and chose a veggie omelet and orange juice from the limited menu. A speaker talked about marketing and ways Eden Falls businesses could help each other with promotion.

Izzy hadn't thought about that part of the business yet. She'd done plenty of marketing for the art gallery, but they'd never been involved with cross-promotions. Baron wouldn't have been open to the idea, but it made business sense to help each other, especially in a small town.

She left the breakfast with several ideas for promotions and good wishes from the business owners of Eden Falls.

On the sidewalk out front, her phone rang. She expected Baron, but it was a number she didn't recognize.

"Hello?"

"Izzy, it's Troy. Joanna wanted me to call. We had a baby girl this morning just after six."

"Oh, my gosh! She's early. Is everyone healthy?"

"Everything went great. Momma and baby are doing well."

"Congratulations! How is dad doing?"

"I'm very proud of my girls."

"I hope they're both up for a visit."

"I think Joanna would love to see you. I have to go by the office for a few hours."

She waved as Alex passed by on her way to Pretty Posies.

"Tell Joanna I have a couple of errands to run, then I'll be there."

"Will do, Iz."

She hung up and headed to the flower shop.

~

*A*fter the monthly chamber breakfast, Gunner ran home to pick up a forgotten tool for his first job. When he passed the Eden Falls Cemetery, his gaze automatically strayed toward the small hill where his mom and sister —his family—were buried. The leaves on the maple that grew near the plot were just beginning to change, and soon the headstones would be covered in a layer of withered burgundy foliage.

Usually he could spot the flowers he delivered once a month, but today someone stood on the hill blocking his view. That someone looked familiar even from the road. His chest tightened unexpectedly. Izzy visiting his sister's grave raised emotions in him that he'd rather keep dormant.

She'd been doing that to him a lot since coming back to town.

He automatically slowed his truck and pulled to the curb. Occasionally he spotted people he knew visiting the only cemetery in Eden Falls, but he'd never seen anyone standing over his family's headstones. Yet there she was, holding a fistful of bright yellow sunflowers, one of Ariel's favorites.

He wanted to get out and ask what she was doing. Completely stupid question. She was paying her respects to someone she'd been close to years ago.

He wanted to go stand next to her and do the same.

He wanted her to go back to California so his life could return to what it was before Rowdy and Stella's wedding.

He wanted to kiss her.

Jessica had never visited the cemetery with him. Maybe it was just as well he didn't have a memory of her offering him sympathy and hugs, or holding his hand while he shed guilty tears when he came to ask his sister's forgiveness again.

Gunner rolled down the window of his truck and breathed deep, trying to get air into his constricted lungs. If Ariel had lived, he liked to think she'd be married now. Going through her things after her death, he found a shoebox of little trinkets, things girls liked to keep. A pressed flower, a bubblegum machine ring, a "meet me at our spot after school" note—possibly from a guy she never told him about. A guitar pick with the words "I pick you" and a heart embossed on one side. He didn't know she'd played the guitar until he found one in a beat-up case under her bed. Vague journal entries alluding to a boy that she'd kept secret. Gunner never found a name, so he had no idea who she was meeting.

She might have married this high school boyfriend, or met the love of her life in college. No matter what she chose as a career, she would have lived here or nearby. He wouldn't allow himself to imagine anything else.

He shouldn't have left Ariel alone with a mother who most of the time was too drunk to know what year it was, let alone if her daughter had enough to eat. Instead of trying to hook up with the gorgeous girl he'd met at the bar the night before, he should have gone ice skating with his sister on that cold December day. If only he could change that one moment when he told her no, everything would be so different now.

Gunner pulled away from the curb, drove into town, and turned in to the employee parking lot behind Patsy's Pastries. Carolyn Garrett answered his knock on the back door. She wore a look of frustration and a smudge of flour on her cheek. A pink bandana held her red hair away from her face.

"I am so glad to see you."

"I love it when a woman says that to me."

Her cheeks flared with color, just like he knew they would. Sweet Carolyn had always been a blusher.

The sparkling clean kitchen of the pastry shop was filled with the scents of citrus, cinnamon, possibly pumpkin spice, and powdered sugar. This was the place to hang out after school. Of course he could never afford to, but Patsy had usually found odd jobs for him, mopping floors, cleaning the front windows, washing out the trash cans. And she always sent him home with more money than she should and a box of baked goods—treats he could pack in Ariel's school lunch —when he finished.

"Hi there, handsome," Patsy said pushing through the kitchen door. "This guy gets better-looking by the day, don't you think, Carolyn?" She laughed when Carolyn's cheeks burned brighter. "If you weren't already married, this would be the guy to go after. He can fix anything. Can't you, Gun?"

"So, which oven is giving you problems?" he asked to move the conversation off Carolyn and himself.

"This big baby right here," Patsy said, patting one of two industrial ovens in the kitchen. "He wouldn't heat up this morning."

"He?"

Patsy grinned. "Tom Hanks. The other is Rita Wilson. They work well together."

"Oka-a-ay, so Tom was working fine yesterday?"

"Yep. This is the first time he's ever given us a problem."

Gunner pulled the oven away from the wall.

"How about a piece of coffee cake and a cup of joe while you work?" Patsy asked.

"How about a cup of joe now and two pieces of coffee cake when I'm finished?"

"You gotta watch out for this guy, Carolyn. He can sweet-talk a woman right out of her panties."

"Pat-se-e-e," Carolyn groaned.

Gunner got to work with another chuckle. Patsy never had much of a filter.

~

*I*zzy left the Eden Falls Cemetery with a feeling of melancholy she didn't like. She wished, when she talked to Ariel, that her friend could talk back. Ariel had always been full of advice, and Izzy could use some right now. Baron's offer to triple her salary... She would never have another opportunity to make that much money—ever. What was she thinking to buy a huge house and try to open a business in a town as small as Eden Falls?

She was angry with Baron for calling. He couldn't have offered to triple her salary when she worked for him? He couldn't have expressed a moment of appreciation? He couldn't have just let her take a week off for her sister's wedding without going off the deep end? If he'd given her the vacation she deserved when she requested, she wouldn't be here right now. She'd be in her beautiful office at the gallery, working on the next exhibit event. For Van Buren Gallery. For him.

She climbed out of her car in front of Patsy's and procrastinated for a few minutes by perusing the tempting treats through the front window. Most looked too beautiful to eat.

Inside, she was met with smells as tempting as the pastries looked. Two young people, a boy and girl she didn't recognize, were working behind the counter. The line, about ten deep, moved quickly, and soon the boy was smiling at her. "What can I get you?"

"Actually, I was wondering if Carolyn and Patsy are in?"

"Patsy," the guy hollered. "Someone is here to see you."

A moment later, Patsy pushed through the kitchen door,

not a plantinum-blond hair out of place. Her smile was always like a warm hug on a rainy afternoon. "Well, look who's here. A little birdie told me everything's a go on the Victorian. I know you'll paint. Thank you for that. The color Madam Venus chose... Wow!"

Izzy leaned against the counter. "I bet that little birdie was Rita."

"You would win that bet. Not sure where she heard the news, but she's spreading it all over town. She said you were going to open an event planning business. Love! That! Idea! I have people in here all the time asking if I know someone who can help organize an event, and I don't."

"Well, now you do."

"Have you got business cards? I'll hand them out."

"I'll get some to you, but first I'm going to wait until I actually close on the property."

Patsy raised a perfectly arched brow. "You don't have to live in the Victorian or have an office to plan events."

She'd been holding off until she had an office set up, but why? Patsy was absolutely right. She could plan events in a coffee shop. And money coming in would be excellent. "If you know someone, give them my name. I'll get business cards to you as soon as possible."

"Perfect. I'm excited about this. Remember, if it's a wedding you're planning, Carolyn's your girl for the cakes."

"I will. And that brings me to why I'm here. If you have a minute, can I talk to you and Carolyn about something?"

Patsy waved her into the kitchen. "We're kind of at a lull at the moment. One of our ovens is on the fritz. Until Gunner can get it working, we have too much time."

Gunner's head was behind the oven, which suited Izzy just fine. She didn't need his hostile stare aimed at her a second time this morning. Though they'd made a slight connection—at least in her mind—last night, he seemed back to his usual self at the Chamber of Commerce breakfast. Sad that the end sticking out was more amiable than the handsome front end.

"Carolyn, look who's here for a visit. Coffee, Izzy? Maybe a cup of herbal tea?"

"I'd love some tea."

"Tea," Gunner muttered from behind the oven.

"You two have a seat in my office. I'll be there in just a minute. How are things going, Gunner?"

He mumbled something else Izzy didn't catch.

She and Carolyn took a seat in front of Patsy's desk and spent a quick minute catching up before Patsy stepped into the office and pushed the door almost shut with a foot. She set two cups of tea on her desk and moved around to her chair. "Now, what can we do for you, Iz?"

"I'm not sure if you know about the house I'm buying," she said to Carolyn.

"Everyone knows," Carolyn said. "Congratulations."

"Well, I also thought I'd add a small tea and sandwich shop on the dining room side of the house. It would overlook the side garden—when I get the yard in shape. Anyway, I was hoping I could buy some pastries from your shop daily to offer. I could pick them up every morning before I open."

"How many pastries do you think you'd need a day?" Patsy asked.

She lifted her cup of tea. "I'm not sure. I guess a variety of about two dozen. Things people can eat with their fingers like muffins, scones, or pound cake, maybe a few cupcakes or a specialty cake each day." She glanced at Carolyn. "That chocolate bundt cake you made for the restaurant in San Francisco was to die for."

"What do you think, master baker?" Patsy asked.

"A couple dozen shouldn't be a problem," Carolyn said. "Are you sure that's all you'll need?"

"Some cookies might be nice," Patsy added.

Gunner tapped on the open door. "The heating element is bad. I'll have to run into Harrisville for the part. Should be an easy fix. I'll have it working by this afternoon."

"You are my hero, Gun. You're Carolyn's hero too, but she's too shy to admit it."

"I'll settle for being your hero," he said to Patsy with a wink. "Carolyn's husband carries a gun." He flashed a quick smile and Carolyn's cheeks lit up like brake lights. The look he gave Izzy said, *Oh, it's you again? Yawn.*

She was tempted to throw her cup of tea at him. That would wake him up. Instead, she looked at Patsy. "You're right, cookies would be nice."

Before heading to the hospital, she bought a pink frosted donut to go with the pink roses she'd picked up from Alex. Joanna looked radiant propped up by several pillows, a sweet baby nestled in her arms.

"Beautiful roses. Thank you," she said when Izzy set the bouquet on the windowsill.

"For a beautiful momma. And look at this little doll," Izzy said, mesmerized by the tiny pink bundle. "She's gorgeous."

"Troy and I think so."

Izzy sat on the side of the bed. "How are you feeling?"

"Other than tired, I feel great. Third time's a charm."

Izzy laughed. "I'll have to remember that."

An hour later she rushed into Noelle's Café. Gertie Rollins pointed to where Phoebe sat in a booth at the front window.

"You're late."

"I know. I'm sorry. Joanna had her baby last night, so I ran to the hospital for a visit."

"How is she?"

"Fabulous, and the baby is darling."

"Good. Hey, did you ever find out who owns all the stuff in the attic?"

Izzy sat back against the red vinyl of the bench. "No. Madam Venus said it was there when she moved in. She checked with several of the previous owners, who all said it wasn't theirs."

"What are you going to do with it?"

"Drag everything downstairs. I'll store it in the sitting room at the back of the second floor until I can sort through it. If I can't find anyone to claim the stuff, I can refurbish some of the furniture and use it to decorate the house."

Phoebe waved someone to their table. "Hey, Gunner. Want to join us?"

Izzy turned in time to see his smile drop when he spotted her.

"No, thanks. I'm in a rush." He backed toward the counter.

Gertie stopped next to their table. "What can I get you today?"

Izzy held out her menu. "I'll have the chef salad."

"I'll take the BLT with a side salad. Leo wants the bacon burger and fries."

"Leo's coming?" Izzy asked after Gertie walked away.

"You don't mind, do you?"

"Not at all." She leaned forward, resting her forearms on the table. "Actually, I wanted to talk to you about Leo."

"What about him?"

"Is something going on between you two?"

Phoebe snorted. "Not you, too. We're friends, Izzy. We've been friends since kindergarten. Why is that so hard for everyone to understand?"

Izzy bit back a smile. "The lady doth protest too much."

"I'm serious."

"So, there's nothing going on? Just friends with nothing else...happening between you?"

Phoebe wrinkled her nose. "Between us...like sex? Is that what you're trying to ask in a very unsubtle, roundabout way?"

"Yes, that's what I'm asking," Izzy said, feeling kind of uncomfortable with the conversation. Not sure if she should tell Phoebe that Madam Venus's prediction for Leo and babies was the same as hers. "Madam Venus said you're having twins."

Phoebe snorted out a laugh. "She said I'd have twins, not that I'm having them right now. And what does that psychic have to do with this?"

Leo slid into the booth next to Phoebe and wrapped his arm around her neck. "Hey, beautiful ladies. What are we talking about?"

"Madam Venus," Izzy said.

"Me and you having sex," Phoebe interjected at the same time.

"We are?" Leo flashed a wide grin, looking from her to Phoebe. "How come you didn't tell me?"

Izzy was relieved when Gertie delivered their lunch. "Time to change the subject."

"I don't know," Leo said, stuffing a fry in his mouth. "I kind of like this subject. How'd it come up?"

"I think I'll ask Lily if she wants all the old magazines in the attic. Kids could use them for collage projects at school and stuff, or maybe a history report. And I'd love your opinion on my design for the attic. Did I tell you that's where I'm going to live, Leo? Or maybe Phoebe did. That way I won't be taking up the extra room at her place for long—"

"In case we want to have sex?" Leo asked.

"No. Well, yes if that's what's going on"—she pointed from one to the other—"between you two."

"Izzy, stop. Leo and I are just friends. No benefits involved. The end." Phoebe shook some ketchup onto Leo's plate and dipped one of his fries in.

"Why don't you ever order your own fries?" he asked.

"Because I'd eat them all."

"So instead you eat all of mine."

Phoebe turned to Izzy, ready to say something, then stopped. "Why are you looking at me like that?"

"Okay." She smoothed a hand over the napkin on her lap. "I'm just going to say this. Yesterday, Madam Venus knew Leo was in the car before she even looked outside."

She glanced up in time to see Leo frown. "She did?"

"So what?" Phoebe said. "She probably saw him through the window."

"The windows are all covered in heavy black fabric, and she came in from another curtained-off area." Izzy made eye contact with Leo. "She said to tell you congratulations...on the twins you're going to have."

Oh, to have a camera to capture the faces across the table from her. The color drained from Phoebe's face as her mouth fell open, and Leo looked like he might throw up.

Phoebe was the first to recover. She shook her head with another snort. "Somehow she saw Leo and decided to play a joke."

"I told you, all her windows have black curtains. The only light in the room came from a thousand candles."

Phoebe and Leo glanced at each other.

"Okay, then," Leo said. "She just assumed you hadn't gone to her house alone and figured I'd driven—"

"Oh, right, out of all the people in this town, she assumed *you* drove me, because she sees us together all the time."

"This is ridiculous. She's wrong." Phoebe took a swig of her water and choked. Leo patted her on the back. "Why are we even talking about this? I don't believe a thing that crazy lady says."

"Phoebe's right," Leo agreed. "She probably saw us together when she lived in town and thought she'd play a trick on you."

Izzy looked from her gorgeous, blond, blue-eyed sister to outrageously handsome Leo with his sandy hair and sapphire-blue eyes. "You guys would make beautiful babies. And I'm looking forward to being an aunt. Plus you're already best friends. Perfect way to start a marriage."

"Your girlfriend is going to be pretty mad when you tell her you're getting married to fulfill a psychic's prediction," Phoebe said to Leo.

"And your doctor boyfriend probably won't take the news any better," Leo piped in.

"Leo, you were the one who said how great it would be to get two prizes in a box of Cracker Jacks," Izzy reminded him.

"Right, but I said it for Phoebe's benefit. It doesn't pertain to me. I can't have kids. Have you met my parents? Do you remember my childhood? Look at me. I'm not parent material."

"You are not your parents, Leo," Phoebe said around a huge bite of her sandwich.

"How can you eat at a time like this? We're having twins."

"We're not having twins," she said pointing a finger at his nose. "We're both dating other people. Madam Venus is a fake. We have been friends forever. Just friends."

Now it really was time to change the subject before a fight broke out. "So, what do you think I should do about Baron's triple-my-salary offer?"

"Way to change the subject, Iz," Leo said, picking up his burger. Phoebe snatched another of his fries and he frowned.

"What about the Victorian?" her sister asked and quickly stuffed the fry in her mouth.

"I could hire a manager. Someone to run the tearoom."

"Izzy, you have to be here for the renovation."

"Triple her already great salary," Leo said. "That's a whole lot of money."

Astronomical. Plenty to make all the renovations without hesitation. Izzy forked a slice of boiled egg. "I have to give him an answer by Friday morning."

~

*G*unner sat at the counter hearing bits and pieces of Izzy, Phoebe, and Leo's conversation. They went from using hushed tones to raised voices, which soon dissolved to laughter. He caught snippets—sex, twins, psychic predictions, and a triple-my-salary offer. Which meant Izzy would go back to San Francisco and he'd be out of a job.

He hated the jealousy that rippled through him just watching Izzy and her sister eat lunch together. That he couldn't call Ariel to meet him for lunch was a daily regret. She'd been such a tiny baby. He'd learned to change her diaper, make a bottle, and set her feeding schedule the first day his mom brought her home from the hospital in a taxi. He was determined to hate her, but instead fell a little more in love bit by bit. First her little chin, then her tiny fingers. Each day something new captured his attention. Even though Ariel had a different father, someone she never knew, he always considered her his little sister.

She was so innocent, so helpless. As she grew, she depended on him for everything. And he gave her as much as possible.

"I have to give him an answer by Friday morning," Izzy said.

The quote for the Victorian was in his truck. He'd get it after he ate. He was bothered by the fact that he wanted this job. He wanted to work with—for—Izzy as much as he didn't. The space she'd drawn up would really look great when finished.

He wanted to see the finished product. Wanted to be a part of what she was building.

He knew Neil Adams, being in the real estate business, worked with other contractors and had probably given her a few names. He wondered how his quote would compare.

Noelle stopped in front of him. "You look deep in thought."

"Thinking about work."

"Actually, I might have some work if you're not too busy."

"Whatcha got?"

"Not sure if you remember that ugly paneling in my office. I had you leave it when you remodeled the café."

He nodded, definitely remembering the eyesore.

"Suddenly—Mac says irrationally—I want it out. Immediately."

"Can I take a look?"

She beckoned him toward the swinging kitchen door.

He set his napkin on his empty plate. "I need to go out to my truck first. I'll be right back." He wanted to give Izzy the quote before she finished her lunch and left.

Outside, he grabbed the manila envelope from his passenger seat and went back inside.

"Hey, Gunner," Leo said, when he stopped next to their table.

Phoebe looked up and grinned. "Hey, Gun, did you change your mind about joining us?"

"I ate." He handed the envelope to Izzy. "I have your quote."

"Thanks. I'll look it over and get back to you."

After, he followed Noelle into her office. Even the ceiling was covered in fake paneling. He fought a smile.

She grimaced. "I know. Worse than awful. I can't stand to be in here anymore. Will it cost me a small fortune?"

"The cost will depend on what's behind the paneling."

"Mac said he'd take it down, but it will take him months between work and Beck's football schedule."

"What do you want done?"

"Simple walls, maybe with a little texture?"

"Let me get some tools from my truck and pull one of these panels back. Then I'll be able to give you a pretty close estimate."

When he went back through the café, Izzy was gone.

～

"Hey, sis," Izzy said when Stella came out of her second-grade classroom. She had her dark hair pinned up in a cute bun and looked very school marm-ish yet adorable in a plaid dress with a thin belt and sneakers. "Don't you look darling?"

Stella rolled her eyes as she extracted a pencil from her hair. "I've never looked darling a day in my life."

They exchanged a tight hug.

"What brings you to elementary school?" Stella asked.

"I heard Rowdy has the night shift and thought we could have dinner together. Phoebe and I planned to take you together, but she has to work tonight."

Stella slung her purse over her shoulder. "Sounds like a plan. I had playground duty and ate my peanut butter and jelly sandwich standing."

"Your choice. What are you hungry for?" Izzy asked.

"Since Eden Falls doesn't have a huge selection of places to choose from, I'm going with Renaldo's Italian Kitchen."

"Perfect."

Stella pumped her fist in the air. "I haven't had pizza in forever."

On their walk, Stella filled in details of her honeymoon. Once they got a table and placed their order, Izzy settled back in her chair. "So, how's married life, little sister?"

A goofy grin spread across Stella's face. "Pretty wonderful. I never really imagined what it would be like to share bathroom space with a guy and watch him get ready for work, which I love to do."

"Not exactly the answer I expected."

"I know it sounds completely crazy, but I love watching Rowdy brush his teeth." She blushed—which was one for the records. Stella wasn't a blusher.

"Brush his teeth? This revelation just confirms what I always knew. You are the weird sister."

Stella shrugged "There's just something about the way Rowdy brushes his teeth." She ran her fingertip between her eyebrows. "He gets this cute little line right here when he concentrates. He's so adorable."

"Sorry, Stella. The words *Rowdy* and *adorable* don't work in the same sentence for me. Try again."

Stella rolled her eyes as only Stella could. "You'll see. One day you'll be watching some guy brush his teeth and think, 'Huh, Stella was right. Watching *insert name here*'"— she used air quotes—"'brush his teeth is downright sexy.'"

Yeah, no. "We'll see."

Stella waved at someone behind Izzy. "Hey, Gunner. How're you doing?"

No way! Eden Falls was small, but running into Gunner four times in one day was ridiculous.

Gunner stopped next to their table, smiled at Stella. "Good. I heard you and Rowdy were back. How's married life?" He held up a hand when Stella's goofy grin reappeared. "Never mind."

He glanced at Izzy with the same *today-can't-get-any-worse* expression he probably saw on her face.

"Want to join us?"

Izzy tried to kick Stella. The table jolted when she connected with one of the legs instead. Indecision crossed his face while she internally chanted, *Please-say-no. Please-say-no.*

"Sure. I've got nowhere to be." He pulled out a chair and sat. The waitress hustled over and was granted a smile that had never been bestowed on Izzy. "I'll take a large pizza with the works."

Stella leaned toward Gunner. "So, we were discussing how sexy a guy looks while brushing his teeth."

His brow wrinkled. "Uh...yeah. I can't really contribute to that conversation."

"Stella thinks *Rowdy* looks sexy while brushing his teeth," Izzy said, feeling like she needed to clarify.

Gunner looked pointedly at her. "Still can't contribute," he said flatly.

"Okay, let's talk about the house Izzy is buying. Dad said you walked through, Gunner. What did you think?"

His gaze bounced from Stella to her. "It's big."

Stella laughed and crossed her forearms on the table. "Seriously, tell me what you think."

"My opinion doesn't matter."

"Well, I love the idea of someone making that house pretty again. I can't wait to see the magic you two create."

"Your sister hasn't hired me yet."

Stella looked at her like she was nuts. "You have to hire Gunner. He's the best in the area. In the state."

"Thanks for the sales pitch, Stella. Your pizza is on me tonight."

"In my defense, I haven't had time to look over his quote," Izzy said. She'd met with another contractor after lunch who said he'd get her a quote by Monday, and she was meeting another contractor tomorrow morning. Four quotes. Someone *had* to come in below Gunner.

Though now she'd feel guilty if she didn't give him the job. But why should she? She was being business smart. People in town would probably overlook her trying to be *business smart* in favor of hiring Gunner. She'd be shunned, stoned, run out of town as a horrible person. *Thanks for bringing up the subject, Stella.*

"Dad said he's going to rent the second story for his offices and you're going to live in the attic," Stella said. "Which I don't get."

Izzy pulled out her phone and scrolled to some pictures. "I'll keep the first two levels true to the era it was built. But my living space will look like this."

"Oh, wow, I love this." Stella handed the phone to Gunner.

As he scrolled through the pictures, Izzy tried to read his expression, which was impossible. At least he didn't look bored. "Your sister got some drawings to me last night."

"And Gunner got a quote to me today. I'll look it over and make a decision. Soon."

Gunner didn't acknowledge that she'd even spoken, but gave his full attention to Stella. "I hear you and Rowdy are living in Alex's rental. I bet that's close quarters after seeing Rowdy's mountain home."

Stella laughed. "I wouldn't know. I was living in a small apartment with Phoebe before Rowdy and I got married. I love Alex's rental. It's so quaint and homey." She glanced at Izzy. "I hear you moved into my room. Phoebe will be happy, especially if you're clean. I definitely didn't live up to her sanitary expectations."

"I won't be there long."

"Right. The attic," Stella said. "Still don't get it."

After their pizzas arrived, Izzy ate while watching Gunner and Stella carry on a comfortable conversation. She found herself watching his lips, the expression of his face, his mannerisms. She'd studied those same mannerisms from behind a veil of hair as a teenager. She'd memorized every angle of his face, every raised brow, every time he quirked his mouth. She wondered what his wife had seen. What had attracted her to him? She couldn't help but be very curious about the woman he'd loved.

He was always subdued around her, but he smiled and laughed with Stella like they were the best of friends. Feeling like a third wheel, her irritation rose. Tonight was supposed to be sister time, and here was Gunner, horning in on their dinner.

Which wasn't exactly fair of her, because Stella had invited him to join them. What was up with her sisters, that they asked him to join them at every meal?

He and Stella discussed things going on around town and people they knew. They talked about the Harvest Festival and a fund-raiser the library planned each year. She'd been gone too long to know all the goings-on of Eden Falls anymore.

Stella's buzzing phone interrupted their conversation. She stood up abruptly. "I completely forgot I told Alex I'd help her with a couple of arrangements after work."

Izzy pulled the napkin off her lap. "I'll just have them box up the rest of the pizza and come with you."

"No. Stay and enjoy your dinner with Gunner." Stella pulled out her wallet.

"My treat," Izzy reminded Stella.

"I've got the pizzas covered. Thanks for letting me crash

your dinner together," Gunner said, as if reading her earlier thoughts.

Stella patted his shoulder. "Thanks, Gun. You're sweet. Rowdy and I will have you over for dinner soon."

"Sounds great."

After Stella disappeared, Izzy smoothed her napkin back into place. "You should know before you accept, Stella is a horrible cook."

"Forewarned," he said, with no hint of a smile.

"If I go with your quote"—*which I won't*—"the next three or four months will be miserable if we can't get along."

"I didn't realize we weren't getting along."

"I don't mean like we're fighting. I mean we should be civil to each other."

"I didn't realize we weren't being civil."

She studied his expression of indifference for a moment before forcing out a huff. "You know what I mean."

"No. I don't."

If he wanted to play dumb, she could too. "Okay, so we're besties now. Yay! How is your cute puppy?"

"You're going to crush his male ego."

"I didn't know dogs had egos. If you ever need someone to watch him, I'd be happy to help out."

She could tell by his expression she'd surprised him. *Good.*

"I'll keep that in mind."

Her phone rang. *Baron.* She flipped the sound off.

"You need to get that?"

"It can wait." She motioned to the waitress. "Can I get a box?"

"Leaving me to eat alone?"

"I don't think I can handle any more of your bubbly personality today. I'm going to Pretty Posies and spend a little more time with my sister." She boxed up the leftover pizza and dropped thirty dollars on the table. "And I'll pay for Stella's and my dinner."

~

*I*zzy ignored Baron's phone calls until Saturday morning. She knew what his reaction would be before he answered the phone.

"It's about time. Instead of calling yesterday, you kept me waiting, which you know I hate."

"Hello to you too, Baron. I'm great. Thanks for asking. You sound like you're the same"—*controlling maniac*—"as always."

"So you'll be in today? I need you here, Isadora. The gallery is falling down around my ears."

"I'm pretty sure everything is fine. You're just getting worked up about little things that probably don't matter."

"You're going to make me wait until Monday, aren't you?"

She was glad this wasn't face-to-face. Baron was a professional at badgering her into submission. "Actually, I'm calling to turn your offer down."

"No. You cannot be serious. You *are* coming back. I'll give you another week. One more week, Izzy."

He was struggling to keep his voice under control and losing the battle. "I'm buying a house here, Baron. I'm not coming back."

"Iz—"

She decided to hang up first this time.

CHAPTER 9

*G*unner wasn't sure what to expect at a Sunday dinner since he'd never attended one in his life.

Though he wore jeans, he put on a nice shirt and something besides work boots. He even stopped at Pretty Posies the day before and asked Alex for a small bouquet he could take to Beverly Adams. Alex, who was savvy about these things, fixed him up with some pink roses, green Fuji flowers that started with "ac", Peruvian lilies, and yellow Asiatic whatchamacallits in a short, square vase. It looked pretty, and he hoped the flowers said, "Thank you for including me."

He arrived a few minutes before five and walked to the door, nervous in a way foreign to him. Two big trees in the Adams' front yard were already shedding, their orange leaves carpeting the grass underneath. Though tidy, the house of the area's most successful real estate agent was surprisingly unassuming. Neil knew his business and made sure he knew his clients, their tastes, and budget—case in point, he'd found Gunner's fixer-upper for him in two days.

Since Gunner had no way of knowing Sunday dinner protocol, he silenced his phone before knocking.

At some point during the evening he hoped he'd get a chance to speak with Izzy. He probably should have been a little nicer after Stella left Renaldo's. He hadn't been very agreeable—not the best way to get a job.

He heard female voices before his knock was answered. Leo opened the door with a grin. "Beware. The sisters are in rare form today."

Gunner stepped inside to a heated argument that didn't make sense. "Do I want to know?"

"I've learned it's safer not to. If you know, they expect you to take sides."

"How can you even say that?" Phoebe hollered from another room. "You're just siding with Stella because she'll make you sleep on the couch if you don't."

"Whoa, leave me out of this," said a male voice.

"Rowdy hasn't learned that trick yet," Leo explained, leading Gunner into an open kitchen-family room area.

"He's siding with me because I'm right," Stella said, hands on hips, standing nose to nose with Phoebe. "Just because you're the oldest doesn't make you the wisest."

"Welcome, Gunner," Neil said, separating the sisters. "Pardon our dust. I wish I could say this will be the end of it, but I'd be lying."

"Girls, table the discussion for now," Beverly said, making her way over to him. "Gunner, so glad you could make it."

He held out the flowers, feeling like a dork. "Thanks for inviting me. It's been a long time since I've had a home-cooked meal."

"Oh, thank you. This will make the perfect table center-piece." She set the bouquet in the middle of a long table set for eight. "Neil, will you carve the roast? Stella, offer Gunner a drink."

Stella took his arm and guided him to a garage fridge filled with drinks. "Glad you could make it. I like even numbers better."

"Even numbers?"

"Yeah, Izzy moving back makes odd numbers at the table. You even things out."

"Glad I could make you feel better," he said, not sure how he felt about her comment.

"Sorry I had to bail on you the other night. I completely forgot I told Alex I'd help. My wedding and honeymoon have messed with my schedule."

"Not a problem." He hoped her schedule was messed in a pleasant way. Rowdy was a good guy and, after what happened to Stella with her last boyfriend, she deserved a good guy.

Izzy rushed into the house. "Sorry, I'm late. I went over to Joanna's and lost all track of time." She skidded to a stop when she spotted him. "Oh, hey. I forgot you were coming."

"That isn't very nice," Phoebe said.

"What isn't nice? I stated a fact. I forgot."

"It's the way you said it."

Izzy looked from Phoebe to him. "Sorry. I didn't mean anything by what I said."

Before he could answer, Stella jumped in with, "Ignore Phoebe. She's in a mood."

"I'm not in a mood," Phoebe argued.

"Enough girls," Beverly said on a sigh. "We have company."

"Who's company?" Phoebe asked. "Leo is family, Rowdy is family, and when Gunner starts working on the Victorian, he's as good as family."

He heard Izzy blow out a breath but didn't look her way.

Phoebe was trying to paint her into a corner with words, and he didn't want her to feel like she *had* to hire him. He believed in quality over quantity, and he knew his work was top-notch. He did what he was hired to do and more, but he'd respect her decision.

"How is Joanna?" Beverly asked. "Is she home?"

"She went home this morning. She and baby are doing well."

"The baby is a girl, right?" Phoebe scrunched her nose at Izzy. "Haven't they given her a name yet?"

"Not yet."

"How do you bring home a baby without a name? They've had nine months to decide."

Izzy glanced at him for some reason. "I don't know, Phoebs. It's none of my business," she said.

"Why do you have to start a fight about everything today?" Stella asked her older sister.

"Okay." Neil clapped his hands. "Let's get seated."

"Yep, everything's ready," Beverly added. "Girls, grab a dish. Leo, will you pull the rolls out of the oven?"

Gunner stood back, waiting to see where they wanted him to sit. Neil and Beverly took either end, Rowdy and Stella sat together as did Leo and Phoebe, which left him and Izzy on opposite sides of the table, staring at each other. Not a hardship on his part.

They all bowed their heads as Neil offered a prayer—another first for him. Gunner hadn't prayed before a meal in his life.

Dinner was delicious, the company was entertaining, and eating here beat eating at home or alone in a restaurant.

Phoebe was determined to start an argument, picking at everything anyone said. Leo kept trying to defuse the situation. Stella and Rowdy were ready to make a baby right there in the dining room, and Izzy was quiet as a mouse. The whole evening was like watching an Adams family soap opera.

~

*J*zzy tried to look everywhere but at Gunner, which was impossible since he was sitting right in front of her. Whenever she peeked his way, he was already looking at her. Steady as a heartbeat. She was furious at Phoebe for sticking her nose where it didn't belong, opening her mouth about hiring Gunner when she hadn't had a chance to look over all the quotes yet. Phoebe didn't understand everything that was involved in making such a major decision.

"Gunner, would you like another roll?" her mom asked.

"I would love one."

"Izzy, honey, can you pass the butter?"

She picked up the butter dish between her and Stella and held it toward Gunner, making eye contact.

He smiled and her brain screeched to a halt. He was smiling. At her. She tried to smile back but her face was frozen in astonishment.

"Thank you."

She nodded once, unable to respond any other way.

He kept smiling as he buttered his roll and told her dad that he was tearing out the paneling in Noelle's office.

"I'm surprised she didn't have you do it when you remodeled the café the first time."

He set his knife on the edge of his plate. "She had a lot going on at the time just moving to town and looking for a place to live. We concentrated on the kitchen and the dining area."

"I bet Noelle is a sweetheart to work with," Beverly said. "She's always so good-natured."

Gunner nodded. "Yes, she is."

Izzy looked at her plate, forked some green beans.

"Hey, we should all go bowling in Harrisville next week," Phoebe said.

Stella snorted. "Who flipped your crabby switch to happy?"

"I wasn't crabby," Phoebe retorted. "And I'm serious, we should go bowling next week." She patted Leo's arm. "Don't you think that sounds fun?"

"Yeah, sure. I like to bowl," he said around a bite of pot roast.

Phoebe glanced from one end of the table to the other. "Mom and Dad, you want to come?"

"I think we'll leave bowling night to you kids," her dad said.

"Rowdy, I have Tuesday night off this coming week. Can you get off that night?"

"I can go Tuesday," Rowdy said, glancing at Stella. She nodded.

"Gun, can you go Tuesday night?"

He glanced at Izzy, held her gaze. "Sure."

Everyone looked at her. Her family knew she didn't have any plans. "I'm free."

"Perfect," Phoebe said. "We need to invite another couple, so we have four to a team."

Stella shook her head. "Alex is too pregnant, so she and Colton are out."

"What about Carolyn and JT?" Leo asked.

Phoebe pulled her phone from her jeans pocket. "Great idea. I'll text JT."

Gunner was staring at her as he took a bite of potatoes. Everyone going was a couple. Except them. Was the same thought going through his mind? He wasn't smiling, but he wasn't glaring either.

"JT and Carolyn are in. I'll call and reserve two lanes at

Ten Pin Alley in Harrisville. Is seven thirty okay with everyone?"

Izzy nodded along with everyone else.

~

*S*he sat at Phoebe's kitchen table the next morning, looking over the numbers from four different estimates for the fifth time, not that any but Gunner's mattered. Though not the lowest, his estimate was the most detailed, which made her believe his work would be just as precise.

Once everyone left the house after Sunday dinner, she had her dad look over the estimates and he agreed. Still, she searched for a reason not to hire him. Other than his orneriness, that reason wasn't evident.

His timelines for the different areas of the renovations were spot-on. Gunner even remembered her telling him she could help with painting and took it into consideration when working up his quote. None of the other contractors even listed her help as a possibility. If everything ran smoothly, the renovations would be complete by the middle of January.

Gunner's number was at the top of his estimate. She picked up her cell phone and tapped in the number...but didn't press the send button. Did she really want to be in a house with a guy who made her uncomfortable for three months?

On the other hand, the house was big. She could always find somewhere else to work. In another room, far, far away. When he was in the attic, she'd work on the second level. When he started on the second level, she'd go to the kitchen. The night she'd dropped her plans at his house hadn't been awful. They'd actually held a brief, civil conversation. And last night there'd even been a smile. At her. *Probably because my mom and dad were there, but it was still a smile.*

Her finger hovered over the send button. He was grouchy and made her feel awkward, but she could handle that for a few months. She'd never have to see him once the Victorian was finished. Well, they'd run into each other around town, but he'd just have to accept her as a resident of Eden Falls.

She set the phone down and shook her head at her silliness. Time to adjust her attitude and get over his gruff intimidation tactics. Despite his glaring, someone had found him loving enough to marry him. His sister had idolized him. And everyone else in Eden Falls seemed to think very highly of him.

Picking up the phone, she stopped just short of pushing send. He didn't glare at Phoebe or Stella, but they hadn't spent the last moments of his sister's life standing on the sidelines in horror.

Gunner, with the intense but very pretty heterochromia iridium eyes.

After all these years, she still thought about the kiss they'd shared. The only boy she'd ever kissed until then had been Tim. They'd been dating for four months when Gunner kissed her. And she let him, which made her a cheater. She imagined it had been Gunner's gazillionth kiss. He probably didn't even remember.

She pressed send and listened to his phone ring three times.

"Gunner Stone."

His deep voice sounded just as seductive over the phone as in person. She released the breath she was holding in a schoolgirl whoosh. "Gunner, it's Izzy," came out too breathless. She had to suck in another deep breath to get the rest out. "I'd like to hire you for the Victorian renovation. Would you be able to start the Monday after I close?"

"When do you close?"

She put a hand to her heart. "The day before the Harvest Festival."

"I should be able to finish my outstanding jobs before then."

Her next question was asking a lot, but... "Since I don't know much about roofing, do you think you could contact the company you suggested about starting that same Monday?"

"I'll call them today. You'll have to pick out the color of shingles you want."

"Apple Valley Roofers, right? Do they have samples at their office?"

After a pause so long that she wondered if the call had been disconnected, he said, "Maybe we can go to Harrisville a little early on Tuesday and stop by their place before we meet the others at the bowling alley."

Be in the same car with him for the fifteen-minute drive? "Oh, uh...sure. That will work."

"You'll need to make some decisions about bathroom fixtures for the attic."

"Okay. Do you want me to—" And he'd already hung up. *Yep, this was going to be a barrel of laughs.*

She got in her car and drove to Eden Falls Hardware and Lumber. She'd only been in once since the store was rebuilt after a fire leveled the place. Beam Garrett came around the counter when she entered and engulfed her in a bear hug.

"Look who finally came in to see me."

"You saw me at the Chamber of Commerce breakfast."

"Yes, but not in my store." He held her at arm's length. "So you really are going to renovate Madam Venus's house."

"I am."

"Do you close soon?"

"The day before the Harvest Festival."

He clapped his hands. "So, what can I do for you?"

"Exterior paint. I need samples."

With his arm around her shoulders, he led her to the paint aisle. "I have a few brochures. My best advice it to take several samples that you like, tape them in different places on the exterior of the house, and then go back when you can view them in different light."

"That's what Gunner told me to do."

"You hired Gunner? Good," he added at her nod. "Do the same with the interior colors. Pick them out, tape them up, and check them at different times of the day."

A wave of uncertainty washed over her. "What am I doing, Beam? Am I completely crazy?"

"Not crazy at all." He selected several color brochures from a display and handed them to her. "Adventurous, which is a good thing. I stepped out of my comfort zone when I partnered with Mason on this place. Now I can't imagine being anywhere else."

Gunner suddenly appeared next to them. "You helping her with colors?"

"Hey, Gun. Yeah, giving her some different combinations."

Izzy wandered over to the wall of paint samples while Gunner and Beam shook hands and discussed something Gunner had ordered.

When she had a handful of colors, she headed for bathroom fixtures, but nothing she saw was right.

"They don't carry a lot of choices, but Beam has a catalog you can look through," Gunner said from behind her. "The items can be delivered here or to the house. You should pick out what you want and get them ordered as soon as you close."

"How long does it take to get special orders in?"

"Beam can tell you dates of delivery. I called the roofing company, and they can start the Wednesday after you close. That will give me a couple of days to start on the saggy porch. They said we could stop by tomorrow to pick out shingles. I'd go with a color close to what's already there." He pulled a chunk of shingle from his back pocket. "We'll take this piece with us."

For some unexplainable reason, she knew she'd made the right choice in contractors.

He held out his hand. "Let me see your paint swatches."

She didn't dare not hand them to him.

"These are better," he said leafing through the colors.

"Glad they meet with your approval."

He glanced at her with raised brow.

"What? I am. Quit being so ornery all the time."

His frown was immediate. "I'm not ornery."

"What do you call this"—she circled his face with an index finger—"frowny, grouchy face?"

"I'm not ornery."

Except around me. She took the paint swatches he held out. "I'm going to hang these around the house and try to decide on colors."

He didn't respond, just stared at her. Whatever had transpired between them last night was gone. If she let herself, she could get lost in his eyes. Lucky for her, she was in complete control. Well, except for the little tingle low in her belly. "Okay. So glad we had this chat. Have a nice day."

After going through catalogues, and with Beam's expert help, she picked out a toilet, tub, vanity, and sink for her attic bathroom.

She held up a hand. "Can you hold this order until after I close?"

"Not a problem. Want to pick out a few tiles to take to the house and see what you like?"

"I can do that?"

"No charge unless you break them."

"See, this is how a normal guy acts. Nice. Pleasant to be

around." Between Baron and Gunner... She didn't even know what normal meant any more.

"Well, my wife would probably beg to differ."

Izzy got up on tiptoe and kissed his cheek. "You are a sweet, sweet man. You should look into cloning yourself. You could make millions. Women all over the country would be ordering. In fact, I'll take the first one off the belt."

He chuckled. "Millions would be good. With that kind of money, I could fund Misty's shopping habit. Actually, *obsession* would be a more accurate description."

"I'm right there with her."

Izzy's next stop was the library. Lily came around the front desk and gave her a tight hug. "Rita said you're buying that wonderful Victorian. You'll paint right away?"

"Rest assured, painting the exterior is number three on the list. Number one and two are a new roof and fixing the saggy porch."

"I can't wait to see the results."

"I'm here for two reasons. The house has boxes and boxes of old magazines. I wasn't sure if the library could use them for school projects or... I don't know."

"If I can't use them, the schools probably can. Are they in decent condition?"

"Some don't look like they've even been opened."

"Bring them over anytime."

"Next, I'm going to need a library card."

She walked out with a card and several library books thirty minutes later. Heading to Noelle's, she decided to settle in a booth for something sinfully yummy, relax for five minutes, and read. Her cell phone rang as soon as she sat. "Hello?"

"Hi, Izzy, it's Alex. I hope you don't mind me calling. I got your number from Phoebe."

"I don't mind."

"Ready to go to work?"

Izzy laughed. "I don't know what that means."

"I have a bride here at the shop who'd like to meet with you. Do you have a minute to stop by and talk wedding plans?"

Money coming in would be great. "I'll be right there."

～

*G*unner drove around the square looking for a parking spot. He'd be glad when the Harvest Festival was over. Never would he agree to be on the committee again. If Alex wanted to hold jobs back unless he volunteered, so be it. Haggling over every tiny detail once a week was not in his DNA.

He spotted Izzy walking into Pretty Posies. She'd called him ornery this morning and maybe he was. At least around her. She sparked something in him, something he hadn't felt since the day he kissed her. Like a tornado, she swirled around him, and his nerve endings came alive in the electrically charged air. She made him imagine there could be more to life than work and...Domino. He felt such a strong pull when she was around. Stronger than he'd ever felt with Jessica, and he'd given his heart to her. He couldn't risk losing his heart again, but he could at least try to be more pleasant around her.

Izzy with her soft lips and beautiful eyes, and the way those eyes lit when she took a moment to share her plans for the Victorian and her living space. All those things uncovered vulnerable spots he wasn't ready to expose.

He pulled into a spot in front of One Scoop or Two and parked near where Rowdy and Manny were hanging a banner over Main Street advertising the festival.

"Manny, your side needs to go up," Phoebe said from below.

"I say this year after year, and still I get assigned to hang the sign," Manny said, reaching as far as he could. "I'm vertically challenged. Blame my parents."

"Gunner's here. He can take your place." Phoebe grabbed his arm and pulled him to the ladder.

"Gladly," Manny said. "Hanging the town's banners for all celebrations and holidays is now your official job, Gun. Hear that, Rowdy? From now on, call Gunner."

And here he was, being volunteered once again. He took the end of the banner Manny handed over and climbed the ladder.

"That's what I'm talking about, Gun. Woot! Look at that view." Phoebe clapped. "Sorry, Manny, you're married, so I can't look at your butt, and Rowdy is my new brother-in-law so, *ewww*. But Gunner, you seriously need to look into a contract for jeans commercials. I'll be your business manager, accompany you to all the photo shoots. All you have to do is show up in jeans."

"Phoebs, quit looking at his butt and tell us if the banner is straight," Rowdy said from the other side of the street.

"Two inches lower on your side, Gun."

When the banner was level, he tied the ends of the rope off and climbed down. Rowdy crossed the road. "Thanks for the help."

"No problem. You headed for the meeting?"

"Yep. I hear Alex roped you into volunteering for the committee this year."

"She has a way of getting what she wants."

Rowdy chuckled. "Yes, she does. She might be tiny, but she's a force to be reckoned with if you don't follow directions. Hey, thanks for getting my property cleared so fast.

Even though we won't rebuild until next spring, I hated having to look at the ruins."

"Sure."

Once inside the library, Rowdy, Manny and Gunner plodded down the stairs and took their seats. Patsy started on time and moved down her list as she'd done at every meeting. When she got to him, she folded her hands on the table and smirked. "Did you get a chance to ask Izzy about the face-painting booth?"

Just by the way she asked, he knew she had the answer already. "Yes."

"And she agreed?"

He sat back in his chair and stretched out his legs. "You know she did."

"For a two-hour shift?"

"Yes. Ten to twelve." The pastry shop owner swore she wasn't a matchmaker, but he'd heard over a couple of poker games that she liked to meddle. More than once she'd reminded him of his single status—like that was something he was going to forget.

"The booth you're manning is right next to the face-painting booth. That's wonderful. You can check up on her."

"To make sure she's painting faces correctly?" he asked.

"Subtle, Patsy," Rowdy said with a laugh. "Watch out, Gun. Patsy has her eye on you."

Gunner gathered his few papers together. "Set your sights on someone else, Patsy."

CHAPTER 10

From Noelle's, Izzy dashed into the Corner Drug Store for a notebook before going to Pretty Posies. Alex and the bride-to-be were in an intimate sitting area—a love seat and two comfy chairs pushed very close together—in the corner of Alex's shop, going through books of flower arrangements. She made a mental note to create a similar place in her office. A spot that would stimulate the imagination.

Alex jumped up and hugged Izzy. This let the bride know Alex trusted her or she wouldn't have called.

"Hi, Iz. Sorry for the short notice."

"I was just across the square at Noelle's." She held out her hand. "Hello, I'm Izzy Adams."

"Hi," the young girl breathed. "I'm Ariel Walker."

Izzy felt the bite of cold trickle down her spine as Madam Venus's prediction came rushing back. *Your first client will be Ariel.*

"You okay, Iz?"

Izzy glanced at Alex, who was four years younger. She probably didn't remember much about Ariel Stone or the accident. Izzy nodded and sat in a chair to ease her shaking knees. "I'm fine. I...you just reminded me of someone I used to know."

Alex sat next to the bride again. "Ariel and her fiancé have picked a January date. They've also picked the venue, On The Green, which is an events barn in South Fork."

"I'm not familiar with that place, but I'll go visit," Izzy said, scribbling in her new notebook.

"Her colors are silver and sage. The centerpieces for the tables will be very simple, eucalyptus and the palest of pink roses in mason jars." Alex held up a picture. "She's already picked out a dress for herself and her four bridesmaids."

"It sounds like you've made a great start."

Ariel nodded. "I've dreamed of my wedding since I was a little girl, so I know what I want. Simple yet elegant, but not so elegant that my guests can't relax. I'm good with picking the big things, but I'd like someone to help me with the details."

Alex stood. "Since we have a solid idea of the flowers, I'll let you two talk."

"Thanks, Alex," she and Ariel said in unison. Then Ariel leaned forward. "Alex didn't really tell me much about you before she called. Can I ask about your qualifications?"

"Absolutely," Izzy said pulling out her phone and opening an events album under her photos app. She let Ariel scroll through the pictures. "I worked for a large art gallery in California until just recently. Those photos show just a sampling of the events I planned, including weddings."

"I don't have this kind of a budget," Ariel said, handing the phone back.

"I've also planned much smaller events, but those photos are on my computer. I can give you a list of references. They're all in and around San Francisco, but they can share details and tell you my prices are very fair. Do you mind if I ask, what is your budget?"

Ariel was the only child of a widowed father. Her mother died when she was young. "He'll tell you the cost doesn't matter, but he isn't wealthy by any means."

"We can make your special day very elegant without breaking any banks. If you'll give me your email address, I'll send out a list of referrals, my prices, and pictures of some smaller wedding and events I planned. I'll also visit the venue, which sounds like a fun place for a wedding."

After a few more minutes of conversation and another thank-you to Alex, Ariel left.

"You have a wedding to plan," Alex said.

"I'm not hired yet." But yes, things were starting to roll forward.

She let herself into Phoebe's apartment a few minutes later. Phoebe was on duty tonight, which meant she had the place to herself. Time to take her event planning business seriously.

She got busy drafting contracts, designing and ordering her business cards, and organizing the photos of events on her computer. Tomorrow she'd build her website. Luckily she had some professional photos taken for the gallery that she could use and, though Baron had hired an expert, she'd taken several coding classes to help her manage the gallery's website.

~

Gunner stopped at the curb in front of Phoebe's apartment late Tuesday afternoon. Izzy stood waiting for him, trench coat hood up against the light rain falling. He planned to get out, but she jumped into his truck before he could open his door.

"I could have met you there."

He put his truck into gear. "We're going to the same places. No need to take two cars."

She lowered her hood and fiddled with the straps on her purse like she was nervous. "How was your day?" she asked.

He wasn't great at small talk, but he'd make an effort to put her at ease. "I'm tearing out the paneling in Noelle's office at the café." He turned down the radio. "I've been working nights, while the café's closed."

"Is that hard? Going from days to nights?"

"It's only for a few days. I'll have most of the dusty work done by Friday, then I'll go back to days."

She nodded and turned toward the window, where rivulets of raindrops trickled down the glass.

"How was your day?" he asked.

The question seemed to surprise her. "Good." She turned on her seat, facing him. "Do you have a website for your business?"

"No. Why?" he asked when she didn't elaborate.

"I spent my morning setting up a website for my business."

He'd thought about a website a time or two but never did more than that. "I've usually got enough work to keep me busy."

"But if you listed all your qualifications, potential clients would have an easier time finding you. It would cut down on the calls you get asking if you know how to do something, like fixing sagging porches."

"True. I'll have to think about it."

The rest of their short drive into Harrisville was comfortably quiet. Izzy's perfume filled the cab of his truck in a pleasant way. She seemed lost in her thoughts, which made him wonder what became of the triple salary offer he'd heard her discussing with Phoebe and Leo, and who the offer came from.

He pulled into the lot where the roofers' office sat among the rows of packaged shingles. The rain had stopped during their drive, but the gray, cheeky clouds still hung low. This time he was able to get out and get her door. She flashed a timid smile of thanks.

He'd brought several pieces of broken shingle with him, and they were able to find a close match. Izzy seemed happy with the choice. The owner of the company said they could start the following Wednesday after she closed, which seemed to make her even happier.

The whole process reminded him of his time with Jessica. They'd picked out the house where they lived together, but Jessica hadn't participated in any of the details. She was content to stand back and let him make all the decisions, when what he wanted was her input. He was trying to build their future, a safe place where they could start their family.

In hindsight, he realized that's when his wife started pulling away, distancing herself. She told him she had some credit troubles, so he put the house in his name. Now he wondered if that was true, or if she already knew she'd be leaving and didn't want a house or any shared property to complicate a quick divorce.

They met the rest of the group at a mom-and-pop pizza joint down the street from the bowling alley. Phoebe had requested a table in the small back room, which made for a cozy setting. Everyone talked and laughed while they shared several large pizzas.

And he felt completely out of place, but in a good way. He chuckled at the contradiction. Sure, he went out with buddies once in a while, played poker with a group of guys he worked with occasionally, but this...dinner and bowling night with people who were acquaintances more than friends was...

nice, in an unexpected way. They made him feel like part of the group, pulled him in by asking questions and including him in the conversation.

He sat next to Izzy, and naturally their knees connected under the round table. Both times she jerked away and mumbled a *sorry* with a blush. He liked that he flustered her. He didn't like that she flustered him right back.

He'd have to remember this restaurant. The pizza was excellent, and this back room was a nice place to bring a date. Chuckling to himself a second time, he tried to remember the last time he went out on a date. It was with Dahlia, but he couldn't recall where they went.

"Are you okay?" Izzy asked, low enough that the others wouldn't hear.

She was looking at him, her amber eyes intense.

"The pizza here is good."

A flash of a smile. "I love this place, but I haven't been here since high school. We used to come after football games."

With Tim.

"Hey, Gun," Leo called, "remember the time you and Beam skipped school and drove over to the coast?"

Gunner laughed at the memory.

"What happened?" Stella asked.

"We were hitchhiking back, and this psychedelic VW van pulled over with Leo's parents inside," Gunner said, still chuckling. "Beam was terrified they'd rat him out to his mom and dad, but they were so high—sorry, Leo—they didn't even recognize him."

Gunner, on the other hand, hadn't been concerned about his mom finding out. That was the month she disappeared, leaving him and ten-year-old Ariel alone to fend for themselves. His sister was his only reason to get home, because he didn't want her spending the night alone in their rundown trailer with faulty locks on the doors. He was just grateful for the ride, whether the driver was stoned or not.

At the bowling alley, he and Izzy teamed up with Rowdy and Stella. He helped Izzy choose a ball that wasn't as heavy as the first one she picked out.

"When was the last time you bowled?" Leo asked.

"College."

So far tonight, Gunner had laughed more than he had in ages. "I hope Stella and Rowdy aren't set on our team winning tonight."

"Phoebe's team against Stella's," Leo groaned. "There will be blood before we get home. Those two compete at everything."

"Sorry in advance, Stella," Izzy said to her sister.

Gunner smiled down at her. "Just do your best and have fun."

~

*I*zzy almost laughed. She took bowling as seriously as she took golf. It was a game among friends, not the Olympics. The winner gloated for a few days, and the losers bought dinner or drinks. If her two sisters competed so fiercely, how had they shared the same apartment for so long?

They made her go first. Of course she rolled a gutter ball and Stella rolled her eyes.

With her second ball she knocked down four pins and was quite proud of herself. Stella, on the other hand, was less impressed.

Gunner rolled a strike right off the bat. Stella rewarded him with a hug.

Rowdy also rolled a strike.

This went on until the fourth frame, when her ball curved before hitting the center pin, knocking five others down.

Gunner rewarded her with a high five and Rowdy gave her a hug. "Well, at least you're getting better," Stella muttered.

Her next ball dropped into the gutter.

She looked in the next lane to see how Phoebe's team was doing. They were up by twelve pins.

When she sat down, Gunner scooted close and placed his arm along the bench behind her. "Are you aiming for the center arrow on the lane?"

She nodded, looking at his mismatched eyes, so very close.

"You've got a slight hook to your throw. Start aiming for the second or third arrow on the right."

"I'll try."

The next time she was up, she did as Gunner told her. Again, the ball hit the center pin and knocked everything down but three on the left side. She waited next to the ball return, determined not to look at Stella's disappointed expression. She picked up her ball and moved into place. Before she took a step, Gunner put his left hand on her waist and pointed at the lane with his right. "Breathe, Izzy." He was close enough she felt his chin touch her temple. "This time, aim for the arrow closest to the gutter."

She sucked in a breath.

"Now, exhale and relax."

She released the air in her lungs, but couldn't relax with him standing so close.

"Take another breath and release as you step forward." He backed away.

She took another breath and again did as he said. Her ball went straight until mid-lane, then curved right for the pins. Every one of them dropped. She turned and shot her arms in the air, hooting in triumph. Gunner grabbed her in a hug and spun her around. His arms around her caught her by surprise, but she didn't have time to react before he set her on her feet and Rowdy picked her up around the waist and lifted her a second time.

"Yay," Stella said, flatly. "It's about time."

"Come on, Stella," Rowdy said. "She did good."

Izzy dropped on the bench next to her sister. "Admit you're jealous. I just got hugged by two handsome guys, and one is your husband."

"Don't let one spare go to your head, sis."

Oh, but she was going to. She got a spare, and she was going to enjoy the high until the next gutter ball she threw.

Gunner sat next to her.

"Are you going to try and steal my thunder too?"

"No, I'm stuck on the handsome part."

She felt the heat flare over her cheeks and she glanced away, wishing she had Harry Potter's invisibility cloak.

He chuckled.

The rest of the night was fun. More fun than she'd had in a very long time. She didn't care about the score, or the rivalry, or her bickering sisters. She just wanted the...whatever this easygoing thing between her and Gunner was...to continue. They talked and laughed like they'd been friends forever.

She was looking forward to the ride home with him, but Phoebe nixed that. She'd driven, and they were going to the same place, so Izzy said her goodbyes outside the bowling alley and climbed into Phoebe's car.

～

*A*fter running into Izzy almost every day since she moved back, Gunner barely caught a glimpse of her for the next two weeks. He finished Noelle's office, tiled a kitchen backsplash in Harrisville, and repaired a shed in

Glenwood. He found more flowers left in the cemetery and assumed they were from Izzy, but he never saw her.

He was disappointed when Phoebe said she'd drive Izzy home after they bowled. It would have been nice to have a little more time with her. He'd experienced an epiphany that night. Gunner realized Izzy affected him the same way she had his little sister. She was a touch of sunshine on a cloudy day. She was a positive happy person and probably struggled around his dark moods. From now on he'd make an effort to be a little nicer.

One night after he finished a job, he decided to drive past the Victorian. Izzy's SUV was in the driveway. He noticed as soon as he got out of his truck that she'd been working in the yard. Though the grass was still brown and brittle, the leaves, branches, and vines had been cleared away. He walked around the side of the house and spotted her leaning against a tree trunk in the back, flexing her hands. A stack of garbage bags and debris took up one whole corner of the yard.

"You've been busy," he said as he neared.

She jumped and stuffed her gloved hands into the pockets of her oversized hoodie. "You scared me."

Her hair was pulled into a ponytail and her cheeks were rosy from exertion. He pointed to the pile of branches. "What if something goes wrong at the closing?"

"Whoever does buy the house will have a lot less yard-work to do."

"You close this Friday?"

"Yes."

He got close enough to tug her hand out of her pocket.

"What are you doing?" she asked, making a fist.

He slipped his thumb under the edge of her fingers and wiggled it. "Let me see."

She opened her hand and he pulled off her glove. She had

raw, angry blisters at the base of each finger. The one between her thumb and index finger was wrapped with tape.

He looked into her eyes. "You need to stop for a few days and let these heal."

She narrowed her eyes as if gauging him, then pulled her hand free. "Why are you being so nice?"

"Ulterior motive. Patsy will be all over me if you can't paint faces at the Harvest Festival because your hands hurt from cleaning the yard of a house you don't own."

Nodding, she picked up the rake and headed for her car. He followed at a safe distance, feeling like he was being tugged by a rope attached to the hollow in his chest. He shouldn't have stopped when he spotted her car. He shouldn't have gone bowling with the group. And he probably shouldn't have accepted the job on this house.

Although he wasn't quite sure why, he still considered her off-limits. Ever since that kiss…

Back then she was a teenager, jailbait. She wasn't a little girl anymore, but she was above him in social status, education, and worldly experience. Even though he'd pulled himself up out of the dregs of his upbringing, he wasn't sure he'd ever feel worthy of Izzy, which made him mad.

~

*I*zzy signed her life away at a title insurance company in Harrisville. Madam Venus sat across from her, colorful as ever.

Izzy had been able to clear out the attic and clean up most of the yard, and her hands were still stiff, but the blisters were starting to heal.

As she flexed her fingers, she pictured Gunner. He was never far from her thoughts, floating in and out at the most inopportune times. Just when she imagined they could work together without him biting her head off, his animosity reared its snarky head again. Except in the Victorian's yard, his touch—and his voice—had been gentle. Different than usual.

"Life is so funny, don't you think?" Madam Venus asked.

"Are you saying in general or talking about something specific?"

"Both, I guess. I bet you never imagined buying the house you've loved since childhood."

Another detail this woman shouldn't know.

The closing attorney set another piece of paper on the pile for her signature. "This is saying there are no liens on the property."

"You're right," she said to Madam Venus. "A line of events starting with my sister's wedding brought me here." She smiled. "You know if the yard hadn't been overgrown, I probably would have walked right past." *Despite the putrid color.*

"Sounds like letting the yard take care of itself was a blessing for both of us."

Izzy thought of the brittle grass and wilting shrubs. "The yard didn't look like it was capable of taking care of itself."

"Keeping a yard nice was never something I've cared much about. I like my environment natural."

"Flowers and green bushes are natural."

Madam Venus quirked a brow. "Not if there's no rain to water them."

True, but even with the little bit of work she'd done so far, the Victorian already looked much happier.

"Your neighbors will be excited to have a new owner. They love green lawns and flowers everywhere. The attorney went so far as to offer his lawn-care service's number."

Izzy smiled. She could just imagine Owen, who kept the property around his office pristine. She'd be happy to get the lawn service's number once she got the yard the way she wanted.

She glanced over two more papers and added her initials to the places indicated.

"Here is the last form for you...Madam Venus," the attorney said.

She signed with a flair and a jingle of her bracelets and stood. As she passed Izzy on her way out the door, she touched her shoulder. "Keep an open mind about the people you deal with. Things aren't always as they seem."

CHAPTER 11

The Harvest Festival was one of Eden Falls' oldest, most widely attended celebrations. The two-block area around Town Square was a hive of activity.

Gunner spent three days erecting tents, running power cables, and setting up booths along with others on the committee. His last Saturday morning job was connecting microphones for the bands who'd be entertaining the crowd. From the stage, he watched Patsy line up the pies for her pie-throwing booth. With a team of elementary school teachers, Stella set up a fishing booth, ring toss, and cake walk for the little kids.

The Fire Department hauled in a dunking booth to raise money for new equipment while Phoebe and JT circled the square in their police uniforms, helping where they could. Carnival rides which had been assembled two days earlier were going through test runs before the ankle-biters descended.

As the sun peeked over the mountains, artists and crafters began arranging their wares. From his vantage point, he could see framed artwork, leather goods, and autumn decorations.

Luckily the day dawned golden rather than cloudy. Trees that hadn't already shed their leaves were showing off their fall finery with colors varying from bright red to sunny yellow and every shade in between. Evergreens added the strength of endurance to what would soon be stark branches against a cold sky.

Ariel used to love the Harvest Festival. He'd save and stash money for months so she could hit every ride at least twice and play every game. She'd wait anxiously all year for this magical day that she dubbed better than Christmas. Which in her eyes was probably true, since Christmas didn't bring much cheer to the Stone household.

His sister would beg him to stay until every last ride stopped running for the night. She always saved a bit of her own money to buy their mom and him special handmade gifts at one of the craft booths. She could never wait until Christmas to wrap them up and hand them out, though. He still had the wallet she gave him his senior year. The faux leather was in tatters, but he couldn't bring himself to throw a gift from her away.

"Hi, Gunner. How are you this morning?" Alex asked as she walked up the stairs to the stage.

"Good."

She looped her arm through his. "I hear you'll be working on the Victorian with Izzy."

"Yep. Thanks for recommending me."

"Always. Is the sound system up and running?"

"Ready for a test." He jumped off the stage. "Let me get across the street before you try it."

Alex unhooked the microphone from the stand and waited until he reached the sidewalk in front of Noelle's Café. A flock of geese heading south honked loudly overhead, their formation a little lopsided on one end.

Though he was confident about his work, he always held his breath at the moment of truth. He signaled Alex.

"Testing, testing."

He blew out a whoosh of relief, and held up a thumb.

"Patsy, can you hear me okay?" Alex asked.

Patsy waved.

"How about you, Stella?"

Stella held up a hand from the other side of Town Square.

After the sound check he walked over to the food tents to make sure everyone had the power they needed. One of the vendors was having trouble with a grill earlier, but Gunner could tell from the smiles at the booth that everything was working fine now. He crossed the street.

"Hey, handsome," Patsy said as he approached her booth. "Here for some sweet treats?"

"That and a mega cup of coffee."

After picking up something to eat, he went out to enjoy a semi-quiet moment before Eden Falls was inundated with people. Izzy and Leo arrived at the face-painting booth. She threw back her head and laughed at something he said, before he wrapped an arm around her neck in a playful way. Then she squatted and petted the one-eyed dog Leo had on a leash. He watched the two banter back and forth for another minute, struck by an unexpected slap of jealousy.

His ex-wife had loved doing little things to make him jealous. Jessica reveled in knowing she had that kind of power over him. She loved drama. He should have recognized early on that their relationship would tank. They were too much alike in some ways, and incredibly different in others.

She would run a petty argument into the ground to prove she was right or to get her way. She'd start a fight over anything from what to have for dinner to the color of his shirt.

The only things they didn't fight about were sex and

money. They were happy in the bedroom, and she insisted they keep their bank accounts separate, which made their eventual split straightforward. Again, in hindsight, she must have anticipated their eventual separation.

Dahlia was unloading pumpkins from a huge cardboard box in front of her salon and lining them up on long tables.

He crossed the square. "Need some help?"

She smiled. "Hmmm. Let's see…good-looking man with muscles offering to help. Of course I'm going to say yes."

He looked at the banner hanging from the canopy she stood under. *Pumpkin Painting* was written in spooky orange and black letters. "This is new. What's pumpkin painting?"

She picked up a stack of papers. "The kids paint a face or design on their pumpkin instead of carving. It's easier for the little ones."

He took the designs she held out and thumbed through them. "Do you have help today?"

Dahlia glanced at her watch. "I closed the salon until this afternoon. The girls will help until then. High school students will fill in after that."

"I like the haircut," he said.

"Thanks." She touched her blond hair, which wasn't blunt at her shoulders anymore but feathered in layers around her face. "Most guys wouldn't notice."

"I think we notice, we're just too dumb to say so."

They made quick work of emptying the pumpkins from the cardboard box. He set up another table while Dahlia unfolded chairs, then they lined up bottles of paint and brushes.

"I heard Izzy hired you for the Victorian renovation."

"Should keep Dom and me fed for the winter."

She studied him for a long moment. "You okay?"

"Sure."

"Still not dating?" she asked, looking away, but not before he saw her sad eyes.

"Nope. Not dating."

"I heard you went bowling with Izzy."

Small town gossip, faster than the speed of light. "I went bowling with a group of people. Izzy was there."

He turned her chin with an index finger. "You still dating the same guy?"

"Yeah. He's a good man. Wants to take me to Vancouver to meet his family next weekend."

"Sounds like it's getting serious."

She wrinkled her nose. "I'm not sure how I feel yet."

"Don't settle for the good man," came a voice from behind him. Gunner turned.

Madam Venus stood in all her colorful, swirling-skirted, scarf-covered glory. She smiled past him to Dahlia. "Good Man is fun and a little exciting. He'll treat you right, but he's not the one." She nodded toward Gunner. "Neither is he. Your knight will ride in"—she looked skyward, then back at Dahlia —"possibly next year. If you'd like to know more, come see me. My tent is at the far end of Town Square. If not, date Good Man, but don't make any commitments. Not yet." She pointed at the pumpkins. "This is a cute idea for little ones. Your booth will be a hit."

They both watched her walk away before turning to each other. He was the first to laugh. "Aren't you glad you didn't waste any more time on me? I'm not *the one*."

"Do you believe her?"

"If your knight rides in one day soon, then I'll believe."

She leaned into him and he wrapped both arms around her, held her for a long moment. She got on tiptoes and kissed his cheek. "Thanks for the help, Gun. And congrats on the job."

He nodded when she stepped back. "Good luck with your booth today."

~

*I*zzy looked up and caught Gunner and Dahlia holding each other in more than a friendly hug. She could tell by the emotions on Dahlia's face, and by the way they held on a minute longer than necessary, that maybe things weren't over between them. *None of my business*, Izzy told herself.

Leo's friendly dog rested at her feet. "Don't you give this guy any attention, Leo?"

"Sure, but like any man, he'd rather have the love of a pretty woman."

"Flattery will get you everywhere. Where'd you get him?"

"I found him at my parents' farm. He was dirty and beat up. We just kind of adopted each other. Two peas and all that. Hey, Gun."

Gunner stopped next to her. "Do you have everything you need?"

"Paint and brushes. I think we're good."

He took her hand and ran the pad of this thumb over her healed blisters. "They look better."

Though she liked the feel of her hand in his, she pulled away. "They are."

"Good." He thumbed over his shoulder. "I'll be next door if you need anything."

"Hi, Leo!" A little boy came to a screeching halt at their booth.

"Looks like we have our first customer," Izzy said, turning her attention to Leo.

"Have you met Charlie? This is Alex's son."

She put a hand on the boy's shoulder. "Charlie? Oh, my goodness, I haven't seen you since you were a baby. You're all grown up."

"Yep, I turned eight in the summer."

"What are we going to paint on your face today?" Leo asked, guiding Charlie to a chair. "How about Spiderman?"

"Yes!" Charlie yelled, pumping a fist in the air.

Izzy's first cheek was Beam and Misty Garrett's black-haired, blue-eyed daughter, Sophia. She sat on Beam's lap and held still as well as any two-year-old could. She got a little butterfly. Before long the line to their booth was fifteen deep and she lost track of time.

Gunner was working the ring toss booth next to her. While she painted a face with tiger stripes, she overheard the sweet way he talked to the children. Even the ones who lost the game got a prize. Who'da thunk gruff, ornery Gunner had a sweet side?

The smell of food all around made her stomach growl.

"Hungry?" Leo asked with a laugh.

"I guess I am. And here come our reinforcements," she said when two high school kids entered the booth. She finished up the dragonfly she was painting and turned her brush over to a darling brunette. "Want to grab some lunch?" she asked Leo.

"If you can wait until Phoebe gets off duty. I told her I'd meet her."

Izzy remembered Madam Venus's prediction and was surprised to discover that she believed it just might happen. "Too hungry to wait that long. I'll see you later."

Izzy decided on a grilled chicken wrap and ate while wandering among the craft booths. She bought a blown-glass ornament for her mom's Christmas tree, and a leather wallet embossed with his initials for her dad.

She watched some boys try to drop a fireman at the

dunking booth. He didn't go down until a dad stepped in, but the boys had a great time trying. When the big guy fell into the water, all three boys cheered in victorious delight. She couldn't help but smile at their happiness.

Life was good at the moment. Attending the Harvest Festival after all her years away reminded her how much she'd missed this town. She loved seeing all the kids running free and feeling safe. She loved seeing people she'd known since she was tiny having a great time. She loved Eden Falls.

As she rounded a corner, she noticed Madam Venus sitting in a booth alone. She walked inside. "Looks like business is slow."

"Things aren't always as they seem." Madam Venus flashed a smile. "How is the new homeowner?"

"I'm good."

"And the house?"

"My family had a little congrats party for me last night and I've been here since nine thirty, so I haven't had time to go there yet."

The psychic cocked her head to the side. "You're wondering when the twins will come."

The lady really did give her the heebie-jeebies, because, yes, that was exactly what she'd been thinking.

"Have patience. Two people who have been best friends their whole lives will have to navigate some rough waters first." She indicated the vacant chair on the other side of her table. "Come sit with me for a minute. People will think I'm seeing your future and become curious to spend a few dollars of their own. Soon I'll have a line as long as your face-painting booth this morning."

Izzy laughed as she took a seat. "You're using me to make money?"

Madam Venus shrugged as if to say, why not? She picked

up a deck of cards and turned over the top one. "This signifies an unexpected visitor."

Which could be as simple as her mom's sister coming for a visit.

She flipped another card. "The event"—she squinted her eyes as if trying to read something—"Oh, you're planning Ariel's wedding."

"How can you know that?"

Madam Venus smiled. "The wedding will be a success and will bring you several referrals. You might want to give the bride a tiny discount for spreading the word." The third card she turned over brought a smile to her face. "Love is on the way."

"Though that would be nice, I don't really have time for love."

The psychic laughed, a fun, hearty sound. Under different circumstances, Izzy imagined they could be friends. Instant shame cloaked her. Why did she automatically discount the woman as a friend because she was a little—or maybe a lot —eccentric?

"Does love ever find us when it's convenient?"

Izzy shrugged. "I don't know. I've only been in love once —or thought I was—when I was in high school, but things didn't work out." When Izzy started dating Baron, she knew his feelings would never grow into love. She had hoped but didn't exert much effort in that department.

Madam Venus flipped another card and her smile dropped away. "Things won't be as they seem."

"That's the second time you've said that. What do you mean?"

She studied the card and then Izzy. "I'm not exactly sure, but I would advise you to be careful."

Squawk!

Izzy jumped and put a hand to her heart. "Rita, would you stop sneaking up like that! You scared me to death."

"Isadora Adams, don't tell me you're wasting your money on this woman!"

"Rita Reynolds," Madam Venus said, "you are about to come into a nice amount of money."

"Hogwash," Rita said, waving a hand, But she didn't leave.

"Have a seat and let's talk."

Izzy stood, and Rita slid into her chair. "How much money?"

When she turned to leave, she locked gazes with Gunner, who stood at the curb across the street. She smiled, he frowned.

Had she really expected anything different? Yes. After their night of bowling and him interrupting her yardwork, she thought they could actually strike up a friendship. Yes. She had expected him to be pleasant several times now and he always disappointed her. *Silly me.*

She wandered over to the pie-throwing booth, where Alex was attempting to hit her husband in the face.

"Come on, Alex," Patsy coaxed. "You hit him last year."

Alex ran her free hand over her baby bump. "I didn't have a football player trying to run a touchdown last year."

"Hit him, Mom," Charlie cheered.

"Hey!" Colton chided his stepson. "Your mom has one more try. Then her turn's up."

Alex's burly cousin took the pie from her, hefting it with an ominous look at Colton. "I'll get the job done, Low-rider."

Before Colton had time to protest, Beam tossed the pie and hit him square in his face. Charlie doubled over with laughter.

Alex patted Beam's chest. "Thanks, cuz. Honey," she

called to Colton, who was wiping banana cream from his face. "I'm going to waddle over to Pretty Posies and pee."

"Yup. Be right there." Colton blew whipped cream out of his right nostril.

Beam smiled at Izzy. "Colton's going to get back at me in some diabolical way. Writing murder mysteries gives him the creative edge."

Izzy nodded. "Should have thought of that before you smashed a pie in his face. Where is your darling daughter?"

"Misty has her at the apple toss." Beam pointed across the square.

"Your turn, Izzy," Patsy said, holding out a pie. "Five dollars a pie. All proceeds are donated to the humane society."

Izzy glanced at the board where a clown's body was painted in bright colors. And who should stick his head through the hole where the clown's face was supposed to be? Gunner. *Sweet justice*. She smiled. He glared. As tempting as the thought of his face covered in chocolate and whipped cream was, she decided she didn't want to risk losing her contractor.

"You'd make a mint off of me, Patsy. I don't have much of a pitcher's arm."

Patsy waved at Beam. "You have a big, brawny man right here to help."

So-o-o tempting. "No, I better leave the pie-throwing to someone else." She handed Patsy a ten-dollar bill. "But here's a donation for the humane society."

Beam picked up a pie and nailed Gunner in the face. "Sorry, Gun. Couldn't let a chance like that go to waste."

Instead of glaring at Beam, Gunner was staring at her as he wiped chocolate off his face with the towel Patsy provided. She patted Gunner's shoulder. "You'll get a chance at revenge. Beam is up in half an hour."

"Can't wait," Gunner grumbled.

Beam laughed and took Izzy's arm, leading her away. "I'm thirsty. Want a lemonade?"

"I'd love one."

Beam held up two fingers to the teenager manning the stand. "When do renovations start on the Victorian?"

"Gunner was going to work on the porch Monday, but texted that he had to pull a permit first—whatever that means."

"Hi, Iz. Hey, Beam."

Inwardly, she groaned, but turned with what she hoped was a pleasant smile. "Hey, Tim."

"I saw you and thought I'd say hi. I heard you're moving back to town."

"She's already moved," Beam said, handing her a cup of fresh-squeezed lemonade.

"Rita said you're buying the Victorian next to Owen's. I told her she's crazy. That place is a dump."

"She already bought it. Gunner starts renovations next week," Beam said, echoing her before taking a gulp of his lemonade.

Tim smiled. "I'm pretty handy with a hammer."

Oh, joy. "The renovation is going to take a little more than a hammer, and Gunner is a contractor." She glanced around. "Where's your girlfriend? I'd love to meet her."

"She's coming later. She had to work."

"I've got to relieve Misty of terrible-two duty," Beam said.

Izzy held up her drink. "Thanks for the lemonade."

"Thanks for letting me throw your pie."

"I'm sure paybacks won't be pleasant."

"No, I'll be cleaning out my sinuses in another twenty minutes. Good to see you, Tim."

She wistfully watched Beam walk away, leaving her stuck with Tim.

"So, you already bought the Victorian. You must have made really good money in California."

Rude. She didn't answer.

"How long will the renovations take?"

"Gunner plans to be finished sometime in January."

Tim stepped closer. "Do you have bats in the attic of that old place?"

"I haven't seen any bats—thank goodness. The attic is going to be my new home."

He rubbed his jawline with a laugh. She recognized the move from high school. He thought she was being silly or irrational. "There have to be half a dozen bedrooms in that house. Why would you live in the attic?"

"My dad needs more space for his business, so he's going to move his offices to the second floor."

His crinkled brow used to mean he was getting irritated. "That's crazy."

"Why? Owen has his offices next door. The zoning for that area says it can be a business."

"You bought a huge house so your dad—"

"Tim!"

A pretty brunette waved as she moved through the crowd toward them. "I got off early. I didn't think I'd ever find you in this mass of people."

She puckered and waited. He looked from her to Izzy and back, then gave the brunette a quick peck. "Hannah, this is Isadora. Iz, Hannah."

Hannah smiled as she threaded her arm through Tim's. "Hi."

"It's nice to meet you," Izzy said.

She looked at Tim. "How do you know each other?"

"High school," Izzy quickly said, not anxious for the

news that they'd dated to get out. "I have to go find... Phoebe." She glanced at her watch. "Her shift should be over. Nice to meet you, Hannah. Good to see you, Tim."

She didn't wait for a response, just turned and jogged as far from him as possible. Grateful his girlfriend showed up to end their conversation. She wondered if Hannah knew about their dinner together. *None of my business* ran through her mind again.

~

*G*unner made the rounds after two pies to the face. Food tents that had power running to them were all working fine. And when darkness fell, the lights came on, just the way they should. Gertie eyed him when it was time for square dance lessons. He wasn't sure whether she expected him to participate or if she was waiting for the sound system to fail...which it didn't. He watched tiny Gertie and her bear of a husband Albert move gracefully around the raised dance floor, showing their moves with a style that always surprised him. Both, who were usually stone-faced, wore smiles. People watched, mesmerized by the couple's fast-paced teamwork.

When the music stopped, they took a bow to vigorous applause.

Albert and Gertie had been dancing together since he was a kid. Ariel used to clap along as they twisted and twirled to the beat of the music.

He caught sight of Izzy sitting at a picnic table with her parents, Leo, and Phoebe. She pointed at something and they all laughed.

"Why don't you come over and sit with me?"

Madam Venus had come up behind him for the second

time that day. "I don't think so. I'm just fine not knowing what my future holds."

"Isadora wasn't afraid."

He'd been surprised to see Izzy sitting in the psychic's booth earlier. "I'm not afraid. I just don't believe you can predict what will happen in my future."

She nodded toward Izzy. "Has she told you about her sister having twins?"

"Phoebe's pregnant?"

"In time, by the man she's sitting with."

"Leo?" He chuckled, unable to imagine bachelor Leo with twins. Just as quickly as she'd floored him, he realized Madam Venus had snared him in her trap. He looked at her. "You're good."

"I don't trick people, and I don't lie. I just tell what I see. If I don't see anything, people get their money back."

He hoped she was telling the truth.

She smiled. "I am telling the truth." Her bracelets jangled when she touched his arm. "Keep her safe."

"Who?"

With a swirl of her skirts, she walked away.

CHAPTER 12

*G*unner bolted upright, drenched with sweat, his heart hammering like a machine gun blazing out a magazine of bullets. He sucked in air, trying to expand his constricted lungs. Domino, on the floor in his own bed, jumped up and whined. Taking deep gulps of air, Gunner ran the fingers of both hands through his damp hair.

Domino rested his head on the bed, worry in his eyes. "It's okay, boy. Just a bad dream." He reached over and patted Domino's head. "I'm okay."

His dog gave a yip.

He picked up his phone and glanced at the time, knowing he wouldn't go back to sleep. Two hours before the alarm was supposed to go off. He slid out of bed, stripped off the clammy sheets, and headed for the laundry room, Domino on his heels. He opened the door to let his dog out. "No barking."

Domino grinned and bounded into the backyard.

He started the coffee maker and stared at his reflection in the window over the sink while he waited for his heart to settle into a calm beat.

His Ariel PTSD had replaced his Army PTSD ever since Izzy came back to town. The guilt that he wasn't at the pond that day with his sister had ramped up to mammoth levels.

She'd been so excited when he called to say he'd be home for his birthday, though he hadn't planned his days back in the States that way.

The trailer was a wreck when he arrived. Ariel had tried to fix a hole in the bathroom floor with a piece of plywood and some roofing nails, because that was all she could find and she couldn't afford to buy what she needed. The damage from the fire his mom started when she passed out before removing the canned biscuits from the oven wasn't worth repairing. Luckily Ariel came home in time to drag her drunk mom to safety and call the fire department before the whole place burned down.

That on top of kissing his sister's best friend had driven him to Harrisville for a stiff drink. He justified his decision with the fact that Ariel had some school activity she had to attend his second night home. He planned to be back in Eden Falls by the time she got home, but several drinks and a woman later had him stumbling into the trailer way past midnight. Ariel sat at the tiny kitchen table eating a cake that said *Happy Birthday Gunner* in blue frosting.

"Oh, honey."

She looked up with tear-filled eyes.

He blew out an alcohol-saturated breath, feeling worse than he had a few hours earlier. "I'm sorry, Ari."

"Yeah, well, hope you had a happy birthday." She pushed back from the table, stomped down the short hall, and slammed her bedroom door without making eye contact.

He sat up most of the night, feeling guilty and wondering if he'd even see his mom during his few days home. He called her cell, which went straight to voice mail. Big surprise. Once his overwhelming guilt subsided, he covered the cake, cleaned out the disgusting fridge, and straightened the living room. He'd planned to stay awake until Ariel woke up the next morning, but the alcohol in his system had different ideas. His sister woke him at noon—having forgiven his selfishness—begging him to come ice skating with her.

"I can't, Ari," he groaned. "My head is splitting."

"Gun, come on. You're only home for a few days and I've barely seen you."

He reached for his phone when it pinged with a text. It took him a second to focus on the screen and then try to remember Kaylie was the reason he'd come home so late last night.

Meeting some friends at Chet's in Glenwood. Can you make it?

He quickly typed, **Yes.** He glanced at his sister sitting on the foot of his bed. She was already dressed for skating in the pink puffy coat she'd bought with the money he sent home. A crazy, colorful knit hat with yellow tassels was in her hand.

"Your head hurts too bad to skate, but not too bad to meet some girl?" Ariel asked, trying to sound angry, yet he detected the hurt in her voice.

"I'll take you skating tomorrow."

"I have school tomorrow."

"Tell you what, after school we'll go to dinner. And a movie. Your choice. Dinner and a movie tomorrow, right after school."

She sank back on the palms of her hands. "One hour, Gun. You can't spend one hour at the pond with me? Please," she begged in her guilt-trip tone. "I haven't seen you for six months."

The directions to Chet's popped onto his screen. "Not today, Ariel. Tomorrow, I promise."

She blew out an exaggerated sixteen-year-old breath and stomped out of his room. When he heard the door of the trailer slam, he crawled out of bed and showered while thinking of blue-eyed Kaylie. Before he left her house last night, she'd taken his phone and entered her number in with a promise to keep in touch. Glenwood was fifteen minutes away and he only had five more days before shipping out again.

He towel-dried, then swiped the mist off the mirror. What he saw looking back was his little sister. She'd asked for an hour of his time, and here he was trying to hook up with a girl he'd just met instead. He had come home to see Ariel. *You're a jerk.*

Snatching his phone, he pulled up Kaylie's name and quickly texted, **Sorry, can't make it.** He threw on jeans and a sweatshirt, took a couple of aspirin for his pounding head, and dug his skates out of the back of his closet. He would spend the afternoon skating if that's what his sister wanted to do.

Eden Falls residents had been skating on Riker's pond since he was a kid. It was built as a retention pond that caught spring runoff and emptied into the river. Once the water froze over in the winter, kids skated on one side and the high school hockey team used the other for practice.

He parked in the small dirt lot and rounded a hill. While the walk in the frigid air woke up his dull mind, it also allowed his headache to really shine through. The snow-covered mountains stood tall and majestic in the background.

He was glad to be home. And glad he'd decided to come. He could already imagine Ariel's smile, though she'd try to act *ho-hum, you-made-it-after-all* teenager-cool when she spotted him. After skating, he'd take her to Renaldo's Italian Kitchen for pizza, or to Harrisville for a burger and hot chocolate. He could sneak off to meet Kaylie after Ariel went to bed tonight.

He rounded a huge pine and the pond came into view.

Only a few people were on the ice. The hockey team stood off to the side, attention focused on a dark spot across the pond from them. Two people were on their stomachs close to the...

His misfiring brain finally kicked in. The dark spot was a hole in the ice. Scanning the area for a pink puff coat and crazy-colored hat, he broke into a run. Where was Ariel? He spotted Izzy and called her name. She turned, her amber eyes wide, tears streaming down her face. The second she saw him, she covered her mouth and glanced toward the pond. He knew. Without being told, he knew.

*H*is reflection in the window came into focus when Domino scratched on the door. He scrubbed at his wet eyes and let his dog inside.

An hour later he pulled to a stop in front of his new jobsite for the next few months. He'd pulled a permit Monday morning and spent the rest of the day taking measurements and purchasing the supplies he'd need to repair the porch. He wanted to get the porch shored up before the roofers—who said they could start a day earlier than originally scheduled —arrived.

The air was chilly, but the day was supposed to warm up by noon.

After unloading his truck, he started working on the new supports. He heard a car, but didn't look around, assuming it was Apple Valley Roofers.

"Good morning." Izzy climbed the stairs. "You're here early."

"Have you turned on the electricity yet?"

"Morning, Izzy. Then I say, How are you? You answer, Good. How are *you*? I say Wonderful. I can't wait to get started. Me either, you say" she said switching between a deep tone and her normal voice. "I say, Oh, I meant to tell you, you're welcome to bring Domino with you. Thanks, you say. He'd love to come rather than stay home cooped up in my house all day.' That's called a civilized conversation. And I know you're capable, because I've heard you hold perfectly pleasant conversations *with other people*."

She jammed the key into the lock and twisted until the door swung open on rusty hinges. "Yes, the electricity is on," she said, spitting like a wet cat.

"I'm going to need a key."

"Then you're going to have to change the locks, because I only have this one, and I'm pretty sure I can't get another of these ancient things made at the hardware store."

Next to-do on my list.

～

*J*zzy walked through the house and unlocked the back door. Next she moved her car around to the back so she wouldn't have to pass Gunner every time she went out for another load. She carried in—and up the stairs— two ladders, eight gallons of paint, brushes, rollers, paint trays, and drop cloths.

Last, she brought in a coffee maker, beans, and several mugs. Thank goodness the refrigerator Madam Venus left was usable until she could buy another, which wouldn't happen until after she decided what to do with the kitchen. She plugged the coffee maker in, added beans, water, and flipped the switch.

Determined to be civil, she decided to start over. Gunner's crabby attitude had made her just as crabby. Not a good way to start a three- to four-month renovation.

She opened the front door and came face-to-booty with Gunner on a ladder. At least she wouldn't be growled at.

"Fresh coffee will be ready in a minute. There are clean mugs on a paper towel on the counter."

"You said you don't drink coffee," he replied, without turning around.

"I don't." She shut the door and headed up the stairs.

While she washed the walls in the big front bedroom, she heard the roofers arrive, and the scraping and banging soon followed. For a split second she thought she should go out and meet them, then changed her mind. She'd hired a contractor for a reason. He could handle the details. She did glance out the window and watched him shake hands with one of the men, then fitted headphones over her ears and the noise disappeared.

When the walls were clean and dry, she taped around the windows and door trim and the beautiful built-in bookcase, then spread drop cloths. The prep took her longer than she'd planned, but at least Gunner wouldn't get after her about paint on the floor.

The sun had shifted by the time she started painting the front wall around the windows. She didn't check the time, because she didn't want to know how long the job had taken. The sun shifted again and she flipped the overhead light on.

Again she lost track of time—until someone touched her shoulder. She spun around. Gunner jumped back, but not in time to save his T-shirt from getting a punch of color from the roller in her hand.

Several emotions swept over his face, and his jaw tensed as he pulled his shirt away from his chest.

He slowly raised his eyes to meet hers and shook his head, his jaw cocked to the side.

She bit back a laugh. "Sorry about another T-shirt."

"I'll add it to my growing pile. Thank you for the coffee this morning."

"You're welcome," she said in surprise.

He thumbed over his shoulder. "I would have washed out the coffeepot but couldn't find any soap."

"I'll add that to my list of things to bring." *Along with toilet paper, hand soap, paper towels, et cetera.*

"Is it okay if I keep my tools and ladder in the living room overnight?"

"Sure. I'll lock up."

"I'm going to run to the hardware store and pick up new locks. Do you need anything?"

He was full of surprises tonight. Maybe her rant this morning had softened him a little. "No, thank you." She glanced around at her mess. "I've got everything I need to finish. What do you think of the color?"

"Not really my area of expertise," he said without looking around.

"Yea or nay? Not that hard to say whether you like it or not. Not that it matters. The color was my dad's choice. This room will be his office." The calm, gray-blue color looked gorgeous with the wood.

Gunner scanned the room. "I like it. The color looks nice with the wood."

She laughed. "That's exactly what I thought. I did what you and Beam said. Hung samples around the room and checked them at different times of day."

Hands on hips, he nodded and studied the wall she'd painted.

Gunner was extremely handsome when he wasn't scowling. Maybe she shouldn't be in such a hurry to rid him of his ornery streak. Otherwise her girlhood crush might come crashing down around her heart, and that wouldn't be good.

"I don't hear banging. Are the roofers finished for the day?"

His brow creased. "It's dark out, Izzy."

Wow, she'd really been in the zone. She hadn't even noticed. "Did they find any damage?"

"Only the spot I pointed out when we were in the attic. They'll be finished by Thursday afternoon."

"Perfect. I'm glad they could start a day earlier. When do the exterior painters start?"

"They'll prep Friday and Saturday, painting starts Monday."

Things were moving along as quickly as she'd hoped. "Thanks, Gunner."

He stopped at the door. "I didn't bring Domino because I didn't want him to get a roofing nail in a paw."

"Right. I didn't think about that, but he is welcome. And I don't mind if he comes inside. I hate to think of him alone all day."

"Thanks. Do you want help cleaning up?"

"No," she blurted a little too quickly. "It won't take me long."

He disappeared, but she stood still, listening to him walk down the stairs and close the front door.

～

*G*unner waited in his truck until the light in the front bedroom went out. He was having a hard time separating how he felt about the woman and how he should feel about his boss. He went into the house a couple of times today and never spotted her.

He turned the heater up against the chill of the night and drove to Eden Falls Hardware and Lumber. Beam was inside at the register.

"Has Izzy come in and set up an account yet?"

"No." Beam grabbed some papers from under the counter. "I can send a form with you."

"Yeah, I'll give it to her tomorrow. I need a couple of new locks. The ones on the house are rusted and sticking."

Beam pointed him in the right direction. He picked out two. When he did the walk-through, he hadn't really checked all the window and door locks. He'd do that tomorrow. Eden Falls was a safe town, and Izzy wasn't living at the house yet, but tonight he'd left expensive equipment inside.

He set the locks on the checkout counter. Beam rang up the purchase. "I'll put these toward her account once she's set it up."

"Thanks, Beam. How's your daughter?"

"Lucky that she looks like her mama, unlucky that she also has Misty's fiery temperament."

Gunner wasn't touching that statement with a ten-foot pole. Everyone in town knew it wasn't wise to cross Misty. "Time for that baby Madam Venus mentioned."

Beam looked up. "I forgot you were there that night. Do you know she was right? Misty is pregnant and angry as a rabid dog, snarling and biting every chance she gets."

"What?"

"I know. Madam Venus swoops into that Harvest Festival committee meeting, makes a prediction, and Misty is pregnant."

Unbelievable. "Good luck to you for the next eight months."

"You can find me here"—he pointed at the floor—"where it's safe. Doing lots of inventory."

Gunner waved before walking into the cold night. He couldn't wrap his head around the fact that Madam Venus had foreseen Misty's pregnancy. Misty worked at Dahlia's Salon and probably cut the psychic's hair, and they talked about... whatever women talk about and Madam Venus made a wild guess from their conversation. That made sense.

Still...

~

*H*e and Izzy fell into a routine over the next two weeks. The roof and the front porch were finished, and the exterior painters got to work. Gunner had framed the attic and started hanging drywall. Izzy was making progress on painting the second floor. She'd moved her belongings into a back bedroom the second weekend after closing. Every morning he'd poke his head into the bedrooms as he passed, to see what she'd done the previous day.

Before the sun came up, Gunner let himself in the back door. Domino made his way to the doggy bed Izzy provided, circled twice, and plopped down for a nap. Just as a faint glow appeared on the horizon, he started the coffee maker and grabbed a donut from a box on the counter, hoping Izzy had meant to share.

He filled dog bowls with food and water, then poured coffee into his huge travel mug and headed up the stairs. In the attic, he got to work on the drywall. He hoped to finish by the end of the week, then he'd start on the bathroom. Izzy had insisted on three different sizes of white tile. He had to admit, once installed, it would look great, but he'd never tell Izzy. She'd driven him crazy asking his opinion, then doing the exact opposite.

"What are you doing?"

He turned and tried not to laugh. "What are you wearing?"

Izzy stood at the top of the attic stairs, looking all sleepy and cute. Pushing her long hair off her face, she glanced down like she'd forgotten she'd put on cow-covered pajamas before bed. "I got cold. I don't think the heater is working."

He walked over to a register and held out his hand. "Has it been off all night?"

"I was asleep. What are you doing?"

"Trying to finish the drywall."

"It's five thirty. In the morning. Why are you here at five thirty in the morning? Why aren't you home? In bed. Like a normal person."

He tried not to react to her smoky, sexy voice. The sight of her baggy, bright yellow pajamas alone should have done the trick, but no. His whole body buzzed with lust. He turned away and inserted another drywall screw. "I wanted to get an early start."

She walked up close, forcing him to look at her. "I think we need some ground rules. Or house rules. No starting before eight."

"Six thirty," he countered.

"Seven. No eating the last raspberry-filled donut," she said pointing to the half-eaten donut on a napkin with wide eyes. "No Pearl Jam before nine and no Led Zeppelin before ten. No using Domino to soften me up so I'll change my mind about something we don't agree on. That is totally unfair to use a sweet dog against me."

He fought a smile, because he had totally done that several times already. Despite the dog, she'd won.

~

*G*unner nodded. Izzy liked that she could bring a smile—well, almost a smile—to his face every once in a while. Of course, it wasn't the full-on smile he flashed to Phoebe or Stella. Or Dahlia. But it was a tiny curl at the corners of his mouth, something she'd never been able to evoke before he started working on the house.

Phoebe shouldn't have mentioned jeans commercials, because her attention shot straight to Gunner's butt every time he had his back turned. Which was often.

Heading down the stairs, she paused to look at three of

the five bedrooms she'd painted. The blue-gray of her dad's office looked lovely with the built-in bookcases and mahogany trim. So did the sienna room. The taupe in the third room wasn't something she'd ever pick, but it was growing on her.

She had a meeting with her bride and groom later this morning, then she'd tackle the fourth bedroom.

After brushing her hair and teeth, she ran down to the kitchen. Domino flipped over, offering her his belly for rubbing, his tail thumping against his bed.

"Good morning, happy dog. How are you this morning? Feeling tired and out of sorts because some grump made you get up so early? I don't blame you a bit. I'm probably going to be grumpy by this afternoon." She shouldn't have stayed up so late last night finishing that third bedroom.

She put a kettle on the burner to warm water for tea just as someone knocked on the front door. "What is up with everyone being out and about so early today?" she asked. Domino hopped off his bed, happy to accompany her.

Passing through the house, she made a mental note of a few things that needed attention soon, like the strange black wire sticking out of the wall with no switch nearby. She opened the front door expecting a sister or her mom or dad. Definitely not Baron Van Buren. Domino barked.

"Baron."

He looked her up and down like he'd just been greeted by an alien. Gathering her hair in a fist, she glanced down at her pajamas for the second time this morning. "I was cold."

Domino barked again. She touched his head. "Quiet, boy."

"You actually bought this place?" He cast a look inside at the black walls in the living room.

"I'm going to paint." She opened the door wider, waiting

to feel something that didn't come. "What are you doing here?"

He stepped inside. "Eden Falls could use another hotel. I had to stay at The Dew Drop Inn last night. They don't have room service."

Poor rich guy. "There's a café, a coffee shop, and a pastry shop in town. All exceptional."

"I saw them. Can't imagine eating in any of them." He glanced around again, the look on his face a little on the I-just-walked-into-a-horror-movie side.

"I can offer you a cup of coffee and a donut."

"A donut."

"I know. Completely disgusting." Baron followed mindful eating practices. He believed in connecting with his food. Well, she was ready to connect with a sugary treat, though the raspberry donut she'd anticipated was upstairs, half-eaten by a guy who wore his jeans really well.

"This house is much larger than it looks from the outside. What do you plan to do with all this space?"

She gave him an edited version. He was probably worried she'd open a gallery.

He stepped into the kitchen and the horror in his eyes grew to gargantuan proportions. "Please tell me the walls were this color when you bought the house and that you didn't do this."

"I didn't do this, and yes, I plan to repaint."

Domino sniffed Baron's expensive pants, making him take a step back. "When did you get a dog?"

"Domino isn't mine." Gunner's dog sat at her feet, his attention on Baron. "He belongs to my contractor."

"You allow him in your house?"

"Who? The dog or the contractor?" She laughed. Baron didn't. "Yes, I allow him in the house. He's a sweetheart." *Unlike his owner.*

"You were right about Eden Falls being small."

"But quaint, and the residents are very friendly. Unless you run into Rita."

"Oh, I had the privilege of meeting Rita. She's the one who showed me where you live. She's..."

She waved a hand. Rita was much too unique to explain in just a few sentences. "Let's get back to my very first question. Why are you here?"

"To bring you to your senses. To hire movers to get you back to San Francisco."

"I'm not going back."

"Stop being so ridiculous, Isadora. What are you going to do in this small town?"

"I told you. I'm opening a business. I already have clients."

He grunted out a laugh. Very unsophisticated, for him. "Time to wake up from your fantasy now."

"It's not a fantasy. I'm meeting with a bride and groom later today."

"Okay, how long does it take to plan a country wedding? Two meetings? Three? Then you move back." He pulled his phone out of his jacket pocket. "What's the name of a local real estate company? We'll put this place on the market today."

"I'm not moving back."

Gunner chose that moment to stroll into the kitchen, travel mug in hand.

"Stop being juvenile, Isadora. It shouldn't take long to get rid of this monstrosity."

She grabbed Gunner's arm and pulled him close, cozying up to his side. "Baron, meet my fiancé, Gunner Stone."

Baron's jaw dropped. "Fiancé?"

Gunner was looking at her like she'd lost her freaking mind, and maybe she had, but she used the first thing that popped into her head. She had to make Baron believe she wasn't coming back.

"Gun, honey, this is my previous boss, Baron. He's here to try and talk me into going back to work for him."

"You left San Francisco less than two months ago. How are you already engaged?"

"Oh, um...Gunner and I had a thing when I was in high school. We ran into each other after my sister's wedding, it was like...bam!"

"Literally," Gunner said, with his usual scowl.

"We just...fell in love all over again." She squeezed his bicep. "I mean, what girl could resist these muscles?"

Gunner moved his arm slightly, his elbow brushing her breast. She tried to pinch his side, but there wasn't enough to grab between finger and thumb.

Baron's eyes zeroed in on her left hand. "No ring?"

Revenge could be so sweet. "No, sadly, Gun here is still on parole and a little short on cash, thus the contractor job. He's really great at drywall. Aren'tcha, hun?"

"You're engaged to a convict?"

"Small town, slim pickings, yada-yada," she said, rolling her hand.

Gunner extracted his arm from her grasp and wrapped it around her waist. "Sorry you had to drive all this way, but Izzy is here to stay." He hauled her against his hard body. She opened her mouth to protest and he took that opportunity to kiss her like she'd never been kissed before. Fireworks exploded behind her eyelids, her thighs burst into flame. Her insides seized and her knees turned to mush and she melted... simply and completely melted into him.

He released her just as quickly as he'd grabbed her. She stumbled back a couple of steps. He steadied her with a wicked smirk and a hand on her arm before he filled his mug with fresh coffee. "I have to get back to work, sweetie. My parole officer is stopping by later."

"Right." She sucked in a ragged breath. "I'm not going back to San Francisco, Baron."

"Triple. I offered to triple your salary."

She was tempted to put a hand to her chest to hold in her jumping heart, but refused to give Gunner the satisfaction of seeing how he'd affected her. Instead, she clung to the countertop behind her. "Tempting, but still a no."

"I don't know, honey," Gunner said. "Triple your salary? We could go to Vegas and get hitched and still have money left over for a few games of craps."

Baron frowned from Gunner to her. "Come back long enough to train your replacement."

"I'm going to be too busy for any trips, Baron." She turned him toward the front door. "In fact, I need a shower before I meet my bride and groom."

"I guess I could put off finishing the drywall until after a quick shower." Gunner, who'd followed them into the foyer, bounced his brows up and down for Baron's benefit. At least she hoped that was why.

"No time, sugar...pie. I have to work. Maybe later tonight," she said, trying to bounce her eyebrows.

He chuckled at her attempt.

Okay, so she was horrible at flirting.

She opened the front door and pushed Baron onto the porch. "Sorry, Baron. You blew your opportunity to have the best, most hardworking, devoted manager in the world."

She shut the door and turned, relieved to see Gunner disappearing up the stairs.

CHAPTER 13

*M*istake. Huge mistake kissing Izzy... Stupid, stupid, stupid!

A mistake that didn't feel wrong when it was happening. Why was he such a glutton for punishment? First, he took this job, placing him in the same house with her at least eight hours a day for three to four months, thus ruining the possibility of a good night's sleep on the odd night he might be lucky and actually stay asleep. Second, he'd kissed her, effectively ending even those few lucky nights, because now he'd be thinking about her even more than he already did.

How could someone who had just climbed out of bed smell so fresh or look so tempting while wearing bright yellow cow pajamas?

The shower on the second floor turned on, and he tried to resist where his mind traveled.

He'd finished the drywall everywhere but in the bathroom when he went downstairs for more coffee and got tangled up with Izzy and her ex-boss who must also be an ex-boyfriend or she wouldn't have gone to such trouble.

She'd used him to pull off her little engagement charade.

The least he could do was get a kiss out of the deal. He thought his being years older would dilute the impact of her lips touching his, but nope. She affected him now even more than she had at sixteen. To his satisfaction, the kiss had affected her too. He'd seen the flash of desire in her pretty eyes.

He chuckled at the thought of her parole story. Pretty quick on the draw.

After cutting another piece of drywall, he fit it above the bathroom door, then stood back to survey his work.

He usually cringed when a client wanted to do their own work, but felt different about Izzy. She was an artist. The bedrooms she'd been painting were precise and professional.

When he went through Ariel's things after her death, he came across a charcoal drawing of Ariel and him laughing together. Izzy had signed her work in the corner on the pocket of his shirt—right over his heart. The detail and likeness had astounded him. Ariel's dimple, the sweet flash of her smile, her slightly crooked incisor. Izzy had even captured the light in her eyes with a simple drawing on the inside chunk of an IGA paper grocery sack. He had his military haircut, so she must have captured them at the going-away party Ariel had insisted on throwing with his money. He framed the picture and hung it on his bedroom wall.

He'd also kept the guitar pick. He should ask Izzy if she knew who Ariel's mystery boyfriend had been.

Without looking, he knew the second Izzy came into the attic. Her perfume settled around him in a soft cloud. She stood on the far side of the room wearing a skirt and billowy blouse that captured the colors of autumn. Domino, attached to her side, wagged his tail. She chewed her bottom lip, a quirk he was used to seeing when she had something on her mind.

He waited.

"Wow, it looks so big."

Seeing her enthusiasm set his nerve endings on fire. "You'll have plenty of space up here."

"Thank you."

"It's your design and your dime."

"I meant for earlier. Thank you for going along with my ruse. Baron doesn't take no for an answer. I thought if I told him I was engaged it would get him out the door faster. It's the first thing that popped into my mind, and I just blurted it out."

"Did the parole thing just pop into that mind of yours too?"

She pressed her lips together, but he saw the corners of her mouth twitch. "Payback."

"Payback for what? You've ruined three of my shirts."

"The last two times were your fault. You scared me."

"Well, your plan seems to have worked."

"We'll see." She shrugged as if she didn't believe she'd seen the last of Baron. "Like I said, he doesn't take no for an answer."

She walked closer, her fresh smell assaulting him once again.

"I have a meeting in a little while. Can I bring you back some lunch?"

He spotted the tiny spark of hope in her eyes, heard the hesitancy in her voice. He wasn't a commitment kind of guy. He'd tried and failed. Izzy wasn't a woman who would settle for anything less. *Time to shut it down, Gun.* "I brought something."

"Okay." She put her hands together as if praying and rested her chin on her fingertips. "Thank you again."

He knew what she meant but couldn't resist the opportunity to tease. "You're thanking me for kissing you?"

Her cheeks flamed red. "No. Well, yes, the kiss certainly

helped convince Baron, but I mean"—she flapped a hand —"for going along with me in front of Baron." She cut him a look from under a veil of lashes. "You didn't have to use tongue, though. Or cop a feel. That was…"

"Resourceful?"

"I was thinking opportunistic."

"You cozying up against me is hardly my fault."

"I was vulnerable."

"You were using me as a make-believe lover. I was playing the part."

She opened her mouth, changed her mind and closed it, pressing her lips together, another smile twitching the corners, before she walked down the stairs.

He enjoyed volleying back and forth with her a little too much.

Rein it in, Gunner.

~

*I*zzy's system was still buzzing from Gunner's kiss as she walked toward Town Square. He'd leaned down so quickly she didn't have time to stop him. Would she have if she'd known what he planned to do? She didn't want to contemplate the answer.

It actually didn't take any contemplation. She liked Gunner Stone, which made absolutely no sense. He'd always treated her as a child before Ariel's death, and viewed her with contempt afterward.

Clouds were billowing over the mountain peaks and a chilly breeze scattered dry leaves along the sidewalk. She pulled her sweater tighter around her. Halloween was two days away. Hopefully snow would hold off until after goblins and ladybugs filled their bags with candy. Snow wasn't much fun while trick-or-treating.

Alex had provided a place for her meetings until she could get the first floor in order. She entered Pretty Posies to the happy jingle of the bell over the door. Alex waved from behind the counter, her upbeat smile in place.

"Thanks for letting me use your shop for my meeting."

"Not a problem." Alex moved around the counter, hand on her pregnant belly, and led Izzy to her little sitting area. "How are the renovations going?"

"Good. Gunner will probably finish drywalling the attic today."

"Before or after Baron Van Buren stopped by?"

"How…?"

"Small town. Baron stopped by Noelle's Café, asking where he could find you, and Rita happily supplied the information. Even escorted him to the Victorian." She tipped her head with raised brows.

Great. News about Baron's visit would be all over town by now. "Baron wants me to go back to California. He's having a harder time replacing me than he thought he would. I doubt he'll find anyone willing to put in the hours he had me working."

"Baron must have confided in Rita. She came back to report that he offered you triple your salary."

Her previous boss had no idea that Rita was Eden Falls' biggest busybody. She'd be spewing the news like Old Faithful. "He did, and he would have made good on his offer." Though he made any kind of private life impossible for her, Baron paid extremely well.

"She also reported she saw you and Gunner *making out like a couple of high school kids*," Alex said, perfectly imitating Rita's tone.

What? Rita must have peeked in the back window if she saw their kiss. "It wasn't romantic. He was just trying to help me convince Baron I wasn't going back," Izzy said as heat blazed over her cheeks. "Did Rita tell everyone?"

"Everyone who was in Noelle's Café for breakfast. She even included details about where Gunner put one of his hands…"

"Great."

"…and a description of your yellow cow pajamas—"

"I was cold," Izzy blurted, hoping to deflect Alex's commentary.

"Good thing Gunner was there to heat things up," Alex said with a grin. "Rita also said something about an engagement."

Gunner is going to kill me.

Izzy was glad for the interruption when the future bride and groom walked into the shop. She'd have to tell Gunner before someone else did.

The first thing Ariel and her fiancé Craig told Izzy about was a change of date. "We decided instead of January to go with a spring wedding. We found an orchard about thirty minutes outside of South Fork that allows weddings among the cherry blossoms. We reserved the date with them."

Izzy loved the idea of an outdoor wedding, but spring weather in Washington could be tricky to plan around. "Does the orchard provide tents in case of inclement weather?"

"They didn't say, but a tent will distract from the beautiful setting and all the cherry trees in bloom."

"So will rain or, even worse, snow." She jotted down the name and directions to the orchard. "I'll visit them and see what they have to offer. What about food?"

For the next thirty minutes they discussed what they'd like served and caterers, number of guests, and invitations.

The bride decided to add pale pink with her silver and sage color choices so the flowers she and Alex had picked on her previous appointment would still work.

Izzy gave them Carolyn Garrett's name for a cake. "She works a couple of doors down at Patsy's Pastries. She recently did my sister's wedding cake, which was gorgeous, and delicious to boot. She used to be a chef at a San Francisco restaurant," she added, pulling a picture of Stella's cake from her file.

The bride's eyes widened. "Do you think she has other pictures of her work?"

Alex chose that moment to stop nearby. "Carolyn keeps a photo album at the pastry shop. She's made several cakes for local weddings, all very unique and beautiful, but also yummy. She specialized in desserts while in culinary school."

"We'll stop by and take a look," the groom said. "Thanks."

"I'll email prices from a few caterers in the area and find out what the orchard will allow. I recommend Carolyn for your wedding cake, but please ask friends and check out other bakers too."

They set up the next meeting for the first week in December. She knew many wedding dress salons, cake bakers, and stationery stores in San Francisco, but hadn't built her Seattle and surrounding area portfolio yet. Although she did have a folder of Alex's recommendations. Not that she didn't trust Alex's opinion, but she wanted to check with each vendor herself before tossing names out. She'd create a spreadsheet and collect pictures from each venue; baker—though she'd always recommend Carolyn first; florist—same with Alex; and wedding dress shops in the area.

And she now had plenty of business cards to pass around to the different shops when she visited.

Gunner flitted through her thoughts again. She had his cell number and thought of calling, which would be the chicken way out, but would save her from his glowering stare. While he'd done the kissing—though she *had* participated—he'd blame her, because she came up with the engaged idea.

Her and Gunner's relationship was already sticky enough without Peeping Rita sticking her nose where it didn't belong and then blabbing what she saw around town.

~

*G*unner walked into the hardware store, waved at Beam—who flashed a goofy grin—and headed back for more drywall mud. Normally, he was prepared, but Izzy seemed to interfere with his plans almost every day in some way or another.

When he returned to the register, Beam stood in the same place, still wearing his grin. "Hey, Gun."

"Hey." He set the five-gallon jug on the counter. "Can you put this on Izzy's account?"

"Sure thing. So, how's the renovation coming?"

"Good." He was getting the same question a lot.

"Yeah? And how's Izzy?"

At Beam's tone, Gunner looked up. "She's okay, or at least she seemed okay the last time I saw her."

"Which was right after you kissed her?"

Gunner's jaw dropped. Izzy was going around town telling people?

Beam's booming laugh echoed through the hardware store. "Izzy's San Fran boss showed up at Noelle's Café this morning asking where he could find her. Rita was more than happy to accompany him to the house while pumping him for information."

"And?"

"She came back to Noelle's and reported to the breakfast crowd that she caught you two kissing."

"Geez, she's resorted to peering in windows?" Gunner picked up the jug and headed for the door.

"Wait. Aren't you going to fill me in?"

"Nope."

"Misty is going to ask for details."

This might be the last day above ground for Rita. "Later."

His father's abandonment had started Rita's tongue wagging about his family years ago. The man had walked out, found another woman, got a respectable job *for her*, and built a family he actually provided for, completely ignoring the fact that he already had one.

His mother's drinking only made their situation worse. Half the town pitied them. The other half kept their distance, because any kid who raked leaves at the cemetery for a few bucks must be a thug, too, at least to people like Rita. So he acted the part, put on a tough exterior so people wouldn't see just how deeply he was hurting. He took care of the details where his little sister was concerned, which was completely fine with his mom. She checked out of Hotel Stone as soon as their dad drove away.

Fat raindrops started to fall before he got to his truck. Domino sat on the passenger seat waiting patiently. "I knew that kiss was a mistake, Dom. It's already come back to bite me—bite both of us—and I'm sure this isn't the end of it."

Not that he paid much attention to what people said about him. They'd been saying the same thing for years. But Izzy was just starting out, making her place in Eden Falls after a long time away.

Domino's tail thumped the back of the seat.

"Let's go home and get some lunch."

He circled the square and spotted Izzy making a mad dash from Pretty Posies into East Winds. If it was anyone else that observance would pass in and out of his mind without making an impression, but not Izzy. Instead, he imagined sitting across the table from a woman with happy amber eyes and tempting lips that she chewed when she had something on her mind.

He'd told her he brought lunch, but Chinese sounded great at the moment, so he found a parking place while telling himself he was only compounding his earlier mistake. His hunger for Izzy overrode common sense.

Once inside, he glanced around. Before he spotted her, a hand took his arm. "Are you meeting someone, Gun?"

"Nope. Here alone, Phoebe."

"Good. We have some things to discuss." She towed him toward a booth where Izzy and Leo sat. Phoebe and Leo— though unwelcome in his lunch fantasies—would be safe buffers in the long run.

Phoebe slid in next to Leo with a "Look who I found to join us."

"Hey, Gun," Leo said with a grin.

Izzy glanced up at him with a look of horror, then moved her purse from her left to her right on the bench...like that would prevent him from sitting too close.

Okay, so he might have been a little aggressive this morning, but he wasn't going to attack her in a public place. He slid in next to her.

"I thought you brought your lunch."

Even with the smells of sesame oil, seared meat, and scallions, he could still smell her perfume. He wanted to stick his nose against her neck and take a deep breath. And a bite. "Chinese sounded better than a sandwich."

"Okay," Phoebe said, leaning forward, arms crossed on the table. "Spill it."

"Spill what?" Izzy asked, suddenly occupied with her menu.

Gunner decided to sit back and let Izzy take the lead.

"Don't play dumb with me, little sister. Rita is heralding

the news of your kiss all over town, so spill. When did you two start this little fling?" Phoebe pointed from Izzy to him. "And why didn't you tell me, Iz? I'm hurt."

"There's no fling," Izzy protested. She glanced at him, and her face flushed beet red. "Baron showed up this morning, insisting that I come back to California. Gunner happened to walk into the room, and I thought if Baron believed we were a couple he'd go away, so I said we were engaged."

"Congratulations!" Leo said.

"I should have known your lunch invitation had an ulterior motive," Izzy said, narrowing her gaze on Phoebe.

Phoebe held up hands. "I only heard about the kiss. The engagement is news to me."

"Gunner was just trying...to...to...make it more believable."

"Way to step up to the plate, Gun," Leo said with a laugh.

"Yeah," Phoebe drawled. "You're a hero."

"Stop," he said, keeping his expression and voice neutral. "You're making me blush."

"She's the one blushing," Leo said. "How convincing was that kiss?"

"Okay." Izzy picked up her purse and batted his thigh. "Move so I can get out."

"Calm down, Iz. We're just having fun at your expense. You're not going anywhere." Phoebe reached out and caught his arm. "Gunner, don't you dare move."

"Wasn't planning to." He didn't mind seeing Izzy all flustered after their kiss, but felt a little protective of her at the same time. "Like Izzy said, I was trying to make *her lie* more believable. The kiss didn't mean anything." He glanced at Izzy and saw a lightning flash of something... Surprise? Hurt? Then it was gone.

She looked away. "Right. It didn't mean anything. What's

important is that Baron believed us and left. He's like a dog with a bone. He doesn't give up without a fight."

Gunner expected the waitress when someone stopped next to him, but it was Tim. He seemed to be popping up a little too often for someone who lived in Harrisville. This time he was with a woman in scrubs. Everyone at the table turned to him as one.

"I wanted to stop by and say hi," he said, his gaze on Izzy.

"Who's your friend?" Leo asked.

"Oh, sorry. This is Hannah Steed. Hannah, you've met Izzy. This is her sister Phoebe, Leo Sawyer, and Gunner Stone."

"Hi, Hannah," Phoebe said.

"Nice to see you again," Izzy added.

Hannah gave a little wave.

"Well, our table is ready," Tim said. "Have a great lunch."

"You too," Izzy said.

Leo waved. "Nice to meet you, Hannah."

"Another cute couple," Phoebe said with exaggerated kindness. "Never trusted that guy. He has shifty eyes."

"That sounds like a line from a fifties cop show," Izzy said.

Phoebe wrinkled her nose. "Sometimes you have to go with gut instinct, and my gut never liked the guy."

Gunner didn't trust Tim either. Like Phoebe, his was just a gut feeling.

Izzy stayed quiet through most of their lunch. She concentrated on her food, answered when asked a question, and filled in facts about the house, but otherwise remained silent.

Was their kiss the reason for her somber mood? Or was she bothered by Tim being with another woman? He glanced

Tim's way. He and Hannah were eating without exchanging so much as a glance at each other.

The couple of times he'd seen Izzy with Tim, she hadn't acted like she was interested. The night they'd been here eating dinner she seemed ready to bolt. In his experience, that wasn't how a woman acted when she was interested.

"So, Gun, what are you dressing as for Halloween?" Phoebe asked.

"A handyman."

"Same as last year and the year before and the year before." Phoebe sighed and fanned her face. "But I do love a man in a tool belt. Izzy, what are you wearing?"

"I haven't even thought about Halloween."

"Well, you better start. Rowdy has a party every year, and you have to be in costume or you can't get in." She moved a finger between him and Izzy. "Now you're a couple, you should find cute matchy-matchy costumes."

"We're not a couple," Izzy said.

"Help me think of cute couples' costumes for them," Phoebe said to Leo.

"An apple and a banana? Pirate and sexy wench?" Leo offered. "How about a sixties couple? I can get a whole wardrobe for you from my parents."

"Great idea," Phoebe exclaimed. "You two would look darling. How about a crown of daisies, Iz? I bet Alex would whip one up for you."

Leo nodded. "How are your legs, Gun? Tights? Robin Hood and Maid Marian? Beauty and the Beast? Bumblebee and flower? Ketchup and mustard?"

"You're good at this," Phoebe said. "Oh! I know, you could go as that farming couple in that famous *American Gothic* painting." Phoebe pulled out her cell phone and started typing away. "What's the name of the artist who did that?"

"Grant Wood," Izzy supplied flatly.

"You know the one I'm talking about? The couple with a pitchfork standing in front of a barn."

Izzy blew out a breath. "They're standing in front of a house."

"Here it is. The artist *is* Grant Wood." Phoebe flipped the phone around so they could see the screen.

Izzy patted his thigh and made a shooing gesture. Yep, he was ready to escape Phoebe and Leo, too. He scooted out of the booth and pulled out his wallet. "I got your lunch," he said to Izzy.

Leo drummed the table with his hands. "How about a target and an arrow?"

"Or Cupid and a heart?" Phoebe exclaimed.

"Thanks, I'll buy next time," Izzy said to him and headed for the door.

"Poison Ivy and Benadryl?"

"Fred and Wilma Flintstone!"

"Just shorten Wilma's dress to show some leg," Leo hollered as Izzy pushed outside.

Gunner set money on the table and followed her out.

She stopped at the curb, her shoulders hunched against the cold. "Sorry," she mumbled when he stopped next to her. She glanced his way without making eye contact. "I'm really sorry about all of this."

He lifted her chin so their eyes met. "I'm the one who's sorry, Izzy. Remember, *I kissed you*. I hope it doesn't cause you any problems. I plan to have a talk with Rita."

Izzy flapped her hand. "Don't bother. She'll only make things worse by telling everyone you threatened her."

"If I thought it would do any good, I would threaten her."

Izzy's quick smile wiped all intelligent thought from his mind.

CHAPTER 14

The next day Gunner arrived at the Victorian intending to start tiling the attic bathroom. He and Domino entered by the back door and he immediately noticed how cold the kitchen felt. He walked through the downstairs to the thermostat. The white digital numbers read thirty-six, which was the same as the outside temperature this morning.

He went upstairs to the closet holding the furnace.

Ten minutes later, the kitchen door closed and Gunner went down to see who'd come in. Izzy was on the floor cozying up to Domino, an overnight bag next to her.

She glanced up, her pretty eyes still looking sleepy. "Morning."

"What happened to the furnace?"

"Good morning to you, too, Izzy. How are you?" She lifted her brows. "Remember, we had this conversation?"

"Good morning, Izzy. What happened to the furnace?"

"I don't know. The heat wasn't coming on, so I spent the night at Phoebe's."

"The power to the circuit board was unplugged."

"Uh, is that something that happens often?"

"No. Someone would have to remove the access panel." Gunner didn't believe it had suddenly come unplugged, but he didn't have an answer as to how, either. He, Izzy, and her dad and mom were the only ones who'd been in the house that he was aware of. Though he couldn't say who she might have invited in after he left for the day.

~

*H*alloween was Gunner's least favorite holiday, right behind Valentine's Day—both a ridiculous waste of money. The only good thing about the day was he didn't have to change clothes, just make sure his hammer and measuring tape were secure on his utility belt for Rowdy's annual party.

Darkness had fallen and the only ghouls out now were too old to be trick-or-treating. They were more the egg-throwing, shaving-creaming, toilet-papering age.

"Gotta go, Dom. I won't be late."

Yip.

"I know you want to go, but Rowdy won't let dogs into the bar and grill. Something about health department rules and regulations." He squatted and gave his dog a good belly rub. "No scary movies or reality shows, and no more potato chips."

Domino grinned.

Gunner decided to walk. Jack-o-lanterns and scarecrows decorated porches along the way, and dry leaves crunched with almost every footstep.

The town hung on the cusp of the calm before a storm—literally. Snow was supposed to sweep into Eden Falls tomorrow. Clouds already eliminated any light from the moon and stars, and he could smell snow in the air. Ariel had always laughed at his ability to predict snow before the official weather report, but his nose was never wrong, forecast or not.

He could hear the music coming from Rowdy's as soon as he turned the corner. Cars were packed into the parking lot.

Batman and Catwoman reached the door before him, and a suggestively dressed Cleopatra gave him a flirty wink.

Stella rolled her eyes when she spotted him. "Oh, that's an original costume, Gun."

"What are you supposed to be?" he asked. She was wearing a green dress covered with leaves and flowers.

"A woodland fairy." She curtsied.

"Woodland fairies wear horns?"

"They came with the costume."

"How are they attached?"

She rolled her eyes again, a Stella signature expression. "Lot and lots of glue." His questioning look had her laughing. "Geez, joke around much? Or are you always this uptight?"

"I'm not uptight." Was he? Yes. Izzy would be here, and he was feeling things for his boss that he shouldn't. She put him on edge every time she was around. And she blushed too much not to be feeling something too. He just wasn't sure if they should act on those feelings or get through the renovations and let the spark of light die.

"Hi, Gunner."

Dahlia. He turned, glancing at her costume. "I like the skirt."

She turned from side to side. "It's called a poodle skirt."

"And there's a poodle on it."

Her hair was tied into a high ponytail with a pink scarf. "I see you wore your usual costume."

"I'm going for a record win with the most boring costume four years in a row."

A man dressed in a white T-shirt, rolled jeans, and greased

hair joined them. "Gunner, I'd like you to meet Ryan Wardin. Ryan, this is Gunner Stone."

He shook hands with a guy he remembered seeing Phoebe with some time ago. Another downfall—besides gossip—of living in a small town.

Ryan nodded toward him. "Construction worker?"

Dahlia smiled. "Gunner is very creative."

"You know me, creative is my middle name."

He glanced around and spotted Izzy. Dressed as Mary Poppins, she stood at the bar talking with Rowdy. Slowly, she turned and their eyes connected. Unblinking, they stared for a long moment.

And something happened.

It was as if she'd cast a lure and snagged him right in the chest. Then, she began reeling him in with her amber eyes. He felt the pull, so tangible he took a step forward.

She broke their gaze by turning back to the bar when Rowdy set a drink in front of her.

Gunner flopped back into the stream and glanced at Dahlia, who was looking from him to Izzy. Her sad eyes made their way back to him. "Have fun tonight."

"You too, Dahlia. Nice to meet you, Ryan."

He turned his back on them and Izzy.

~

*W*hen Izzy glanced back for more of Gunner's magnetic pull, he was gone. She looked around but couldn't see him. Okay. Obviously, the whole hypnotic moment was hers and hers alone.

Leo walked over and bumped shoulders with her. "Hello, Mary Poppins," he said with an English accent. "Love your hat."

"Why thank you. My, what a big smile you have, Mr. Joker."

"Totally sincere."

"I can tell." She looked behind him. "You here alone?"

"Between women."

"You say so flippantly. Do you think you'll ever want to settle down?"

Leo held up a hand. "Don't start with the me and Phoebe thing."

"I wasn't going to say a word about Phoebe. I'm just wondering. Don't you want to do the traditional thing? Marriage? Family?"

He flashed his devastating grin. "Are you asking me to get married?"

"Would you accept if I was?"

"Though the offer is very sweet, I'd have to say no. I am not your type."

She slid onto a stool. "I have a type?"

He scooted close and put his arm around her shoulder. "You just said 'traditional, marriage, family.' That's your type."

"What's your type?"

He pointed at a blond in a roaring twenties flapper dress. "I think she's my type tonight, but who knows? The woman dressed as Elvira just might be the one. Who can resist long black hair and a dress that dips to the navel? Think she'll like my smile?" He tipped Izzy's hat slightly. "Wish me luck."

She wanted to be disgusted. Leo floated from blonde to brunette to redhead. She'd been back in Eden Falls for two months now and had never seen him with the same woman more than twice. The same could be said about Phoebe. She and the doctor she'd been dating at the time of Stella's wedding were ancient history. And now she wasn't dating Brad anymore either. Madam Venus's predictions didn't look too promising for two people who were so opposed to settling down.

"You look deep in thought."

Tim. She pasted on a smile. "Hi, Tim. Or President Trump. Hope you have your phone. Can't go an hour without blasting out a few thousand tweets."

Tim held up his phone and laughed. "Right. Wait, let me tweet that."

"Where's Hannah?"

"She had to work. Hopefully she'll get off in time to stop by."

"She's beautiful."

Tim smiled and nodded in time with the music playing from well-hidden speakers. "Can I get you a drink?"

She held up her glass.

"Right." The stool next to her was vacant and he slid aboard. "So, how are the renovations going?"

"Good."

"No problems?"

"Not so far. Fingers crossed it stays that way," she said crossing the fingers of both hands.

"Mind if I stop by sometime to see what you're doing?"

Yes. "Stop by anytime."

"Is Gunner on track?"

She looked at Tim, wondering why he'd ask that, or would even care. "Seems to be. He's got my attic apartment all framed and drywalled, so it's actually looking like a reality. I figured we'd run into some hiccups along the way. If something takes longer or if we have a problem, it won't be a big deal. I'm not in any rush."

"What about your dad's offices?"

"The second floor will be ready to move into by the end of the year." Her mom was getting excited about choosing artwork and furniture for her dad's new office. She'd been by the Victorian taking measurements and visiting antique shops in the area.

"Glad things are working out for you."

When she raised her glass to take a sip, she noticed Gunner across the room. He was watching, wearing his usual glare. Every time she thought they might be having a breakthrough, something happened to knock them back to being uncomfortable with each other. "Tell me more about your girlfriend, Tim. Does she live nearby? Does she come from a big family?"

Madam Venus appeared next to them. She was wearing the same costume she always wore. Wildly colored skirt with lots of bangles and scarves. Izzy wondered what she looked like without the heavy eyeshadow and liner.

Tim leaned back on his stool, as if she'd invaded his space.

She held up a finger and twitched it back and forth as if reprimanding a naughty child. "You need to move on."

"Excuse me?" Several expressions moved over his face. He opened his mouth, then closed it and held up his phone. "I'm going to check in with Hannah. I'll see you later, Izzy."

"He wants you back," Madam Venus said, watching Tim retreat.

"He has a girlfriend."

"Still an unbeliever." She smiled at Rowdy. "I'll have my usual."

"Coming right up."

Izzy was surprised Madam Venus—she remembered the psychics name was Vera from the closing papers—had a "usual," and even more surprised that Rowdy knew what it was.

"Thank you," the psychic said when Rowdy delivered a milky-looking drink. She slid onto Tim's vacated stool. "My father named me Vera after a rich aunt in hopes of an inheritance."

"Did it work?"

"Not for him."

"Did her cats get the inheritance?"

"No, I got the money."

That kind of explained how she bought the Victorian and why she'd been in no rush to sell.

"What is that?" Izzy pointed to the psychic's glass.

"A White Russian. Would you like a sip?"

"I don't drink alcohol."

"Right. A vow you and your sisters made after your grandparents' accident."

"Still freaking me out here." Izzy glanced in the mirror behind the bar. Dracula stood behind her, laughing with Little Bo Peep. Cleopatra, in an obscenely revealing dress, had her hand on Gunner's chest, and he was smiling. *Of course.* She turned to Madam Venus. "Tell me about your childhood."

"I grew up in a Seattle suburb. Inherited my gift of seeing from my maternal grandmother. Using your word, I still *freak* my dad out."

"Have you ever been married? Can I call you Vera when it's just the two of us?"

She smiled. "Yes, you can and no, I've never been married. I see things, therefore I scare men."

Izzy imagined a very lonely life for Vera.

"Don't pity me." Madam Venus lifted her brows. "I see it in your expression."

"You didn't see pity, just…"

"I had a nice childhood, loved school, most kids thought I was weird or scary so I was bullied a bit, but that didn't really bother me."

"Stephen King's *Carrie* was bullied."

"Fiction versus reality," Madam Venus said. "Unlike

Carrie White, I had friends other than the high school gym teacher." She nodded toward the mirror. "The man in the mirror who keeps watching you is pretty cute."

Gunner. "What you call watching, I call glaring. Gunner Stone has glared at me since—"

"The death of his sister." Vera lifted her drink and swirled the contents. "You couldn't have done anything to save her."

"I know. Still, I feel so guilty. I keep thinking if I'd gotten there earlier, I would have been on the ice with her. Maybe I could have done something. But my mind was on one thing. *The glarer.* I had such a crush on her brother." She cut her eyes to Vera. "He was in the Army, home on leave. I knew Ariel would invite him. When he was in Eden Falls, she wanted to spend every second with him, so I took my time getting ready, primping in front of the mirror." Izzy tried to swallow around the lump suddenly clogging her throat.

"Ariel was so beautiful. She wanted to be a professional skater. I was jealous of how gracefully she moved across the ice."

Vera turned on her stool, giving Izzy her complete attention. "Tell me what happened."

"You already know."

Madam Venus touched her hand. "In your words."

"Ariel arrived at the pond before I did. She was already on the ice. The hockey team was practicing on the far side. Their coach always let ice skaters have the end nearer the parking lot. While I put on my skates, I watched her gliding over the ice with such grace. She was mesmerizing to watch." The vivid image hurt her heart.

Then a memory... "She kept looking at the hockey team like she might be trying to impress someone."

"Who?" Gunner's voice so close by startled her. She couldn't read his expression, but he took the stool on her other side.

Izzy shook her head. "I don't know. I was watching her, but she kept looking their way and smiling. I'd just finished lacing up my skates and stood when I heard this sickening crack. Ariel skidded to a stop and looked down. In a split second, yet in slow motion, she glanced at me in...surprise, shock, I don't know. I still remember her face, her eyes wide."

She realized tears where trickling down her face when Vera dabbed at her cheek with a napkin. "Sorry. This is a Halloween party and I'm—"

"Finish your story," Gunner said.

Vera nodded, encouragingly. "Finish."

"I'll always remember the look on her face the moment before she..."

"Disappeared," Gunner said.

Vera covered her mouth. "I'm so sorry for both of you."

Gunner raised a brow. "A psychic didn't know the story already?"

"Not the details. But I now understand the guilt Izzy carries and the shame you can't get past, because you both think if you'd been there you could have saved Ariel." Madam Venus held up a hand when Gunner started to interrupt. "Though there was nothing you could have done, you feel like it's your fault because Ariel was already on the ice when you arrived," she said to Izzy. She glanced at Gunner. "And you feel shame because you would have been there if not for trying to meet up..." She narrowed her eyes as if in thought "...with a girl who'd get your mind off of your sister's best friend."

Izzy glanced from Vera to Gunner, whose mouth dropped open.

Vera leaned forward, resting her forearms on the bar, looking at Gunner in the mirror. "Your sister asked you to come skating, just as Izzy assumed, but you said no because you knew Izzy would be there and you were very attracted to her. What you feel is shame for letting your sister down."

Vera reached across Izzy and touched Gunner's arm. "There was also nothing you could have done. Ariel would have gone skating with or without either of you, because someone on the hockey team had asked her to be there for him. Even if you'd been there, you wouldn't have been able to save her. Both of you need to let go of your feelings of guilt and shame."

Vera stood and pulled bills from the waistband of her skirt. "I have to go. Be very watchful through this renovation, Izzy."

She stopped next to Gunner. "Keep Izzy safe."

Both she and Gunner watched Vera flit out of Rowdy's. Then he turned toward her. "Why did she say to be watchful and to keep you safe?"

Izzy shrugged a shoulder, still stuck on Vera's statement about Gunner being attracted to her. "I...have no idea."

"Who was the hockey player, Izzy?" Gunner asked, leaning very close, his different colored eyes intense.

"I don't know. Ariel never said anything to me."

"Would Joanna know?"

"Maybe."

He leaned away and rubbed an index finger under his lower lip. "Would you ask? Please? For me?"

"Of course."

Draining the liquid from his glass, his Adam's apple bobbed with each swallow. "Madam Venus is right," he said, setting the empty glass on the bar. "You shouldn't blame yourself, Izzy. Ariel would have gone skating anyway."

"Yes, she would have. Especially if a guy was involved." Ariel had been a daydreamer who believed a guy would sweep her up into a world of luxury, away from the life she led. She expected someone else to bring happiness into her life rather than searching for that joy herself. She believed she'd find a pot of gold at the end of the rainbow. Skating was the only thing she ever put any real effort into. "Can you let go of the shame she said you were hanging onto?"

"I should have gone with her when she first asked." He held up his hand. "Rowdy, can we get refills here?"

Rowdy tapped the bar as he passed. "Coming up."

Gunner studied her for an uncomfortable moment. "How could you be Ariel's best friend and not know which hockey player she was seeing?" he asked, his accusing tone low.

"Uh…maybe because we didn't share every tiny detail with each other." She had never told Ariel about Gunner's kiss. Even if they'd had more time, she didn't think she would have ever shared that detail.

Rowdy delivered the drinks and they both mumbled their thanks.

"I guess it doesn't really matter." Gunner lifted his glass and took a swallow. "Knowing won't bring her back."

"No."

"Izzy!" Stella grabbed her by the shoulders, almost toppling her off her stool. Gunner caught her with a hand around her waist. "Why are you hiding at the bar? We have a table over there. Come join us, Mr. Originality."

Gunner shook his head. "I think I'll head home."

"You can't go home. My fabulous husband hasn't given out the most boring costume award yet." Stella leaned across the bar and gave Rowdy a smacking kiss.

Izzy glanced at Gunner, who was watching her again. She lifted a shoulder to say *why not*? "You might actually have fun."

He scooted off the stool and picked up both their drinks.

Stella led them to a corner, where several tables had been pushed together and a crowd had gathered.

While everyone laughed and joked together, Izzy

mentally pictured each of the high school's hockey players from that year, wondering who Ariel had been seeing and why her friend hadn't shared the information with her. And why did she believe Madam Venus? Sure, the woman seemed to know a lot, but she couldn't be right one hundred percent of the time. Everyone made mistakes.

CHAPTER 15

*I*zzy sat up in bed, coming awake from a fuzzy dream about Gunner dressed as Robin Hood. In a boat. On a river. The sound of water...rushing. Her brain moved slowly through sleepy fog to awareness. She sat up. Why was water running? She jumped out of bed and slipped on the wet floor.

Maybe an inch? She couldn't tell, but didn't dare flip on a light. Making her way to the bedroom door, she found a few dry spots along the way. Once in the hall, she flipped on the overhead light. Water was streaming down one wall of the bedroom. She ran down the stairs to the main level. Water was dripping from the ceiling onto the laundry room floor.

Running back up the stairs, she grabbed her phone from the nightstand and scrolled to Gunner's number. After two rings, she hung up and called again.

"Why'd you hang up?" his voice barked out, gruff and sleepy after, the first ring.

"There's water running down the wall of the bedroom I'm sleeping in. The floor is wet and it's dripping into the laundry room."

"I'll be right there," he growled in his now-alert-but-still-grumpy voice.

The sound of water was louder as she ran up the stairs to the attic. She flipped on the light and gasped. Her just-tiled bathroom was completely flooded, water spouting from behind the newly-installed-yesterday toilet. She knelt down, water soaking her face and pajamas, and twisted the nut that hooked the hose to the tank, but it wouldn't budge. Next she tried the knob that she assumed would turn off the water. Nothing. She put a little more muscle into it. Still nothing.

Wrench. She needed a wrench. At least that's what she thought she needed. A search of the attic didn't turn up Gunner's toolbox, so she ran back downstairs and grabbed the towels she'd thrown in the dryer last night. Up three flights again—maybe an attic room wasn't such a great idea—she tried to tie a towel around the spraying water. That only worked to soak her even more. She grabbed the dry towels and made a dam in the doorway to stop more water from flowing into the attic.

Suddenly the water stopped spraying.

"Why didn't you turn off the water main?" came an angry voice from somewhere below. "And why is your back door unlocked? Anyone could walk in."

Why *was* her back door unlocked? She'd checked it before bed and, in her haste to grab towels, she hadn't thought to unlock it for Gunner.

He thundered up the attic stairs. "Why didn't you shut off the water main?"

"I don't know where it is," she said as he pushed her out of the way.

"Why didn't you at least turn the water to the toilet off?"

"I tried. The knob wouldn't turn."

He grunted as he twisted the stupid little knob, but nothing happened. He tried again. Nothing. "Grab a wench."

"I looked for your toolbox and couldn't find it."

Gunner mumbled a curse word.

"Is that directed at me?"

He stood up and lasered her with a look. "Did you use this toilet?"

"Why would I use this toilet when there's one in the room I'm staying in?" She heard the defensive tone in her voice. "Besides, you didn't tell me I couldn't use it."

"So, you *did* use this toilet."

"No." She crossed her arms, defiantly. "I told you I didn't. Even if I did, you never told me not to."

"You should have some basic tools of your own. Why don't you have a toolbox?"

"Why are you yelling at me?"

He looked at the ceiling, his jaw bulging like he was grinding his back teeth.

"Whatever." She headed down the stairs to put on dry clothes. "Just add this to the list of things you blame me for."

"What does that mean?"

She'd call Beam once the sun rose and have him put together a toolbox with essentials a girl might need. Not that she'd know what to do with most of them. She started into her bedroom when a firm grip on her arm stopped her.

"I asked you what you mean by that last remark."

She turned, hands on hips, a glare of her own. "Why, if you dislike me so much, did you take this job? You can't be that hard up for cash."

"I'm not hard up for cash, but I also can't breeze into town and buy a huge, historic Victorian because the fancy strikes me."

"A Victorian you're trying to ruin by not tightening the doohickey on the toilet."

"Do you honestly believe I wouldn't have tested that fitting before I left last night? That toilet was installed right."

"Then why can't I use it?"

"So you did use it," he spouted accusingly.

"No!"

"The grout around the base has to set. That's why you can't use it."

"You could have told me that." They were nose-to-nose now, his eyes dark with...what?

"Everything you say makes it sound like you used the toilet." He put his hands on his hips and turned away. "This will set me back a couple of days." He made eye contact. "Some of us have to work hard for what we have."

"Believe me, I worked hard for the money I used to buy this *huge, historic Victorian*." She wouldn't go into the hours and hours she'd spent in what most people would clock as overtime.

"Right, sitting in a cushy gallery, hobnobbing with the rich and famous at cocktail parties and fancy dinners. I'm sure you worked really hard. And Baron, what did you have to do for him to—"

Her hand was faster than her brain. She reached out and smacked him across the face before she even realized what she was doing. She gasped and covered her mouth as his hand rose to his cheek.

"Based on your reaction, I assume I was on the right track."

She stepped back and slammed her bedroom door in his face.

~

*G*unner stalked away as soon as the bedroom door closed, angry that he'd started a fight with her over his own frustrations, annoyed that he'd barked at her for something that wasn't her fault. In the attic he mopped up the water. Luckily, he'd spent the last week tiling halfway up the walls, so no drywall had been damaged. She said she'd applied three coats of grout sealant over the last weekend, so there shouldn't be a problem with water absorption. Once the floor dried out, he'd check the seal around the toilet.

Only two pieces of drywall just outside the bathroom door would have to be replaced. The damage could have been worse. The room right under him was Izzy's. She said water was running down the wall. He'd check there after they both had time to cool off.

He shouldn't have implied something inappropriate was going on between her and Baron. Another stupid blunder because Izzy wound him tighter than a cat in water.

When he reached the second floor, he checked the room next to the one she was using. No water spots on the ceiling was a good sign. The walls didn't feel damp, and the floor was dry. On the main level, water dripped from the ceiling into a laundry basket. The top layer of clothes was wet, but the leak wasn't bad enough to have soaked everything. He'd check the ceiling after it dried out.

He glanced out the laundry room window before realizing he was looking for footprints. This was the second time he suspected someone had tried to sabotage either his work or Izzy's house.

He'd rushed out of his house so fast he hadn't fed Domino. When he went home, he'd grab the two industrial fans he kept in the garage. They'd dry the walls and floor pretty fast.

Next he examined the back door. The new lock—that Izzy hated—didn't look damaged. He couldn't spot a forced entry. The window in the mudroom was painted shut for eternity, like most of the others in the house—one more thing Izzy had added to their long list of repairs.

The teakettle whistled and he guessed Izzy was in the

kitchen making a cup of her disgusting tea. When he rounded the corner, she was pouring steaming water into a soup-sized mug. She added a teaspoon of honey and turned. When she saw him watching her, her gaze dropped to the floor.

"I need—"

"Sorry," she said at the same time.

"—to apolo—what?"

"I'm sorry I hit you. I shouldn't have done that. I've never hit anyone in my life." She glanced up through a veil of lashes. "Well, I did hit Phoebe once, and pulled Georgiana's hair, but that was when we were teenagers. And I hit Tim the first time he tried to kiss me, but only because we'd been friends and I didn't expect him to lean in and kiss me so unexpectedly. Oh, and I slapped Oops's hand when she tried to touch the stove one—"

"Oops?"

"Adelaide. We call her Oops because she came as such a surprise, even to Mom and Dad." She shook her head like she was trying to clear her mind. "I did hit Billy Crane in the fourth grade but he put a spider on my arm and—"

"I'm sorry too," he said because he was, and he wanted to stop her confession that might run on until tomorrow.

She looked at him, her eyes wide with surprise, like she thought he was incapable of an apology.

He rubbed the back of his neck. "I shouldn't have said what I did about you and your boss."

"It wasn't like that, you know. We dated but it wasn't like...what you insinuated."

She wasn't gorgeous like Jessica, but she was down-home, cheerful, let's-have-babies-together beautiful—his thought screeched to a halt, his pulse jumping like a bird in his chest, wildly beating its wings in an attempt to escape.

He thumbed over his shoulder. "I need to look at the damage to the room you're sleeping in."

"It's kind of early. You could just come back later. When the sun is up."

"I'm already here."

"Want me to start a pot of coffee?"

"That would be…nice. Thank you." He started up the kitchen stairs, then stopped and turned back to her. "You never answered my question earlier."

"What question?"

"You said something about a list of things I blame you for. What were you talking about?"

She set her cup of tea down, crossed her arms, looked at the floor. "Ariel for one."

He came down a step. "I never blamed you for Ariel's death."

"You've glared and snarled at me ever since that day."

"I don't glare and snarl."

"Hold that face you're making right now and go look in a mirror," she said pointing at his nose. "I'd love to know what that face is called if not glaring."

He tried to relax his facial expression as he came down the last step. "I don't blame you. I never did. Like that psychic said, I blame myself. Ariel wanted me to go with her and I…said no."

"So, explain the glaring."

He leaned against the wall and crossed his arms to match her stance. "Do you remember what happened the day before?"

Her cheeks flamed red, making it obvious she did.

"I didn't think I should be around you, and I knew you would be there. That's why I told Ariel no."

"You glare at me because we kissed?"

"I don't glare. I tried to stay away from you because you were young and I was attracted. *Very* attracted."

She put a hand over her mouth, eyes wide and unblinking.

"You were? I thought you kissed me to scare me out of having a crush on you."

"I did. You were a child."

"I was *not* a child. I was a teenager."

"You were sixteen as opposed to my twenty-two."

"Too young."

He chuckled. "Illegal."

She pointed at him. "You just laughed. I didn't think you were capable."

Twenty-two or thirty-seven, he was still very attracted to her.

Unexpectedly, she pulled coffee beans out of the cupboard, filled the carafe with water, poured it into the coffee maker, and ground some beans, releasing their rich, heady scent.

He wasn't sure what he expected, but it wasn't her sudden detachment, as if they hadn't been discussing something kind of serious. "Are we done here?" he asked.

"Guys are dumb," she said without turning around.

He walked over to her, not really sure he wanted to know why she thought that, but not ready to walk away either. "Because?"

"How do they show they like you? They pull your pigtails or hit you with spitballs or put spiders on your arm." She spun toward him, hands on her hips. "Why can't they just say they like you? Why is that so hard?"

"As opposed to how girls act when they like you? They flirt with another guy to try and make you jealous, or follow you and hope for a chance meeting then act all surprised that you happen to be in the same place at the same time."

She snorted, her pretty eyes sparkling. "I have never flirted with another guy to make someone jealous or followed a guy hoping for a chance meeting."

He nodded. "So that time you *accidently* ran into me at

the library and dropped all your books was just that, an accident."

Color bloomed over her cheeks again, and her bottom lip went between her teeth. "Okay. I'll admit I had a crush on my best friend's big brother."

He nodded and turned to go up the stairs, but she grabbed his arm to stop him. "Wait. I think my admission deserves an admission."

"I already admitted I stayed away because I was attracted to a child—sorry, teenager," he quickly added when her eyes narrowed.

"So you *did* like me."

"I never said I liked you. You were as irritating as Ariel. I said I was attracted to you. There's a difference."

Her smile was slow in coming, her hand warm on his arm. "But now you like me."

"Now I tolerate you." He turned away when her smile grew. "I'm going upstairs to check on the damage done by the toilet you say you didn't use."

"I did *not* use that toilet!" she hollered up the stairs after him.

He smiled. At four o'clock in the morning, slogging through indoor puddles, he was smiling.

Izzy did that for him, just as she'd made Ariel smile.

While he looked around, she carried in more towels, and they mopped up the floor together. They'd been like two warships closing on each other, circling warily. Today something shifted. Were they ready to raise a white flag? He glanced over where she was drying the wall, standing on bare tiptoes, her nails painted a frosty blue to match the cold outside.

"I've got to run home and feed Domino. When I get back, we can move your things into one of the other rooms."

She paused. "You're going to bring him back with you?"

"Might as well. He likes you better anyway."

"That's because I don't spend my day glowering," she said, flashing a smile before walking out the door with an armload of wet towels.

~

*I*zzy arranged the towels in the washing machine, added soap, and closed the lid. On her way into the kitchen, she stopped to examine the back door lock, which didn't look like it had been tampered with. Crime was low in Eden Falls, so she had a hard time believing someone broke in. She got her phone and called Phoebe's cell. Her sister was on duty for another two hours.

"Hey. What are you doing up so early?"

"I had a leak. I called Gunner and he said my back door wasn't locked when he got here, but I checked it before I went to bed last night."

"I'll be there in five minutes."

"Thanks, Phoebs."

By the time Izzy poured a cup of coffee, Phoebe was walking through the back door. "The lock looks fine."

Izzy held out the coffee mug. "That's what I thought. I didn't see any scratches on the wood or the metal, but what do I know about locks?"

"That one's ugly." Phoebe took a sip and hummed in pleasure.

"I know. I've been looking for one online that matches the period of the house."

Gunner walked into the kitchen, and Phoebe stared at him over the rim of her cup. "So, a contractor who makes middle-of-the-night house calls. I might need to look into that. What services are available?"

"Phoebe," Izzy groaned. "Learning to filter words from thoughts is a real thing."

"Uh-huh," Phoebe said, taking another sip. "Did you make a mistake, Gun? Or do you suspect someone was in the house?"

He filled his travel mug with coffee. "The toilet was connected before I left because I check my work. Izzy said she locked up before bed, but the door wasn't locked when I got here."

Phoebe selected an apple from the basket on the table and took a bite. The crispy crunch sounded loud in the quiet house. Her sister glanced at her. "Ghost?"

"No. Madam Venus promised me there are no ghosts in this house."

"Maybe they just didn't manifest themselves to—"

"Stop talking ghosts, Phoebe. There are no ghosts."

"Maybe they don't like what you're doing to their house, or maybe they moved back in when they saw you were fixing the mess Madam Venus made."

"Time to be serious, Officer Adams," Izzy said to her sister.

"Okay. If someone came through a window and left through the door, it would be unlocked when Gunner arrived."

"Most of the windows are painted shut," Gunner said, screwing the lid on his travel mug. "I'll check them all before I leave tonight."

"I'll check around outside, Iz. Have you noticed anyone strange hanging around?"

Izzy took advantage of the question and glanced at Gunner.

"You're insinuating me?" he asked.

Izzy turned to Phoebe, hiding a smile. They'd shared a moment earlier. She hoped, this time around, that moment morphed what they had into a friendship so she wasn't the only female in town he didn't smile at.

Phoebe took another bite and wiped a knuckle under her bottom lip. "Maybe Madam Venus is the one in the house. Has she seen the color you painted the exterior? An affront to flamboyant psychics everywhere." Phoebe tugged the flashlight off her utility belt. "I'm going outside to look around."

"I'll be back in a little while." Gunner grabbed his coat from the back of a kitchen chair and turned toward the door.

Phoebe whistled like a guy. "There goes the next jeans poster boy, Iz. We can say we knew him when."

Gunner glanced over his shoulder and raised a brow.

Izzy felt her cheeks heat, but decided to go for broke, since he'd caught her ogling again. "I like the stitching around the pockets."

Phoebe snorted out a laugh, choked on her bite of apple, and Izzy patted her back.

$\mathcal{L}$ater that day Izzy was painting the last bathroom on the second floor. She kept hearing thumps above her, but wasn't sure what Gunner was working on. Domino lay close by in a sunny spot on the bedroom floor.

Phoebe had circled the house and come back to report she didn't find anything, then she helped Izzy and Gunner move her stuff from the wet bedroom to a dry one when he came back. He didn't think the damage was so bad he'd have to pull down the wall, but said he'd keep an eye on it.

Domino yipped at a knock on the front door. Izzy slipped her paintbrush into a plastic sandwich bag and wiped her hands as she went down the stairs. Domino beat her to the door. When she saw who stood on the porch, she was sorry she'd answered the knock.

"Tim, how are you?"

"I had the afternoon off and thought I stop by and see the house."

"Sure." She stepped aside so he could come in.

He glanced around the grand foyer, then wandered into the living room. "This place is awesome, Iz. What are you going to do with all this room?"

She'd already explained her plan to him once, but if answering his questions would get him out of her house sooner... "This room will be for small events, retirement parties, that kind of thing. I'm going to turn the dining room and sunporch into a tea and sandwich shop," she said, leading him toward the kitchen, only stopping when he lingered at the gargoyle chandelier.

In the butler's pantry, his eyes popped wide. "The colors."

"Yeah, I'm not sure what I'm going to do about this room and the kitchen yet."

"How about a match?" he said on a laugh, following her in the room.

"It's pretty bad, but it's only paint."

He stepped close enough that she could smell his minty breath, and he ran a finger over her cheek. "You have some paint."

Domino growled low in his throat.

Gunner chose that moment to walk into the kitchen. "Iz— Oh, sorry to interrupt."

Izzy stepped away. "You're not. I was just showing Tim around the house."

"Right," he said in a way that meant he didn't believe her.

"Did you need something?" she asked with just as much sarcasm, glancing at Domino, whose neck hair stood at attention. She bent to reassure the sweet dog that everything was okay.

"I'm going to run to the hardware store. Do you need anything?"

"No thanks."

Gunner walked to the back door, yanking his coat on. "Come on, Dom."

Domino didn't budge from her side.

Gunner looked from his dog to her to Tim, his eyes narrowed.

Izzy petted the dog again. "He can stay."

With a nod, Gunner left, shutting the door a little harder than necessary.

"What's up with him?"

"We're both tired." Izzy led Tim into the rooms on the other side of the house. "A toilet sprang a leak in the middle of the night and we had to clean up the mess before it ruined all our hard work."

Tim's eyebrows jumped. "Gunner was here?"

"Well, I called him and he came." She swept a hand in front of her. "This will be my office. My dad thinks it used to be the billiards room."

Upstairs she showed him the bedrooms that would become her dad's offices.

"This must be the room you were working on, since the color matches the one on your cheek."

"Yep. I was actually painting the adjoining bathroom."

He stepped inside and looked around. "So where was your leaky toilet?"

"Attic. It was bad enough that water leaked all the way down to the laundry room."

"Wow. Much damage?"

"Until everything dries out, we won't know for sure. Hopefully not."

"Show me the attic."

Gunner's smart dog kept positioning himself between her and Tim, which was fine by her. She wanted to keep as much space between them as possible.

"There isn't much to see," she said, leading him up the stairs. "Just a big open space."

"Nice and roomy. So that must be the leaky toilet," he said pointing to the bathroom.

"Luckily Gunner tiled up here last week, so everything should be fine."

He nodded toward each side of the bathroom door. "Looks like a couple of pieces of drywall took the brunt of the water."

"Gunner said that's an easy fix. I'm just sorry he has to do it over again."

"The place is going to look great."

"Thanks. I think so." She glanced at her watch, hoping he'd take a hint.

"I guess that's my cue to go."

"Sorry. I told Joanna I'd babysit her new daughter so she and Troy can take the boys to a movie." She pointed to her face. "And I need a shower."

She walked him to the front door with a quick goodbye and flipped the lock as soon as his feet hit the first step.

$\sim$

*W*hen Gunner got back to the house, Izzy's car was gone. Domino greeted him at the back door. "Hey, boy. Where's Izzy?"

Yip.

"Gone, huh? Did you watch out for her?" Oddly, the psychic's words came back. She'd said, *Keep her safe*, but from what? Or who? The hair on Domino's neck was bristled up when he walked in on Tim and Izzy earlier. Remembering that made him nervous.

"Where's Izzy, Dom?"

Yip.

He dug out his phone and scrolled to her name. **Where are you?** he texted.

He waited impatiently, watching the bubbles on his phone bounce while she texted. **I forgot to tell you I'd be at Joanna and Troy's house watching their sweet new baby girl. I asked Joanna about Ariel's mystery guy. She didn't know anything.**

Thanks for asking.

Want to come and help babysit?

Yes, he did, but he wouldn't text that. He'd run into Joanna and Troy at Noelle's two days ago, and their daughter was a tiny doll with a shock of hair that stuck straight up in the air.

Some of us have to work.

Before he could shove his phone back into his pocket the bubbles started bouncing again.

Quit being so ornery. Take off early and bring pizza. My favorite is pepperoni and mushroom. Oh, and black olives.

Was she asking him out in a roundabout way? He'd been telling himself dating Izzy wasn't possible, but why? He wished he didn't already have plans. He'd like to go over and sit with her. Or maybe he was very glad he had a standing poker game. Dating would make things between them complicated.

Okay, you can pick the toppings!

Here he was, smiling again.

You'll have to order delivery. Tonight's poker night.

CHAPTER 16

*A*fter Tim's visit, a knock on the front door worried Izzy, but the Town Car parked out in the driveway assured her the visitor was a different nuisance. She opened the door to Baron's astonished look. Obviously, he didn't approve of her paint-spattered jeans and T-shirt, or her messy ponytail. He on the other hand was dressed impeccably in a suit and tie, his black shoes shined to perfection.

She smiled. "I told you this town was small but has a way of growing on you."

"Like a fungus?"

"Ah, I see you dug your positive attitude out of some old trunk and polished it up." She opened the door wider. "Would you like to come in?"

"I wouldn't be here otherwise."

So, he'd moved beyond their nonexistent relationship as quickly as she had.

"I'm here on business," he said, stepping inside.

"In Eden Falls or my house?"

He glanced around. "Is there somewhere we can sit?"

"Come into my soon-to-be office." She beckoned him into

the billiards room, which she'd furnished with her unimposing desk and a small sofa from San Francisco. They took up a lot of space in her California room, but here the large room made the pieces look small and very insignificant. Baron scoffed. To not care what he thought was so freeing, she almost laughed when she waved him to the sofa. The view of the yard wasn't very impressive, but the snow-covered mountains in the background were. At least to her.

She sat at an angle so she faced him. "To what do I owe this pleasure?"

"I've decided to buy this house and turn it into another gallery, which you can run."

"No."

His frown was instant. Baron was an extremely handsome man, with dark, brooding, and sometimes very sad eyes. Every black hair on his head was always in place. She used to be so attracted to him. He'd enter a room and she could barely breathe. Now...nothing. It was as if him threatening to fire her had erased everything.

"You haven't heard my offer."

"I don't need to, Baron. You could offer the moon and I'd still say no. Eden Falls couldn't support a gallery, and the tourists we get—mostly fishermen and sports fanatics—wouldn't visit a gallery of the Van Buren caliber. The place would fail, you'd sell it out from under me, and I'd be back where I started."

"In California where you belong."

She smiled and shook her head. "Eden Falls is home."

He raised groomed eyebrows. "With your parolee?"

"Yeah, I lied about that. Gunner's never been in jail—that I know of. And we're not engaged. He's a contractor here in town. His sister and I used to be friends in high school."

Baron stared at her with a puzzled frown. "I'm not sure I like this new Izzy."

A feeling of freedom expanded in her chest, making her a little breathless. "You would if you got to know her. This is the Eden Falls me. The small-town girl who loves this Victorian, nature, cold pizza for breakfast, and jeans."

"Cold pizza?"

"Barbaric by your standards, I know." Domino trotted into the room and leaned against her leg so she could love on him.

"So you're really leaving me. Nothing I can say or do will change your mind?"

She reached over and took his hand. "I left in September, Baron. Thank you for saying you'd fire me if I came to my sister's wedding. You changed my life for the better with that threat."

~

*I*zzy woke to a strange sound. Something that made her sit up in bed.

Not water this time, which was good. She climbed out of bed and creaked her door open, peering into the hall. All was dark and quiet. Turning back to bed, she stopped after one step. A thud echoed through the empty house, sounding closer than it probably was, but still too close for comfort. She was on the cusp of one of those too-stupid-to-live moments—investigate or grab her cell phone and call the police? She decided on number two.

"911, what's your emergency?" Her sister was working dispatch.

"Phoebe, it's me."

"Why are you calling 911 at two thirty-two in the morning?"

"I heard a sound in the house." She peered around the door. The hall was still empty, no more thuds.

"I'll send JT over. Stay on the phone with me until he gets there."

Thump!

"Waaa!" A shiver skittered up her spine convulsively.

"What? What happened?" Phoebe yelled.

Izzy slammed her bedroom door and twisted the lock. "Someone's downstairs."

"JT and Mac are on their way. Do you have a gun?"

Izzy snorted. "No, I don't have a gun!"

"Can you get to the front door?"

"No," she wailed. "I don't dare leave the bedroom."

"Can you see out the front?"

"No, the bedroom I'm using is at the back of the house." Izzy stole a look out the window. The backyard was shrouded in shadows, the naked branches of the trees black against the cloudy sky. A movement caught her eye. Someone was standing near the garage, looking at her window. "Oh, my gosh! I see him. He's in the backyard."

"Are you sure it's a he? Do you recognize him?"

"I can't tell. It's too dark. Who would be in my backyard? Oh, he's leaving. He hopped the back fence."

"Hopped or climbed over?"

"Hopped."

"Athletic. Is he tall?"

"Remember the dark part, Phoebs?"

"Go to the front door. JT is coming up the walk. Mac went around the back, so don't scream if you see someone."

Izzy ran down the front staircase and flipped on the foyer lights, but nothing happened. The porch light wouldn't come on either. She pulled the door open. Police Chief JT Garrett stood, fist raised, ready to knock. "Hey, Izzy. You okay?"

"Yes. He did something to the lights. They won't come on."

He lifted his two-way radio. "She's okay, Phoebs. I'll let you know what we find."

"He was inside," Mac Johnson said, walking down the hall. "Your back door is wide open."

"That door was locked. I checked it before I went to bed."

Using his flashlight, JT led Izzy and Mac through the house to the kitchen.

"Did Phoebe tell you I saw him? Well, sort of saw him. I looked out the upstairs window. He was in the yard looking at me, then he hopped over the back fence."

"Where's your breaker box?" Mac asked.

Phoebe pointed toward the laundry room. "Next to the closet. Gunner just installed a new one."

JT squatted and examined the lock on the back door. "Have you seen anyone hanging around, Izzy?"

"No."

"No strangers?"

"Other than a couple of inspectors and my family, Gunner's the only one whose spent any time in the house."

"Whoever was here turned off the main power to the circuit breaker box and cut all the wires to the individual circuits," Mac said, coming back into the kitchen.

"Why?" Izzy looked from Mac to JT. "Who would do that?"

JT straightened and pulled out a small notebook. "What alerted you that someone was in the house?"

"A strange sound woke me up. A thump, like furniture being moved or a door hitting a wall. I don't know."

"I'll take a look around the yard," Mac said, slipping through the door.

"What did the guy in the backyard look like, and are you sure it was a guy?" JT asked.

"It was too dark." She looked out the window to the spot

where the man had stood. "I'd say he was more tall than short, and he hopped over the back fence with ease."

"No one you recognized?"

What was it with police officers not understanding the too-dark part? "No."

"Gunner should install dead bolts on the doors as soon as possible."

Izzy nodded.

"And you should stay somewhere else until he does."

"I still have a key to Phoebe's place. I'll stay there tonight."

"Get everything you need. One of us will follow you over and make sure you get inside safely."

Mac stepped inside. "I didn't find anything but possibly some disturbed dirt along the fence. The ground is too frozen. He probably came through Mr. Harrison's yard. The man is deaf enough that he wouldn't hear a thing."

"Are you suggesting the guy in my backyard would know Mr. Harrison is hard of hearing?"

"The typical intruder lives within two miles of their target," Mac said.

"But this is Eden Falls. People don't break into other people's homes in Eden Falls."

"The name of the town doesn't give you instant protection, Izzy," JT said. "Have you had problems before tonight?"

"Uh…"

"Is that an *uh yes*, or an *uh no*?" Mac asked after he and JT exchanged glances.

"Well, the furnace was mysteriously disconnected and a nut on a toilet malfunctioned and caused some water damage."

"You didn't report the other two instances because…?" JT asked.

She felt her cheeks heat. "I thought maybe Gunner was making mistakes."

Mac rubbed the back of his neck. "Gunner is pretty meticulous about his work."

"You also mentioned inspectors, so someone is coming through and looking at Gunner's work," JT stated.

Izzy nodded.

"I noticed bars on the basement windows when I circled the house," Mac said.

"Dad had the bars installed. He'll be storing people's personal information down there once his business moves onto the second floor."

"I would suggest you add a security system," JT said.

Of course, because bars on the basement windows aren't security enough. "Have there been any other break-ins in the area?"

Mac shook his head.

"Pack a bag, Izzy," JT said. "Phone Gunner in the morning about dead bolts."

"Okay." Izzy ran up the stairs and packed what she'd need. When she came back downstairs, JT and Mac were checking for broken windows.

"I'll circle the neighborhood a few times while Mac follows you to Phoebe's. Make sure you lock up tight when you get there."

"Do you think I'm in danger?"

"Just lock up until we know more," JT said. "And call Phoebe when you get there. She's worried."

∼

As soon as Gunner entered the back door, Domino raced up the stairs to Izzy's bedroom. He flipped the switch in the kitchen, but the lights didn't come on. Cursing under his breath, he walked into the laundry room, then really let go a string of curses. Domino returned looking forlorn.

A feeling of dread threaded through his system. "Where's Izzy, boy?"

Yip.

He took the stairs two at a time and searched for her, but she wasn't in the house. Jerking his phone from his pocket he called her.

"Hello?" she said in a groggy voice after the third ring.

"What happened to the breaker box?"

"Uh…yeah. Someone broke into the house."

"Are you okay?"

"Yes. JT said I shouldn't stay there until you install dead bolts, so I'm at Phoebe's."

Gunner and Domino climbed into his truck and circled Town Square until he found a parking place close to Town Hall. Helen wasn't standing sentry in front of JT's office, so he tapped on the closed door. "Come in," JT called out. He turned from his computer screen when Gunner entered. "Hey, Gun. Have a seat. I guess you heard about the break-in."

"Not much. I was hoping you could fill me in."

"I don't have much to tell. Izzy called when she heard a noise. When we arrived, she said someone had jumped over the back fence. Mac and I looked around and can't find how he got in. Izzy insisted the door was locked."

"I should have installed dead bolts first thing, but Izzy said she wanted to replace the doors and clean up the original locks."

"Whoever broke in cut the wires to all the circuits to the breaker box."

"I saw?" Gunner dropped into one of the chairs in front of JT's desk. "I just installed that box yesterday."

"I didn't look at it. Hopefully they clipped the wires close to the circuits."

"Any ideas who came in?"

"No, but Izzy said this wasn't the first time someone's caused damage."

So she was finally convinced he wasn't an amateur. "Anything else?"

"Not that we could see. Izzy said she heard some noise but couldn't identify the sound."

"I'll get new doors and dead bolts installed today." *Keep her safe.* Why hadn't Madam Venus warned him what to watch for? "Keep us updated." As soon as he said *us,* he wanted to take it back. This wasn't his business.

JT nodded with a smirk. So he'd caught the *us,* too. "Will do."

Fifteen minutes later he knocked on Phoebe's apartment door. Izzy answered wearing jeans and an oversized sweatshirt. He liked the surprise he put on her face when he held out a to-go cup of the nasty tea she liked.

"Thanks. This is…thoughtful." She looked from the cup to him. "You didn't have to come over."

"I thought you'd need a ride."

"I have my car."

He hadn't even paid attention, just assumed Mac or JT gave her a ride. "I wanted to make sure you're okay."

Again, he could see he'd surprised her. "I am. Do you want to come in?"

"Sure." He stepped inside. She shut the door and waved him to the sofa. "JT said you saw someone in the backyard."

"You talked to JT?"

He nodded.

"It was too dark to identify them—him. I'm pretty sure it was a him." She met his gaze. "Mac said most intruders live only two miles away from the houses they break into."

"Most doesn't mean all."

He sat on the sofa and she took a chair kitty-corner from him, almost within reach.

"If it's the same guy, he never takes anything. He just breaks in and causes damage." She rotated the cup in her hands. "Why would he do that? Do you think he's looking for something?"

"Maybe something in the attic belongs to him."

"Why doesn't he just come to the door and ask? I'll happily give him whatever he's looking for." Izzy lifted the cup to her lips, but didn't take a sip. "Madam Venus said she talked to previous owners and they didn't claim anything in the house. Do you think it's someone who thinks they have a claim on the property?"

He could tell she was becoming agitated and he didn't want that. He looked at her a long moment. She evoked a tangle of emotions in him. Lust to frustration and every irritating feeling in between. Each morning he looked forward to arriving at the house to see her, and when he was finished for the day, he couldn't wait to get away from her voice, her scent, her beautiful eyes.

"Are you okay?" she asked, her voice soft.

"I don't want you to be in the house unless I'm there."

"Don't be silly. It's my home. I need to start painting the hallway upstairs. I only have five more weeks before my dad and his agents need to start moving in. Also, it's broad daylight. I'll be fine. The guy was in the house last night. If he was going to do something, he would have."

"Izzy…" He counted to three and exhaled slowly. "I found some doors I want you to see. If you don't like them, this place has plenty more to choose from. JT said dead bolts should be installed today, and I agree with him."

He stood, took her hand, and pulled her to her feet. "Let's go pick out your doors so we can keep you safe."

⁓

*T*hey didn't talk much on the drive to Harrisville. Instead she watched the fingers of sunlight flash through the patchy clouds and touch the towering pines. The acres and acres of orchards, their spindly branches bare of leaves and fruit, looked forlorn.

Domino hung his head over her shoulder, also looking out the window. She reached up and scratched his neck and he licked her ear. "Yuck. Isn't that called a wet willy when someone licks your ear?" she asked, wiping off the slobber.

"Depends on who's doing the licking."

She felt her cheeks heat. Gunner seemed to enjoy throwing out innuendos that made her blush.

He chuckled. "A wet willy is when someone spits on their finger and sticks it in someone else's ear."

"Whatever it's called, no more kisses, Dom."

"Do you think the intruder is your boss from California?"

She glanced at Gunner. Her first thought was absolutely not. Her second was a little more iffy. Would Baron go to such extremes? She wouldn't put it past him. Though the idea of him hopping over a fence with such ease made her smile. He would have split the crotch of his Brioni pants. No, Baron wouldn't go to the trouble himself, but he might hire someone to try and scare her or to sabotage Gunner's work so she'd give up and move back to San Francisco.

"No answer is answer enough. I saw him pull up out front yesterday."

"He offered to buy the Victorian and open an art gallery. I turned him down, which I didn't do very often in San Francisco. Never, actually. He wasn't happy but seemed to accept my decision." She didn't like the look Gunner shot her. "No, Baron wouldn't be the intruder, but...he might hire someone to get his way."

"You need to talk to JT about *Baron*."

"I will," she said, letting her gaze drift back to the passing landscape. The sun wasn't making an occasional appearance through the clouds anymore. The sky was dense and ominous-looking. "I didn't even think to mention him when JT was at the house."

When Gunner pulled into a parking lot, she was startled. She'd expected a box store rather than a salvage yard.

He turned off the engine. "I called ahead with the dimensions. The owner is holding two doors he thinks might work for you."

"I never would have thought of a salvage yard. This is perfect."

"Stay put."

She fought a smile as he got out and hurried around the front of his truck to open her door. "Thank you," she said as she climbed down.

Gunner opened the glovebox and handed Domino a treat with a pat on the head. "Stay here, buddy. We'll be back soon."

Inside the building she stood in awe for a brief moment, making a mental note to come back here another day for more shopping. The place was full of fun items, everything from corbels to banister finials. "Where did you ever hear about this…warehouse of treasures?"

"Your Victorian isn't the first historic house I've worked on." He touched the small of her back. Even though she wore a coat, she felt a tingle of pleasure move up her spine. "We need to go this way."

He led her to a sectioned-off area where doors were lined up on pull-out carts. Two had tags with *Isadora* written on them. He pulled them out for her to see.

Her heart was pounding hard, just like the day she first walked into the Victorian. All the anticipation and excitement pulsing through her veins with every beat. "They're perfect."

"I thought you might like them."

She lifted the price tag. "A little steep. Does the owner allow wiggle room?"

"He will today. Jerry appreciates when people try to restore something old." He touched her again. "Let's go find him."

For the next ten minutes they searched the huge warehouse for the owner. Well, Gunner searched while she stopped to admire a stained-glass window or tin ceiling tiles.

"I found some old ceiling tiles in the attic. Do you think they used to be in the kitchen?"

"Possibly. I'll take a closer look when we get home."

When we get home sounded kind of nice to her ears. And maybe to her heart, too.

She shook her head at her silliness and wandered over to examine an antique mirror that would look perfect in the entry. Then to search through light fixtures. Most of the fixtures throughout the house had been exchanged for more contemporary ones. She couldn't afford to replace them all at once, but maybe a couple at a time. She'd be making frequent stops here in the future.

Gunner pointed out a beautiful kitchen sink with drainboards on each side. "That would have been more original to the house than what's in the kitchen now."

"I love it." She flipped over the price tag and choked. "Three thousand dollars?"

"You pay for quality. That piece is in mint condition."

"Well, it's out of my price range for now. Maybe someday."

"Gunner? Is that you, boy?" a voice bellowed from somewhere behind them. Gunner wasn't small by any means, but the man who appeared in a doorway made him look like a child. He walked forward swiftly, and yanked Gunner into a bear hug, both patting each other on the back.

"How are you, Buzz?"

"Couldn't be better. Who is this lovely lady?"

"Isadora Adams, this is Buzz Standish."

Izzy held out her hand. "Nice to meet you, Buzz."

"What is a beautiful woman like you doing with a bum like Gun?"

"The beautiful woman is here to haggle with you over the price of the doors you set aside," Gunner said.

A glance at him told her Gunner was just as astonished by the *beautiful woman* comment as she was.

She glanced away when her cheeks heated, feeling like a teenager, but curious why Gunner had such an effect on her, curious about his seriousness—his commitment to Ariel before she died despite a father who left and a mother who drank herself into oblivion most nights, curious about his ex-wife and the relationship they'd shared.

When she looked back, both men were watching her.

Buzz chuckled and indicated they should follow him.

He gave her a run for her money in the haggling department, but he did come down when she told him she was also interested in the sink and the antique mirror. He also said he'd take the old light fixtures in trade when she took them down, then he helped Gunner load her purchases into the truck.

Suddenly, Izzy couldn't wait to get back to the Victorian to see how her mirror looked in the foyer she still needed to paint.

On their way home, Gunner glanced at her. "Can I ask some questions about Ariel?"

She turned toward him in the seat, petting Domino, who was resting his head on Gunner's shoulder. "Okay."

"After her death, I found her diary. She kept mentioning a

guy, but never named him. Are you sure you don't know who she was seeing?"

"If I did, I would tell you," she said, feeling slightly betrayed. She'd thought she and Ariel shared those kinds of things with each other. Shame followed immediately behind betrayal. She'd never told Ariel about her crush on Gunner, so how could she have expected more of her friend?

"Not that it matters now, but will you look at the entries I've marked to see if you can figure out who it might have been? I put the diary in the glove box."

"Okay." She opened the compartment and pulled out a leather-bound book. She ran a hand over the cover, feeling irreverent for reading something her friend had kept secret. "Are you sure?"

"I'd like to know, but don't read it if you feel uncomfortable."

Gunner had lost his only sister. He had no family left. She could do this for him. Opening the cover, she read aloud, "This Book Belongs To." Underneath, her friend had written *Ariel* in loopy cursive.

She flipped to the first page Gunner had marked with a blue sticky note. Reading Ariel's entry didn't give her any clues. She was meeting someone behind the school gym at eleven. The date recorded was September twenty-eighth. Out of the blue, she remembered that was Ariel's birthday. In the next paragraph she wrote that her friends Joanna and Izzy were taking her to East Winds for dinner. Izzy recalled that day. She even remembered what Ariel ordered. Izzy had dropped a cake off beforehand, and East Winds staff came out of the kitchen bearing it with a sparkler for a candle and singing "Happy Birthday." Ariel had been so touched she cried.

The other entries mentioned the boy without giving any details about his features, or even revealing his initials.

At the last entry, the day before she died, Ariel mentioned she would see her "love" at the pond the next day. She would skate while he practiced with the hockey team, then they'd meet at their secret spot later that night. Her last sentence said he'd given her a special gift since they both loved to play guitar. Izzy had forgotten about the used guitar Ariel bought after saving every dime for several months.

She glanced at Gunner. "Do you know what the special gift was?"

"My guess is the guitar pick taped to the next page."

Izzy turned the page, and there was a guitar pick with the words "I Pick You," followed by a heart. At once, she couldn't breathe. She'd given that pick to Tim right after they started dating.

Her best friend and her boyfriend had been seeing each other all along.

"Any clues?"

Gunner's voice startled her.

"Uh…" Should she tell him? This small unresolved detail must be nagging at him or he wouldn't keep asking, but what did it matter now?

So far she'd only read the entries he'd marked. Had he missed something that would give her a better clue? Would telling him what she suspected taint his memory of Ariel, since Tim was supposed to be Izzy's boyfriend? A guitar pick wasn't proof of anything.

"No." She shook her head without making eye contact. "No clue."

CHAPTER 17

Gunner couldn't help but smile. Izzy was in the shower, singing at the top of her lungs. Convinced she was making up the words to a popular tune as she went along, he was proved right when she fired out the words to Bon Jovi's "Living on A Prayer". Though he liked her version when she substituted "naked" for "make it." Naked was always better.

From the attic, he heard the water turn off. He imagined the stream rolling out of the bathroom in a cloud of her perfume when she opened the door.

The new front and back doors were hung, dead bolts installed, and there'd been no more problems with intruders. He made sure she talked to JT about her California boyfriend. JT came back with a report that Baron had been in San Francisco at a function the night someone was in the backyard. Gunner agreed with Izzy, though. Baron wasn't the kind of guy who would—or could—hop a fence.

Someone knocked on the front door. He hadn't heard Izzy emerge from her bedroom, so he clomped down the stairs and stopped at her door. Her scent wafted into the hall, surrounding his head in a floral halo of intoxication. He would be content to stand right here and enjoy it if someone wasn't hammering on the door again.

"Izzy," he yelled. "Someone's at the door."

"Will you get it? I'm shaving my legs."

"I didn't need to know that," he mumbled. They sounded like a married couple.

The thought froze his brain and his insides.

He never imagined he'd want to do the married thing again, but maybe he shouldn't judge the entire institution by one failure.

She wanted the attic done so she could move up there, yet he was constantly having to stop to answer the door or help her with a project.

Though he wouldn't complain aloud. He was getting paid whether working on the house or answering the door, and the money was good. The remodel was ahead of schedule despite the setbacks caused by the intruder. Izzy let Domino stay here while he worked, even bought a bed, food, and treats for his dog. And she fed him. Yesterday she made a lasagna and sent half home with him.

On his way down the second flight of stairs, he studied the shadowed figure through one of two frosted rectangle windows on the new front door. His steps slowed to a stop as his heartbeat sped up to heart-attack level. He knew that profile.

Domino stood at the door sniffing, already detecting something unpleasant.

"Hello!" was followed by another pounding knock.

Izzy came around the banister, wrapped in a bathrobe, towel-drying her wet hair. "Why aren't you answering the door?"

She started down the stairs, but he held out a hand to stop

her. "I'll get it. It's probably the sconces you ordered for the upstairs hallway."

"Open up, Gunner. I know you're here. Your truck's in the driveway." He glanced at Izzy, his feet frozen in place.

"I don't think it's the sconces," she said as she passed him to open the door. "Hi. Can I help you?"

"Who are you?"

"The owner of the door you're pounding on."

Gunner stepped between them before Jessica pushed her way inside.

"Gunner, sweetheart!" His ex-wife jumped into his arms and wrapped her legs around his waist before he had a chance to stop her. When she tried to kiss him, he turned his head.

She laughed, then bit his neck. "I was hoping for a warmer welcome home."

"This isn't your home," he said, unhooking her ankles so he could set her on her feet.

"I know that. I went by the house, but you weren't there so I stopped by the post office figuring the bird lady would know where I could find my husband."

"Ex-husband."

"She said I should try here. Said you were playing house with an event planner."

"I'm not playing house. I'm working."

She looked a robe-clad Izzy up and down. "Looks like you're playing house to me." She held out her hand. "Hi, I'm Jessica Stone. Gunner's wife."

"Ex-wife."

"Izzy Adams," Izzy said with a smile.

Jessica ran a hand down his chest. "You look mighty fine in a tool belt, but I still like you in your birthday suit the best, hubby."

Gunner took a step back. "Our divorce decree says I'm not your hubby anymore."

Jessica must have taken his moving away as an invitation to walk further into the house, which she did. "Your color choices are interesting," she said to Izzy.

"We haven't started on the main level yet. Gunner's been working in the attic and I'm painting..." Izzy's words petered out with his pointed look.

Jessica smiled. "I'd love to see the place."

"Jess—"

"Of course. Gunner can show you around," Izzy said at the same time. Through a veil of lashes, she gave him an apologetic smile. "If you'll excuse me, I have to get ready for a baby shower."

Gunner rubbed the back of his neck, trying to ease the tension as Izzy ran up the stairs. What did Jess want from him? He'd had a hard time getting over her and here she was, mocking his efforts.

When he glanced back at Jessica, she was watching him with interest. He nodded toward the parlor or sitting room, not sure of the correct terms for Victorian houses.

"Why are you here?"

"I had some vacation time," she said, stopping in the dining room to examine the gargoyle chandelier like everyone before her. The light fixture and the shocking colors of the kitchen were the highlights of every house tour.

She tried out one of the two lawn chairs in the sunporch. "I could get used to this. Is whatshername going to flip the place when you're done?"

"No, her dad is going to run his real estate offices from the second level and she's opening a shop on this level."

Jess feigned interest as they moved from room to room. She'd never cared about his work but was trying hard to pay attention.

"Where are you staying?"

"With you." Jessica tipped her head and flashed her

suggestive smile. At one time that smile made him do all kinds of crazy things. Now he saw it for what it was—manipulative.

He shook his head. "The Dew Drop Inn is two blocks past Town Square. I'll pay for your room."

She laughed and took his arm, cozying up close. "I don't need your money, Gun."

"Why are you here?"

"I told you, I have vacation time and want to spend it with you."

Just as they reached the foyer, Izzy bopped down the stairs carrying two gift bags with blue tissue sprouting from the tops. She wore a gray sweater over a white shirt paired with a black skirt and knee-high boots. Simple. Unassuming. He found her sincerity and confidence very attractive.

He didn't want her to leave him alone with his ex-wife... and wanted her safely away at the same time.

"When is the baby shower?" he asked.

She stopped at the bottom of the stairs. "In a couple of hours."

"For Alex and Noelle?"

Holding up the packages, she nodded. "Two baby boys."

"This is an interesting place," Jessica said.

Izzy glanced around with a smile. "Thank you."

Gunner studied Izzy as she and Jessica exchanged a few words. Though he detected a wariness in Jessica, Izzy seemed at ease.

When Izzy headed for the kitchen with Domino trotting happily behind her, Jessica turned to him. "What's going on between you two?"

"I have to get back to work, Jess."

"So, something *is* going on."

He refused to answer. His life didn't concern her

anymore. "Do you want me to call The Dew Drop and see if they have a room?"

"You're really going to make me stay in a rundown motel?"

"It's a quaint inn."

She smiled. "I'm here to change your mind about us. I ran off too quickly. I think we should try again."

Why didn't you come back six months earlier? Then maybe… "I think it's too late."

"You know you still care."

"I do, but that doesn't mean I think we should go backward."

She wrapped her arms around his waist and thrust her chest against his. "Then let's go forward from here. Restart our life together."

He shook his head.

"You'll love LA. There's so much to do. I bet you could get a gig working on a movie set."

"I'm not moving to LA."

"Why? This town is dead, Gun. There's nothing here for you. And you still care about me. I see it in your eyes. We could build a nice life in the Golden State." Her arms tightened around his waist. "We can try for a baby."

Like most people, Jessica liked to get her way. Unlike most people, she used whatever method she could to get there, trampling feelings along the way. She knew how disappointed he'd been when she lost their baby, and she expertly hit below the belt.

Yes, he'd loved her once, with all his heart, but he refused to go back. Didn't want to even try. She was still so exotically beautiful and deadly at the same time, but her feelings ran skin-rather than heart-deep.

"I need to get back to work, Jess." He disengaged her arms and opened the front door.

She got on tiptoes and kissed his cheek. "I'll see you for dinner."

"I'll be working through dinner."

"I'll bring something here."

"No, Jess—"

"Tomorrow night, then. And I won't take no for an answer." She bounded out the door before he could finish his sentence.

After she left he headed for the back of the house, feeling like he should apologize to Izzy for his ex-wife's intrusion. As soon as he entered the kitchen she swiped a chip through something and held it up. "Open."

She popped the chip into his mouth. Such a simple, yet seemingly intimate act—at least to him.

He chewed. Guacamole. One of his favorites. "That's good. In fact, that's better than good."

"Thanks. I'll leave some for you and Jessica in the fridge."

"No need. Jessica is staying at the inn."

"I left some extra chips in the pantry," she said, as if she didn't hear him.

"Thanks." He caught a glimpse of a layered concoction sitting on the countertop. "What is that?"

"A berry trifle." She opened the fridge to reveal a second trifle. "I made a small one for you to take home tonight."

Their new ritual—she made things for him to take home, but never asked him to stay for dinner.

Of course he could ask her out, but, for reasons unfathomable to his dimwitted mind, he felt she should be the one to take the next step, to let him know she was interested. Unreasonable on his part. Especially after today.

Jessica dropping by without a word since she'd divorced him had been a bit of a shock. Obviously Izzy thought they were together or she wouldn't have left enough dip for both of them.

"It looks too nice to eat."

She smiled, her eyes sparkling. "It tastes even better than it looks."

"Thanks. Look, about..." He thumbed over his shoulder. "I'm sorry."

"No need." Waving away his apology, she slipped into her coat, then picked up the trifle. "I guess I'll see you Monday."

He grabbed the bag she'd put the dip in and her two bags of chips. "Let me help you to your car."

~

*I*zzy drove away from the house feeling...what? Jealous, for sure. Jessica was so gorgeous, with her dark hair and olive complexion. Her deep-brown eyes were dazzling.

When Gunner and Jessica faced each other, she'd tried to read his expression—which was impossible on a normal day—but he didn't seem happy to see his ex-wife.

While she was in the kitchen she heard enough of their conversation to know Jessica was here for Gunner, which left her feeling...again, what? She liked to think she and Gunner had grown close over the past month. He didn't glare at her nearly as much. And, once in a while, he even smiled—which she happily brought to his attention every time.

Her mom had already invited Gunner for Thanksgiving dinner. Should she tell him Jessica was welcome to join him? Would that be awkward for her family? She'd ask her mom today at the baby shower. Though...Gunner and Jessica might want to spend the day alone.

Izzy parked at the end of JT and Carolyn's driveway. She'd never been in the home JT inherited from his grandparents. Stella told her he'd remodeled every room but the kitchen, which he left for his chef bride. The outside was contemporary stark lines and walls of windows. Preferring more traditional architecture, Izzy had never cared for bold, geometric elements and severe lines, but the property with its surrounding forest softened those hard edges, making the house fit perfectly among the trees.

The interior was unbelievably airy and decorated with earthy colors, bringing the outdoors inside.

She'd attended events in San Francisco almost every night, but most of the attendees were strangers. Half the town turned out for the shower—at least the female half of Eden Falls—and Izzy had the time of her life. So many years had passed since she'd been able to hang out with these friends.

They played games and ate all kinds of yummy treats, and Izzy laughed until her eyes watered.

Alex and Noelle looked darling, cradling their tummies, both due dates just weeks away.

After all the fun and laughs, Izzy went home afterward feeling empty. Marriage and children weren't in the immediate future, yet something she craved. In San Francisco she'd looked into adoption briefly, but the idea of raising a child alone scared her. Here, she was surrounded by family. She'd have help.

Snow started to fall as she neared the house. She ran inside, grabbed a blanket, and pulled a kitchen chair onto the front porch to watch the fat flakes float to earth like goose down, enveloping her world in quiet solitude. Though she thoroughly enjoyed the past three hours of noise, she treasured the serenity and beauty of her surroundings, especially now that the snow was covering her yard of horrors. She'd been able to get the worst of the mess cleaned up, but she had a lot of work ahead of her once spring hit. She was glad the huge old tree in the front had survived the years of neglect. It would provide nice shade for the porch during the hot summer months.

Her mind traveled to Gunner. He was probably with Jessica tonight. Whether they were fighting or making up, Izzy didn't want to think about them together. They had history. They'd been married. Maybe they could find the string that had pulled them together in the first place and strengthen the cords, repair the weaker strands to withstand whatever had torn them apart.

She was grateful when a car pulled into her driveway, turning her attention away from her handsome, sexy contractor. The appreciation only lasted for a split second before the car door opened and Tim was illuminated by the interior light. For another split second she was tempted to hide in the shadows of the porch until he left, then decided to put away her childish instincts and deal with him up front.

He came up the walk and climbed the stairs. She waited until he was on the porch, almost to the front door before she said, "Hi, Tim."

She couldn't see his expression, but knew she'd startled him by his quick side-step.

"What are you doing out here?"

"Enjoying the snow."

He walked closer, squinting through the darkness. "I didn't expect—you surprised me."

"Sorry. What can I do for you?"

"Uh…I was just out and thought I'd stop by and see how the work on the house was going."

"Good."

"Can we go in and see?"

She was so tempted to tell him no. If what Madam Venus said was true, she didn't want to lead him to believe she was interested, especially after what she suspected between him and Ariel.

Show him the house and tell him the truth. "Sure."

Izzy led him inside and shut the door on her quiet evening.

"It doesn't look like much has changed," he said after she flipped on the huge foyer chandelier.

"Nothing down here has changed." She motioned for him to follow her upstairs. She'd almost finished the landing where her dad's receptionist would sit. Her mom had found a beautiful antique desk that would fit the area perfectly. "I've painted all the bedrooms and bathrooms on this floor. My dad plans to move in before Christmas."

Tim took a few steps over the threshold and scanned one of the bedrooms. "I remember this room used to be a brown mustard color."

She touched the tip of her nose, something they used to do in high school, to say he'd hit the mark. Now the room was a very light sage green.

"Looks nice."

She led him into the adjoining bathroom with white porcelain fixtures she'd polished until they shone. "This room used to be such a bright yellow it hurt my eyes."

"You know, I could help you paint on my days off."

"I don't have much left to do. Gunner is going to bring in some scaffolding and use a paint sprayer to do the downstairs foyer."

She led him up the stairs, proud of her attic apartment. Though she hadn't done any of the work, she had come up with the design. Her bathroom was luxurious. Her living space was almost complete. And the bedroom area was light and airy, for an attic room. The sun lit the whole space beautifully during the daylight hours. French doors, the windows covered in sheer drapery panels, sectioned off the bathroom on one end and the bedroom on the other, allowing light to flow through all three rooms.

Gunner had even fit in a small kitchenette. "Isn't it perfect?"

"If that's the bedroom, it's pretty far from the bathroom."

Tim was a pessimist, always looking for the worst in situations and people. "I love it, and your cloud of gloom isn't going to ruin this for me."

"You haven't changed."

"Some things about you haven't changed either."

When he didn't respond, she glanced his way. His jaw was tight and his lips thinned to a grimace. The moody Tim she remembered so well had taken the interested one's place as if stepping into the spotlight.

"As long as you're happy, nothing else matters," he said, his words clipped.

"I thought we had matured enough to leave old issues in the past."

He looked down at her, his eyes narrowed. "You just left. Closed the door on our relationship without giving me—us— so much as a chance."

There was truth to his statement. She'd been fond of Tim, thought for a time that she loved him, but her feelings weren't strong enough to want to work on a long-distance relationship. While they'd dated they usually went with his friends, where he wanted to go, so his *As long as you're happy* comment wasn't really fair. How many hockey games had she sat through for him?

"I guess I did, but it was a long time ago. We took different paths, wanted different things out of life. You wanted to stay here and I wanted to get away."

"Yet here you are. Back in Eden Falls, buying a house and putting down roots."

"My roots were always here, Tim."

"So you just didn't want me."

"We were moving in opposite directions. You had a

hockey scholarship. I wanted to study art. We were young. I wasn't even eighteen yet."

"I loved you."

"Right. You *loved* me. Past tense. Thirteen years have passed, Tim. Life is too short to hold onto grudges. We're different people with different goals. You have a great career. And a girlfriend."

"Yes, I do." His gaze raked over her, making her feel uncomfortable. "I would never have done what you did."

"But you *would* cheat on me. With one of my friends."

His stunned expression told her she was right. "Ariel was always coming on to me. *Always* badgering me to be with her."

Tim had stepped into the quagmire without even realizing. "I never said which friend I was talking about."

He snorted.

"She wrote about you in her diary, taped the guitar pick you gave her in the back."

"She stole that pick." He turned his back on her. "Seems to me if Gunner knew what he was doing he'd be finished by now."

"I guess that's why you're a pharmacist and he's the contractor." She walked over to the attic stairs. "Time for you to go."

CHAPTER 18

*G*unner added light bulbs to the new fixture over Neil Adams' desk. Izzy's dad's office had turned out great. He climbed off the ladder and flipped the switch. When he heard footsteps coming up the stairs, he turned, expecting Izzy's delight with the light fixture. Instead Jess appeared in a skintight sweater that showed plenty of cleavage, leather pants—even if they weren't in style, she would make them look hip—and ankle boots, with a fur coat over her arm. Jessica had always been fashion conscious. *Breathtaking* was his first thought, because she was still beautiful enough to stop traffic. His second thought, *How'd she get in?*

"Aren't you going to say hi?" she asked, stopping in front of him.

"I didn't hear a knock."

"The door was open."

"Open?"

"Well, it was unlocked."

"So, you just walked in? This is a private residence, Jess."

"I thought the first two floors were going to be businesses."

"They will be, but it's still a residence." He dropped his screwdriver into his toolbox near the door.

She waved his words away as if swatting at gnats. "What time do you punch out?"

"I don't have a time clock. I leave when I'm finished for the day."

"Okay," she said, irritation edging her tone. "When do you finish for the day?"

As if on cue, his stomach growled.

She smiled. "Sounds like I came at the perfect time. Let's go to Rowdy's Bar and Grill. I remember they had great nachos."

Why not? They'd be in a public place, so she wouldn't be apt to create a scene when he told her he wasn't interested—for the second day in a row.

He used to think he wanted to know why she'd given up on their marriage so easily. Now he didn't care. He used to think he wanted this very thing to happen, for her to come back so they could try again. Seeing her here... All those excited, heart-pounding feelings were gone.

"I'll meet you there in an hour. I want to get cleaned up first."

"Perfect." She turned with a flourish and bounced down the stairs.

An hour later, he walked into Rowdy's. Jess wasn't there yet, so he got a table toward the back, hoping to avoid any extra attention. Which would be a waste of time, since Rita Reynolds was sitting at the bar. Five minutes later Jessica swept through the door. She made her way to his table, waving at Rowdy, who gave her a puzzled nod.

Jess kissed his cheek before scooting into a chair. "I always loved this quaint little town."

"You hated Eden Falls."

"I didn't hate—well, maybe I did at the time, but now, with the snow, it looks like a fairy tale. We could keep your house and travel up for long weekends."

"I'm not moving to LA, Jess."

"I spent the whole day shopping and getting reacquainted with everyone in town," she carried on as if he hadn't spoken.

She must really be at loose ends to go to that much trouble.

"I got a pretty cold greeting from Patsy. She looked down her nose at me like I had a disease."

He understood. In a sense he and Patsy were kindred spirits. He was considered a hoodlum because of his upbringing and, until her marriage to Mason Douglas, Patsy had been looked down upon by some of the townsfolk because of her four previous divorces. She'd always been protective of Ariel and him.

"And that woman who owns the bookstore? She wanted to know why I was here. I told her it was none of her business."

Maude had always had a soft spot for him too, though you'd never know by her snarky comments.

Jess sent him a seductive smile before beckoning to the waitress. She ordered drinks and nachos, then settled back in her chair.

"You can't deny it, Gun. We are perfect together," she stated in her overly confident way.

He'd always admired her assertiveness. Her forthright confidence. Her determination to go after what she wanted. He'd just never admired her tactics. "Were. We had our run. Things didn't work out."

Rowdy delivered their order and gave Gunner a *sorry, buddy* look.

"Why can't we try again?" Jessica asked in studied casualness. She picked up a nacho and nibbled at a corner before meeting his gaze. "Are you seeing someone?"

He saw Izzy every day, but not in the sense Jessica meant, though, over the last couple of weeks, he admitted to himself, he'd like to change that. Izzy was warm and caring, and made him laugh. She was devoted to family and friends, to Eden Falls and her project.

Jessica was beautiful. Pretty eyes, alluring smile. Inside she was cold and self-serving. She'd taken his heart and stomped it flat to fulfill her own agenda. After the initial adrenaline rush of new love and marriage wore off, she moved on to the next high.

That part of Jessica would never change. He wanted a wife. She wanted adventure. He wanted a family. She wanted the world. When he looked at her now, he saw her with different eyes than he did before they were married. Back when he thought they were headed toward the same goal. He had to accept half of the blame for the failure of their relationship. The signs were there, but he'd only noticed what he wanted and blocked everything else out.

"So, you're not seeing anyone or you'd say so." She smiled like she knew something he didn't. "Did you date, or have you been pining away for me?"

Pining and brokenhearted were two very different things. He'd suffered through the hurt, but somewhere around the four- to six-month mark, reality took hold. They were two very different people who wanted something in life the other couldn't give. "I haven't pined."

She smiled over the rim of her drink. "You're not the pining type, are you? You just forget the past and move on with your life like nothing happened."

That wasn't true either. He'd never forget Ariel and the difference he might have made if he'd chosen to go ice skating with her on that cold winter day. And there was one girl he'd thought about for years after leaving her. He hadn't *pined* after Izzy, but he had pictured her in his mind more often than anyone else.

"How long are you staying?"

"Until I convince you to take another chance on me. You loved me with a passion that—"

"Yes, I did. Past tense, Jess."

He glanced toward the door when Izzy and Leo entered. Her cheeks were rosy from the cold. They grabbed a table on the other side of the room. Jessica looked over her shoulder to see what had caught his attention, then turned back with a scowl. "So, you have your eyes on...what's her name?"

He'd wager his house that Jessica remembered Izzy's name.

She leaned forward, almost spilling her breasts out onto the table. "I can make you forget her."

Agreeing to this meeting had given Jess hope, which was wrong on his part. She didn't know him or she wouldn't have come back. But *he* knew *her*. She was here because she was bored. Her life—maybe her love life—wasn't going as she wanted, so she was stumbling around, looking for a new direction or purpose. Once something—or someone—else caught her fancy, she'd be gone again.

"What if I don't want to forget her?" He didn't mean to say the words aloud because he was still trying to define his feelings. He and Izzy had been dancing around each other long enough, though. It was time to act.

Jessica's eyes widened. "You're in love."

Her comment hit him like a fist to the gut. He wasn't sure he knew how to love a woman who didn't need him. His mom had required looking after, keeping the booze hidden, patting her back when her relationships didn't work out. He'd been Ariel's guardian, taking care of her because their mother couldn't. And Jessica, his adrenaline junkie, had to be picked up when the high wore off.

Izzy was different. She didn't *need* him. She was a strong, independent woman. What could he give her that she didn't already have?

He snorted, hoping to stop Jessica, but she looked from him to Izzy. "You've got to be kidding. She's—"

"Not you," he offered.

"Nothing like me. Does she get aroused by anything besides paint and drywall?"

He'd seen the thrill of delight in Izzy's eyes a time or two that didn't have anything to do with the house. Yes, she did get excited about sinks and mirrors and crown molding, but so did he—an interest they shared. Wasn't that what relationships grew from?

He and Jessica had the Army in common. Now that they were both out, they didn't have much to talk about.

Phoebe and Stella joined Izzy and Leo's table. Laughter soon followed, and he wished he was with them rather than struggling through this meeting with his ex-wife, who seemed to finally realize his heart lay somewhere else. Were he and Jess the topic of their conversation? He was sure a few others in the bar and grill were discussing them. Couldn't live in a small town and not expect to be talked about.

When Rowdy laid the bill on the table, Gunner picked it up. "I'll take care of this."

"A parting gesture of goodwill?" she asked, without making eye contact.

"You're the one who left, Jess. I'm the one who can't—won't—go back."

"So, this is goodbye? You don't even want to give us a try?"

Ready to put the past where it belonged, he stood. "This is goodbye."

~

*L*eo turned Izzy's head toward him with an index finger. "I figured you had a thing for Gun," he said, low enough that only she could hear.

"I don't have a *thing*. I admire the quality of his work. He's fastidious—in a good way, and he's honest and—"

He chuckled. "You have a thing."

Grateful her sisters were too busy arguing over something ridiculous, as usual, and occupied, she said, "Don't say anything to Phoebs."

"You think people don't suspect?"

The suggestion surprised her. "Do they?"

"You've been holed up together in that house for the past two months, and send him home with food at night—yes, Rita has reported containers going home with Gun. Not sure where you were going, but you were seen leaving town in his truck. Errand? Date? Speculation is running rampant. Bets are being taken. I have fifty on no date yet, but I'll lose my fifty if something doesn't happen before the lighting of the Christmas tree in the square."

"People are betting?"

"You can't hide much in this town, Iz. You know that. Anyway, what's wrong with people knowing?"

Izzy stole a glance at Gunner. She deliberately sat with her back to him when she and Leo first arrived, but Stella forced her to change chairs so she could watch her husband at work behind the bar. For once Gunner's glare was directed at someone besides her. "What if he doesn't have a *thing* for me?"

Leo chuckled. "Judging by the look on his face, you stand

a much better chance than his ex-wife. She's a looker with a heart of stone."

"You know her?"

"Everyone in Eden Falls knows her. She didn't make many friends while she lived here, and those few friends didn't stick after she left Gunner. He was in love. She broke his heart, but he got over her."

"How do you know?"

"Look at him. Does he look like he's the least bit interested?"

When she turned her head, Gunner was looking at her. Their gazes locked and held for several thumps of her heart. Then the corner of his mouth lifted. Grimace or smile? She couldn't tell.

"What do you two have your heads together about?" Phoebe asked.

"Nothing," Izzy said.

"Actually, we're watching poor Gunner fend off his ex-wife," Leo chimed in at the same time.

"If she leans forward any farther, her boobs will spill out onto the table," Stella said.

"A guy can only hope." Leo stretched his neck. "Come on, Jess, just a little bit more…"

Phoebe punched him in the shoulder. "Rein yourself in until Gunner dumps her. Then you can make your move."

Rowdy offered one special a night, and tonight it was chicken enchiladas, which they all ordered. Izzy got caught up in the conversation and laughs and didn't notice when Gunner walked out, but his ex-wife moved to the bar after he left. She tried flirting with Rowdy, but Stella put a stop to that by going behind the bar and giving him a sizzling kiss before turning a you-touch-this-and-you-die look on Jessica.

Izzy's phone vibrated in her back pocket. Her heart did a cha-cha when she tugged it free and saw Gunner's number. He called very seldom, preferring to text. She pushed back from the table and grabbed her coat. "I have to take this."

Only Leo acknowledged with a nod.

Outside the air was frigid enough that her breath came out in white clouds. She huddled in her coat and connected the call. "Hello?"

"Hey. I was wondering if you'd like to go out to dinner with me tomorrow?"

The cha-cha turned to breathless pounding. She'd faint if she didn't make light of the situation. "Who is this?"

His deep chuckle made her smile. "You know who this is."

"Gunner Stone, are you asking me out on a date?"

"If you want to put a label on the invitation."

A date with grouchy Gunner. She'd waited years for this invitation. "I do."

"Okay, we'll call it a date."

She shivered, and not from the cold. "I'll have to check my calendar."

"Better hurry, the offer runs out in three, two—"

"Look at that! I'm free."

"Good. I'll pick you up at seven."

She did a happy dance right there by the door to Rowdy's.

He laughed. "Go back inside before you freeze to death."

Oh, peanut brittle. She scanned the parking lot until she spotted Gunner's truck, a cloud of exhaust coming from behind. "You could have told me you were watching."

"And miss all the fun?" He disconnected the call. His headlights flicked on and he drove away.

When she got to the table, she was still holding her phone pressed to her chest. Leo raised a brow, a teasing grin spreading across his face. "Good news?"

She lifted a shoulder, trying to keep a neutral expression

when her heart was pounding and her ears were buzzing and she couldn't contain her smile.

Leo leaned close. "You going to tell me, or do you want me to guess?"

"You never will."

"Gunner asked you out."

Izzy turned to him with open mouth. "How did you know?"

"While he sat over there with the ex-wife, he was looking at you most of the time."

"Really?"

Leo sat back in his chair with a smug smirk. "Looks like I'll get to keep my fifty bucks."

~

*H*eadlights flashed into her driveway and Izzy's pulse jumped. She stood back in the deep shadows and watched him get out of his truck and walk to the door lit only by the moon. After he knocked, she counted to ten very slowly before she answered the door to an actual smile on Gunner Stone's face.

"You ready?"

On their way to dinner, they talked about the house — common ground. Something they could discuss with no effort.

He pulled into the parking lot of a quaint Italian restaurant in Glenwood. Inside, the savory scents almost brought her to her knees. The décor was exactly how she'd imagine an authentic Italian restaurant to look, romantic music playing softly in the background, lights dimmed, heightened senses.

She put a hand to her stomach. "It smells so good in here."

A robust woman came toward them with outstretched

arms. "So, you decided to grace us with your presence tonight." The woman and Gunner wrapped their arms around each other in a heartwarming hug.

"Sorry it's been awhile since I've been in."

The woman released him. "No matter. You're here today. Now, introduce me to your pretty date."

"Izzy, this is Carlotta Romano. She and her husband Papi have owned this place forever." He wrapped an arm around Izzy's waist. "My pretty date is Isadora Adams."

"Such a beautiful name. Come." She waved them forward. "Only the best for you."

She led them to a table in a dark corner of the restaurant, the only light a candle in a wine bottle holder marked by colorful wax trails. Unexpectedly, Gunner held her chair.

"Thank you."

"Such a gentleman," Carlotta said on a sigh. "Fresh bread, right out of the oven, coming up." She hustled away.

"How do you know her?"

"I used to work for them after school occasionally."

"Is there anywhere you didn't work?" She covered her mouth. "Sorry. That did not come out very nicely."

"It's fine. And no, there aren't many places around the area where I haven't worked. Carlotta and Papi were…very generous."

"Sorry." Embarrassed by her flub, she grasped for another topic. "What were we talking about before?"

"No more house discussion. Let's talk about us."

She was too astonished to respond.

Carlotta stopped next to their table with a basket of bread. "The best focaccia in the whole valley."

"Thank you, Carlotta," Gunner said.

"Take your time with the menu and just let me know when you're ready to order."

Oh, yeah, she was even more nervous now than she'd

been when he came to her front door. She picked up her menu, so grateful it was tall enough to cover her face. "What's good?"

"Give us two minutes." Gunner chuckled, hooked his index finger over the top, and pulled her menu down. "Everything is good. The spinach and crab ravioli is amazing. The Chicken Milano…" He did the Italian finger kiss and she laughed.

Next he dipped a slice of bread into olive oil and spices and held it out.

Delicious. The taste and texture reflected the baker's passion for what he or she did.

Dinner was…perfect. More right than any date she'd ever been on. They didn't talk about the house, but about likes and dislikes, movies, books, and their strangest moments.

Out of curiosity, she decided to ask a more personal question. "What's the first thing you notice about a person?"

"Eyes," he said quickly. "You?"

"Probably the same. I've always liked your eyes."

One of his brows raised. "Because they're weird?"

"Because they're unique."

He watched her for a long moment, his unique eyes intense. "Where would you go if you could travel anywhere?"

She wiped her mouth with her napkin. She'd ordered the Chicken Milano, and Gunner was right. The dish was amazing. "That's a hard one. There are so many places I'd like to see. Maybe Ireland? What about you?"

"I'd like to see Ireland, Italy, Switzerland."

"Yes, Switzerland." She smiled and he smiled back. "If you won a million dollars, what would you buy?"

"Another easy one," he said. "I'd pay off my house and put the rest in the bank."

"Really? You wouldn't quit work and travel?"

"No. I like what I do. It's different almost every day."

She really liked his answer.

Gunner ordered two zabagliones, which were served with blueberries and raspberries. They lingered over the decedent but light dessert. On the way out she got a hug from Carlotta and Papi.

~

*A*t the front door, Gunner took her keys and unlocked the door. She turned the knob and beckoned him inside where it was warm. "Thank you for a wonderful dinner."

"You're welcome." He looked at her lips. Kissably rosy because she'd been chewing on them. The amber depths of her eyes pulled him into their warmth. She smiled, and that was all the invitation he needed.

He ran knuckles down her cheek, then slipped his hand behind her neck and pulled her toward him.

Their lips met almost hesitantly, which was a first for them. He could tell by the sharp intake of her breath that she was as surprised as he was. Their first two kisses had been fueled by lust and desperation. This was different. His heart expanded, becoming too big for his chest. They'd gone from barely acquainted to friends to...

He wasn't sure what she wanted, but he knew exactly what he was moving toward.

Their kiss deepened. He reached for the zipper of her coat, then stopped. He and Jessica had rushed into a physical relationship. He and Dahlia had done a little rushing too.

He wanted to take things slow with Izzy. He wanted her to be sure. "I'd better go. My boss has really got a temper."

She opened her mouth, most likely a sharp retort on the tip of her tongue, but he took advantage and dipped his tongue in for one last taste. She leaned into him and he wrapped his arms around her. "I'll see you in the morning," he whispered into her hair.

~

*T*he next three weeks flew by, and Izzy fell harder for Gunner every day. Her dad moved his business into the second level, and she started painting her office, while Gunner began construction on what would become public restrooms on each side of the grand staircase.

Madam Venus dropped in occasionally to share a cup of tea, and Izzy welcomed her visits and felt like they were becoming fast friends. And who couldn't appreciate a friend who could see into the future? Gunner usually stayed a safe distance away when Vera was in the house.

Izzy moved into and decorated her attic apartment for Christmas, and Domino spent most of his days lounging up there or in the kitchen while she and Gunner worked.

After dinner or a movie, she and Gunner spent their evenings cuddled on the sofa at her place or his. Gunner's intense gaze muddled her brain, made her forget to breathe. She knew Jessica had hurt him. Would his heart ever be open enough to love again?

She often wondered how Gunner felt about her, if there was a word to describe what he thought, but didn't dare ask, and he never shared. They went to a couple of Christmas parties together and were acknowledged around town as a couple, which was thrilling. Even though she'd dated Baron, they'd never arrived at an event together. Never held hands, only kissed in private.

All but one aspect of life was pretty freaking wonderful. At times, she had a creepy sensation that she wasn't alone in the house. Things were moved, and tools disappeared, to the point where Gunner started locking them up when he left at night.

She and Gunner made sure the windows were locked tight and the doors were dead-bolted each night, and still things vanished.

Madam Venus had been right a few times, but maybe her prediction about no ghost in the house was wrong.

CHAPTER 19

*G*unner stepped onto Izzy's porch feeling more at ease than he'd ever felt in his life. Over the past three months he and Izzy had fallen into a comfortable rhythm that worked for them. He was at a point where he could imagine building a life with her. Something he never thought would happen again.

Normally he let himself in, but never for a date. He knocked. Waited. Then knocked a second time. Finally, he pulled out his key. As soon as he opened the door, he smelled natural gas. "Izzy."

He ran from room to room without switching on any lights. The closer he got to the kitchen, the stronger the smell, almost overpowering. "Izzy!"

The door to the kitchen was closed. He pushed it open and skidded to a stop. Izzy lay on the floor unmoving.

He lifted her into his arms. At the back door, he grabbed her black puffy coat and ran outside, away from the house. Dropping the coat in the yard, he spread it with the toe of his boot before laying her down. He checked for a pulse and closed his eyes in relief when he felt one in her neck. Though her breathing was shallow, she was alive. Removing his coat, he wrapped her tight, tugged his phone out, and called 911.

"911, what's—"

"Phoebe! It's Gunner. Get an ambulance to Izzy's immediately. There's a gas leak."

Suddenly, Tim appeared next to them.

"Stay with her," Gunner ordered as he jumped to his feet and ran to his truck for a wrench.

By the time he reached the gas meter, a patrol car and an ambulance were pulling into the driveway. He waved them to the back, then shut off the gas and called the power company before reentering the house. He propping the front door open. Stupid to go back inside, but he couldn't let Izzy's dream be blown to smithereens. He pulled his coat over his nose and ran from room to room opening windows wide, grateful he'd taken the time to chisel them loose.

Why she had the interior kitchen doors shut didn't make sense. She liked everything open and airy. By the time he got through with the windows, his eyes and throat were burning. Mac stood at the back door hollering his name. Outside, JT looked like he was questioning Tim, while Brandt—Eden Falls' only paramedic—treated Izzy.

"Is she going to be okay?" he asked, dropping next to Brandt, his voice raspy.

"The ambulance is taking her to Harrisville Regional. Did you go back in there?" Brandt asked when Gunner broke out in a coughing fit.

Gunner waved him away. "I'm okay. Take care of her."

"This is your fault!" Tim yelled, pushing past JT, who was on the phone with someone. Mac planted a hand on Tim's chest to keep him where he was. "How many mistakes have you made since Izzy started this renovation? This one almost killed her!"

He hadn't worked with any gas connections recently or

he'd be questioning himself. Brandt and the ambulance driver lifted Izzy onto a stretcher, then loaded her into the ambulance.

"This is your fault, Mr. Handyman!"

"Enough," JT said.

"Arrest him!" Tim shouted.

Gunner took a deep breath of cold air and turned to Tim, who Mac was still holding back. "Why are you here tonight?"

He couldn't read the expression that passed over the guy's face.

Both Mac and JT glanced at Tim.

"Izzy and I are friends. She invited me over."

"No. We had a date tonight. She wouldn't have invited you to be here."

Tim came to life, leaning toward Gunner. "He's the guilty one. He probably did something to hurt Ariel the day she fell through the ice."

Fury flared bright red. Gunner lunged and got in a punch to Tim's jaw before Mac and JT yanked them apart. "Don't you *ever* talk about my sister. *Ever*," Gunner growled, jabbing a finger at Tim for emphasis.

"You threatened her when you found out she was pregnant!"

Gunner stopped struggling against JT's hold. "What did you just say?"

"You heard me."

Ariel drowned. There were witnesses. The coroner didn't see any reason for an autopsy. Could she have been pregnant? And if so, why would she have told Tim and not Izzy or Joanna? Or had she told them and they kept her secret from him?

"Maybe we should all go down to the station and have a talk," JT said.

"We can talk just fine right here while I wait for the power company," Gunner said.

"Mac can wait for the power company."

Tim pulled out of Mac's grasp. "Am I under arrest?"

"Not yet. Let's go." JT took Tim's arm and indicated Gunner should follow. "Where's your car?" JT asked Tim when they got around front.

"I walked over."

"From where? You live in Harrisville."

"I was…visiting a friend."

"Follow us to the station, Gun." JT opened the passenger door of the patrol car. "You can come with me, Tim."

While Gunner climbed into his truck, he watched JT pull out his phone and text someone before he got into the patrol car. Gunner followed him to the station. He was put into a room, the door unlocked, where he waited while JT talked to Tim.

His thoughts were stuck, the same questions running over and over. Was his sixteen-year-old sister pregnant when she died, and if she was, had she told Izzy? If she'd told Izzy, why had Izzy kept that information from him? She said she didn't know who Ariel's mystery guy was, but how could she not know Ariel was pregnant?

He felt as hurt and betrayed as when Jessica left.

JT entered the room and sat in a chair on the opposite side of a small table. "Did you know about Ariel?"

"No."

"Do you believe him?"

"I was home on leave the day she died. I hadn't seen her in six months."

JT leaned back in his chair. "Has Tim been stopping by the house often?"

"I only know of a couple of times."

"He's accusing you of making a lot of mistakes. Not connecting toilets right, taking too long on projects."

"Does that sound like something I'd do?" Gunner asked.

"No." JT pulled his cell phone from a pocket and held up a picture of a car. "Tim said he walked over to Izzy's from a friend's house tonight, but Mac found his car parked on the opposite block."

Phoebe said she didn't trust Tim. Maybe her instincts were right. "Did the power company show?"

"The line behind the stove was disconnected."

"All the doors that led into the kitchen were closed. Izzy never closed those doors."

"What do you think happened?"

"You're the cop. You tell me."

JT rubbed his jaw and looked down at the table between them. "I think, for some reason, Tim is causing trouble and trying to blame it on you. But why?"

Gunner almost repeated that JT was the cop. Instead he didn't respond.

"Tim said he and Izzy used to date in high school."

Gunner nodded, remembering Ariel's letters about her jealousy over Izzy having a boyfriend.

"Do you know what happened between them?"

"No." He waited for another question that didn't come. "Can I go? I want to get Izzy's stove fixed."

JT nodded. "Sure."

∾

*I*zzy woke to a splitting headache. Her mom and dad were in the room along with Stella, Rowdy, Leo—and Phoebe, who started asking questions before Izzy realized where she was, questions she couldn't answer. She'd gone into the kitchen and noticed the smell of gas. She'd tried to pull the stove out but couldn't get the antique thing to move. That's all she remembered.

"Did you let anyone in the house?"

Did she? Her memory was fuzzy. She was waiting for Gunner, but didn't remember hearing a knock… "I don't know, Phoebs."

"Gunner found you on the kitchen floor," Phoebe said. "After he got you outside, Tim showed up."

Why would Tim be there?

"He said you invited him over."

Did she?

The emergency room doctor wanted to keep her overnight, so they moved her to a room. She kept expecting Gunner to come, but he didn't. She wished she had her phone so she could call him. He could tell her what happened.

She slept fitfully and woke to JT standing next to her bed.

"How're you feeling?"

"Other than a headache, I feel okay." She held up a hand. "Please don't ask what happened. Phoebe grilled me for an hour last night."

"I talked to her. I'm not here to ask about that." He pulled a chair close to her bed. "Did you know Ariel was pregnant when she died?"

She tried to sit up, but winced when her heartbeat pounded like a drum in her temples. "No. Where did you hear that?" she asked.

"Gunner and Joanna say they didn't know either."

First she'd suspected Ariel and Tim were seeing each other behind her back, and now this? "Are you sure?"

"No. Tim told Gunner last night."

"He admitted to being the father?" she asked.

JT's brow knit together. "What?"

Izzy told JT about Gunner finding Ariel's diary and the mention of a boy. "I think Tim was that boy."

"Tim told me last night you two dated in high school. Was this before or after?"

JT wouldn't remember since he was a senior her sophomore year. "During."

His mouth made a perfect O.

"I don't have proof. I just suspect. I gave Tim a guitar pick, and Ariel had it taped to a page in her diary. She wrote that her mystery boyfriend gave it to her."

"Guitar picks are pretty common. How would you know it was the same one?"

"I had it embossed as a present. I accused Tim and he didn't deny it."

"Did you tell Gunner?"

"No, because I wasn't sure."

"Do you think Tim is the one sabotaging the house to make Gunner look bad?"

The thought hadn't occurred to her, but yes, she believed that's exactly what was happening. "He's holding a grudge that stems back to when I left for college."

JT leaned forward and rested his forearms on his thighs. "Last night he told me he walked to your house. Mac found his car on the next block."

"Why would he lie?"

"Think he could hop over a fence?"

She thought back to the night the man in the backyard hopped over the fence with ease. "Absolutely."

~

*A*fter JT let him go and the power company declared the property safe, Gunner spent the night airing out the house and repairing the damaged connection to the stove. He was pretty sure Tim had caused the leak, but why? That part puzzled him. Unless he was still in love with Izzy. If that was the case, why would he try to harm her?

He could tell JT suspected Tim too, yet he let him go. No evidence?

Keep her safe.

Very soon, he planned to pay Madam Venus a visit. He needed clarification on that directive.

Another question that weighed…should he exhume Ariel's body to confirm she was pregnant? But to what end? Just to know? To try and find out who the father was? What did any of that matter now? Unless she'd been raped. No. He was certain she would have said something if that had happened. Would Ariel have told him about the pregnancy while he was home on leave, or kept the information to herself?

He needed to get home, take care of Domino, and get some sleep. He felt punch-drunk from being up all night. Satisfied the gas smell had dissipated enough to be safe, he closed the windows, locked up, and drove home just as the sun rose over the mountain peaks, breaking through his gloomy thoughts. Domino greeted him at the door like he'd been gone forever rather than ten hours. While his dog ran around the backyard in ecstasy, Gunner filled his food and water bowls, then grabbed a banana for himself.

After a quick nap, he wanted to go to the hospital. He was desperate to see Izzy, and angry that she might have kept information about his sister from him at the same time. He didn't want that to affect his feelings for her, but was afraid it would.

He dropped Domino at Izzy's on his way to the hospital. Once he pulled into the parking lot, he questioned his reason for being there. To see Izzy because he was concerned? Or to grill her about Ariel?

The information desk attendant gave him Izzy's room

number. When he reached the top of the stairs, he spotted Madam Venus. She got up from a chair in a waiting area and smiled.

"I'm surprised you heard about Izzy so quickly."

She shook her head. "I didn't."

Right. She's a psychic.

"Though I'd like to see Izzy, I came to talk to you."

"Yeah, I need to talk to you, too. You said to keep her safe. A little direction as to why or how or from what would have come in handy last night."

"You kept her safe." She took his arm and led him to a chair. "You saved her life."

"That was it? That's what you were warning about?"

She stared into his eyes for an uncomfortable moment. "Your sister wasn't pregnant."

"How…" Logic verses reality duked it out in his brain.

"She told her boyfriend she was to force him to choose her over his current girlfriend. Not a very nice—or smart—thing to do, but girls do silly things for love."

He wasn't sure whether to be relieved or angry as questions tumbled through his mind. Ariel had to have had sex with her boyfriend to think she could pull off a lie like that. And who was the randy guy who was having sex with his sixteen-year-old sister when he already had a girlfriend?

"Next you need to check Izzy's basement."

That statement took him by surprise. "For what?"

She closed her eyes and a frown pulled her eyebrows together. "A way in."

"A way into the house?"

"Behind a wall," she said, placing fingertips to her forehead, her red nails flashing under the fluorescent hospital lights. Eyes still closed, she reached out as if trying to touch something. "Look behind shelves. No! Under…something, I can't quite make out what. Something I never noticed when I lived there. A false wall…or floor." She shook her head. "A shelter of some sort." Her eyes opened wide and she looked at him. "Ariel knows. I saw Izzy with a man at Rowdy's Halloween party. He's getting into the house through the passage."

"Ariel is dead."

Madam Venus closed her eyes again. "She used to meet her boyfriend there. He wrote the directions on a piece of paper. Blue—no, a ticket stub." She met his gaze. "Ariel put the stub in a box. Find it and you'll know how he's getting in."

~

*I*zzy was dressed and ready to go when her dad showed up at the hospital. She was heartsick that Gunner hadn't come to visit. Phoebe told her how he'd carried her out of the house to safety, then opened all the windows to get the gas out.

"Gunner fixed the stove, so the house is safe, but I'd rather you spend a few nights at home," her dad said on the ride to Eden Falls.

"The house is my home." She smiled at her saintly dad.

He pulled into her driveway and stopped behind Gunner's truck. "I feel better knowing he's here."

Izzy wasn't sure how she felt. Grateful and hurt at the same time.

He started to get out of the car, but she stopped him. "I'm fine, Dad. Thank you for picking me up."

"We'll see you early on Christmas morning?"

"I'll be there. Love you."

"Love you back, sweet roll."

She climbed the stairs of the porch. Before she could

unlock the door, it swung open. Gunner stood on the other side. She waved to her dad and stepped inside. "Hi."

He shut the door and tugged her into a warm embrace. "You had me scared. How do you feel?"

"Tired and a little headachy, but I'm okay." She wrapped her arms around him, taking in the smell of his shirt, the feel of his back under her hands.

He kissed her like nothing had happened.

Domino nudged his way between them.

She laughed, reached down, and petted his head. "Hi, boy."

He smiled.

When she looked back at Gunner, he wasn't glaring, but she couldn't identify the look he gave her. When she straightened, he pulled a piece of paper out of his pocket and held it out. "I came to the hospital early this morning but was waylaid by Madam Venus before I made it to your room. We talked about what's been going on."

"She was at the hospital? How did she know?"

He lifted a brow. "Psychic."

"Right." She took the piece of paper he held, an old ticket stub to a concert she and Tim had attended in Seattle, but why did Gunner have it? "Where did you get this?"

"In a box of trinkets Ariel kept. Flip it over."

On the back was the Victorian's address and directions to a hidden panel in the garage floor. She looked at Gunner.

"Tim and Ariel were meeting there."

So her hunch was right. "They *were* seeing each other."

"Why didn't you tell me?"

"I didn't know for sure The day you showed me Ariel's diary, I wondered when I saw the guitar pick. I gave it to Tim when he asked me to the Homecoming Dance."

"Tim told me last night that Ariel was pregnant when she

died. Madam Venus said it wasn't true. Did Ariel tell you she was pregnant?"

"No. I told you, I didn't even know she was seeing anyone. Let alone my boyfriend."

He ran knuckles down the side of her face. "I'm sorry."

Like she'd told Tim, life was too short to hold onto grudges. Even if Ariel was alive, she didn't think her feelings would be any different.

"There's an old tunnel, possibly a bomb shelter from the fifties or sixties. It runs from the garage to the basement. We—JT, Phoebe, and I—think Tim is the one coming into the house. Him showing up last night when he did was too coincidental."

Phoebe came through the living room and hugged Izzy. "How are you feeling?"

"I'm okay."

"Everything's ready," she said to Gunner.

"What's ready?" Izzy asked.

"We've set up cameras in the garage, basement, and back stairway. We're going to catch creepy lover boy in action."

"Do you think he'll come back?"

"Absolutely," Phoebe said, her eyes wide with excitement. "And I can't wait. People don't mess with my family."

"I never saw a door in the basement," Izzy said.

"It's behind the last set of shelves," Gunner explained. "I completely missed it when we walked through the house the first time. Until today, I haven't been down there."

Gunner took her hand, lifted it up, and kissed her palm. She was mesmerized by his lips touching her skin.

"Want to see the cameras?"

Nodding, she met his heterochromia gaze. "Yes."

She and Gunner followed Phoebe to the basement and the secret door that led to an underground room.

"Madam Venus couldn't quite make out this room in her

vision or whatever she uses to see. Maybe because it's underground. But she told me to look for the ticket stub. I found both doors and called JT."

~

*I*zzy didn't need him like his mom or Ariel had, but he liked to think he could help her anyway.

After she went upstairs for a shower and a nap, he got to work on the bathrooms here on the main level. He had the floor and wall tile finished in both bathrooms, and the toilets installed in the women's room. He'd finish installing toilets in the men's room today. Sinks would come next.

Maybe life could settle into a norm. Jessica had skipped town three weeks ago, leaving him with the bill at The Dew Drop Inn. Fine by him, as long as she was gone. Funny that he'd wanted her to come back after she first left. And when she did come back, he couldn't wait for her to leave. All because of a woman with pretty eyes and a big heart.

He wondered if Tim knew JT suspected him. The cameras were Phoebe's idea. She'd gone to Harrisville to pick them up early this morning, and JT and Leo helped Gunner install each one before Neil went to pick Izzy up from the hospital.

Tim's determination to sabotage his work was still a mystery. His talk with Madam Venus had only cleared up one question. Whether to exhume Ariel or not. Not that he was a believer, but Madam Venus had been amazingly accurate with her predictions so far. Nothing would be gained by taking his sister from her resting place. She would still be gone and, if she had been pregnant, so would her baby.

Phoebe opened the bathroom door. "We need to make a plan."

"*You* need to make a plan. I'm taking Izzy to dinner."

She leaned close and batted her eyelashes. "Aww... Are you going to be my new brother-in-law?"

He'd been thinking about it.

"First comes love, then come marriage—"

"None of *your* dates have led to that. Here, hold this for me."

She took the wrench. "True, but I'm not the marrying kind."

"I have an ex-wife under my belt, so maybe I'm not either."

She leaned against the bathroom wall. "Where did your ex-wife go when she left town?"

"Now or the first time?"

"Now."

"No idea." He reached for the wrench she held. "Why haven't any of your conquests ever led to marriage?"

She laughed. "I'm having a pretty good time being single. And I sure don't think I'd make a very good mother."

"Really?" He liked to think he'd be a good father. He'd do exactly the opposite of what his parents had done.

"You know, if things don't work out between you and Izzy, people will run you out of town."

True. Though he'd always been considered an outcast, he'd be burned at a stake if he hurt Izzy. But he was willing to risk Eden Falls' wrath for the woman who'd been camped out in the back of his mind since she was sixteen. "I'll take my chances."

Phoebe assessed him for a long moment. "You really like her."

"She drives me crazy."

"In a good way or bad?"

He chuckled. "Both."

*I*zzy still wasn't used to having her own apartment. After three months of moving around, she was finally in her own place—a first for her. At home she'd roomed with Phoebe and Georgiana, in college she had a roommate, then she and three others rented an apartment. After she got her job at the gallery, she moved into a house with four others. Every time she'd added another person to the mix, but she was finally alone. She'd never lived alone before. Ever. Scary and exciting at the same time.

She'd slept most of the afternoon and felt much better. After a hot shower in her very own bathroom, she dressed in black jeans, a warm sweater, and boots.

Ten minutes before Gunner was supposed to arrive, she went downstairs to the kitchen, sniffing to see if she could still detect natural gas. After the first of the year she'd add a security system.

"Everything's locked up tight," Phoebe said from the dark sunporch.

Izzy jumped. "I didn't know anyone was still here."

Phoebe stood from a lawn chair and walked into the kitchen. "I have a motion detector on my phone. It will sense anyone who goes near the garage."

"So the police department is going to camp out here?"

"Would you rather be alone?"

"No." She was positive she didn't want to be alone until after Tim, or whoever was coming in, was caught. "Have you eaten?"

"Leo brought something by."

"Do you really think Tim will come a second night in a row?"

"Aww, your date's here," Phoebe said when he knocked. "Bring me some dessert."

Izzy ran to the front door, taking deep breaths to calm her

fluttery stomach. She liked this newness of them, the excitement she experienced every time Gunner was near. She opened the door and her fluttery stomach turned sour.

"Hi, Iz," Tim said. "I came to see how you're feeling."

"I'm fine." Now she had proof from a ticket stub, she considered bringing up Ariel, but changed her mind. It just wasn't important to her anymore.

"I was worried."

He was crowding the door, but she wasn't about to invite him in. Gunner would be here any minute, and she sensed Phoebe nearby. "Nothing to worry about. I'm perfectly fine. In fact I have a date in a few minutes."

Tim narrowed his eyes before he glanced at his watch. "Right. Me too. Hannah and I are having dinner."

"Have a nice evening."

"You too."

She waited until he got into his car before she shut the door, then she ran into the dark billiards room where she and Phoebe watched him back out of the driveway.

Tim lived in Harrisville, worked in Harrisville, so why was he in town so often? He had a couple of much older brothers who'd moved away from Eden Falls before he graduated from high school, and she wasn't sure if his parents were still around.

By the time Gunner arrived she'd changed her mind about going out. "Let's eat dinner here."

"No," Phoebe said. "Get her out of here, Gun."

unner had to almost drag Izzy out of the house. She had a stubborn streak he liked—until she was using it against him.

She was antsy tonight, kept her phone in her hand, and had a hard time paying attention when he asked a question.

"Let's walk through the square," he said when they left East Winds. He took her hand in his and tucked both into his coat pocket. "Talk to me, Izzy. Are you scared?"

"No." She was quiet for a few steps. "Disillusioned is a better word."

"By what?"

"Who. Tim, for one."

"And Ariel?" he asked, squeezing her hand.

She nodded. "Yes. I wish she'd talked to me. If I'd known she was interested in Tim, I would have bowed out. Tim and I dated for three years, but we never had this…" Her words died away and she blushed under the streetlight.

He stopped next to the huge pine bright with colorful Christmas lights and turned her toward him. "Finish what you were going to say."

She chewed her lip and shook her head.

"This connection *we* have," he offered.

Nodding, her glance lighting everywhere but on him.

"Izzy, look at me."

She raised her gaze through a veil of lashes.

"This is as romantic place as any to tell you I love you."

After a tiny gasp, she smiled as her eyes glistened with tears. "I love you too."

"Good to know."

Both of their phones buzzed at once. Izzy got hers out before he did.

She beamed at him after reading the text. "They got him! JT's taking him to the police station now. Phoebe said we should come home."

CHAPTER 20

*C*hristmas with Izzy's family was amazing. They all treated him like he'd always been part of their tightly knit group. Other than pathetic Christmas mornings that he'd tried to make special for his little sister, this was the first year he'd spent time with people other than Army buddies who were trying to forget they were far from home. Even Domino was invited.

Mrs. Adams and her daughters made a dinner he'd never recover from. He was so full afterward he could barely move.

With Izzy's help, he'd picked out small gifts for everyone. They all gave him gifts too. By the time the night was over, he'd choked back tears more than once.

Izzy showed him she understood by touching his hand or arm at just the right moment.

He couldn't deny that he'd loved Jessica, but what he felt for Izzy was much deeper, much truer than anything he'd ever felt before. He loved her and wanted to spend forever with her. He only hoped she felt the same.

Two days earlier he'd asked Neil for permission to marry his daughter. Izzy's dad had welcomed him to the family with a hug, a strong pat on the back, and a husky voice. "It's good to finally be *officially* evening out the male-to-female ratio around here."

"I'm not sure when I'll ask her. I'm waiting for the right time."

Neil laughed. "I'm not sure there's a right time with any of my girls. Good luck."

Halfway through dinner, Gunner decided tonight was the right time. He'd given Izzy a few girly tools she could add to her toolbox and a sweater Phoebe said she'd been admiring. Those were the presents she opened in front of her family. He waited until he took her home to pull out the present still in his coat pocket.

She looked up at him and her eyes filled with tears.

"Breathe, Izzy."

Sucking in a breath, she swiped at her eyes.

He dropped to one knee. "Isadora Adams, will you be my wife?"

For a long moment, he thought she might say no. She stared at him as tears trickled down her face. "Are you sure?"

He chuckled. "Most women wouldn't ask a man who's on one knee if he's sure."

"It's just that you didn't like me for so long."

"That's not true. I always liked you."

"Well, I thought you didn't like me because you glared at me and were so ornery."

He pushed off his knee and led her to the stairs, where he sat and pulled her onto his lap. "That's your misinterpretation of me trying to stay away from a woman I liked more than I should."

"We've only dated for a month."

"Would you like me to wait until summer and ask again?"

"Would you be more sure?"

He tweaked her chin and laughed. "I'm not the one questioning, crazy lady. You are."

"Where would we live?"

"Wherever you want."

"What about kids?"

"I want them."

"You do?" she asked in complete surprise.

He chuckled. They'd talked a lot over the past two months, but they'd never discussed children. "Yes. Do you?"

"Yes." She took a deep breath, and the first of a smile appeared. He knew she'd say yes eventually, he just hadn't realized they'd have a discussion beforehand. "What about another dog?"

She was going to make this as hard as every decision she made about the house. "I wouldn't be opposed."

"If you're working and I'm working, who will clean the house?"

"How about if we share duties?"

"Would you insist I stop working when we have children?"

"We'd work something out."

She pointed to the box he'd propped on her knee, her eyes still sparkling with tears. "What if I don't like the ring?"

"You will."

"How do you know?"

He kissed her nose, her cheeks, each of her eyelids. "I know you." She would love it if it came from a gumball machine, because that was Izzy. He watched her as he flipped the box open with his thumb. She gasped and her amber eyes lit with delight.

"It's beautiful."

"Beautiful enough to wear?"

She smiled. "You have to ask my dad."

"I already did. He likes the idea of a handyman in the family."

"Then yes, I'll marry you."

"Well, that only took thirty minutes." He pulled the ring out of the box and kissed her finger before sliding it into place. "This is forever, Izzy."

She took his face between her hands and kissed him so sweetly. "Forever," she whispered against his lips.

ACKNOWLEDGMENTS

Thank you to my amazing editor, Faith Freewoman at Demon for Details for your encouragement and inspiration. You make my manuscripts stronger. You make sure what I write makes sense. And you make me laugh. I'm so very grateful for our cyber friendship.

Thank you, Jane Haertel of Crazy Diamond Editorial for polishing my manuscript, and for adoring Gunner. I adore him too.

Thank you, Dar Albert of Wicked Smart Designs. Every book cover you send is as amazing as the last. I love opening your emails.

Not only did beta reader, Jeanine Hopping, help with a very early version, but came up with the idea for the title. Thank you, sweet friend.

For all the dinners, for all the work you do to keep the house running smoothly, for the love and encouragement you give me, thank you, Rick. I couldn't do this without your support.

xox

Tina

ABOUT THE AUTHOR

Tina Newcomb writes clean, contemporary romance. Her heartwarming stories take place in quaint small towns, with quirky townsfolk, and friendships that last a lifetime.

She acquired her love of reading from her librarian mother, who always had a stack of books close at hand, and her father who visited the local bookstore every weekend.

Tina lives in colorful Colorado. When not lost in her writing, she can be found in the garden, traveling with her (amateur) chef husband, or spending time with family and friends.

She loves to hear from readers. You can find her at
tinanewcomb.com

For a **free ebook,** sign up to receive my newsletter at
tinanewcomb.com

NOTE FROM AUTHOR

Thank you for reading my book, Fortunes for Eden. If you enjoyed it, I hope you'll leave an honest review or consider telling a friend—the two very best ways a reader can support an author.

I'd like to share an excerpt from Snow and Mistletoe in Eden Falls, Book 8 in the Eden Falls Series. Enjoy!

Warmest Regards,
Tina Newcomb

P.S. - For a **free ebook,** sign up to receive my newsletter at tinanewcomb.com

You can follow me on:
https://www.facebook.com/TinaNewcombAuthor
https://www.bookbub.com/authors/tina-newcomb
https://www.instagram.com/tinanewcomb
https://www.goodreads.com/tinanewcomb
https://www.pinterest.com/tinanewcomb

EXCERPT FROM: SNOW AND
MISTLETOE IN EDEN FALLS

Book Eight of the Eden Falls Series
by Tina Newcomb

Chapter 1

"Hello?"

When he heard the greeting, Kevin Klein checked his cell phone screen. The number was definitely his brother's. *Nice voice—way to go, bro.* "Is Ethan there?"

"Nope. Sorry, you must have the wrong number." *Click.*

After the call disconnected, Kevin looked at the screen again, then scrolled through his contacts and was careful to press Ethan's number.

"Did you think if you called right back the number would magically be Ethan's?" asked the same female with a laugh.

"This has been Ethan's cell number since he got his first phone at fourteen."

"Well, he must have changed his number. Have a good day." *Click.*

She'd hung up on him for the second time. Out of frustration, he hit the number again.

"Look, I don't have time to play this little game with you. Today's the first day of a new job and I won't be able to leave on time if you keep calling."

"Ethan would have told me if he changed his number."

"Maybe you don't know this Ethan as well as you think you do."

"I've known my brother since the day he was born, so yeah, I know him pretty well."

"I don't know what to tell you except to repeat that this is my number and there is no Ethan here, so goodbye."

"Wait! At least tell me how long you've had this number."

He heard her irritable sigh loud and clear. "About three weeks."

Had it been that long since he called Ethan? Kevin checked the Klein's Auto Shop calendar on the reception area wall—the first week of December. He talked to Ethan on Thanksgiving when Mom called him on her landline and they just passed the receiver around. He ran his fingers through his hair. Maybe it had been three weeks since he called his brother.

"Hello-o-o?" the female sing-songed. Even irritable she had a sexy voice, sweet with a touch of rust. "I'm hanging up."

"Yeah. Sorry to bother you."

Kevin stuffed his phone in his back pocket and walked out of the office and into the garage bay. The acrid smell of motor oil, the tangy scent of metal, and the pungent odor of rubber surrounded him in a cocoon of familiarity. Nate, brother number three of five, had his head under the hood of brother number two's 1970s Camaro. The car was a beauty, and Max's pride and joy. Max sat on a nearby workbench, staring intensely at Nate's back. Though two years apart, his brothers looked like they could be twins. Except Max's scowl. None of them could quite match Max's furrow-browed scowl.

Nate straightened and tugged a greasy rag out of the back pocket of his overalls and turned to Max. "Sounds fine to me."

Max threw up his arms. "Come on, bro. How can you not hear that pinging sound?"

"Maybe a worn water pump bearing," Nate said with a shake of his head.

"I know what a worn water pump bearing sounds like. This is different. It's a high-pitched ping."

"Maybe you need your hearing checked," Kevin said as he approached them. "Did either of you knuckleheads know Ethan changed his number?"

Max jumped off the workbench, opened the driver's door, and switched off the engine. "Sounds like the only knucklehead around here is you for not knowing. And Nate for not being able to hear."

Good-natured Nate ignored the remark with a shrug.

"Why would he change numbers?"

"That psycho ex-girlfriend wouldn't stop harassing him," Max said.

Kevin picked a candy wrapper up off the garage floor and held it out for Max. His brother—nicknamed the slob—had a bad habit of leaving his trash wherever it dropped. "You mean the girl who wasn't a girlfriend but thought she was?"

"Yep," Max answered, wadding up the wrapper and aiming for the trash can. "He jumps! He shoots!"

The paper hit the rim and bounced off, rolling under the Camaro, where it would stay until Kevin or Nate picked it up again. He leveled a look at his brother.

"What? You can't sink 'em all."

"You never sink any," Nate said.

"Okay, what's Ethan's new number?" Kevin asked.

Nate pointed to his phone sitting on the workbench. "Check my contacts. I think I have the right number."

Kevin found Ethan's name, entered the new number, and tried again. This time he got Ethan's voicemail.

"Hey, bro, thanks for the heads-up about changing your number. For Christmas we're all pitching in to give Mom and Murray a trip to Victoria Island. Give me a call when you have a minute so I can fill you in on the details."

"Glad you reminded me," Max said after Kevin disconnected the call. He pulled out his wallet and handed over some bills.

"Jolie wrote you a check this morning. I left it sitting on the desk in the office," Nate said, opening the hood of a white Toyota.

Money was tighter for Nate than for the rest of the brothers. He married his high school sweetheart three years ago, and bought a new house. His wife, Jolie, hadn't gone back to work since their darling baby girl—who had the entire family wrapped around her sweet little finger—was born.

Kevin hated the hint of jealousy he felt because a younger brother found love and was settled and starting his own family, while love was elusive as Bigfoot for him.

Sure, Kevin had a nice life and a booming business, but he had no one to share it with. Most of his friends were married, owned homes, and had kids. Going home every night to the apartment he shared with Max was getting harder and harder. He felt discontented, antsy for more.

Kevin nodded toward the Toyota. "When did that one come in?"

"It was parked out front. A lady left a message on the answering machine, said the engine has been overheating," Nate said. "She put her keys in the drop box."

Kevin knew most everyone in town and knew what they drove, but the Toyota wasn't familiar to him. "She didn't leave a name?"

The bell in the reception area echoed through the bay before Nate could answer.

"Time to move your car out, Max. We have customers." Kevin opened the bay door behind Max's car so he could back out.

Inside the office, postal worker Rita Reynolds peeled off gloves and unwound a scarf three times the length of her body from around her neck. The woman never made an appointment. Just dropped off her car and expected them to put it at the top of their list of repairs. "Hey, Rita. What can we do for you today?"

Squawk! She flapped her arms—one of her many birdlike habits—as if she might take flight any minute. "Don't give me any grief, Kevin Klein. I told Nate I needed an oil change and he said I could come in any time."

"I wasn't going to give you grief." *Like that would do any good.* "We can get to it this morning."

"Okay, well, come on then." She started to rewind the scarf.

"Where are we going?"

"I need a ride to work!" She flapped a hand toward the window. "You don't expect me to walk to the post office in this blizzard, do you?"

Blizzard was a bit of an exaggeration, but the snow was coming down steadily. He hit the intercom button on the wall. "Max, bring Rita's car in next for an oil change. I'm going to run her over to the post office. Be right back." Both Max and Nate waved without looking his way. He grabbed his coat from the rack and held the door open for Rita. The tiny woman glared up at him as she passed.

Normally he'd take his truck, especially with the snowy

roads, because the bed was loaded with bags of sand. But Rita couldn't climb up into the passenger seat, and he wasn't about to lift her. He led her to a Subaru. If he trusted her driving, he'd just let her take the car as a loaner, but Rita was forever getting tickets for her fast, reckless driving around town.

He unlocked the passenger door and waited until she slid into place before running around to start the car. He'd scrape the windows while the engine warmed up.

She glared at him through her thick-lensed glasses, her eyes magnified to scary proportions. *Squawk!* "You hurry up now, Kevin, or I'll be late."

The second woman of the morning blaming him because *she* was going to be late. "Yes, ma'am." He turned the heat to high, grabbed the scrapper, and shut the door. Once the windows were clear, he climbed in and drove Rita around Town Square with her complaining the whole way. When they reached the post office, he pulled into the special drive-thru lane lined with mailboxes.

Squawk! "You're not supposed to park here. This is for letter drop-off only."

"I'm not parking. Just trying to get you close to the door, Rita."

"Driving through here without a letter is in direct violation of post office policies."

"I won't ever do it again." He leaned across the console and opened her door. "Out you go. We'll call when your car is ready."

"I'll need someone to pick me up."

"Yep. Got it. One of us will come and get you." *But it won't be me.* He unclipped her seatbelt. "Bye, Rita. Have a great day."

She took two full minutes to climb out of his car, pull her hat lower over her ears, adjust her coat, and sling her purse over her head. The car behind him honked. Bending down, she shook a gloved finger at him. "See, I told you this drive-thru is for mailing letters only. You have three cars lined up behind you. You may just get a ticket for this stunt, Kevin Klein."

They're not waiting for me. They're waiting for you! "Okay, Rita. If you'll shut the door, I can get out of their way." *And she's flapping her arms again.*

"This sidewalk is slippery."

Kevin jumped out, held up a hand to let the cars behind him know he was sorry, and rounded the car. He took Rita's arm to steady her and shut the door. The car behind him honked again.

He looked skyward. *Please, help me get through this morning.*

"You don't have to manhandle me."

"I'm not manhandling. I'm holding your arm to keep you from slipping."

"I'm going to have bruises from your rough treatment."

"Pretty sure I'm not holding your arm tight enough to give you bruises." He got her up on the curb and walked her to the post office's front door. "There you go."

A woman coming down the sidewalk stopped next to Rita. "Are you okay? Is he hurting you?" she asked, her voice muffled by the scarf wrapped around the lower half of her face.

"He's manhandling me."

Kevin threw up his hands in surrender. "I'm not manhandling you, Rita." He glanced at the woman. Everything was covered but a pair of the bluest eyes he'd ever seen. "I was helping her to the door so she wouldn't slip."

Blue-eyes glanced from him to Rita and back, then pointed to his car. "You do know that's a drive-thru lane for dropping off letters. It's not a parking lot."

"Got it," he said over his shoulder as he jogged to the Subaru. "Sorry to ruin everyone's day while I helped an old lady to the door."

Squawk! "Who are you calling an old lady?"

"Sorry, Rita." He climbed behind the wheel and pulled onto the street before he glanced in the rearview mirror. Rita and the woman stood where he left them, both glaring in his direction. "Happy Monday," he muttered.